# The Burning

**M. R. Hall** is a screenwriter, producer and former criminal barrister. Educated at Hereford Cathedral School and Worcester College, Oxford, he lives in Monmouthshire with his wife and two sons. Aside from writing, his main passion is the preservation and planting of woodland. In his spare moments, he is mostly to be found among trees.

THE BURNING is the sixth novel in M. R. Hall's twice CWA Gold Dagger-shortlisted Coroner Jenny Cooper series, following *The Coroner*, *The Disappeared*, *The Redeemed*, *The Flight*, *The Chosen Dead*, and ebook short story *The Innocent*.

m-r-hall.com
facebook.com/MRHallAuthor
@MRHall_books

# M. R. HALL

## The Burning

PAN BOOKS

First published 2014 by Mantle

This paperback edition published 2015 by Pan Books
an imprint of Pan Macmillan, a division of Macmillan Publishers Limited
Pan Macmillan, 20 New Wharf Road, London N1 9RR
Basingstoke and Oxford
Associated companies throughout the world
www.panmacmillan.com

ISBN 978-0-330-52663-0

3 5 7 9 8 6 4 2

A CIP catalogue record for this book is available from the British Library.

Typeset by Ellipsis Digital Limited, Glasgow
Printed and bound by CPI Group (UK) Ltd, Croydon, CR0 4YY

For Will and Tom: tough guys

# ONE

THE EVENTS OF THAT EVENING so long ago had con-
densed over the years into a single scene that he played over
and over in his mind. But the passage of time had not caused
the images to fade or the exquisite sensations to dim. Not
at all. They were as vivid as ever. *Exquisite*. The word came
close to capturing what he had experienced that day, but not
quite. There had been so many layers, so many aspects to his
ecstasy. *Heaven*. That's what it was. Such a simple word, but
the only one that would do. The second he had breathed
into the depths of his lungs as the life left her eyes had been
pure *heaven*. His blood had turned to light; his body had
felt as if it were hovering: quivering and gravity-defying in
mid-air.

And then he had done it again.

He could feel the stirrings already: the tension tightening
the fibres of every muscle; the delicious anticipation like the
first touch from his angel. His angel with the full red lips
that tasted of honey and wine, his angel whose flesh was as
soft as velvet and down. His precious angel: the beginning
and now the end of all this.

Reaching the end of the roughly gravelled farm track, he
struck out across a field frozen concrete-hard and carpeted
with frost, the cold air sharpening his senses until they were
as keen as a wild animal's. The bony knuckles of a solitary,

leafless oak clawed at the silver-bright sliver of moon and an infinity of stars sprayed over a tar-black sky. He looked up like a child in wonder. The universe was smiling on him.

At the hedgerow on the far side, he climbed over the stile and made his way along the rutted path that crossed the stretch of woodland sloping down towards the hamlet of Blackstone Ley. As the darkness of the trees closed in around him he caught occasional glimpses of the lights from the scattering of houses below. His fingers tightened around the smooth, polished butt of the shotgun. The only sounds were of his footsteps and the gentle sloshing of diesel coming from the rucksack strapped tightly across his back.

After a quarter of a mile the path dog-legged sharply through a dense stand of birch, widened slightly, then finally delivered him onto the narrow lane at the foot of the hill. He stood for a moment in the shadow of the hedgerow, safely outside the pool of hazy orange light cast by the single street lamp. He glanced left and right.

All was quiet and still.

It was time.

# TWO

THE MORPHINE WAS SUPPOSED TO make her sleep through the night, but for a little over a fortnight now, Clare Ashton had slept for only two hours before waking again at eleven. It was the same pattern each night. As the grand-father clock on the landing beat out its inexorable rhythm, she would lie cold and restless with the dull pain mounting in her chest and spine while her mind flooded with long-forgotten memories as vivid, sometimes more vivid, than the original events themselves. Tiny, irrelevant details – a stain on her sundress, a patch of unshaved stubble on her father's cheek – would manifest with dazzling clarity. Smells, too: her mother's scent, the smoke from the woodstove in the living room, the damp wool of her winter coat. The odd thing was, these recollections were only of childhood. Her body, and she was always conscious of her body, was flat-chested and slender-hipped. A boy's body, her grandmother had once said in gently mocking tones that still rung hurt-fully in her ears. A little girl with the body of a boy until she was nearly fourteen years old. The last among her friends to grow breasts. The last to bleed.

Yet in most other important respects she had been first. The first to marry. The first to give birth. The first – and only one among them – to lose a child. And soon, aged only thirty-five, she would be the first to die. Something had gone wrong somewhere along the line. Not something that had *happened* to her, but something in her make-up; in her wiring. For as far back as her memory stretched she had always felt more than a little off-kilter. As a girl she had found no words to express it. As an adult nearing the end of her life, Clare had found the perfect encapsulation: it was as if she had always been a reluctant visitor to this world. Part of her, she had come to realize, had never wanted to arrive here in the first place. If the prospect of death in two months' time held any consolation, it was in the hope that she would finally get to meet that reluctant part of herself, and to understand who in fact she really was. And if there was nothing to come, if the lights simply were to extinguish, then none of it mattered anyway. Everything from beginning to end would have been meaningless. A monstrous joke.

It was nearly 11.30 when she heard Philip's footsteps on the lane and the creak of the gate as he returned from one of his increasingly frequent late-night runs. The closer Clare came to the end, the more restless her husband seemed to become. More often than not he would sleep in the spare room. 'I didn't like to disturb you,' he would explain softly, but it was he who was disturbed, not she. A man who ran marathons and began each day with 200 press-ups was never going to feel comfortable lying next to a dying woman. Who could blame him? Besides, he had students to teach in the morning. A classroom full of bright-eyed private-school teenagers brimming with hope for the future. He was too considerate not to meet them each day with energy and optimism.

Of the two of them, it was Philip who had always been the selfless one, the coper, the one who had kept up the daily routines in the bleak months after they lost Susie. Without Philip's strength Clare was certain she wouldn't have lasted one year, let alone ten. Sometimes she pictured him as a widower, alone in the house, quiet and stoical, his hair cut shorter as it slowly turned grey, his body even leaner and harder as he doused his inevitable guilt at surviving her with an ever more punishing exercise regime. There would be women, of course, but she couldn't imagine him falling in love again. He had already done that twice in his life and each time it had brought him nothing but unhappiness. No, despite his best intentions the women he let into his bed would never possess him as she had done, and it would trouble him deeply that he couldn't give the devotion they craved.

Perhaps when he was old, when she had become nothing more than a faded photograph, he might let down his defences again and lay himself open, but by then he would be a stranger about whom, imagining him now, she found it hard to care. That was another thing she had noticed about dying: it was making her selfish. As her life force diminished so did her capacity for empathy. With a little luck, by the time she reached the end, the process would be complete. It would be a small blessing, but a blessing nonetheless, to be allowed to die without pity for those left behind.

Clare closed her eyes and tried to banish a procession of uninvited mental images of her nursery school in the small village on the Welsh borders where she had grown up. She had loathed the place and all but erased it from her mind, yet here was the outdoor sandpit with its weathered boards and plastic buckets and spades; now the grey lumps of Plasticine stored in a biscuit tin and the red-and-white chequered apron with her name embroidered across the chest; now the tightly crammed coat pegs, the beanbags in the reading corner. And here came Miss Allsop, or at least her fat calves and ankles stuffed into heavy brown shoes. Her smell: sour milk and face cream. 'Which book shall we read today?'

Miss Allsop's voice cut through her tiny child's body, demanding and judgemental.

Clare slipped in and out of a shallow doze with the childhood memories still unbanished, trapped inside the emotions of a fearful four-year-old. Monsters and other unknowable horrors lurked around each corner. Miss Allsop led her along the corridor and into her office. She produced scissors from her cardigan pocket. 'Now give me your fingers, Clare.'

She jolted awake. Her heart was racing. Her pyjama top was glued to her body with sweat. The dark was frightening her. 'Philip? Philip?' she called out faintly, hoping that if he had left his door ajar he might hear her. There was no reply. She called louder and was met with the implacable silence of a still and empty house.

A sensation of rising panic began to overwhelm her, but the stubborn quietness of the night was interrupted by the distant sound of a siren; no, several sirens. They were drawing closer, heading into the village from the Thornbury Road. She reached for the lamp at her bedside, and fighting the pain, forced herself to her feet and limped stiffly to the window. She drew back the curtain and lifted the blackout blind to see a column of flames on the far side of the three acres of common around which the dozen or so houses of Blackstone Ley were randomly arranged. The lights from numerous flashlights were converging from several directions. She dimly made out excited voices and wondered if the villagers were having a bonfire, but for what? New Year? Wasn't it three days too early for that?

There was a sudden and violent explosion. A spectacular fireball erupted just to the left of the burning house. The rolling flames surged upwards and lit up the entire common, exposing a small crowd of horrified onlookers whose hands flew simultaneously to the exposed skin of their faces. Seconds later, Clare felt an intense wave of radiant heat travel through the cold glass and in the same moment realized that it was Kelly and Ed's house that was alight, and that the explosion must have been the large tank of propane gas that stood alongside it in the garden. She thought of Kelly and the three children and wondered if they had escaped the inferno. Then of Philip. Had she seen him among those on the common? She hoped he hadn't tried anything heroic. It would be just like him. *Please, no. Not now. Not like this.* She pressed her face to the pane, praying for a glimpse of him. She waited and waited, growing more and more desperate, until at last she saw him captured in the headlights of a fire engine. *Thank God.* He was standing absolutely still: tall, lean, strong, staring into the flames. Even as the fire crew busied themselves all around him, he remained unmoving. Clare could read his thoughts as if they were her own: he was seeing their own lost child among the flames. Their Susie. And after ten long years, he was wondering if this place might at last be about to give up its secrets.

# THREE

A SHROUD OF DENSE FOG had settled over the Wye Valley on Christmas Eve and for several days now, Jenny Cooper had been able to see no further than the far side of the lane. Even the usually raucous crows that nested in the crown of the vast oak in the next-door meadow had sunk into subdued silence. The only sound in this isolated corner a mile up the hill from the village of Tintern was that of her axe as she worked her way through the pile of logs, mechanically splitting one round of wood after another. Each strike issued a report that rang out like a warning shot into the gloom. It was a sound of defiance that mirrored her mood.

Jenny's fingers ached with cold inside the tough leather work gloves that were made for a man. There had been none in the hardware store cut for a woman. No one imagined feminine hands wielding heavy tools or hauling firewood in a hoar frost. She prised another frozen log off the shrinking pile that had been dumped in a heap at the side of the cottage, struck it with her heavy, wedge-shaped maul, and tossed the two halves into the high-sided barrow. It was one of several jobs Michael had promised to do. He was going to have it all split and stacked in the dry before Christmas. But as with most of his promises, he had failed to make good on it.

Jenny hadn't seen him in nearly two weeks – he claimed

his boss had demanded that he work over the holidays. In fact, she had seen him only a handful of times since October, when the small airline for which he worked as a pilot had beaten off the competition to secure a lucrative freight contract. Now, when Michael wasn't ferrying wealthy clients around the country, he was transporting consignments of pharmaceuticals from Geneva and Zurich to the secure depot at Bristol International Airport. Weight for weight, his cargo was more valuable than gold, he had told her. With £50 million worth of product on board a small aircraft, the clients insisted on the most highly qualified pilots. Having flown RAF Tornadoes from the age of nineteen until he was forty, Michael was considered the safest pair of hands in the company.

What neither Michael's bosses nor their Swiss clients knew, however, was that he had started seeing a therapist to deal with the combat stress that still plagued him with regular nightmares. It had been Jenny's suggestion, and to her great surprise he had agreed without objection. He hadn't talked much to her about his sessions, but since the process had got underway Jenny had noticed that, even more than usual, he tended to avoid situations that left him alone with his thoughts. She could only assume that was why he had agreed to work between Christmas and New Year despite knowing it would mean her spending the holiday alone: the quiet days when the world stood still left the troubled mind nowhere to escape from itself.

She reached for another log, set it on the chopping block and channelled her frustration into a powerful swing of the axe. It was just her luck that as soon as she had begun to feel at peace with herself Michael had started to turn inwards and become difficult. Still, if after all they had weathered he could continue to provoke such powerful and tangled feelings in her, she supposed that must mean that somewhere in amongst them there was something approximating love.

The blood ran hotter through her veins and at last reached her frozen fingertips as she hacked through a stubborn, knotted log that resisted repeated blows. Days and weeks of dammed-up anger exploded from her muscles. Michael was hard enough to forgive, but her son, Ross, had taken off to Morocco for the entire university vacation without even calling by to wish her a happy Christmas. Things had been complicated between them since the previous summer, when he had nearly lost his life. He had dropped several hints that he was planning to 'talk' with her at the end of his university term. Jenny had allowed herself to believe this might be it, the reconciliation she had been longing for, but Ross had found another girlfriend (she had lost count of how many there had been in recent months) and his phone calls had dried up.

She was surrounded by men who couldn't cope with their feelings. She always had been. It felt like her cruel destiny.

The work was cathartic. She filled the barrow to the top and hauled it down to the old stone shed at the end of the garden by the stream that had once housed the mill workings that gave her isolated property its name: Melin Bach, Welsh for 'Little Mill'. She set two wide planks on bricks to keep the damp from seeping through the dirt floor, arranged the logs on top then returned for a second load. Crunching over the hard ground, her breath billowing in icy clouds, she felt a small surge of elation at being tough enough to look after herself. Who needed a man if you could chop your own wood?

An hour slipped past in a steady rhythm of splitting, loading and stacking. The comfortable exertion calmed her racing mind until at last her thoughts were entirely absorbed by the task at hand. She was more than halfway through the pile and determined to use the remaining daylight to work her way to the bottom when she heard the sound of a car crawling up the hill from Tintern. The cautiousness of its progress told her that it didn't belong to a local. The two other properties accessed by the loop of lane on which Melin Bach stood were owned by farming families whose social circle was tightly drawn. Over many centuries they had become as deeply woven into the fabric of the valley as its Saxon hedgerows and medieval stone walls. When strangers came, it was not for them.

Jenny buried her axe in the block and wiped the sweat from her forehead as the car drew up outside the front gate. She walked around to the front of the house as the driver stepped out of a black Toyota. He was a young man, thirty-five or thereabouts, and tall, with short, slightly tousled blond hair. He wore a dark wool coat over a business suit and sober tie.

He came to the far side of the gate. 'Mrs Cooper?'

'Yes.' She approached cautiously, noticing his wide green eyes that tracked her unblinkingly as she made her way towards him along the flagstone path.

'Detective Inspector Gabriel Ryan. Gloucestershire CID. You're the coroner, right?'

'I am,' she said, relieved that it was a professional visit and nothing to do with Michael. Having a pilot for a boyfriend had left her fearful of unannounced visits – she was always at least partly prepared for a representative of the company arriving to inform her that there had been a regrettable accident.

'Sorry to trouble you at Christmas,' Ryan said.

'Christmas was three days ago.'

'If you say so.' He shrugged his narrow shoulders and gave a hint of a smile. Up close he looked tired, with dark shadows beneath his eyes. A day's stubble darkened his sharply defined jaw.

Jenny unfastened the iron gate and let him through.

'I tried to call, but could only get your voicemail.'

'No signal. You didn't think to try the landline?'

'Sorry.' He glanced over at the wheelbarrow and the axe sunk into the chopping block alongside it. Jenny watched him adjusting the mental picture he would have formed of a woman with the title 'Her Majesty's Coroner for the Severn Vale District'.

'I'm guessing you've not come all this way to tell me good news,' Jenny said.

'Afraid not,' Ryan answered.

Jenny nodded. She wanted a moment to ready herself, to erect her defences before talking shop again.

'You look like you might have been up all night,' Jenny said. 'Can I get you some coffee?'

'Please,' Ryan said. 'I could do with it.'

She started around the side of the cottage to the back door, stepping past the remains of the wood pile. Ryan followed, tip-toeing over the partially frozen mud in his city shoes.

'You live all the way out here alone?' he inquired.

'Some of the time,' Jenny said, and left it at that.

Ryan sat at the small pine table in the warm, cramped kitchen while Jenny made coffee on the oil-fired range that dated back to the 1950s. From the corner of her eye she watched him glance at the old Welsh dresser and worn quarry tiles with what seemed to be mild amusement. She guessed he had never been a country-dweller.

'I had what the magazines call a "dream kitchen" once,' Jenny said. 'I've never felt more uncomfortable in a room.'

'I like it. It's cosy.'

'I'll believe you.'

She brought the steel pot to the pine table along with two cups and a jug of milk. 'OK. Tell me the worst.'

'You must have heard the news this morning?'

'Only snatches. I try to avoid it if I can.'

'There was a house fire. A place called Blackstone Ley – it's over the river, near Thornbury.'

Jenny did remember a fragment of news bulletin reporting a fire, but at the mention of children she had mentally stopped her ears, as if anticipating that before too long it would become her problem. She sensed that her holiday was about to come to a premature end.

'Stepdad and two kids were killed,' Ryan continued. 'One girl of fourteen and the other eleven. He also had a child of three – a boy – whom we think he murdered and disposed of elsewhere before setting light to the house. Only the mother survived. She works behind a bar in Bristol. Came home to a smoking ruin.' He hesitated. 'I've just spent the morning with her.'

*Whom.* Jenny adjusted her assessment of Ryan. His precise grammar suggested he was a graduate. For reasons she couldn't justify, she trusted graduate detectives less than their unschooled colleagues. Perhaps because they were cleverer at disguising their motives.

'You say the father started the fire?'

'Looks that way.' He reached into his pocket and brought out his phone. 'You have got Wi-Fi, right?'

Jenny gave a tolerant nod.

'Password?'

'What would I need one of those for?'

He tapped the screen and handed her the phone. 'The father's name was Edward Morgan. He was known as Ed. You're looking at his Facebook page. The last entry was made at 11.30 last night.'

Jenny looked at a photograph of a smiling Ed carrying his

three-year-old son on his shoulders through a snow-covered field. He was a big man in his thirties, bearded with broad shoulders and thick brown hair that covered his ears. The date was 21 December – a week ago to the day. The comment said '*Me and Robbie off to make a snowman up Tump field!*' Above it was another comment, text only, dated 27 December, posted at 11.28 p.m.

> For Kelly.
> Robbie is gone but you will never find him. We are all at peace now, but you will be in living hell, which is all a whore like you deserves.

Jenny handed the phone back across the table to Ryan while at the same time fending off mental images of girls trapped inside a burning house. Hardened as she had become to violent tragedy during her six years as a coroner, there were still cases that hit her like a fist in the heart. This was already one of them.

'Kelly is who – his wife?'

'Long-term partner. They weren't married but had been together nearly ten years.'

'What's the family's history?'

'I can give you the few bits and pieces I picked up this morning. She moved up from London in her early twenties with a three-year-old and a baby. Met Ed a couple of years later, settled down, then eventually had the boy by him. She's as confused as everyone else is shocked.'

'He called her a whore—'

'She's a pretty woman, but she insists she's always been faithful. Often as not, in my experience, it's all in the guy's head. Some just have the jealous gene, imagine things that aren't there.'

'Have you got a photo?'

'Of Kelly? Sure.'

Another couple of taps on the phone brought up Kelly Hart's profile page. The picture she had chosen of herself showed her dressed in denim shorts and a bikini top standing barefoot on the beach. She was petite, dark-haired, full-lipped and olive skinned. Beautiful, but not in a provocative way. Her expression was almost demure, as if she'd been a reluctant subject for the camera.

Jenny found herself impatient for more of Kelly's story. 'You said she's from London? How did she end up in this part of the world?'

'From what I can make out the girls' father – his name's Molyneux – worked as some sort of security guard or bouncer type in a West End casino. But according to Kelly he made most of his money dealing coke to the punters. He got four years just before their youngest was born. Kelly wanted a clean break. She stayed with friends near Bristol, found a bar job, then got offered a council house in Blackstone Ley. It's a bit out of the way, but I guess she thought it would be good for the kids.'

Jenny looked again at Kelly's picture. She seemed too exotic to have chosen to live in a small hamlet in South Gloucestershire.

'I know it's unusual,' Ryan said, 'but I get the feeling that there was a year or two after Molyneux was put away when she blew with the wind. Could have ended up anywhere. Just so happened she fetched up on our patch.'

'What about him – Ed?'

'Local boy. Worked part-time for the Forestry and put in a few shifts each week up at Fairmeadows Farm near Sharpness.'

'Why do I know that name?' Jenny asked.

'Fairmeadows? You'll have seen the lorries – all the

happy-looking animals painted on the sides. It's not exactly a farm, though – more of an abattoir and rendering plant.'

'Ah,' Jenny said. The smiling father in the photograph transformed into a man with a butcher's knife and blood up to his elbows. 'Ed worked as a slaughterman, then slaughtered his family.'

'That seems to be about the length of it.' Ryan finished his coffee, then looked at her with what appeared to be sympathy. 'It's a shitty case and my super wants it off our hands sooner than I'd consider decent. He aims to dump the file on you tomorrow.'

'So you've come to give me a friendly warning?' Jenny said doubtfully.

'No. I thought you might want to look at the house before we bulldoze it. If we leave now, we might manage half an hour before dark.'

'Is there anything to see?'

'Not much, but at least we'll have given you fair opportunity.' He shrugged. 'That's all my super wanted. Between you and me, I'm not his greatest admirer.' He stood up from the table with an air of finality. 'Thanks for the coffee.' He turned to the door.

'Hold on,' Jenny said. 'You're right. I ought to have a look at the place.'

Ryan nodded his approval. 'I'll wait in the car.'

# FOUR

JENNY DROVE CLOSE BEHIND RYAN through the thickening fog, their two cars the only vehicles on the road winding through the wooded trough of the Wye Gorge. It occurred to her that she was repeating a pattern: during each of the six Christmas holidays in her time as coroner, she had dealt with either a suicide or a homicide. The cracks in fragile minds tended to work open when the hours of darkness far outnumbered those of light.

She had expected the fog to disperse a little as they emerged from the forest and arrived on more open ground alongside the Severn Estuary at Chepstow, but as they crawled the final mile towards the old Severn Bridge it seemed to grow thicker still. Not a breath of wind blew in from the Bristol Channel. Jenny's senses searched for anchors, a familiar landmark with which to orientate herself in the claustrophobic gloom, but with every passing yard her field of vision grew smaller, until all she could see ahead of her were the two red dabs of Ryan's tail lights appearing and then disappearing again into the grey murk.

Minutes seemed to pass before they arrived at the roundabout just shy of the bridge. Her relief at reaching the mid-point of the journey was short-lived – a dull orange glow sharpened into illuminated letters on an electronic sign as they approached their intended exit: BRIDGE CLOSED.

Now they would have to follow a diversion to the new Severn Crossing along a ten-mile stretch of empty motorway that passed over the Magor flats. Staying as close to Ryan's rear bumper as she dared, Jenny fought against a rising sensation of anxiety that was tightening the muscles beneath her ribcage. 'Toughen up, Jenny,' she said out loud to herself. She was supposed to have left behind the symptoms that had dogged her for so many years. No panic attacks for a year or more. No medication; only a little wine to lighten her mood at the end of a long day. She told herself she should have stayed at home. Most coroners would not have dreamt of visiting a scene of death – the legal requirement to view a body *in situ* had been abolished more than thirty years ago – but despite having every excuse not to, Jenny had never quite managed to quell a compulsion to take the feel of a scene of death herself.

A sharp and unexpected noise startled her. It was only the phone ringing through the loudspeakers, but her heart beat harder as she fumbled for the answer button located in the centre of the steering wheel.

'Hello?'

'Is that you, Mrs Cooper?' It took Jenny a moment to register that the voice belonged to Alison. Her officer had been signed off sick since her accident the previous summer. They hadn't spoken since early December, after Alison's last visit to the consultant neurologist who had brought her back from the dead. She sounded excited, as if she had important news.

'Alison. How are you?' Jenny said, covering her surprise. 'Did you have a good Christmas?'

'No. It was a complete pain. Couldn't wait for it to be over.' Alison had woken from a month-long coma the previous summer minus many of her former inhibitions. 'I could have murdered my daughter and her partner by Boxing Day.

You think old married couples snipe at each other – try sharing your flat with a couple of lesbians.' Her frontal lobe – the part of the brain that controlled appropriate social responses – had had a shard of bone driven through it. On the plus side, Alison seemed untroubled by the fact that a portion of her skull had been replaced by a metal plate. Nor did she seem to regret that she had nearly killed herself by deliberately driving into the path of a car that had been aiming itself at Jenny. In fact, as far as Jenny had been able to tell, the whole horrific incident remained a gaping blank in her memory.

'Sorry about the call from DI Ryan,' Jenny said. 'He was given your number by his super. He can't have known you were off work.'

'Oh, he knows all right. Sam Abbott and I are old mates – we were at training college together. I expect he thought I'd be interested. I was also a DS on the original Blackstone Ley case back when he was just a humble inspector.'

Jenny was confused. 'Which case was this?'

'You remember – the four-year-old girl who disappeared. Susie Ashton. About ten years ago.'

*Ashton.* Jenny repeated the name to herself. *Blackstone Ley.* The village had sounded vaguely familiar when Ryan first mentioned it, but she hadn't known why. But now she put it together with the name Susie Ashton a host of images flooded into her mind: a small, fair-haired girl with pigtails and big, trusting eyes. Dignified, well-spoken parents hounded on their doorstep by slavering journalists. Daily speculation that had grown more and more prurient and grotesque. Jenny had been working for the local authority as a child-protection lawyer at the time and the case had hit a nerve. As she recalled, the mother had left the child playing in the front garden by herself for only a few minutes, during which time she had vanished forever. She remembered the outrage and indignation that had focused on the quiet, unremarkable woman. After the initial round of sympathy, the newspapers had turned, hinting through increasingly vicious innuendo that she was involved in the murder of her innocent child.

'I do remember her. Yes. I just hadn't put it all together,' Jenny said.

'We never found the bastard,' Alison said, 'but I bet we have now. That's why he's done it – guilt. I met Ed Morgan, interviewed him three times. Always played the clueless country boy. He was out in the forest at the time, he said – by himself, of course. No alibi. I hate to think what he did to those girls before he set fire to the place.' She paused, then abruptly changed tack – another symptom of the head injury. 'I've got a driving test tomorrow morning. With any luck, I'll have my licence back by lunchtime.'

'Right. Good luck with that,' Jenny said distractedly, scarcely noticing Ryan's lights fading altogether from her view. Her thoughts were suddenly focused on the realization that she was dealing with far more than a suicidal man who had taken his family with him. The Gloucestershire police had been castigated for their failure to solve the Susie Ashton case; Blackstone Ley held bad memories and the potential for many ugly column inches. It wouldn't have been Superintendent Abbott's decision alone to close the criminal investigation and pass the file as quickly as he could to the coroner: she had no doubt that it could only have been done with the chief constable's approval.

'You know what that means, don't you?' Alison said.

Jenny didn't answer.

'Are you still there, Mrs Cooper?'

'Yes?'

'I can come back to work.' Jenny only half registered her

words. 'I can't wait. You know your life's come to a dead end when you end up playing internet bloody bingo all day.'

'Oh. Right . . .' Jenny floundered, finally realizing what Alison had said. 'We should talk about this. You might need to have an assessment.'

'Sod that, Mrs Cooper. There's nothing wrong with me. You're my employer – it's up to you whether you think I'm fit for purpose. If I'm no use, you can kick me out again.'

Jenny struggled for an answer. 'What are we – Wednesday? Why don't you come in Friday morning? We'll talk then.'

'I'll be there at nine. You know the locals were all lying for each other?'

'I beg your pardon?' Jenny had lost her thread, still absorbed with thoughts of the chief constable.

'At Blackstone Ley. Keep up. Someone there knew about Ed Morgan, I'd bet my life on it.' Alison rang off abruptly without a goodbye.

Ryan's lights had vanished. Jenny found herself alone, floating in white space with no idea what lay ahead.

The fog hung heavily all the way along to Magor and over the river, then, for no discernible reason, began to disperse as Jenny made her way north-east along the southern shore of the estuary, allowing her glimpses of the fields beyond the hedgerows that lined the network of lanes linking the farms and villages of South Gloucestershire. She drove through the deserted market town of Thornbury and headed a further five miles through frozen countryside. She was only thirty minutes from the centre of Bristol, but this was a landscape, sparsely dotted with stone cottages and Georgian farmhouses, that hadn't altered in decades. A piece of old England suspended in time.

A left turn off the main road took her a little over a mile

over a hill and down a steep lane into the tiny village – if it could be called that – of Blackstone Ley. A dozen or so houses were positioned haphazardly around the outside of several acres of rough common set at the foot of a densely wooded hillside. Some were quaint cottages, others were twentieth-century additions. A squat medieval church with a square Norman tower stood at the far end. Denuded of the families of agricultural labourers who at one time would have worked the surrounding land, the community was now too small to sustain a pub or a shop. Continuing around the edge of the common, Jenny spotted a cluster of cars and vans next to the burned-out shell of a two-storey house. Alongside them stood a large bright-yellow caterpillar-tracked vehicle with a three-pronged metal claw at the end of a long hydraulic arm. As she drew closer, she saw Ryan emerge from a group of detectives and forensics officers dressed in their distinctive blue paper overalls. He waved her over, directing her to park her Land Rover on the verge behind his Toyota.

Ryan came up to meet her as she stepped out from the comfort of her car into the piercing cold. 'Got here just in time. Held them off for you. They're just about to lift the human remains if you're interested.'

'Thanks. That'll be a treat.'

Ryan glanced over his shoulder. 'Hold on a moment.'

Jenny followed his gaze and saw two female police offi-cers, one in uniform, the other in plain clothes, with a slightly built woman huddled in a bright-pink hooded anorak. They were leading her away from the house towards a squad car.

'Is that the mother?'

Ryan nodded. 'They wanted her to confirm a few things about the layout. She volunteered.'

Kelly Hart's face was hidden beneath her hood. Her hands were clasped tight under her folded arms. She wore jeans that hugged slender legs and pink trainers that matched her coat. The women police officers shepherded her into the back seat of the car and drove her away. As they passed, Jenny briefly caught sight of Kelly's face as she pulled down her hood and wiped her eyes with the back of her hand. She was unusually pretty, even in the depths of grief.

Ryan led the way through the parked vehicles and past police officers who were sharing a joke with three men Jenny recognized as local undertakers.

'Where's the mother staying?' Jenny asked.

'They've got her a flat in Bristol,' Ryan said. 'We're trying to keep the press off her back for now. You know what those vultures are like.'

They arrived at the front of the house. There was an open gateway in a low brick wall and a short, concrete slab path leading to the ruin. Only the rear and right-hand walls still stood; both were stained black with soot. Three white plastic sheets weighted down with orange cones were arranged in a row on the churned-up patch of lawn at the left side of the house. Nearby was a pile of scorched metal wreckage.

'Sure you want to see them?' Ryan asked.

'Maybe I'll wait,' Jenny said, the acrid smell of charred timber catching in the back of her throat.

She peered at the heap of bricks and tiles, then picked her way across the muddy garden, passing the plastic sheets covering what she guessed were nothing more than blackened skeletons.

'Big place for a council house,' Jenny remarked.

'Not bad at all,' Ryan said. 'But you'd have to stick living next to those woods. I wouldn't sleep at night.'

Jenny pointed to the heap of metal. 'What was that – a gas tank?'

'For the central heating. Set too close to the property. Went off like a bomb, witnesses said.'

Jenny's eyes travelled over the unkempt garden. A child's ride-on tractor lay on its side next to a rusting swing. A deflated football was decaying in a clump of weeds. Glancing back at the side wall of the house she noticed several large, rectangular, light-coloured patches on the brickwork. She stepped closer, realizing that the discolouration had been caused by chemicals used to scrub off graffiti.

'Have you seen this?'

Ryan wandered over and joined her.

'What do you know about it?'

Ryan shrugged. 'First time I've seen it.'

The outlines of the crudely daubed letters remained ghosted in the pits of the bricks: *FUCK OFF NIGGERS*.

'Why that, I wonder?' Jenny said.

'Kelly's ex-husband was a black guy. The daughters took after him in looks. People round here don't get about much.'

'The family must have reported it. There has to be a record somewhere.'

'I'll look into it,' Ryan said, glancing back over his shoulder at his restless colleagues, now anxious to get the job done and go home to their families.

'I need someone to take a picture. This is evidence.'

'Uh-huh,' Ryan said, as if hoping she might change her mind.

'You're not knocking anything down till it's done.'

He looked at her as if he were about to give her some words of advice, then seemed to change his mind. He headed back to the gate, calling out to ask if the photographer was still there.

Jenny already knew his problem. Somewhere there'd be an entry on a file that said Kelly and her family had been racially harassed, and the chances were the police would have done nothing meaningful about it. It was the sort of nugget that would make for news copy of just the kind they were hoping to avoid, which made it even more important that she herself didn't overlook it.

She walked around to the rear of the house and found a long stretch of lawn, a little wider than the house, that backed onto woodland covering the hillside rising up behind this side of the common. Jenny registered for the first time that the three sides of the property that didn't face onto the road were bordered by a head-high post-and-wire fence with a single strand of barbed wire running along the top. She recognized it as the type of fence that the Forestry Commission erected to keep deer from newly planted saplings, except that to her knowledge Forestry fences didn't tend to incorporate barbed wire.

Jenny turned at the sound of voices and saw Ryan giving instructions to a police photographer, telling him to make sure he got clear shots of the faded graffiti.

Leaving him to it, Ryan came and joined her.

'Certain you don't want to look at the bodies? Last chance. They're about to go in the van.'

'I'll leave it till the morgue,' Jenny said, preferring to avoid any disturbing sights that could wait until another day.

Ryan called over to his colleagues out in the lane. The undertakers pulled on facemasks and, carrying a pair of hand-held stretchers, went with two forensics officers to gather up the remains.

'What do you make of this fence?' Jenny said, turning her back on the scene. 'And if he's gone to all that trouble, why does it only run around three sides?'

'I think it went along the front, too,' Ryan said. 'The fire crew must have ripped it down.'

'Looks like Ed Morgan might have put it up himself – got the tall posts from Forestry supplies. You said he worked for them.'

'That's right,' Ryan said vaguely. He glanced at his watch. 'Seen enough yet? There are a lot of impatient people out there.'

'Do you think it's anything to do with that graffiti? Could Ed have been trying to keep someone out?'

'More likely trying to keep his daughters in,' Ryan said. 'We are talking about a family annihilator. Controlling types, aren't they?'

'Do you know if he had a lot of locks on the doors? Was the place hard to get out of?'

Ryan gave a tired smile. 'You're wondering could they have been trapped inside? Maybe Ed didn't do it after all?'

'Why is that funny?'

'Aside from his goodbye note and the fact that his three-year-old son is still unaccounted for, nothing at all.'

Jenny felt herself blush. Ryan had made her feel foolish.

He continued: 'Our forensics people are saying both girls had been shot through the chest with a twelve-bore shotgun. The back of Ed's skull was blown off and the gun – the metal part of it, at least – was found next to what was left of him. I can tell you now – he's been licensed to own a shotgun and hunting rifle all his adult life. I doubt there was a day went by that Ed Morgan didn't kill something, but this time –' Ryan glanced over at the undertakers loading the stretchers into their black van marked 'Private Ambulance' – 'this time he took it to the next level.'

Jenny felt a rush of icy wind against her face. The first hint of breeze in days. 'Were there any witnesses?'

'Plenty to the fire. A few others. You'll get their statements tomorrow.'

'Susie Ashton was taken from her garden, wasn't she?'

Ryan met Jenny's gaze. 'I wouldn't know. Before my time. Aren't you getting cold? I am.' He started back towards the front of the house. 'I'll see if the photographer can't email you those pictures before he goes.'

The dull afternoon light was fading to grey. The breeze, now picking up to a light wind, carried a whiff of coal smoke from a neighbour's chimney. Somewhere up in the woods Jenny heard a dog barking and men's voices – officers combing the countryside for Robbie Morgan's tiny body. There was something about the scene – a *feel*, nothing she could put into words – that told her she should try to remember it. She reached out her phone, called up the video camera and swept it slowly across the garden and hillside behind, keeping it rolling as she followed Ryan back to the road.

# FIVE

THE BULLDOZER – if that was the right term for a machine with a giant metal claw – crushed the brick wall at the front of the plot under its caterpillar tracks and came to a halt in front of the burned-out house. DI Ryan had accompanied the undertaker's van to the mortuary to book the remains, but several of his colleagues had stayed behind to enjoy the fun. Jenny stood a short way off on the common, feeling a strange obligation to witness the demolition as a mark of respect. The big diesel engine issued a low, threatening rumble as the machine's single arm rose in several jerky movements then unfolded to its full length. The three steel talons grasped the top of the wall and squeezed, taking a huge, jagged bite out of the brickwork. Several of the watching officers gave a muted cheer.

Jenny's attention began to drift as the machine worked its way down the wall and she found herself wondering about the people behind the drawn curtains in the other houses around the common. Every village she knew had a soul, an atmosphere all of its own, that told you something about its inhabitants. The houses of Blackstone Ley were spaced out, each home, even the smallest, its own fortress surrounded by its individual parcel of land. It was the kind of place city people might come to live thinking they would have privacy, only to realize there were ten pairs of eyes watching each time you stepped out of the door. It was a place where the truth about one's neighbours would be hard to untangle from the myth; where reputations, good or bad, would never be shaken off.

'I suppose it's for the best.'

Jenny turned to see a woman dressed in a battered wax jacket. A springer spaniel was running in excited circles off to her left, its nose close to the ground as it chased a rabbit scent. As she approached, Jenny saw that beneath her coat she was wearing a priest's collar which sat somewhat incongruously with the rest of her appearance. She was probably the same age as Jenny, but she exuded a natural vitality that made her elegant features look far younger.

'Are you with the police?' the woman inquired.

'No. I'm the coroner. Jenny Cooper.'

'Ah.' She offered her hand. 'Helen Medway.' Her gloved fingers were warm to the touch. 'I'm the vicar here. For three parishes, actually, but this is the one where I happen to live.' She pointed across the common to a black-and-white half-timbered cottage next door to the church. 'Any news on Robbie?'

'Not that I've heard. Did you know the family?'

'Yes, though more as neighbours than parishioners.' Helen glanced over at the machine, which had made short work of the house and was now most of the way through the last remaining wall. 'I've heard it was the father – he left a message.'

'That's what the police tell me.'

Helen nodded and fell silent for a moment. Jenny sensed she was puzzled by something.

'I expect they've asked you for a statement, living so close by?' Jenny said.

'I told them what I could, which wasn't much. Pardon me for asking, but isn't it quite soon for a coroner to be involved? Isn't this a police investigation?'

'It is at the moment,' Jenny answered guardedly.

'Sorry. I always ask too many questions. Force of habit. I used to be a probation officer.'

'Bristol?'

'No, Gloucester. I was made redundant when they shut the prison. I've only been doing this a year so haven't quite learned to be properly vicarly, or whatever the word is.'

She gave an apologetic smile and Jenny found herself warming to her.

'Between you and me, I get the impression the police don't think there's anything to investigate,' Jenny said. 'The culprit's dead. All that's left for them to do is to find out what Morgan did with his son.'

'He was a proper countryman. Knew every corner, ditch and hedge. I expect they'll have a job.'

'I think they know that.'

Helen Medway bit on her bottom lip and glanced away. Jenny could see that, despite initial appearances, she was suffering.

'Do you mind if I ask you something?' Jenny said. 'There had been some racist graffiti daubed on the side wall of the house. It had been scrubbed off, but you could still see the words.'

'I know. It appeared in the summer. About August time.'

'Before the fence went up?'

She nodded. 'I expect Ed was worried. Well, you would be.'

'Any idea who did it? Or why?'

'Well – ' Helen's eyes flicked left and right, as if she were checking for unseen spies. 'I don't want to be disloyal to my flock, but most people around here would tell you in private they believe the family did it themselves. Or at least—' Helen stopped herself. 'I really am saying too much now.'

'No. It's very helpful,' Jenny said. 'Were you going to say

they did it to try to get their neighbours painted as racists – so they could be re-housed elsewhere?' Helen's expression of surprise told her she was on the right track. 'Did they have a problem here? Had they fallen out with anyone?'

'I'm afraid they were that sort of family,' Helen said. 'The oldest girl, Layla, was a bit of a handful. From what people tell me, Kelly had been quite a divisive figure in the past. All that's just gossip, of course. I don't really want to . . .' She sighed, annoyed with herself. 'I'd rather you got all this from those who were here and not second-hand from me. It's not really appropriate for me to pass on hearsay.'

'I understand.' Jenny offered a diplomatic smile.

Helen Medway gave a grateful nod. 'Thank you.' She started to turn, as if going on her way, then looked abruptly back. 'The message Ed left – it didn't say anything about Susie Ashton, did it? You do know who I mean?'

Jenny weighed her options and decided to err on the side of safety. 'I'm afraid it wouldn't be right to discuss that now.'

'It's only that her mother, Clare, is very ill. She's got cancer. Her oncologist has told her months, but her husband confided in me that it could be weeks or days. Another indiscretion, I know, but I do know how much it would mean to her. It's been ten years. That's their cottage opposite – the Old Post Office.' Helen buried her hands deep into her coat pockets and strode off into the gathering dusk.

Jenny looked back at the house and saw that the machine had nearly finished its work. In a few short minutes the building had been reduced to a silent heap of rubble. The following morning lorries would arrive to ship the detritus away. Within twenty-four hours all traces of the former family home would be gone.

*

CID were still hazy about their protocols respecting who they could allow to befriend a dead murderer on Facebook, so the best DI Ryan could do was to email Jenny a screenshot of Ed Morgan's final message. When she read it again from her phone, as she stepped under the tiled porch of the Old Post Office, it took on an even bleaker resonance.

The door was answered by a tall, wiry and heavily preoccupied man in his late thirties. Fresh bandages covered both his hands, leaving only the tips of fingers and thumbs exposed.

'Good afternoon,' he said gravely.

Two short words were enough to remind Jenny of the voice which, for a few short months ten years ago, had played repeatedly on the TV and radio. It was a little deeper now, but it could not have belonged to anyone other than 'father of missing child, Susie Ashton'.

'Sorry to disturb you, Mr Ashton. I'm Jenny Cooper – the local coroner.' She presented him with a business card that had curled at the edges. 'I'll be dealing with the family that died in the house fire.' She swallowed, feeling self-conscious in Philip Ashton's serious presence. 'I just bumped into Reverend Medway. She suggested your wife, or you and your wife, might like to be kept up to speed – given past events.'

Ashton handed her card back to her and was silent for a moment, looking over her shoulder to the lights across the common. Jenny waited, unsettled by his lack of reaction. She wondered what had happened to his hands.

Then, sharply, he said, 'Why don't you come in, Mrs Cooper?'

He ushered her through a carpeted hallway and into a formal sitting room in which a Christmas tree decorated with coloured lights stood incongruously in one corner. It was a space in which everything was in its place, and in which a visitor couldn't help feeling self-conscious. Jenny had the impression of a house devoid of life; a house lacking the scuffs and disorder of children.

Philip Ashton motioned her to a chair. 'I'll fetch my wife.' And then, as an afterthought, he said, 'I apologize if it's too warm in here. She requires it to be at this temperature – I'm afraid she's very ill.'

'Yes. I heard.'

Ashton gave a stiff nod and retreated. Jenny heard him climbing the stairs calling, 'Clare – it's the coroner to see us.'

She glanced around the unnaturally tidy room and noticed the absence of family photographs. Not even a wedding picture. With only a few exceptions, parents of dead children fell into two distinct camps: those who erected morbid shrines on the mantelpiece and those who banished all traces. It was debatable which response was healthiest, but Jenny preferred dealing with a family prepared to weep; those that had locked their grief down tight made her feel an uncomfortable urge to experience emotion on their behalf.

They took a while coming down, Clare snapping at her husband in a stage whisper that she could manage the stairs perfectly well by herself. He entered first, holding open the door for her. A pale woman, whose face bore only a passing resemblance to the one Jenny remembered from TV, shuffled in behind him on matchstick legs. She was dressed and made up, but nothing could disguise her hollowed-out features and wasted body. She still had her own walnut-coloured hair, but it was flattened at the back of her head where it had been pressed against her pillow. Nevertheless, she was putting on a brave front. Ashton held his wife's arm as she lowered herself onto the sofa.

She looked at Jenny with eyes made unusually round and childlike by the thinness of her face. 'Thank you for coming, Mrs Cooper.' Her voice was clear and steady, but less familiar than her husband's. It echoed only faintly in Jenny's memory. 'We appreciate it. We really do.'

Jenny decided to leave the niceties aside and get straight to business. She was aware that, for Clare Ashton, maintaining her composure would be taking all of her strength. 'I'm afraid I don't have anything definitive for you, but I can tell you the police think Ed Morgan was responsible for the fire and the deaths of his stepdaughters and probably that of his son. He left a message to that effect. Would you like to see it?'

Clare and Philip Ashton exchanged a glance. Philip nodded. Jenny handed him her phone with Morgan's final words on the screen. He read it quickly and without emotion before handing it to his wife.

'I'm afraid it doesn't say anything about your daughter,' Jenny said. 'But if the police's reading of the situation is correct, it does tell us what he was capable of.'

Clare looked up and passed the phone back to her husband, her expression as unreadable as his. 'Thank you, Mrs Cooper.' She hesitated. 'Thank you for sharing this with us.'

Jenny glanced at Philip Ashton. He was reading the message a second time, this time appearing to subject it to close critical analysis.

'What is it?' Clare said, a note of apprehension entering her voice.

'He wouldn't be the first man to kill his family, suspecting his wife was being unfaithful,' he said. 'In fact, from what I read in today's papers, not to mention what I've researched privately over the years, it's not at all uncommon. Child abductors, though, are very rare, and invariably sexually motivated. In the present day, such a person is likely to be heavily involved with the worst forms of child pornography. You would also expect to see a pattern of offending behaviour from adolescence onwards.' He fixed Jenny with a searching, sceptical look. 'As far as I know, Ed Morgan had never been in trouble with the police. Is there any suggestion that he was sexually abusing his stepdaughters?'

'I'm sure that's something my inquiry will examine,' Jenny said, remembering now that, even though he had been a young man at the time of his daughter's disappearance, Philip Ashton had always employed an acid eloquence when dealing with questioners.

'Was she cheating on him?' Clare Ashton asked. 'I know she's a very beautiful woman, but since being with Ed I got the impression she'd settled down.'

'I know nothing about her, Mrs Ashton. Not yet.'

Clare's eyes darted warily towards her husband's. Jenny sensed there was something she wanted to share.

'I'll probably have to ask you for a statement in due course,' Jenny said, 'the same with all the neighbours. But if there's anything you'd like to tell me that you think might prove useful?'

Another glance passed between them. Philip Ashton gave a slight shrug as if to say that if Clare wanted to speak it was up to her.

'Kelly cleans for us once a week. She has done for years. I wouldn't say I knew everything about her, but I always got the impression she and Ed were close. She said he was good with the daughters, especially Layla – she'd been behaving quite badly lately. Fourteen going on twenty.' Clare smiled faintly. 'According to Kelly, he hardly ever raised his voice, even when Layla was being impossible.'

'I'm not in any position to draw inferences,' Jenny said, 'but in these cases a man's violent behaviour can sometimes appear completely out of character.'

'Yes, but – ' Clare's eyes seemed to lose their focus. Her body stiffened. 'Sorry, I'm feeling a little discomfort.' She reached under her cardigan to what Jenny assumed was a morphine pump.

'I should go,' Jenny said tactfully.

As she rose from her chair, Clare said, 'Philip, tell her about Darren Brooks.'

'What about him?'

'Their history.'

'I don't think repeating village gossip—'

'Please,' Clare said sharply. 'And it's hardly gossip.'

Jenny remained standing while Philip relayed his information in clipped, staccato sentences.

'Darren Brooks is a local builder. He lives around the corner at The Forge – the place that looks like a gypsy encampment. He and Kelly were together years ago, then when she met Ed she moved him out – or rather, as I recall, had him ejected. He's had other relationships since, several possibly, but those who claim to know hold that his affections continued to lie with Kelly. He also has a fourteen-year-old daughter named Nicky, by his former wife, though I think they may be together again – I lose track – but you get the idea.'

'Tell her about last night,' Clare croaked.

Philip Ashton gave a tight-lipped nod. 'I was among a number of people who came out of our homes when we saw the house had caught fire. It had clearly taken hold very quickly. You wouldn't have thought anyone inside could possibly still be alive, but Darren Brooks . . . well, he ran towards the flames. I don't know quite what he hoped to achieve. I think I heard him call Kelly's name. Then came the explosion – the gas tank. He was thrown off his feet and quite badly burned. His clothing caught light. Fortunately for me it was just my hands. I must have used them to shield my face.'

'I see,' Jenny said. 'So Mr Brooks was prepared to run into a burning building for her.'

'He made an attempt to get inside, but I couldn't comment on his precise motivation.'

'My husband teaches maths and physics,' Clare said. 'He doesn't like to form opinions without evidence.'

'My wife trained as a journalist and has always made up for my reluctance to speculate.' He touched Clare's shoulder with his bandaged hand. 'You'll understand we've endured a decade of false dawns, Mrs Cooper. We have remained living in this village in the hope that if anyone does know what happened to our daughter, our constant presence will one day prompt their conscience. We learned long ago to be patient, so you mustn't feel under any obligation to us. I'm sure your job will be hard enough without any extraneous pressures.'

Jenny glanced into Clare Ashton's eyes and saw she had no strength left to fight her corner. Her husband's will had triumphed and drawn the life out of her. Jenny felt certain that it was he who had purged the house of visual reminders of their daughter and stifled any thought of having another child. Photographs aged people and placed them and events in the past, where they belonged; new lives displaced old realities as surely as dawn dissolved the night. It was plain to see: Philip Ashton wouldn't move an inch until he had his answer, and if possible, his revenge.

Flecks of snow were slanting from a moonless sky as Jenny left the Ashtons' cottage and picked her way across the common. The police vehicles had left and the bulldozer stood silent, its folded arm partially illuminated by the single street lamp to the left of the razed house. She could see the lights of ten or so nearby houses, yet somehow their occupants felt distant and indifferent. Whether it was an accident of geography or something in the landscape's soul, she felt in her gut that Blackstone Ley was and always had been a private and a lonely place.

Eager to reach her car, she drew her arms tightly across her chest and quickened her step. As she walked the final yards, an uneasy sensation – she attributed it to drawing closer to the ruin – caused her to glance along the margin of the woods on the far side of the road. For a fleeting second she thought she saw movement: a human silhouette against the hedgerow. Feeling suddenly vulnerable, she fumbled for her keys with cold, clumsy fingers and hastily let herself into the Land Rover. She locked the doors and started the engine, telling herself her mind was playing tricks. But as she turned her car around and her headlights picked out the tree trunks behind the pile of rubble, she was sure she saw it again: a figure vanishing into the trees.

# SIX

THE RAW EASTERLY THAT HAD picked up in the late after-noon had blown away the fog but brought thickening snow flurries that by the time Jenny reached the Severn Bridge were becoming a swirling blizzard. The few drivers fool-hardy enough to make the crossing into Wales crawled slowly along the single open lane, uncertain of reaching their desti-nations. A winter that had started early and bitterly in mid-November was biting deeper.

Jenny tried to concentrate on the road ahead, but her thoughts kept returning to the village she had left behind. It was the story Clare and Philip Ashton had told her about Kelly's former lover, Darren Brooks, that was weighing most heavily on her mind. As the gossips would have it, when Kelly left Darren for Ed, Darren had continued to live in a house set back from the opposite side of the common, and remained a rival for her affections. Jenny could see perfectly how that might happen. Country people born and raised in the same place weren't inclined to move out and move on. They'd sit and brood on the same hurt feelings for decades, and if they remained unresolved, even take them to the grave. She would have to find out the truth about the graffiti and whether Kelly had been trying to move house. Perhaps Brooks had made a pass? Maybe Kelly had responded, or Ed thought she had. One thing of which she could be certain was that ten years of sexual jealousy between three people could lead to anything, and would almost certainly have led to something.

The storm grew heavier as Jenny left the estuary behind and struck out alone on the valley road. Driving as fast as she dared, she travelled six winding miles without seeing a single vehicle, making the first tracks through snow that was already lying inches deep. It grew thicker still as she turned off the main road at Tintern and headed up the lane to Melin Bach. Even with four-wheel drive the Land Rover struggled against the steep gradient. Pitching from side to side, with her foot pressed to the floor, Jenny wondered if she really was a little mad to live out here by herself. What sort of woman chose to live by herself in a cottage in the woods? Faced with a long evening alone, the thought of a sleek harbour-side apartment five minutes' walk from the office became more attractive by the moment. But then she caught a glimpse of lights up ahead, and sliding around the final bend before home she saw that they were coming from the windows of her cottage. A steady stream of white smoke was rising from the chimney. For a moment she allowed herself to believe that Ross might have come home early to pay her a surprise visit, but then she reminded herself that she had never known him do anything as practical as light a fire on his own initiative. She was right. Drawing closer, she made out the familiar shape of Michael's elderly Saab under a covering of snow.

It had been weeks. He had better have a good explanation.

'Can I come in?'

'What if I said no?'

Michael nudged through the bathroom door carrying two large glasses of red wine.

'What do you say now?'

'Hmm.' Jenny wrestled with conflicting emotions. 'All right. You win.'

He sat on the edge of the roll-top bath and handed her a glass, pretending not to glance down at her breasts, which were only partially hidden beneath the foam. Jenny felt she ought to have mounted at least a small display of anger for his abandoning her over Christmas, but lying neck-deep in the hot, rose-scented water she could no longer summon the energy. Life felt too short.

'I tried to get leave, Jenny, but there's only a couple of us the Swiss clients truly trust in this weather.'

'They get to choose who flies your planes?'

'It's written in the contract – only pilots with military experience or at least 10,000 hours for a passenger airline. Cuts their insurance premium in half.'

'You didn't get that suntan flying.'

'I had a day skiing near Geneva. One of the guys from the office took me out.'

'You could have emailed.'

'I should have done. I'm sorry.'

Jenny took a sip of wine and sensed that he meant it. 'You must have been having a good time.'

'You know what it's like – the longer you leave it, the worse you feel.'

'What did you think I was going to do, dump you like some teenage girl?'

'I guess.'

'Honestly, Michael?'

'I kind of deserve it.' Changing the subject, he leant over to the window and lifted a corner of the blind. 'Can you believe it? There must be eight inches of snow out there. It's still falling.'

'Is it worrying you?'

He looked at her, puzzled.

'The thought of being snowed in with me.'

'Why would that worry me?'

'I couldn't help wondering if you'd been avoiding me – since you started seeing the therapist. I thought maybe it had stirred you up.'

Michael smiled. 'I'd have been better off taking you out to dinner. Would have been a hell of a lot cheaper and a lot more fun.'

'You're not going any more?'

'I gave it three sessions, then she invited me to her "Men's Group". There's a misnomer for a start. But I had your voice in my head telling me not to be judgemental, so I swallowed my pride and took myself along. Now bear in mind these were meant to be her worked-out ones, the successes,' he paused to take a mouthful of wine, enjoying telling his story, 'and certainly if your measure of success is the ability to squeeze a middle-aged body into a pair of pink jeans or give the world's limpest handshake, these guys had made it.' He held up his hand, anticipating her protest. 'And before you tell me I'm being a macho idiot, I was actually fine with all that. The problem was, none of it felt real. They'd all give you the same placid smile, but there was no one behind it. And they all talked in the same creepy, measured way. There's "Call me Vicky" busy telling us we've got to be "whole people" – whatever that means – and all the while I'm surrounded by these empty shells whose personalities have gone missing.'

Jenny slid deeper into the water, wriggling her shoulders beneath the warm surface. 'You do sound a bit of a macho idiot.'

'We each had to give our definition of perfect mental health. I told them I thought it was being able to live with your own stink.'

'That's nice.'

'It's true. We're all messed up to some extent. Healthy people admit it and get on, the others go to Men's Group.'

Jenny watched him suddenly get lost in his thoughts and stare intently into space.

'So you're feeling better now?' she asked.

'Hmm?' He looked at her vacantly.

'Are you happy?'

'Much more for seeing you.' He dipped his fingers into the water and brushed her knee. 'Do you think you might have room for one more in there?'

'We'll see. Let me finish my wine.'


Snug beneath the thick winter duvet, they lay for a long while in peaceful silence, Michael telling her all she needed to hear in the way he gently stroked her hair. She liked the way he was content just to be with her in these moments. Her ex-husband, David, had always angled for words of reassurance or praise after their rare moments of intimacy, never realizing that if you had to fish for them, they weren't worth having. She reached out and touched the back of her hand to Michael's chest, feeling its slow rise and fall.

'I'm glad you came,' she said.

'So am I.' He leant over and kissed her softly on the lips. 'And I'm sorry you were alone at Christmas.'

'It's OK. I don't much like it anyway. I should have copied Ross and taken off to the sun somewhere.'

'You're missing him, aren't you?' Michael said.

'I can't blame him for staying away, especially after one of my cases nearly cost him his life last year. I should just be grateful he survived.'

'You were only doing your job.'

'If I were him, I'm not sure I could ever forgive me.'

'Hey, don't cry.'

'I'm not.'

He drew a finger across her cheek and Jenny felt the dampness on her skin. 'What's that?'

'I always wanted to be a good mother. I tried. Honestly, I did. I was never going to be the stay-at-home kind, but I at least thought he might be proud of me one day.'

'Even if he isn't now, he will be. Think how much you've achieved.'

'But I've never made him feel secure, never made him feel loved the way he wanted – not like a proper mother does.'

Michael stroked his fingers along her neck and shoulders. 'I don't think there's any such thing as a proper mother. It's a myth designed to make women feel bad about themselves.'

'It works.'

'Don't you think it's time to move on from that now? The one thing I did take from therapy was that raking over the past gets you nowhere.'

'I try, but it feels like unfinished business.'

'Everything's unfinished business. While we're still here there's no other kind.'

Jenny drifted into silence, asking herself if she really could forgive herself and move on. The thought of a life without Ross's affection felt like wandering through a desert.

'It will all work out, I promise you,' Michael said, and Jenny allowed herself to believe him.

She rolled onto her side and felt herself yield as he slid his hand behind her waist and drew her closer. She'd been alone for long enough, and there was plenty of night left for sleeping.

# SEVEN

'HEY. WAKEY-WAKEY!'

Jenny forced her eyes open, squinting in the glare of the snow-reflected light streaming through the bedroom window.

'Phone for you. Someone called Ryan.'

'What time is it?' Her voice was thick with sleep.

'Just gone eight.'

Michael was standing naked at the foot of the bed with his hand cupped over the phone. 'Shall I tell him you'll ring back?'

'I'd better take it.' Jenny eased herself upright, shivering at the cold air on her bare shoulders. She couldn't remember the last time she'd fallen asleep without pulling on a T-shirt. She felt an unaccountable twinge of shame as Michael handed her the phone. He grabbed his clothes and headed out to the shower.

'Good morning, Inspector.'

'Mrs Cooper. Sorry to disturb you.' She thought she detected a hint of mocking humour in Ryan's voice. 'I thought you'd want to know that my super has formally closed our file. He sat down with the CPS last night and they decided there was no evidence warranting further investigation. Do you want the physical statements or will email do?'

'I suppose I'd better have the originals.'

'I'll be at the Vale mortuary around ten, if that suits you. I'm taking dental records over to Dr Kerr just to confirm the identifications – not that there's any doubt.'

'I'm not sure I'll be able to make it this morning,' Jenny said. 'You've seen where I live.'

'I'll leave it up to you . . .' Ryan paused, as if he was holding something back.

'Is there anything else?'

'Well, just between ourselves, I'm feeling a little guilty on my department's behalf – towards Kelly Hart, I mean. I know it's not for me to tell you how to do your job, but it feels wrong just to leave her hanging. It'd be nice if she felt someone was looking after her interests, moving things along.'

'You're still searching for her son, aren't you?'

'Of course. But finding his body isn't the same as delivering closure with Ed.'

'She accepts he did it?'

'I think so.'

'You only *think* so?'

'It's only been thirty-six hours. Look, all I am asking is would you mind paying her some attention.' Another pause. Jenny sensed there was something he was avoiding saying.

'What exactly is it that you think I ought to be doing?' Jenny asked.

'It's just I've seen one or two similar cases, not exactly the same, but I know this is the danger time – while the bereaved is waiting for all the wheels to start turning.'

'You're worried Kelly might do something stupid?'

'I saw her again last night. She was very quiet. I can tell she's very bright – more than you'd think – but she's fragile. We offered her a counsellor but she's not interested. That worries me a little.'

'Are you sure you're in the right job, Mr Ryan?'

'I beg your pardon?'

'You're not sounding much like a detective.'

Ryan laughed. 'You're right. I'd probably have been happier without the psychology degree.'

There. He wanted her to know he wasn't just any detective inspector. He was a DI with an education. Her equal.

'Has she mentioned a man called Darren Brooks?'

'Not specifically. Why do you ask?'

'I heard she was involved with him before Ed. He tried to get into the burning house.'

'I knew that.' Jenny heard another phone ring at Ryan's end. 'Hey look, that's my super chasing me. I'll catch up with you later.'

'Just one more thing – Kelly's number.'

'I'll send an email.'

Ryan rang off. He'd played it very cool, but she'd got the message: he was worried that Kelly Hart was a suicide risk and Superintendent Abbott didn't give a damn. In fact, it would probably suit him if she were to swallow a handful of pills – that way there would be no victim left for the media to parade as a reminder of his past failings.

Ryan's warning was still weighing on her mind as she made her way downstairs in her robe. She had no idea how little sleep she'd had, but the heaviness in her limbs told her that it could only have been a few hours. She was making coffee at the stove when Michael appeared wrapped in a towel.

He came up behind her and kissed her neck. 'What's the hurry? I thought we were being lazy.'

'Change of plan. I've got to go to Bristol this morning.'

'Have you seen outside the window?' He rested his hands on her hips. 'You're not going anywhere.'

'Want a bet?' She slipped out of grasp and reached into

an overhead cupboard. 'And while I'm gone, you're going to cook lunch and stack the last of those logs like you promised.'

'They're under a foot of snow.'

'You're full of beans, you'll enjoy the exercise.' She handed him a cup. 'Deal?'

'And I get what, exactly?'

She looked playfully into his eyes. 'To be a real man.'

The Land Rover seemed at home with the deep snow hugging its wheels, and held steady around the tight series of bends leading down to the foot of the valley. Briefly forgetting the purpose of her journey, Jenny soaked up the vivid cloud-flecked sky and the whitewashed fields that seemed to offer the hope of new beginnings. It was one of those rare and precious mornings on which anything seemed possible – even Michael being content to stay with her for more than a few hours. He had set to work outside without a word of objection, and she had even felt a twinge of guilt as she pulled away from the house leaving him shovelling snow. But now that she thought about it, wouldn't any decent man have done the same? Wasn't this how people who loved each other behaved?

*Love*. It wasn't a word she often used when thinking of Michael – *frustrated, exasperated, mystified* more often came to mind – but this morning had been different. Talking easily over breakfast they had seemed to mesh in a way they had never previously managed, as if they'd both let down defences and been surprised at what they had found. It was nothing urgent or melodramatic, simply a sense of peace in each other's presence; an effortless and unconditional connection. If that was love, Jenny was more than happy. She could dare to acknowledge its name and find courage to hope it might last.

Death, like the British weather, seldom relented. Jenny followed a black undertaker's van along the untreated roadway around the outside of the Vale Hospital to the separate and unmarked single-storey mortuary. While Jenny carefully manoeuvred over the icy tarmac into a parking space, she glanced over to see two body bags being unloaded. The undertakers chatted amiably as they wheeled the corpses through the loading bay; theirs one of the few businesses to which the freezing weather was a boon.

Jenny sensed the busy atmosphere as soon as she was admitted through the security door and stepped into the vestibule. She was met with the sound of voices, the high-pitch buzz of surgical saws and the clang of metal gurneys being moved. Entering the main corridor she found several technicians rearranging the queue of twelve or more gurneys, each loaded with a body awaiting its turn in the autopsy room. At peak times, when the mortuary had more corpses than fridge space, the staff operated a complex system of rotation in an attempt to keep as many chilled as possible. The foul smell of human decay indicated that they weren't being entirely successful. Jenny instinctively reached a hand to her face as Joe, a sprightly sixty-year-old with an ex-boxer's flattened nose and slightly vacant, punch-drunk eyes, approached her.

'We're snowed under, Mrs Cooper, if you'll pardon the pun.' He spoke not with the local Bristol accent, but with the slow, rich Somerset vowels that seemed to emanate from a previous century.

'I can see.'

'D'you think anyone would mind if we parked the buggers outside?'

'I should imagine they would – very much.'

Joe grinned, showing missing front teeth. He was a recent addition to the mortuary team and seemed to relish his work a little too much for Jenny's comfort.

'Is Dr Kerr on duty?'

'Dealing with them fire victims.' He nodded towards the door to her right. 'And I thought I'd seen it all.'

Jenny proffered a stiff smile and turned quickly into the autopsy room, keen to be out of his presence.

Her relief was only momentary. Jenny entered the large, brightly lit space to find the senior pathologist, Dr Andy Kerr, working at one table, and his locum, Dr Jasmine Hope, opening a cadaver at the other. Dr Kerr was a tall, muscular Ulsterman; Jasmine a beautiful Ghanaian woman with an air of constant melancholy behind a kindly smile. Not yet thirty, she had already lost her only child in infancy and been deserted by a husband who had disappeared back to Accra. Andy had taken her under his wing and was angling, in his understated way, to get her a permanent contract. Jenny suspected he had other plans, too. Jasmine nodded in greeting. Jenny had seldom heard her speak.

'I didn't think a few inches of snow would keep you away, Mrs Cooper,' Andy said, glancing up from his work. He invariably stuck to formal titles in a professional setting, which suited Jenny very well. Informality and dead bodies had never seemed to her an appropriate combination.

She took a paper mask from the dispenser on the wall and pulled it over her face as she crossed the room. At first she couldn't bring herself to look directly at the blackened skeleton laid out on the steel autopsy table. Thankfully, what she took to be the other two recovered from the house in Blackstone Ley remained on gurneys in cocoons of white PVC. Drawing closer, she was no longer able to avert her eyes. It was only bones – no tissue could survive the extreme temperatures in the heart of a house fire – but they smelt disconcertingly of burned fat, like the remnants of a summer barbeque.

'I always have the same reaction. It's enough to put you off your chops,' Andy said dryly. He was peering inside what remained of a skull with a slender LED flashlight.

'I take it this is Ed Morgan,' Jenny said.

'I'm still waiting for the police to arrive with the dental records, but yes, it's a male, mid-thirties or thereabouts.'

Jenny noticed that the rear of the skull was missing and that the surrounding bone was jagged and shattered. 'The police said they found a shotgun next to him.'

'There it is.' He pointed to a clear plastic evidence bag on the dissection counter to his right. 'I measured the barrel – it was physically possible for him to have placed it in his mouth and pulled the trigger.'

'So you'll corroborate their conclusion it was suicide?'

'It seems the most likely explanation. The angle the shot was fired at was slightly unconventional, though – in most cases the victim will hold the gun more upright and blow the top of the skull off rather than the back – but I'm sure this fellow was strong enough to have held it out in front of him.'

'I've seen a picture,' Jenny said. 'He was a big man.'

Andy nodded, satisfied with his observations of the skull, then turned to look at Jenny thoughtfully over his mask.

'What do we know about what happened before the fire?'

'Very little, at this stage. Why, what have you found?'

He leant over the table and indicated the bones of the right arm. 'The right ulnar and radius are fractured midway between the elbow and wrist. He suffered a violent impact – a strike from a blunt object.'

'The building collapsed on top of him,' Jenny said.

'It could have been falling debris, but it's in a very specific spot – just where your forearm might be if you were protecting your head from a blow. There are no other broken bones. It's only circumstantial evidence, but not insignificant, especially when you take into account the injuries of the other victims. Particularly the older one.'

He went over to the nearest of the two gurneys and pulled back the flap of plastic, revealing not just skeletal remains, but a shrunken, carbonized body that bore more than a passing resemblance to an unwrapped Egyptian mummy.

'She was shot in the back, between the shoulder blades,' Andy said dispassionately. 'The entry wound is nearly 100 millimetres wide. I'll need some data on the scatter pattern from this particular gun, but I say she was shot from a range of twenty feet of so. In a small house you're probably talking about a shot fired in the hallway and stairs. She was found amongst the debris from the upper storey, so I'd be tempted to speculate that it was fired from the foot of the stairs while she was at the top running away.'

'Shot by a man whose right arm was broken?'

'It's not impossible to imagine, but you've got to wonder if there was some sort of altercation between them downstairs. She could have flung a chair at him, or hit him with something else in self-defence.'

Jenny's mind filled with violent and disturbing images of Layla Hart fighting off her murderous stepfather. At moments like these she envied Andy Kerr his ability to remain so relentlessly forensic.

'What about the other girl?' Jenny asked.

'A single shot through the chest from the front,' Andy said. 'Close range.'

'Any other significant injuries on either girl?'

'None that I can see, but that's not proof of very much, given how little I've got to work with.'

Andy glanced past her to the door. Jenny turned to see DI Ryan entering. He was dressed casually in well-cut jeans and a brushed suede jacket over a plaid shirt and sweater. Expensive, designer clothes that told Jenny that Ryan was either gay (though he seemed a little deadpan for that) or liked to have women competing for his attention.

Ryan addressed Andy, handing him a buff envelope. 'Dr Kerr. I chased down those dental records.' Then he acknowledged Jenny, 'Hello again, Mrs Cooper.' He smiled, but made no offer of a handshake.

'Inspector.'

'I've got a file in the car for you. I can't pretend it'll leave you much the wiser.'

'Dr Kerr has just pointed out that Morgan had a broken arm.'

'Really.' Ryan gave an entirely neutral reaction.

'It's possible he and Layla struggled. She was shot in the back, possibly fleeing upstairs.'

'That would make sense—'

'Interesting.' The comment came from Andy Kerr, who was examining the dental records. He went back to the autopsy table and shone his flashlight into the skeleton's mouth cavity. 'There's no doubt this is Morgan, but the right canine incisor is missing.'

'Has he lost it recently?' Jenny asked.

'Hard to say. His last check-up was eighteen months ago. Hold on.' Andy went to the cupboard under the bench and came back with a hand-held ultraviolet lamp. He ran the narrow beam of light carefully over the teeth. 'What I can tell you is that we have some hairline cracks in the teeth either side of the missing incisor. I'd say he lost it traumatically, rather than through disease.'

'Kelly should be able to help you with that,' Ryan said to

Jenny. 'I've left her details in the file. When were you planning to see her?'

'I thought tomorrow,' Jenny said.

Ryan looked at her, studying her face as if he were able to read her thoughts. 'You don't have to worry, Mrs Cooper. She'll be fine with you. I made sure not to build up her expectations.'

'Thanks,' Jenny said with a pronounced note of sarcasm.

'You know what I mean.'

'Tomorrow will be fine. I'd like to be prepared.'

'You'll have my reports on these three later this afternoon,' Andy said, drawing their meeting to a close. 'Is that all for now?'

Jenny nodded. 'For now.'

She followed DI Ryan out, noticing him cast a subtle glance over at Dr Hope and catch her eye as he passed the foot of her table. She looked away quickly as if he had caught her out. Jenny believed that he had made her blush.

'What's your theory, Mrs Cooper?' Ryan asked, as they stepped around the gurneys cluttering the corridor.

'I don't have one,' Jenny answered honestly.

'I've been doing some reading up on family annihilators,' Ryan said. 'Ed Morgan was textbook. Quiet guy in a low-status job who drew his self-esteem from the respect of his family. I expect if you look far enough into his childhood you'll find something that set the syndrome in motion – abuse, violence, some catastrophic blow to his self-confidence.'

'Has he got any extended family?'

'I think there may be a cousin or two dotted about.'

'Any suggestion of violence in his recent past?'

'Not that I can find. But that's consistent with annihilators, too. They tend to erupt all at once and out of the blue.'

'He was questioned in connection with Susie Ashton's disappearance.'

'Like I told you, that was before my time.'

'You haven't gone back to the file?'

'Make even more work for myself? I don't think so.'

Jenny went ahead of him into the vestibule and paused there. 'You're not curious to know if it really was Morgan who did it?'

'I was hoping you might cast some light on that.'

'Whether it's me or you, your boss still faces the same embarrassment.'

'All Sam Abbott wants is for his name to stay out of the papers. If he finds the right doctor, he might even get himself retired early on health grounds and manage to hold on to his pension. Not exactly noble, but maybe in his shoes I'd do the same.'

Jenny met Ryan's gaze and couldn't decide whether she trusted him or not. He was bright and more than polished enough to take on any number of high-flying careers, but here he was in the South Gloucestershire CID and wearing a £1,000 outfit to visit the morgue. She wondered whether he had pride to match his vanity and couldn't function unless he was confident that he was the sharpest in the office.

'Or maybe you wouldn't, Mrs Cooper?' Ryan said with the subtly knowing look that was becoming familiar to her. 'I've heard you don't always go by the usual route.'

'I go whatever way I have to,' Jenny said. 'Now where's that file?'

Jenny sat behind the wheel of the stationary Land Rover sifting through the bundle of documents DI Ryan had handed her with the growing suspicion that Superintendent Abbott had something to hide. Besides statements from police officers and neighbours who witnessed the fire, the file contained a fire-investigation report, photographs of the destroyed house and a full forensics report from a private laboratory that had tested debris from the heart of the building. It identified the accelerant as diesel, and not only that, diesel refined and sold by BP. An accompanying map detailed the handful of BP filling stations within a twenty-mile radius. It all amounted to a comprehensive piece of police work that in any normal investigation would have taken a week, or more likely a month, to complete. This had been assembled more or less overnight, in the dog days of December. She had never known detectives move as quickly.

Leaving the file stowed under the driver's seat, Jenny made her way into the main hospital building and attempted to track down Darren Brooks. She eventually located him in a side ward next to the intensive-care unit on the third floor. His room was at the end of an empty corridor with no staff in sight. Jenny glanced through the observation pane and saw that he was alone. His upper body was propped up on pillows and most of his torso and forehead were bound with pressure bandages. Three IV bags hung from a stand at the bedside delivering fluid and drugs. She suspected he would be on maximum doses of drugs: the pain from burns was reputedly worse than any other kind. There was still no nurse to consult, so Jenny decided to take a chance and went inside.

Brooks, a man in his late thirties – though it was hard to tell beneath the bandages – looked up at her through heavily lidded, bloodshot eyes.

Jenny introduced herself and explained that she was investigating the deaths at Blackstone Ley. Then she asked if he was able to talk.

'What about?' He answered in a hoarse and fractured whisper, with a broad Gloucestershire accent.

Jenny had second thoughts. 'If you're in too much pain, this can wait.'

'I can't feel a thing,' he said, his eyes rolling upwards and exposing the whites.

Jenny brought out her phone and searched for the email Ryan had sent her. 'I'm not sure if you've been told that the police think Ed Morgan started the fire at his home deliberately—'

'My wife told me.'

Jenny held the screen up in front of his face, showing the goodbye message Ed Morgan had left for Kelly. 'Can you read that, or shall I?'

'I can manage.'

Brooks stared at it for a moment, then looked away. After a long stretch of silence, he said, 'You'd see her, the way she dressed, and she'd look like she might. But she never did, not to my knowledge. Not since she's been with Ed.'

'I was told you were close with her once.'

'Long time ago.' His gaze turned inwards. 'How is she?'

'Unhurt. She was at work. Her son's missing and her two daughters died in the fire.' Jenny stopped herself from adding extra detail. Brooks was going to be in enough pain without her adding to it.

'Kelly's a good girl,' he said slowly. 'Makes the women jealous and turns every man's head, but she's worked hard for her kids. Cleaning, bar work, not above none of it. You've got to respect that.'

'Did Ed?'

'I'm sure he did. We didn't talk much.'

'Did he strike you as the jealous kind?'

'Not 'specially. Always been a quiet bloke.'

Brooks seemed to slump, the effort of talking sapping his energy. Jenny decided she could afford one more question. It had to be a good one.

'You don't have to answer this, Mr Brooks, but did you ever suspect Ed of murdering Susie Ashton?'

He thought for a moment. 'No. Kelly would've known. She's one of those women, like – you'd tell her everything.'

Jenny couldn't stop herself from following up: 'Why do you say that?'

Brooks turned his eyes towards her. 'It's like this,' he said, his voice fading so Jenny could barely hear. 'Once in a man's lifetime he'll fall for a woman who is not of this earth. That was Kelly.'

# EIGHT

'Do you know what he means?'

'Kind of.'

Jenny was warming her legs in front of the log fire, feeling guilty that Michael had not only cooked but was now insisting on carrying their plates through to the kitchen.

'Is that it?'

'What do you want to me say?'

'It's obviously a male thing – "not of this earth".'

'You think?'

'I've not heard of women turning men into imaginary angels. It's certainly never been a fantasy of mine.'

'I suppose somewhere in their minds, most guys, well – ' he paused to correct himself, 'immature guys, have this image of a woman being pure. And if she's pure, then she's no longer quite human, is she?'

'How do you define "pure"? I mean, what are the criteria?'

'Aren't we going to watch a film now?'

'In a minute. Stop changing the subject.'

Michael came back into the room and tipped the last of the wine into their glasses that were standing empty on the mantelpiece. 'I can't speak for him. How do I know what he thinks?'

'Tell me what a pure woman is. Come on – you must have discussed this kind of stuff in the Air Force.'

Michael gave her a look, and decided to humour her. 'I think maybe we're talking about two different things. There's the one who's sweet, innocent, maternal and only has sexual feelings for you—'

'Or pretends she has.'

'You're a woman – you see through it.'

'I'm not sure Kelly Hart fits that category. She's got history. What about the other kind?'

'Well, I suppose she takes you somewhere else altogether. And she can have as much history as she likes. In fact, the more the better.'

'And still be pure? Really?'

Michael looked at her warily, as if nervous of where she was pushing him.

'Go on,' Jenny prompted. 'No need to be embarrassed.'

'I suppose what she's about, or seems to be, at least, is *pure* sex. Which means she's buying into it as absolutely and completely as the guy.'

'You think most women don't buy into sex?'

'We're keeping this in the abstract, OK – I don't want you taking this personally.'

'I won't,' Jenny insisted, but she was already comparing herself with the mythical female Michael was conjuring.

'I'm not saying most women are lacking something, I'm just saying that some women seem to possess a sort of black magic.'

'You mean the femme fatale?'

Michael stared thoughtfully into his glass and then slowly shook his head. 'No. It may not be that obvious.'

'This is interesting.' Jenny couldn't help wondering whom he was picturing – she felt sure he was thinking of someone from his past, and felt a childish twinge of jealousy. 'Go on. Describe her – theoretically, of course.'

'Quiet. Self-contained. Drops unspoken hints but makes

you come to her. Knows when to look right into your eyes – and beyond them – then how to kill you by looking away. She's not a coquette, she's somehow more direct than that, like there's something oddly male about her.'

'*Male*? Now you really are confusing me.'

'Maybe that's not the right word.' He paused to reconsider. 'This is going to sound strange, but it's as if when you're sleeping with this woman—'

'You don't meaning *sleeping*—'

'No, but the point is, it's like she's a man in a woman's body – she's after the same thing as you are. The same hit. And that's what tips it all over the line – having sex with her is like heroin, or devil worship. It's beautiful because somehow it's unnatural and dangerous.'

'Dangerous how?'

'I don't know.' He shrugged, becoming embarrassed.

'It's your word. It must mean something.'

'I suppose she's gives you everything you could dream of between the sheets, but when it's over, there's not a shred of nurture in her being.' He tipped back his wine and swallowed. 'And that, of course, is what makes her not of this earth – when it comes down to it, she's a witch. A demon.'

'Meaning she's not pure after all,' Jenny said.

'She's pure lust. And that's not a good thing.'

'But it's a drug.'

'For a while, until you realize what's missing. This woman is not going to be the mother of your children.'

'What if she's a mother already?'

'There my powers of speculation end.'

'You've never thought of me that way?'

'Oh yeah, all the time. What do *you* think?' He went in search of the TV remote.

'You've worried me, Michael.'

He flopped onto the sofa. 'You have compassion in your soul, Jenny. And that's what I love about you.'

She was touched. 'You mean that?'

'You think I'd chop wood and cook lunch for a witch?'

Jenny sat next to him and tucked her arm under his. He hadn't exactly said *I love you*, but he was getting there.

Jenny drove through the deserted Clifton streets experiencing an unfamiliar sensation of peace. Her drive into work usually involved a steady ratcheting of tension as the tasks of the day ahead lined up against her in formidable rows. But this dull December morning she felt light and unencumbered. She had a man at home who, through his actions at least, was expressing something akin to devotion. Michael had volunteered to not only go to the supermarket, but to deal with the peeling paint on the bathroom ceiling and to have dinner ready for her. In the twenty or so months they had known each other, he had never stayed at Melin Bach more than two nights in a row, and she had only ever spent single nights in his tiny rented house outside Stroud. It was difficult not to let her imagination run away with what it might portend. Was this the beginning of real commitment? She scolded herself – *Stop it, Jenny!* – but she couldn't help it. She was desperate to know.

The snowploughs had cleared the main streets of the city, but any roads smaller than major thoroughfares remained treacherous rivers of frozen slush. It was 29 December, a Friday, and Bristol seemed to have sunk into a torpor from which it would only awake on New Year's Eve. There was no traffic, the shops were shuttered, and along the entire length of Whiteladies Road the only signs of life were a vagrant pushing a heavily laden shopping trolley, and a postman. She had no trouble parking outside her office in Jamaica Street, but the cafe where she bought her morning coffee was shut up for the rest of the week, and even the convenience store that she had never once seen closed for business had given up hope.

There was a reason all sane people abandoned their workplaces between Christmas and New Year, and as she strained to turn the key in the frozen lock of the heavy front door, Jenny remembered what it was. The inside of the Georgian building felt even colder than it was outside. She could see her breath as she made her way along the ground-floor passage to the entrance to her modest offices. Inside the reception area a vaguely damp smell hung in the air. She switched on the heaters and went to the kitchenette in search of instant coffee, which in the absence of milk she would have to drink black. She hoped she could make it a short day.

Films of ice had formed on the panes of the large bay window overlooking the pavement, making huge snowflake patterns that stretched the entire width of the glass. Jenny's room felt as if it had lain abandoned for years rather than days. Eager to make progress, she huddled at her desk still wearing her coat and ski-hat, and lifted the phone to call the number for Kelly Hart that Ryan had jotted on the file. After six rings there was no answer and Jenny was ready to give up, when she heard a quiet female voice.

'Hello?'

'Good morning. This is Jenny Cooper. I'm the coroner for the Severn Vale. Am I speaking to Kelly Hart?'

There was a momentary silence. 'Yes. That's me.'

'I don't know if you're familiar with what a coroner does—'

'The police explained. Inspector Ryan told me you'd call.'

Kelly spoke with a soft Gloucestershire accent, but Jenny also detected a subtle hint of her London origins in her vowels. It was an oddly distinctive voice, and after hearing her speak only a few words, Jenny knew that she wouldn't forget it.

'Did he tell you I'd like to talk in person?'

'Yes.'

'Would midday suit you?'

'Where?' A note of alarm sounded in Kelly's voice.

'Why don't I come to you?'

'No, I—'

'That's all right.' Jenny appreciated her concern: the police would have promised to keep her whereabouts strictly confidential. 'Are you able to come to my office?'

'Can we meet outdoors somewhere?'

Jenny wondered if perhaps the fire had left her phobic about confined spaces.

'Where would you like?'

'The Observatory.'

'That's fine,' Jenny said, confirmed in her suspicion. The old Observatory stood on the edge of the open parkland of the Downs high above the Avon Gorge and commanded a view across the entire city. Nowhere in Bristol was less confined. 'I'll be the one in the pink anorak.'

'I remember what you look like – I saw you at the house.'

Jenny hesitated for a moment before answering. 'Good. I'll see you at twelve.'

Setting down the receiver, she tried to remember seeing Kelly catch sight of her face, but couldn't. She'd seen her with the female officer and watched her climb into the car and drive away. But as far as she could recall, Kelly had been staring at the ground or straight ahead. Memory could be fickle, though – you only had to spend a day in court and hear five different witnesses give an account of the same event to be left in no doubt of that.

Jenny turned back to the papers on her desk and searched out the map of BP filling stations. With a little luck she might recover CCTV footage of Ed Morgan buying the diesel he used to start the blaze. There were three of them within a twenty-minute drive of Blackstone Ley. The closest was six miles away, at a service station on the M5 motorway. Seven miles to the west there was another at the south end of the Severn Bridge. The next closest was more than ten miles distant on Gloucester Road in the north of Bristol.

Her flow of concentration was interrupted by the sound of the front door opening and closing. In the silence of the empty building she could hear footsteps in the passageway making their way to her office. She recognized them at once – Alison's.

'I'm back,' Alison called out brightly as she stepped through the door into reception. 'Passed my driving test. All legal again.' She was dressed in her best navy suit and snow boots and was carrying a carton of milk. She took it through to the kitchenette. 'I didn't think you'd remember. Am I right?'

'Yes,' Jenny said, trying to hide her surprise. She had been so absorbed in her case and with Michael that somehow she had managed to forget Alison's threat to return to work this morning.

'No wonder you've kept your coat on. It's arctic in here.'

'I haven't been in for a week.'

'I can see that,' Alison said, bustling over to her desk. 'I've never seen it so tidy. I don't know how you've managed that, we're usually rushed off our feet this time of year.' She settled in her chair and adjusted its height. 'You've had a temp in? I hope she hasn't interfered with my things.' She opened and closed the drawers in her desk, checking her belongings.

'The last one was a man, actually.'

'Oh yes? Young and good-looking, I hope.'

'Not bad.'

'No condoms or girly mags. He must have been vaguely civilized.' Satisfied that her space had not been violated, Alison looked up expectantly. 'What would you like me to get on with?'

For a moment Jenny allowed herself to believe she was looking at the Alison she had always known, but then she couldn't help notice the deep scar across her temple that was only partially hidden beneath her dyed blond fringe. Her eyes had altered subtly, too: they were slightly misaligned and seemed to stare intently and demandingly, the damage to her brain having dulled the subconscious reflex that keeps healthy eyes making constant tiny movements. Jenny realized she had no choice but to confront the issue head-on.

'I appreciate you want to get back to work,' Jenny said, 'but didn't we agree that you'd be declared fit by your consultant first?'

'I still know how to wipe my own bum, Mrs Cooper.'

Jenny ignored the uncharacteristic crudeness of the remark. 'What if it all proves too much for you?'

'You'll be able to tell, won't you? Far better than any doctor would.'

'You may not appreciate my honesty.'

'I think I might have lost the part of my brain that gives a damn about dressing things up. Shoot from the hip, Mrs Cooper, I can take it.'

The phone on Alison's desk started to ring before Jenny could reply.

'Severn Vale District Coroner's Office,' Alison answered with exaggerated politeness. 'Yes, I am,' she glanced up at Jenny, 'all things being well. Now don't tell me you've called up to wish us a happy New Year.'

Jenny knew that she had already lost the fight. Alison was perfectly aware that she wouldn't pass the detailed competency assessment recommended by the Chief Coroner's office, so had called her bluff. She had offered Jenny a bald choice between taking her back on trial and betraying her. While Jenny hadn't asked her to lay down her life for her that night in the Savernake Forest, she could hardly claim that she would have preferred to take the head-on impact from a Range Rover herself. And it wasn't only Jenny's life that had been saved; Jenny had escaped from the scene of the confrontation with the antibiotics that had pulled Ross back from the brink of death. Viewed that way, there was no question of Jenny refusing her.

Alison took notes in large, childlike script as the caller, a DI Ballantyne from Broadmead, passed on details of another traumatic death.

'Yes, I'm sure Mrs Cooper will want to see for herself,' Alison said, giving Jenny a look that said she knew the answer without needing to ask. 'If you can leave him where he is for now, she'll be along shortly. Thank you.' Alison rang off and handed Jenny her note. 'Suspected suicide in Henleaze. Male, mid-thirties, found hanging in his flat. Been there a few days, apparently.'

'He lived alone?'

'Apparently so.'

Jenny looked at the address and recognized it as one of the smarter streets in the North Bristol suburb. Solitary hangings were more usually the stuff of tower blocks and bed-sitters. A lonely suicide at Christmas. There was always one.

'I could go if you like, but I thought you'd prefer to,' Alison said. 'I mean, you don't know how many of my marbles I've got left, do you? I could be a complete nutcase with all this grey matter missing.' She tapped her flattened temple with the end of her pen.

Jenny smiled, grateful to see light return to Alison's eyes. 'We'll play it by ear, shall we?'

'I'm happy with that if you are, Mrs Cooper.'

'It's good to see you.'

'There's no need to over-egg it.' Alison switched on her computer. 'We both know the score.'

'You'd think they'd clear the pavements. What the hell did we elect a mayor for? Look at it – solid ice. Someone's going to break their bloody leg.'

Detective Inspector Jack Ballantyne smelt of last night's booze and had cut himself shaving. Last time they had met at a scene of death his beef had been what the lawyers were charging him for the privilege of divorcing his unfaithful wife. Living alone hadn't been good for him: the broken veins across his cheekbones had migrated upwards into his eyes and he looked more like sixty than forty-five. Jenny suspected he spent most nights alone with a whiskey bottle.

She ducked under the cordon tape and followed him over the few yards of pavement the police had shovelled clear leading to the Edwardian terraced house in Janus Avenue. It was a family area to which young middle-class professionals flocked for the schools, but number 15 had been divided into two single-bedroom flats. The occupants of the ground floor had been away for the holidays, Ballantyne said, and had returned home to a choking smell that had permeated the whole building.

He dug into his coat pocket and pulled out a crumpled paper mask. 'Here, have mine. I'm used to it.'

'Thanks,' Jenny said, trying to sound grateful, and pulled it uncertainly over her face as they approached the front door. The mask was impregnated with a sickly pine scent that was invariably as hard to stomach as the odour that started to reach them as they stepped inside the tidy communal hall.

Ballantyne led the way up the single flight of stairs to the first-floor landing, breathing heavily with the effort. 'Our forensics boys have done their bit, but I doubt we'll be looking for a third party.' He paused to catch his breath at the top, then pushed open the door to the flat. 'After you, ma'am. You'll find him at the end there.' He pointed along the short passageway.

The detective hung back where the air was still breathable, as Jenny made her way to the partially open internal door ahead of her. The flat felt light and modern, with cream-coloured walls and matching carpet – not what she had been expecting. It told her to expect a neat suicide: the kind where the deceased left things in order for those who would have the unpleasant task of cleaning up. She encountered several such cases each year: often a man who had been diagnosed with a terminal illness or who was facing investigation for a shameful crime. Alison called them 'considerate suicides'.

She pushed the living room door open gingerly, resisting the impulse to gag as she connected the stench of decay with its source. She fought the urge to close her eyes. 'Is this how everything was, with the chair on its side?'

'Just like that,' Ballantyne answered.

Jenny stepped forward into a sitting room which the dead man had used partly as an office. There was also a mini-gym against the far wall. Barefoot, and dressed in tracksuit bottoms and a training vest, Daniel Burden was hanging by a short length of nylon rope from the steel pull-up bars. He was a small man, probably no more than 5'6", with a closely shaved head and of stocky build. He had worked hard on his biceps and had a neat goatee beard. To the right of the mini-gym and lying on its side, was an office-style chair on castors, which it seemed he had stood on to gain the height he needed to hang himself. His flesh had started to decay and was speckled with large patches of gangrene that were slowly joining up, like ink blots on blotting paper.

Apart from the upended chair, the room was in perfect order, right down to the plumped-up cushions on the sofa and the DVDs lined up precisely on a shelf above the TV. Opposite the mini-gym was a small, orderly workstation. A laptop sat on the desk, its standby lightly blinking unerringly.

'What's on his computer?' Jenny called over her shoulder.

'Take a look,' Ballantyne answered. 'You won't be long, will you? I think I might puke.'

'Give me a moment.'

Keeping her eyes off the body, Jenny crossed over to the computer and pressed the on button. The screen flickered into life. Burden had been watching porn. As far as Jenny could make out, the movie clip involved men and women in various combinations, all having fun in a hot tub. By internet standards it was relatively innocent. She opened a new tab to call up his browsing history and found that, apart from the record of his final visits to the porn site on the night of 23 December, it had been cleared. It was what she would have expected, and hinted that his usual interests might have been a little stronger.

Reaching the limits of her tolerance, she swept the room one last time with her eyes, looking out for anything that might lend an insight into Burden's state of mind, or even evidence that his death could have been what she had learned to call a '3A' – an accidental autoerotic asphyxiation. There was nothing. He'd been thorough. All she noticed was that a pair of training shoes lined up at the side of the desk were only a size six. She wondered if they might belong to a girlfriend, but on the way out she checked a pair of loafers in his wardrobe. Size six again. Burden simply had small feet.

Jenny kept her questions until they had left the building and could breathe easily again. Ballantyne said there were two DCs back at the station checking out Burden's history, and all he could tell her for certain was what they had gathered from the paperwork in his desk. He was thirty-five years old, single, owned an eight-year-old Ford Galaxy which was parked across the street, and had worked at the passport office in Newport for the past seven years. He commuted to work by train from Bristol Parkway station: they had found his season ticket in his wallet.

'What about a next of kin?'

'None listed on his passport or his driver's licence. We'll find out and let you know.'

'Did forensics find evidence of drink or drugs? I didn't see any.'

'Couple of beers in the fridge. No more than that.'

'December the 23rd. I didn't see any Christmas decorations in there, did you?'

'It doesn't take a lot of working out, does it?' Ballantyne said. 'Poor lonely bastard.'

# NINE

Jenny left her car at the edge of the Downs and made her way through the hard-frozen snow that crunched underfoot. Up ahead, a solitary female figure dressed in a pink anorak with the hood up was standing by the railings to the side of the observatory. There was no mistaking that it was Kelly. She was looking out at the view: the narrow Clifton Bridge spanning the gorge, the Avon four hundred feet below snaking down to the docks; rows of pastel-coloured Georgian houses clinging to the hillside.

Jenny expected Kelly to turn at the sound of her approach, but she remained with her back to her, looking out, until Jenny arrived at her side.

'Kelly Hart?'

'Yes.' She spoke in a faint, disinterested voice. The recently bereaved, particularly those who had suffered a catastrophe as huge as she had, often spent days or even weeks in what Jenny could only describe as a state of mental anaesthesia. Kelly was clearly in such a condition: numb and remote. It might take many days before she would find herself able to cry.

Catching a glimpse of her face from close quarters, Jenny began to understand what it was that Darren Brooks had meant when he had described her as not of this earth: deep-green eyes, skin the colour of polished olive wood and full red lips. It was an effortless, unselfconscious beauty that she almost seemed to shrink from.

'Are you sure you're all right to talk out here?'

'I prefer it,' Kelly said.

'Fine.' Jenny stamped her feet, trying to get blood into her aching toes. 'Did DI Ryan tell you what I'll be doing?'

'Kind of.'

'I have to determine the cause of your daughters' deaths. And your partner's.'

'What about Robbie?'

'Well, if it comes to it—'

'He's dead.'

'Right.' Jenny struggled for an appropriate response.

'I'm his mother. I know.'

'Let's hope the police have some news for you soon.'

'It doesn't matter if they do or they don't.' She spoke in the same even, detached voice, her gaze fixed on the view.

Jenny let a silence open up between them, hoping she could use it to read Kelly's state of mind. She was fearful of pushing dangerous buttons, especially up here, with the cliff edge so close. It suddenly felt a foolish place to be having this kind of conversation.

It was Kelly who spoke first. 'What did you want to ask me?'

'I'm trying to find out a little about Ed. You've seen the message he left.'

Kelly nodded.

Jenny trod carefully. 'Is there anything you'd like to tell me about what he said?

'Like what?'

Jenny became acutely aware that the railings in front of them were barely waist height. A few yards away was a drop all the way down to the foot of the gorge. Several people with far more reason to live than Kelly jumped each year. It was Jenny's job to deal with the aftermath.

'Are you talking about him calling me a whore?' Kelly shook her head. 'Life was complicated enough without adding another man to it.'

'Oh? Could I ask in what way?'

Kelly shivered suddenly. 'Would you mind if we walked for a bit?'

'No problem,' Jenny said, relieved to be moving away to safer ground.

Kelly set off in no particular direction across the Downs, her hands thrust deep into her coat pockets. Sensing their conversation might not last long, Jenny gently prompted her.

'You said life was complicated.'

'Work, kids, you know. Ed was cut down to two days at Fairmeadows last year, so I ended up working six nights a week behind a bar. And more hours in the day.'

'I spoke to Mr and Mrs Ashton. She said you helped her out.'

'She's been good to me. I mostly work at the Grants' – the big house outside the village. The one with the tennis court.'

'I must have missed it.'

'You can't miss that place if you've driven by.'

Jenny pushed a little further and coaxed out the fact that, because of her hours, Kelly had left Ed with most of the childcare. He'd been great when the girls were young, but struggled to cope with Layla, who at fourteen had discovered boys and alcohol and developed an attitude.

'All she had to do was swear at him and he'd back off.' Kelly said. 'He didn't know how to handle her and she knew it.'

'What about your youngest?'

'Mandy's never been any trouble. Not so much of her father in her, I guess.'

Kelly quickened her pace and turned sharply to the right across an open, empty expanse. Jenny got the feeling that she had already had enough.

'I'll leave you alone,' Jenny said. 'But if you could just tell me about the graffiti on the side of your house—'

'Nothing to tell. It just turned up one night.'

'When?'

'Around August, September.' She seemed unsure.

'Do you have any idea who did it?'

'Something to do with Layla, I expect. Probably borrowed money from someone and didn't pay it back.'

'Is that why Ed built the fence?'

'That's always been there. He built that after Susie Ashton. I always said to him it wouldn't happen twice in the same place, but . . .' Her voice trailed off. She took several more steps then stopped abruptly and turned to face Jenny for the first time. 'You try your best. You try to be a good mother – ' Her eyes flashed briefly with anger and bewilderment, then just as quickly emptied again. She stared at Jenny as if she had suddenly found herself lost in a hostile and alien landscape.

'My car's not far,' Jenny said. 'Why don't I drop you home?'

Kelly sat in silence with her hood up as Jenny drove through Clifton towards the address in Fishponds she had given her. It was at moments like this when Jenny appreciated why other coroners only ever met face to face with the bereaved in the formal surroundings of their office, if at all. She told herself that it was still open to her to keep things at arm's length, to treat the case as a paper exercise which she could deal with at her desk and file away. All she owed Kelly was a fair examination of the evidence, and despite his attempt to make her feel guilty, she owed DI Ryan nothing.

For the second time in their meeting, it was Kelly who broke the impasse.

'You didn't ask me if I thought Ed was, you know – interfering with the girls.'

Jenny felt her heart start to race. She tried not to let her anxiety sound in her reply: 'I didn't think it was a good moment to go into those kinds of details.'

'I've been thinking about it. I don't think he was. I would have known.' A pause. 'Have you got kids?'

'A son. Grown up now.'

'I thought I knew everything about them. Maybe it's different with boys, but I thought I knew my girls. I usually do know things about people. I can tell what they're thinking. Like Clare Ashton – I know she likes me, but she's always been jealous of my kids. You can't blame her, but I'd never bring Robbie to her house.' She was still for a moment, then shook her head. 'But I thought I knew Ed, didn't I?'

They were approaching Kelly's street. Jenny's time with her was running out. 'Look, I don't want to burden you with any more questions now, but maybe if you were to talk to my officer on Monday. I'd like you to make a statement – anything you think I ought to know.' She turned the corner.

'Whatever you want.' She pointed to a modern, three-storey block of flats on the right. 'I think that's the place.' She didn't seem altogether sure.

Jenny pulled up at the kerb outside, but Kelly remained seated, as if unable to bring herself to step out into her new reality.

'Is this the place?'

Kelly nodded.

Jenny spoke to Kelly's reflection on the inside of the windscreen. 'Tell me what you think happened.'

'If I didn't know Ed, I can't know anything, can I?' Kelly

said, staring straight ahead. 'You read in magazines about couples where the woman goes cold and never wants to know. I was never like that. I was always there for him.'

'That's what I'm here for,' Jenny heard herself say, 'to see if I can't put those missing pieces together.' She felt suddenly frightened for Kelly, and reluctant to let her go into the flat alone. 'Is there anyone who can stay with you? I'm not sure you should be by yourself.'

Kelly glanced across at her, making eye contact for the first time. 'I know what you're thinking, but no, I won't. I can't tell you why, but I do still believe in something. I do still have a reason to live.' She reached for the door handle. 'Thanks for dropping me back.'

Jenny watched her pick her way over the pavement to the front door of the block. The slender figure in the pink anorak could have been anyone, but she wasn't. She was the woman whose partner had just murdered her children and then blown his head apart.

# TEN

'DETECTIVE INSPECTOR RYAN CALLED,' Alison announced as Jenny arrived back in the office.

'Did he say what he wanted?'

'Got something for you, he said. He's going to bring it down. Nice voice – has he got looks to match?'

'I haven't noticed,' Jenny lied. 'Would you like a sandwich?' She offered her one of the two packets she had picked up at a service station. 'I think they've been made this side of Christmas.'

'Thanks.' Alison grabbed one and tore the packet open. Jenny watched, unsure how to react as Alison bit off half a sandwich in one bite. A large fleck of mayonnaise stuck to her chin, but she didn't seem to notice as she took a second huge mouthful. 'God, I was starving'.

'So I see,' Jenny said mutely and turned to her office.

'Oh, and Dr Kerr emailed the reports – the bodies from Blackstone Ley,' Alison called after her through a mouthful of food. 'He said he's not in this afternoon but you can call him if you want to talk.'

Jenny tried again to make it across the threshold of her private space.

'I used to think he had a bit of a thing for you,' Alison persisted, 'but I hear his interests may lie elsewhere at the moment.'

'I think that was probably in your imagination.'

'That's what Paul's always telling me, but he doesn't notice anything. It took him twenty-five years to realize he should have got together with me in the first place. But I can't believe you didn't notice it.'

'Andy Kerr is ten years younger than I am.'

'All the more reason to feel flattered. You've still got that pilot of yours, have you?'

Jenny avoided the questions. 'I'd better start looking at these reports.'

'No change then – one foot either side of the door, has he? I suppose you know what you're doing.'

'We're fine,' Jenny said, praying this wasn't what she had to look forward to at all future lunch breaks.

She had made it to the far side of her office door and was about to push it shut when Alison called out yet again. 'I looked up some of the old newspaper reports on the Susie Ashton case yesterday. There were some pretty dark theories going around about who took her.'

'I'm sure.'

'I'll get them to you. You ought to see. I had half a mind to talk to the papers myself when we wound that investigation down. It does make you wonder.'

Against her better instincts, Jenny felt herself caving in to curiosity. 'Wonder what?'

'Who decided to call it off. And why.'

'Presumably you chased up every lead and had none left?'

'You can always look for more. Personally, I never thought it was Sam Abbott's choice or even his super's at the time. Call me a nutter, but my theory was the order came from much higher up.'

Jenny couldn't remember ever hearing Alison insinuate against her former colleagues in the police, still less entertain conspiracy theories about the higher ranks.

'You tell me why you thought that,' Jenny said, 'and I'll tell you if it's nutty or not.'

Alison swallowed the last of her sandwich and sat back in her chair, the spot of mayonnaise still clinging stubbornly to her chin. 'We talked a lot about paedophile rings in CID. Went through every known offender and dragged more than thirty men out of their beds in this city alone. But what I hadn't known about rings is how many different kinds of blokes you'll find in them. Back then it was all word of mouth – X knows Y, meets Z and puts them in touch. You'd have all sorts – an army officer, a clergyman, a teacher and a hospital porter, all in the same circle. And the richer the blokes in the ring, the more likely they'd be to use blue-collar types to do their dirty work. Pay them a few grand in cash to set them up with a victim and away you go.'

'You're talking about the police protecting a powerful and influential suspect?'

'I was just a humble DS, but Sam Abbott and his DIs were talking to convicted nonces all over the country. You remember the pressure the press were putting on? It was unbearable. Anyone who led them to a conviction would have been given a big fat envelope. And if they were already inside, they wouldn't have stayed there for long. It was that sort of case. Abbott would have sold his mum on the town bridge for a result.'

Jenny smiled at the turn of phrase that Alison must have picked up during her twenty-five years' frequenting the police canteen. She touched a finger to her chin: 'Mayonnaise.'

'Bugger!' Alison wiped it away with the back of her hand and grinned. 'You'll tell me if I start dribbling, Mrs Cooper?'

'I will.'

*

Dr Kerr had emailed three characteristically concise post-mortem reports, each confined to a single sheet. Ed Morgan's was the first Jenny opened.

Name of Deceased: **Edward Morgan (Male)**
Age: **36 yrs 4 months**
Weight: **85.7 kilos**

I
Disease or condition directly leading to death: (a)
  **Gunshot wound to the skull and tissues of the brain**
Antecedent causes (b)
  **None**

II
Other significant conditions contributing to the death but NOT related to the disease or condition causing it
  **None observed**

Morbid conditions present but in the pathologist's view NOT contributing to death
  **None observed**

Is any further laboratory examination to be made which may affect the cause of death?
  **No**

Comments:
  **The deceased's remains were recovered from a dwelling house that had been destroyed by fire. All soft tissues had been incinerated. A shotgun wound inflicted from close range entered the skull through the back of the mouth. An exit wound of 6 cm diameter was observed in the parietal bone. The upper-right canine incisor was absent. Cracks observed to right lateral incisor and right first pre-molar**

indicate recent trauma, possibly caused by recoil from the discharged weapon.

Jenny turned to the second report. Dr Kerr had reported Amanda Hart as being eleven years eight months old and weighing thirty-six kilos. He had listed two conditions as causative of death: gunshot wound to the chest / asphyxiation by smoke inhalation. In his comments he wrote: Circumstantial evidence indicates that death was caused by a gunshot wound. Due to the condition of the remains, it is impossible to determine if smoke had been inhaled before the infliction of this injury. Knowing that his conclusions on Layla Hart would be much the same, Jenny skimmed the final page, noting that the shot had entered the upper back between the third and fifth thoracic vertebrae. Again Dr Kerr commented that it was impossible to say whether she had inhaled smoke before death, but concluded with a remark that Jenny had to read twice: Close examination of charred tissues of lower abdomen reveals evidence of foetal remains. Estimated fifteen weeks' gestation.

Jenny grabbed the phone and dialled Andy Kerr's mobile number. She impatiently counted eight rings before he answered with a cautious hello. Small children were squealing excitedly in the background.

'Sorry – it's not a good time,' Jenny said.

'Family gathering. Hold on, I could do with a moment's peace.' She heard him step outside and close the door on the noise. 'That's better. I expect I know what you're going to ask, Mrs Cooper – is there any retrievable DNA from the foetus? The answer is maybe, but maybe not. It'll take some expensive work that probably won't yield anything conclusive.'

'I'll find a way of paying for it. It won't come out of your budget.'

'We're talking about multiple samples – it'll be £5,000 at least.'

'I'm owed a few favours. I'll call them in.'

'If you're sure. I'll have Jasmine ship it to the Home Office lab this afternoon. I can't promise they'll be quick.'

'It can wait a few days. Enjoy the party.'

'I'll try,' he said, with more than a hint of resignation. 'Oh, one more thing, while we're talking – I've been thinking about the father's broken tooth. If you're getting the gun's scatter pattern tested, you might want to think about getting an opinion on its recoil. It could be that it knocked the tooth out jumping back after it was fired. It's bagged up at the mortuary, if you want to collect it. I'll be in tomorrow.'

'On the Saturday before New Year's Eve?'

'You're not telling me you've got a better offer?'

'For once, yes. Have fun.'

The list of death reports in her inbox awaiting attention had grown by six during the course of the morning. Aside from Daniel Burden's case, the others were largely routine matters – four deaths in hospital and one suspected coronary in a 45-year-old male who had crashed off the motorway seemingly having fallen asleep at the wheel – but each required tough decisions and form-filling. With a flavourless sandwich in one hand and working her keyboard with the other, Jenny tried to force herself to stick to these mundane tasks, but her mind refused to be distracted from the mounting questions she had about the deaths at Blackstone Ley.

Losing the battle, she grabbed a pen and a blue legal pad and, in no particular order, started to commit her disjointed thoughts to paper. Behind it all was the question of what had lit the fuse on the night of the 28 December, and how far she felt obliged to go in finding the answer. Would she take the evidence at face value and return a simple verdict of unlawful killing by Ed Morgan, followed by his suicide, or would she feel compelled to dig deep into the reasons and come up with a narrative that explained the whole chain of events? Before learning of Layla's pregnancy, she might have been tempted by the easy road. But the more she thought about it, the less she could square the prospect of leaving questions unanswered with her conscience. Ed, Layla and Kelly all had complicated histories that needed excavating; she would have to talk to friends, neighbours and employers. She would need medical records, bank statements, lists of phone calls made and received. She would have to sort rumour from fact and lay it all out in a public inquest that risked churning up painful memories and turning a community inside out.

In the space of a few minutes she filled two whole pages with a complex web of questions, theories and fragments of evidence. Her sandwich lay half-eaten and the pen poised, trembling in her hand. She had tackled big cases before in her modest inquests, held in village halls in unlikely corners of the county; she had embarrassed corporations, exposed corrupt public officials and even uncovered heinous crimes, but there was a peculiar kind of darkness that loomed out of her spiralling frenzy of notes. The fatal fire no longer seemed to carry the violent energy of an explosive conflagration, but rather its opposite: the dark, inky centre of a very black hole. And underneath it was the nagging fear that what had happened just a few nights before was a strange and not-unconnected echo of Susie Ashton's vanishing.

'DI Ryan for you.'

Jenny looked up from her computer, having finally managed to turn her mind to other things.

'Shall I show him in?' Alison asked.

'Please do.'

Alison smiled, as if to say 'I wouldn't say no', and ushered him in.

Gabriel Ryan came through the door dressed in a well-chosen outfit and greeted her with an amused smile.

'Your officer's very friendly.'

'She had an accident,' Jenny said quietly. 'It's her first day back.'

'I heard about that. Sam Abbott told me. Drove into the path of a couple of mad Saudis out in the woods.'

'I'm sure it lost nothing in the telling.'

'I heard you handled yourself pretty impressively, too.'

'I didn't have a lot of choice.' She pushed the painful memories of that night from her mind. Ryan wouldn't have known what had happened to Ross. Her son's connection with events had remained a closely guarded secret. Even he didn't know the whole story that had led to him nearly losing his life to a genetically modified bacterium.

Ryan gave her a look that was partly admiring, partly amused. He cast his eyes around her office in the same way he had done in her kitchen the day before. 'When you hear "coroner" you think – well, I didn't think you.'

'My officer mentioned you had something for me,' Jenny said, in what she hoped was a convincingly formal tone.

He reached into his inside pocket. 'I got hold of the passwords from Ed and the kids' Facebook accounts. I haven't asked for them to be taken down yet – you never know if someone might post something useful.'

He handed her a single sheet of folded paper containing three email addresses and passwords. Ed's was the vaguely poetic *Viewfromthew00ds*. Layla had chosen *Sexylilbitch*, and Mandy *My89Hart*.

'Says something about them, don't you think?' he said.

'Really?'

'Look at Ed's, those two zeros like eyes staring out at you.'

'Or the barrels of a shotgun?'

'I hadn't thought of that. Are you sure you didn't study psychology?'

'I sometimes feel like I have.' She tucked the passwords away into her pad, aware of Ryan's eyes on her. 'Is that it? You came all the way over here just to give me these?'

'Not exactly.' He tugged at his shirt cuff, the nervous gesture telling Jenny he was holding something back. 'Have you spoken with Kelly?'

'I met her this afternoon.'

'You asked her about Ed's message?'

'I did. She denies there was anyone else in her life.'

'That's what she told me. I *think* I believed her.'

'Meaning you did or you didn't?'

'Meaning I was worried that she felt it was her fault in some way. Even if there *was* someone else, it would be no excuse for anything.'

Jenny tried to read him, searching for a motive other than one that seemed too unlikely for a detective. 'Are you worried about her? I am, though she did her best to reassure me, which isn't always a good sign. Her precise words were "I do still believe in something. I do still have a reason to live."'

Ryan gave an uncertain nod. 'You were right in what you said on the phone – a real detective would forget about it and move on.'

'There's something you might be able to help me with,' Jenny said. 'Have you seen the post-mortem reports?'

He shook his head. 'Not yet.'

'Layla was pregnant. Nearly four months. There's only a slight chance of recovering DNA. You can't help wondering if it was Ed, and if she was going to tell her mother.'

'Does Kelly know?'

'No. I didn't hear until after I spoke to her.'

'That would put it all together,' Ryan said. 'I'll ask around off company time, see if I can turn anything up.'

'You could just leave that to me,' Jenny said, giving him a way out.

'I can't seem to help myself,' Ryan responded. 'Something about this case.' He glanced off into space. 'I guess they're bound to come along.' He looked back at Jenny. 'Do you ever get angry?'

'All the time.'

'I've never been angry with a dead man before – it's a peculiar feeling.'

'Maybe you should talk to someone.'

Ryan smiled, amused at the thought. 'Maybe I will.' He got to his feet. 'See you around.'

As he made his way out, Jenny heard Alison collar him in reception.

'I don't think we've been properly introduced.'

'No—'

'Alison Trent. I used to be DS in Bristol CID before I fetched up here. Spent my last eight years on serious crimes. I was on the team seconded to the Susie Ashton case – Gloucester didn't have enough bodies to deal with it on their own.'

'Right.' Ryan was showing little enthusiasm for the conversation.

Alison failed to notice. 'I learned a thing or two about country coppers out there. Nice blokes, clever enough in their own way, but definitely old-school. Not what you'd call sophisticated.'

Jenny heard Ryan move towards the door.

'Give my best to Sam Abbott,' Alison called after him. 'He

could be a right calculating bastard sometimes. Can't think what he must make of a pretty boy like you.'

Jenny imagined Ryan giving her a tolerant smile as he walked out of the office and closed the door quietly behind him.

# ELEVEN

THE FORESTRY COMMISSION DEPOT WAS a mile north-east of Blackstone Ley, at the end of a lane. It was not yet four o'clock, but after only a few brief hours of daylight, the countryside was sinking rapidly into another sixteen-hour midwinter night. Jenny eased the Land Rover along the single-track lane with still more questions accumulating in her mind. She had spent the hour after Ryan's visit trawling through Ed's and the two girls' Facebook histories and had found no evidence that he was a man who had harboured murderous tendencies. He had posted once or twice each week, mostly with photographs of Robbie, animals he'd spotted out in the woods or birds that had visited a feeder outside his kitchen window. His few online friends appeared to share similar harmless interests. The only reference Jenny found to violence was a brief account of his running into a couple of poachers the previous October, one of whom had broken his ankle struggling to haul a deer carcass back to their truck.

Layla's posts had been more colourful, but from what Jenny could see, all the talk between her and her friends was of meet-ups, parties and who fancied who. Once you learned to see past the code in which it was written, it was just the same kind of harmless, posturing stuff kids of Jenny's generation used to share at the bus stop. Far from trading secrets, the kids in Layla's circle seemed to hide behind carefully constructed personas. Jenny searched hard for evidence of a boyfriend, but found nothing that could be called intimate. Layla seemed to conduct most of her online conversations with a girl named Nicky Brooks. Nicky's security settings allowed Jenny to access only basic information, but it was enough to establish that she also lived in Blackstone Ley. Jenny assumed that she was Darren Brooks's daughter.

Mandy Hart had opened her account only two months before, and had used it very little. Contrary to all the scare stories that filled the newspapers, Jenny's observation was that eleven-year-old girls behaved quite innocently online: it was all pictures of pop stars, harmless chit-chat about boys, and playground gossip. Layla and Mandy hadn't become online friends (Layla had ignored Mandy's request), and Ed, it seemed, had kept entirely away from them both.

Kelly Hart had used her account even less than her youngest daughter. She had left it open to the world, with the loosest security settings, but had made only three substantial posts: each one a photograph of herself in a different setting. In the first she was in cut-off jeans, paddling in the surf on a Cornwall beach; in the second she was dressed up for a party in a short black frock. The third was very different: a soulful portrait of Kelly standing next to a pond in autumnal woodland, dated the previous October. Whereas the first two pictures had been smiling and optimistic, this one had left Jenny with an impression of a woman who, whether she was aware of it or not, was suffering from a sense of melancholic longing; resigned to, but not fulfilled by, the life she was leading.

A solitary pick-up painted in dark green Forestry Commission livery was parked outside the small, timber-clad office building. Beyond it was a fenced-in area of hardstanding in which several items of heavy plant – two tractors and a tree harvester that did the work of fifteen men – were slowly disappearing under a thick covering of snow. The sweep of Jenny's headlights across the office windows as she entered the yard brought a face to the glass. The man inside squinted out into the gloom, not expecting visitors. He came to the door as Jenny mounted the short flight of steps leading up to it. He was around fifty, with heavy-set shoulders, and weathered, bovine features.

He greeted her suspiciously. 'What can I do for you?'

'Jenny Cooper. I'm the coroner. I left a message on your machine.'

'Oh, that was you, was it?' He looked her up and down once more, with the slow, patient gaze he might have used to size up an awkward piece of standing timber. 'Bob Bream. Come in.'

Jenny followed him into an office heated by a large pot-bellied stove. Of the three desks, only one showed signs of activity. Bream stepped behind it.

'Everyone else on holiday?' Jenny asked by way of small-talk, as she took a seat.

'Best place for them, this weather,' Bream said, easing his huge body into a swivel chair.

Jenny noticed his hands: palms the size of tea plates, with thick, calloused fingers. 'I'm right in thinking you're the local manager?'

'*Forestry Officer*, not that it makes any odds. A couple of full-time staff and a few machines. Not exactly an empire.'

'Does that include Ed Morgan?'

'No. Ed was part-time. He'd fell the odd bit of tricky stuff the machines couldn't get to, and keep the deer down – and the odd boar. He'd no head for desk work.'

'Had you known him long?'

Bream nodded. 'About thirty-five years. He was a cousin,

well, half-cousin, strictly speaking. Known him from a babe in arms.'

'You sound as if you were close?'

'Close enough. My mother's side never much cared for the Morgans – no one remembers why – but Ed was all right. Yes, he was a good lad.' He shook his head. 'What do you think happened, then? None of us can work it out – he was the sort of bloke you'd trust with your life.'

'What have you heard?'

'All sorts – gunshots, this and that. You know how people talk.'

Jenny took out her phone and for the second time that day called up Ed Morgan's parting message. She handed it across to Bream who read it with a puzzled expression, then read it again with a growing look of disbelief.

'No,' he scoffed. 'Pardon my French, Mrs Cooper – that's bollocks. Total bollocks.' He pushed the phone back across the desk. 'One of the sanest men I knew.' Bream sat back in his chair, which creaked under his weight, and shook his head firmly. 'That's just someone's sick joke, that is. Ed didn't write that.'

'It seems he posted it before the fire broke out.'

'He might have posted something, but that's not to say someone else didn't get in and edit it after. My kids get up to that stuff all the time.' Registering Jenny's evident look of surprise, Bream said, 'You hadn't thought of that?'

'Yes, of course,' Jenny lied. 'It's a possibility, I suppose.' She made a mental note to have Alison investigate; better still, DI Ryan. 'But who do you think might do that?'

'How would I know?'

'Did Ed have any enemies?'

'The odd poacher, maybe. Even then, he'd not refuse a drink with most of them.'

'What about Darren Brooks?'

'Brooksy's over all that. Been settled back with Sandra for years.'

Jenny thought of Brooks's words to her from his hospital bed – about Kelly being a woman not of this earth – but decided that, for the moment, she would keep them to herself.

'Do you know if Ed and Kelly were happy?' Jenny asked.

'He never said any different. And it wasn't as if he was the silent type. I've known some of those in this job, guys you wouldn't be surprised to find hanging from a rope out in the woods somewhere, but that wasn't Ed. He was a contented sort.'

'I've been told he didn't much like Kelly having to work as hard as she did.'

'You've not come across people making up stories before?'

'Sorry – I'm just repeating what I'd been told.'

'Well, if I were you, Mrs Cooper, I would treat whatever folk tell you round here with a shovel-load of salt. As far as half of them are concerned, we've been harbouring a child-murderer for ten years. No matter that it's never happened again, once people get the rumour disease they can't seem to shake it.' He fixed her with a steady look. 'Ed's been working out of this place ten years. I think I knew him better than most.'

'Perhaps I ought to make myself clear, Mr Bream. I'm not here to make accusations. I'm just searching for anything that might shed some light. Let's just imagine Ed did write that message—' Bream interrupted her with a dismissive grunt. Jenny persisted: 'Is there anyone you can think of whom he might have imagined – correctly or incorrectly – Kelly had become involved with?'

'Now you're asking me to make up stories?'

'No—'

'Listen,' Bream interrupted, placing his outsize palms on

the desk, 'I don't know how I can put it any more plainly. Ed was a gentleman. Loved his kid, and Kelly's. He never had a bad word for anyone, not even Harry Grant when he sacked him off his estate. He even let Kelly go back and work for him – so what does that tell you about the man?'

'What happened with Grant, if you don't mind my asking?'

'Ed used to run his shoot for him, had a cottage with the job. When Susie Ashton went missing, Ed was one of those the police were talking to. Grant accused him of stealing diesel oil, just to give him an excuse to sack him. Dirty trick, but that's lawyers for you.'

'Not Grant as in Grant & Whitman?'

'So I believe.'

'But Kelly still works for that family?'

'When you live out here, you take whatever you can get.'

This detail came as a curious surprise. Jenny had had dealings with Grant and Whitman twice in her tenure as coroner and didn't care to repeat the experience. They were a small but highly successful firm of Bristol solicitors, who in the space of only a few years had earned a national reputation for protecting wealthy and famous individuals who found themselves attracting the unwanted attention of the media. Corrupt bankers, politicians caught cheating on their wives, and disgraced celebrities beat a path to their door. If you could afford them, they knew how to close a story down faster than any in the business. Jenny remembered Hugo Whitman as a man who hid a vicious streak behind well-practised charm. Harry Grant was more enigmatic and let his partner do the talking, preferring to conduct his business as privately as possible.

'I'll tell you what, Mr Bream,' Jenny said, 'why don't I leave you one of my cards, and if you think of anything else, you can drop me an email.'

'Such as?'

Jenny made a stab in the dark. 'Did Ed ever mention that someone graffitied his house?'

'That? That was all down to Layla. She and Nicky Brooks got mixed up with a group of lads down in Bristol. They took to coming up here at weekends with their cars and motorbikes. Blackstone people didn't like that.'

'Ed knew who painted it?'

'He might have had his suspicions, but he knew better than to mention any names.'

'You're suggesting that it was someone local?'

'Come on, Mrs Cooper. I have to live here, same as everyone else. And we all know what a man does in drink mightn't be what he'd do next morning.'

'Maybe so,' Jenny said, deciding not to pick a fight here, but to leave the hard questions to the courtroom. 'You know how to reach me. Thank you for your time.' As she rose from her chair, she said, 'Nicky Brooks – am I right in assuming she's Darren Brooks's daughter?'

Bream nodded. 'She was a good girl, too, till she fell in with Layla. Funny how you can't cheat your blood.' Responding to Jenny's questioning look, Bream continued on his theme: 'Layla's father was a villain, wasn't he? And she was showing all the signs of taking after him. I wouldn't be surprised if she started the fire.'

Jenny suppressed the urge to tell Bream that Layla had been shot through the back while she fled upstairs, but decided she would leave that until the courtroom, too. The witness shocked with unexpected facts invariably spilled more truth than the one who was prepared. She was looking forward to shocking Bob Bream. She had the feeling it might do him good.

\*

Jenny had one more call to make before turning home. She travelled four miles north-east along deserted, snow-covered lanes towards the estuary port of Sharpness. Amid a flat expanse of fields sloping down to the river, the lights of Fair-meadows Farm were visible from more than half a mile away. She started to smell it soon afterwards: the sharp ammonia of animal dung mixed with a foul, yeasty odour. Its source became clear as she turned off the lane onto a straight, wide stretch of driveway, leading to the illuminated yard in front of the complex of barns and industrial sheds: a solid column of thick, steamy smoke rose from a steel chimney into the windless night.

Jenny pulled up next up next to an empty stock lorry. The car's thermometer said the outside temperature was minus three. A shapeless, androgynous figure came down a flight of external steps from an office on the first floor of the adjacent building. As the figure approached, Jenny saw that it was a sturdily built young woman hidden beneath a thick fleece jacket and woollen hat.

'You must be Mrs Cooper. Annie Preece, Assistant Manager.'

'That's right. I was hoping to speak to Mr Johns, the managing director.'

'I'm afraid he isn't here. Sorry.' She didn't sound in the least apologetic.

'I thought my officer had spoken to him?'

Annie Preece gave a defensive smile. 'The police wanted a word. You know – they're still looking for the boy. Mr Johns had to go up to Gloucester. He should be back tomorrow.'

Jenny felt herself start to shiver. She hadn't eaten in hours and the biting cold seemed to reach inside her clothes and grip her bones. 'I was hoping to have a look around.'

'Oh. Right.' She appeared nervous. 'I just work in the office mostly – accounts and that.'

Jenny was determined not to have to make a return trip. 'I'm conducting an investigation. I need to see where Ed Morgan worked. I'm sure it won't take long.'

Offered no choice, the young woman reluctantly turned and led Jenny across the gritted concrete towards the largest of the buildings. En route they passed a long, low shed about thirty yards in length. Heavy-duty stock railings created several narrowing channels through which arriving animals would be funnelled until they arrived inside in single file.

'That must be the abattoir,' Jenny said.

Annie Preece nodded. 'Ed Morgan wasn't a qualified slaughterman, so he didn't work in there. He was mostly over this side, feeding the machines.'

She opened a large sliding door and took Jenny into a cavernous building of warehouse proportions that smelt overpoweringly of boiling offal and ground bones. Jenny surveyed the array of steel hoppers, conveyors and cylindrical tanks, which gave the impression of operating as a single, seamless entity. The machinery emitted a low, steady, clinical throb. There were no staff in evidence apart from a solitary male figure dressed in nylon overalls and white calf-length boots, who was patrolling an overhead gantry running alongside the conveyor. Occasionally he would stop and prod at the conveyor's contents with a bloody plastic paddle. He glanced disinterestedly down at them and continued with his work.

'What do you want to see exactly?' Annie Preece asked, failing to disguise her impatience.

'You said Mr Morgan fed the machines. I'd like to see them.'

'You might wish you hadn't.'

'I think I can cope.'

With a shrug of indifference, Annie Preece headed under the gantry and between two huge steel containers that stood over ten feet high and emitted waves of intense heat. 'The main boilers. Softens everything up before it goes into the centrifuges.'

They emerged into a large open space that was brightly lit from above. To their left were two steel hoppers feeding the grinding machines that commenced the rendering process. To their right was an expanse of concrete separated from the outside yard by a twelve-foot-high doorway, through which a JCB appeared. It was fitted with a 500-gallon bucket loaded with meat waste. The driver edged up to the hopper closest to them and tipped the contents of the bucket inside. An electric motor started up with a rising, high-pitched whine like an aircraft engine readying for take-off. When it reached a steady note, Jenny heard a mechanical clunk as a trap opened and flesh and offal began to drop into the spinning blades. Seconds later, garish pink gobs the consistency of toothpaste dropped onto the conveyor beneath and continued on to the next stage of the journey.

'That's all Ed did,' Annie Preece said, 'brought the waste over in the bucket and tipped it into the grinders. Aside from that, if a machine broke down, he'd give a hand trying to fix it.'

Jenny watched as the JCB backed out of the door, blood dripping from its bucket.

'I've only seen two workers,' Jenny said, 'is that all it takes to man this place?'

Annie Preece shifted evasively from one foot to another. 'Mostly. Depends what work's on.'

Jenny nodded and left it at that. There was no need to state the obvious. It was plain to see why the boss was spending the afternoon with detectives in Gloucester: if anyone had had the opportunity to get rid of a body without leaving a trace, it had been Ed Morgan.

'How long had he worked here?'

'About twelve years. Two or three shifts a week.'

'That must be unusual. I imagine you have quite a high turnover in this kind of work.'

Annie Preece answered with another shrug.

'Did he ever cause any problems?'

'I never heard about it if he did.' She seemed keen to bring their encounter to an end. 'Is that it now? I've got a lot to do, with the boss away.'

Jenny turned to see the JCB returning with another load. Ignoring Annie Preece's edgy glances, she stood and watched the grinding process a second time, wondering what it would do to the mind of a man, let alone a sensitive one, seeing the remains of living animals reduced to pulp day after day, year after year.

'It may sound a strange question,' Jenny said, 'but have any of your employees suffered mental health problems, or been in trouble with the police?'

Annie Preece turned to her with the dumb, mouth-slightly-open look of someone unexpectedly caught out.

'You don't have to answer now,' Jenny said, heading back the way they had come. 'If you'd prefer, I can call you as a witness to my inquest.'

'No . . .'

'Good. That makes it easier for both of us.'

# TWELVE

FACED WITH THE PROSPECT OF being called to give evidence, Annie Preece had found her tongue and come up with quite a list. She had worked at Fairmeadows Farm for close to five years, and during that time could recall the names of at least half a dozen employees – all male; no women had ever worked on the floor – who had suffered from depression, alcoholism or both. Of these, two had found their way into prison. One had been convicted of battering his girlfriend in a drunken rage, and the other had pleaded guilty to charges of extortion, having moonlighted as a collector for a Bristol loan shark. Having blurted out this information, Preece then succumbed to a sudden attack of nervousness and tried to persuade Jenny that the problems with their staff were nothing to do with the nature of the work – when men could earn the same wage driving a van or stacking shelves, you were left with only the dregs to choose from.

Jenny had no reason to doubt what Annie Preece had said, but an instinct told her that it wouldn't be safe to rely on her word alone. Following their conversation, Jenny sought out the employee she had seen up on the gantry and found him outside the main building, smoking a cigarette. His name was Tomasz, a young Polish man, with soft blue eyes that didn't seem to belong in these ugly surroundings. Unlike Annie, on learning that he was talking to a coroner, he decided that the safest course was to cooperate from the outset. He told her that he had held his job for nearly two years and had been working all the hours he could get in order to send money home to his young family in Krakow. Some of the English workers had a problem with his being Polish, but Ed Morgan had always been a friend to him. Whenever they found themselves working the same shift, they would spend their break-times talking about football or their kids. Ed was crazy about his boy, Robbie, Tomasz said, but he was also fond of the girls and mentioned them almost as much. He'd never known him angry – on the contrary, he had always seemed relaxed and content with what life had dealt him.

When Jenny asked Tomasz about the other workers, he told her that he wasn't the kind to ask prying questions. If people wanted to talk about themselves, that was their business, but on the whole they didn't. It was that kind of place. The one man he did mention was Don Stephens, the foreman of the abattoir and the boss's brother-in-law. He had also gone to Gloucester with the police earlier that afternoon. Stephens was the one who hired and fired those workers whose jobs involved getting their hands dirty. The office staff all reported to Mr Johns and didn't come downstairs if they could help it. Responding to a hunch that had been growing stronger since she arrived, Jenny asked Tomasz whether all his co-workers were employed legitimately – with paperwork, and taxes deducted. It was the only question to which he refused to give a straight answer. Instead, he gave her a pointed look as he stamped out his cigarette and headed back to work. She read it as meaning that there were two sides to Fairmeadows Farm: the one you could see, and the one you couldn't.

*

Jenny kept an eye on her rear-view mirror as she left the rendering plant behind and turned towards Thornbury. Something in Tomasz's look and Annie Preece's prickly, defensive demeanour had unsettled her. It had been more than just the natural caution of employees scared for their jobs; it was as if they had been in fear of something – or possibly someone – in particular. She wondered if that person might not be Kenneth Johns, the boss; or perhaps Tomasz was dropping her a hint with his mention of Stephens, the foreman and Johns's brother-in-law. The family angle was interesting. A coroner only had to investigate a few deaths connected with family-run businesses to know how toxic they could become when personalities clashed. She painted herself a picture of Kenneth Johns trying to manage an operation that would bear the scrutiny of officials and inspectors, while Stephens ran the shop floor according to a different set of rules. It occurred to her that, in a business that was so highly regulated, temptations must present themselves to those prepared to turn a blind eye to the law. An outfit prepared to slaughter unregistered stock or process unfit carcasses stood to make money, perhaps a lot of money. And as the man who fed the machines, Ed Morgan would surely have known more than most.

The phone rang just in time to stop her imagination running away with itself. The call was from Alison's mobile number.

'Would you believe the office phones are buggered? Ice shorting out the connections, or some bloody nonsense. There's a man who's been fixing them upstairs. He says he can come and sort ours out first thing next week.'

'You're not still there?' Jenny said with a hint of rebuke.

'I'm fine. You don't have to treat me like a cripple.'

'It's half past five on a Friday night before New Year. You're released.'

'CID turned up an address for Daniel Burden's next of kin. A brother in Somerset. We think he might be away on holiday – he's not answering his phones.'

'Then leave him a message.'

'I can't relax with that hanging over me.'

'Go home. Have a glass of wine. Forget about it.'

'I've been at home for six months, Mrs Cooper. I've drunk France dry.'

'You won't mind if I have a weekend? On recent form, I might not see Michael again till Easter.'

'There's always DI Ryan. I'm sure he wouldn't say no.'

'Call me unadventurous, but one man at a time tends to be enough.'

'The CCTV footage from the petrol stations,' Alison said.

Getting used to her non sequiturs, Jenny went with her. 'What about it?'

'I phoned round. There are four sets of tapes to collect. I thought I'd start going through the footage over the weekend, to look for Morgan.'

'Won't Paul have something to say about that?' Jenny could only wonder how Alison's partner had coped with her dramatic change in personality.

'It doesn't take much to keep him sweet,' Alison said suggestively. 'Leave him to me.'

Jenny decided it was time to close the conversation down before she heard something she wished she hadn't. 'Don't work too hard. See you Tuesday?'

'Tuesday?'

'Monday's a bank holiday, remember – New Year.'

'Oh.' Alison sounded lost, as if what Jenny had said made no sense. 'How did I forget that?'

'I'd say you were doing pretty well.'

'You mean not bad for an old bird with a plate in her head.' She laughed, but it wasn't a laugh Jenny recognized.

It seemed to belong to someone else. 'I'll see you on Tuesday then, Mrs Cooper. If I can remember who I am.'

Alison rang off, leaving Jenny with fresh doubts about the wisdom of letting her return to the office. Come to think of it, she wasn't entirely sure how she had allowed it to come about. But every time she thought about putting Alison through the ordeal of an official assessment that she was bound to fail, she was overwhelmed by guilt. This was the woman, after all, to whom she and Ross owed their lives. It didn't leave her with a lot of choice.

Jenny listened to the local radio news as she drove gingerly through the Wye Valley along roads coated with a skin of freshly formed ice. In an interview with an exaggeratedly sombre reporter, the Assistant Chief Constable of Gloucestershire gave assurances that the search for Robbie Morgan wouldn't cease until he or his body was found. Responding to the suggestion that the police were also investigating whether Ed Morgan had been responsible for the disappearance of Susie Ashton ten years before, the Assistant Chief Constable insisted that there was no evidence whatsoever to connect the two incidents. Jenny waited for the reporter to press him on Morgan's connection with the abattoir, but the follow-up question never came and the announcer moved seamlessly on to the next story.

The staged interview left Jenny with the impression that the police were working extremely hard to play down any connection with Fairmeadows Farm. In all probability, the Assistant Chief Constable would only have agreed to go on air on condition that it wasn't mentioned. It was possible that his force was motivated simply by a noble desire to prevent an outbreak of panic over the possibility that human flesh had found its way onto supermarket shelves, but the more probable explanation was that they were trying not to scare off potential witnesses. It was obvious that they were more than interested in Fairmeadows Farm, if for no other reason than that, if all other lines of inquiry failed, it provided the perfect explanation: Ed Morgan dumped Susie Ashton and Robbie's bodies in the plant's industrial grinders, knowing they would never be traced.

The smell of cooking floated pleasantly through the air as Jenny picked her way up the path to the front door of Melin Bach: spaghetti carbonara, one of only three decent dishes she had never known Michael cook. Still, it was three more than she was capable of. One of her ex-husband's most often-repeated complaints had been that her lack of interest in cooking for her family demonstrated a lack of love. No matter that at the time she was working fourteen-hour days trying to protect the county's most troubled kids; devotion that wasn't channelled directly towards him didn't count.

Jenny paused on the doorstep and tried to clear those unhappy memories from her mind. It had been seven years since she had finally found the courage to leave her marriage and strike out on her own. David and his judgements on her failings as a wife and mother belonged to the distant past. It was her time now. Her opportunity to start again.

An unfamiliar and welcoming warmth enfolded her as she entered the hallway and hung up her coat. She unlatched the door to the sitting room and was greeted by a fire leaping in the grate.

Michael called through from the kitchen. 'Don't move. I'll be right with you.'

She did as he asked, noticing that he'd tidied the room and opened out the leaved oak dining table she reserved for the rare occasions when Ross came to stay.

Moments later Michael appeared, dressed in a freshly pressed linen shirt (the one he had worn the first time they had met for a drink), carrying a bottle of champagne and two slender glasses.

'I thought the occasion demanded it.'

'Aren't we a day early for New Year's Eve. Hi, by the way—'

'Not that – *this*.' He kissed her. '*Us*.' He started to unwrap the foil from around the cork. 'How was your day?'

'OK, but I could do with jumping in the shower before starting on the champagne.'

'Had to visit the morgue again?'

'I'd rather forget about it.' She turned to the door.

'Oh, someone called Dr Hope rang.'

'Did she leave a message?'

'She said it could wait till morning. I told her it would have to.'

Jenny smiled. 'I won't be long.'


'What's so funny?'

'You.' Jenny took another sip of her champagne, savouring the last few inches in her glass. It hadn't taken them long to empty the bottle.

'What about me?'

'You seem . . . happy.'

'That's so surprising?'

'No. It's nice.' She reached out with her toes and brushed his leg beneath the table.

'I could always give up flying and keep house for you.'

'You'd love that.'

'Maybe I would.'

'For about three days. Then you'd take off and leave me again.'

'Come on, Jenny,' Michael said, 'I've never left you.'

He seemed hurt, and Jenny felt sorry for wounding him.

'I didn't mean it like that. You know I didn't.' She reached across the table and took his hand. 'The spaghetti was delicious. Too nice. I could get used to it.'

Michael was silent for a moment. His eyes dipped from her face to the table.

Jenny waited, sensing his effort to put feelings into words.

'I missed you,' he said quietly. 'I always do when I'm away, but . . . oh God, now I'm sounding like an idiot.'

'No. Tell me.'

The corners of his mouth curled in an awkward smile. 'This time it became almost like a physical pain.' Embarrassed, he started to pull back from the table. 'I'll make some coffee.'

'No you won't.' Jenny tightened her grip on his fingers. 'Stay. You don't have to feel ashamed every time you admit to having feelings. And don't tell me I sound like your therapist.'

'Now you mention it . . .'

Jenny frowned in rebuke.

'You have to admit it. But if I have to hear something, I'd much rather it came from you.' He looked at their hands clasped in the centre of the table. 'So, what do you think?'

'About what?'

'You know . . .' he began hesitantly, 'it just seems like a good time to put things on more of a solid footing.'

Jenny felt a nervous flutter in her chest. 'What did you have in mind?'

'It's entirely your call, but the lease on my place runs out at the end of next month. I could always give notice and come and live here.'

'You want to live together?' Jenny's heart was pressing hard against her ribs, expressing emotions she had yet to form into coherent thoughts.

Michael raised his gaze and looked her squarely in the eye for several seconds, as if reassuring himself. 'Yes. I do.'

'Why now?'

'Why not? I love you, Jenny. I want to be with you.' He let go of her hand, sat back in his chair and waited for her answer.

On the spot, Jenny found herself tongue-tied. A confusion of conflicting feelings – happiness, uncertainty, excitement, fear – combined in a bewildering mix of contradictory responses that clamoured in her head.

'Sorry,' Michael said. 'I've ambushed you. I didn't know how else to do it. Why don't we leave it for a couple of days, give you some time?'

Jenny felt her anxiety retreat. 'Good idea.'

She leant across the table and kissed him gently on the mouth. It was intended as an affectionate, reassuring gesture, but as their lips touched, all that had remained unspoken between them found its expression in a rush of desire that sucked the breath from their lungs. Without a word, they left the table and made their way up the stairs to Jenny's bed.

Jenny's eyes snapped open and were met by total darkness. For several disconcerting moments she struggled to comprehend whether she was actually awake or still trapped in the netherworld of her strange and disturbing dream. She had been searching for a child in a rocky landscape stalked by faceless, semi-human creatures that issued siren calls as soft as a mother's whisper. She pressed a hand to her chest and felt her pounding heart. She drew in a slow, deep breath. She was awake, but the dream remained horribly vivid in her mind and refused to fade. The young child she had been desperately seeking had been hers, but it wasn't Ross – it had been an idealized and more perfect rendering of her son. It had been Ross without flaws. Recalling the dream-child's slender and beautiful face, she felt ashamed that her subconscious mind was even capable of forming such dark and disloyal fantasies.

'Bad dreams?'

Michael's voice came not from next to her, but from the foot of the bed. Jenny pushed up on her elbows and as her eyes adjusted to the faint slivers of moonlight filtering around the edges of the curtains, she dimly made out his naked silhouette. He was standing, looking at her.

'Me too,' he said, before she could reply.

'What are you doing?' Jenny asked.

'I'm not sure.'

'What does that mean?'

'I just found myself here.' He sounded confused, or was it frightened?

'You probably forgot where you were sleeping. Too many nights in strange hotel rooms. Come back to bed.'

Michael groped his way through the darkness and climbed in under the duvet next to her. Jenny touched his arm: it was icy. She pressed her fingers between his.

'You must have been there for ages,' Jenny said.

Michael murmured in reply, already slipping from consciousness.

Jenny rolled onto her side and stroked his forehead until his muscles slackened and his breathing sunk into the slow, steady rhythm of sleep. Whispering goodnight, she gently kissed each of his eyelids and tasted the salt of his dried tears.

# THIRTEEN

JENNY WOKE TO THE SOUND of Michael singing along loudly and badly to the kitchen radio. The house was filled with the smell of fresh coffee and pancakes. If she really was going to live with this man, she would have to teach him some weekend etiquette. Saturday was her lying-in day; her feet weren't meant to touch the floor until at least nine o'clock. She groaned and buried her head under the covers, willing sleep to reclaim her.

Her peace lasted less than five minutes. First the telephone rang, then Michael appeared clutching the handset.

'Someone wishes to speak to the coroner,' he announced.

Jenny emerged from beneath the duvet with a pained expression. 'Who is it this time, for goodness' sake?'

'Some woman,' was all the information Michael could give her.

Jenny sighed and dragged herself to a sitting position. Her limbs were leaden. She took the phone and tried to pretend that she wasn't still half asleep.

'Hello. Jenny Cooper speaking.'

'So sorry to have disturbed you, Mrs Cooper. I do hope I haven't woken you.' The pretence had failed. 'It's Clare Ashton, from Blackstone Ley. I wanted to speak to you while my husband was out.' Her voice was thin and apprehensive.

'Yes?'

'He'll be gone half the day, you see – he's out with his running club.'

'I see. How can I help you?'

'Since your visit the other day I've been thinking back. I looked out all my old notebooks. I wrote everything down after Susie went. I knew I wasn't capable of thinking straight at the time, so I tried to put all my thoughts on paper.' She dried up, as if the emotion of the past had swept back over her.

'What have you found?'

'I'm not sure,' she hesitated. 'There are a few things. I'd need to explain—'

'How long is your husband out? Would it help if I came over?'

Jenny ignored Michael's silent gestures of protest as she waited for Clare Ashton's response.

'Yes. I think it might, if it's not too much trouble. He's not back until one.'

'I'll be with you in an hour.'

'Thank you. Thank you, Mrs Cooper.'

'What's that all about?' Michael said, as Jenny tossed the phone aside and swung out of bed.

'Quick house call. You can be my driver.' She kissed him. 'Won't take long. Promise.'

'You're worse than me. You can't say no to anyone.'

'Including you.' She kissed him again. He smiled. 'Let's have some breakfast.'

The police had set up a roadblock across the main route into Thornbury, and the small amount of traffic was being stopped in both directions. Teams of officers swathed in thick black anoraks were thoroughly searching every vehicle with the help of black Labrador sniffer dogs. Michael pulled up in a queue of three cars heading east. Until that moment he'd been in an unusually ebullient mood, entertaining her with stories from his days in the RAF and admitting to her that, far from being a one-off, his sleepwalking episode the previous night was just the latest in a long line of unfortunate nocturnal adventures. The most embarrassing had been during the period when he'd been flying sorties over the Balkans. He'd taken three days' leave in Italy and had woken naked in the corridor of a Rome hotel to find himself locked out of his room. With nothing but a vase to hide behind, he'd made his way down to the lobby to explain himself to a bewildered night porter. They had both laughed until her sides ached, but now that Michael found himself unexpectedly stuck in a row of waiting cars, his mood shifted abruptly. Jenny felt his tension climbing. His whole body had become rigid and tense.

'What is this? What the hell's going on?' he said impatiently.

'They're searching for the missing boy,' Jenny said. 'It's not unreasonable.'

'Can't you pull rank, show them your card or something?'

'Relax. There's no hurry.'

'But you shouldn't have to wait. You're the coroner.'

Jenny thought that perhaps the sight of the roadblock had sparked painful memories of one of the many war zones he had been posted to during his military career. She tried to distract him. 'Think about something else. Switch the radio on.'

Michael's hands gripped the steering wheel tightly. He didn't seem to hear her.

Jenny reached out to the radio console to find a music station.

'Don't!' he snapped.

His response was sharp and instinctive and carried more than a hint of menace.

'Michael?'

'Shut up.'

The car at the head of the queue was waved through. The Ford van in front of them eased up to the barrier, but Michael made no attempt to move the Land Rover forwards. He stared straight ahead with a fixed, belligerent expression that drew the gaze of one of the three police officers standing on their side of the road. Sensing trouble, the officer peeled away from his colleagues and made his way towards them.

'Michael, please – ' Jenny urged.

He remained silent and unmoving, tracking the approaching police officer with his eyes.

'Michael, lower your window.'

He didn't react.

The police officer arrived. A burly man with a battered, rugby player's face. He tapped the driver's window with a large, gloved hand.

Jenny felt her toes curl as she waited for Michael to respond.

The officer knocked again, loudly this time. Jenny made to lean over and lower the window herself, but Michael suddenly broke into a smile and pressed the switch.

'Sorry, officer, I was miles away,' he said charmingly. 'I should have moved forward, shouldn't I?'

The policeman nodded, regarding him suspiciously. 'If you would, sir.' He glanced at Jenny. 'Everything all right, ma'am?'

'Fine, thank you,' she lied, aware that he was carefully scanning her features for signs of physical abuse.

Detecting none, and with no solid reason to do otherwise,

he finally stood aside as Michael pushed the car into gear and closed the gap.

The search took less than a minute. The dogs found nothing to interest them and Michael maintained his cheerful demeanour even as they drove away from the barrier in the direction of Blackstone Ley.

Jenny remained silent for a while, bracing herself for the moment when the mask slipped, but as they left the town behind and headed out into the country lanes, the angry persona she had glimpsed showed no sign of returning.

'Michael, are you all right?'

He seemed surprised, as if her question had sprung from nowhere. 'Fine.'

'Then what was that about?'

'What?'

'Back there. You got so tense. I thought—' She stopped herself mid-sentence.

He kept his eyes on the road. 'Bit of a flashback. Soon passes.'

'Is it happening often?'

'Hardly ever.'

'You should probably go back to the therapist.'

'You're all I need.' He glanced over, with a smile intended to put the matter to rest. 'It's nothing. Just an echo from the past. I'm sorry. Forget about it.'

Jenny nodded, hoping he was right.


Jenny left Michael to take a walk in the snow, while she called on Clare Ashton. As she made her way towards the cottage it dawned on her that in no sense would this be an anonymous visit. She already had the sensation that she was being watched from behind the windows of the neighbouring properties. People would recognize her car and know that she was the coroner, and Clare would know that they knew. While Jenny waited for her to come to the door, she wondered whether that was part of the reason she had asked her over – that she wanted her neighbours to see that she hadn't let go, and that if any of them still harboured secrets, she remained determined to root them out.

Clare Ashton appeared even paler and more fragile than she had two days before, as if the tumult of the fire had loaded her with an extra burden. She thanked Jenny for coming, especially in such bad weather, and steadying herself against the wall, led her along the hallway to the snug kitchen at the rear of the house.

'I prefer it in here,' Clare said, easing herself into one of the upright pine chairs. 'It feels more homely. My husband's the orderly one. I always say I like a house to feel lived in.'

'I can only dream of being this tidy,' Jenny said, noticing that to the left of a shelf containing a neat arrangement of cookery books, there was a solitary framed photograph: Clare and Philip with their small, dark-haired daughter, all three of them dressed up in their best clothes, standing outside a church.

'My sister's wedding,' Clare said. 'Susie was one of the bridesmaids. It's the only one of her Philip can bear to have up.'

Jenny stepped over for a closer look. It slowly dawned on her that something about the picture was familiar. 'I think I recognize that church.'

'It was over in Monmouthshire,' Clare said. 'Penallt Old Church.'

'I know it well,' Jenny said, dismissing the odd sensation that Clare's mention of one of her favourite buildings had prompted. The church at Penallt was a little further north along the Wye Valley from her home, and unusually it stood alone amongst fields, rather than at the centre of a village. It was one of the handful of places to which Jenny would often return on her solitary weekend walks, for no reason other than it seemed to exert a sort of magnetism, as if there were hidden truths locked up in its ancient stones.

'Why did she choose there?'

'It's where we grew up. You take a place like that for granted when you're a child. You don't see how beautiful it is. I long for it now.'

Again pondering the strangeness of this coincidence, Jenny took a seat at the table. Clare reached several hard-cover notebooks from the counter behind her. She opened the one on top of the pile, her frail fingers shaking from this small effort.

'I told you I'd been looking back at my notes. I'd forgotten I wrote this about Ed Morgan.' She pushed the notebook across the table. 'On the right-hand page.'

Clare's handwriting was educated and precise. The journal entry she had indicated was dated 4 April, and in brackets she had written, '*D+6*', meaning, Jenny guessed, six days after Susie's disappearance. It read:

*The police interviewed Ed Morgan under caution today. Helen M told me he looked very frightened as they led him to their car. Mrs Davies (Three Chimneys) once told me that he was badly beaten by his father as a child, which explains why he's so quiet and withdrawn. He had one older brother who died in a car accident when Ed was fourteen. Apparently he worshipped him and was quite depressed throughout the rest of his teens. Mrs D contacted the police six years ago to register an objection when she heard he had applied for a shotgun licence, but was told by the sergeant there were no grounds for refusal.*

*I often see him with Layla (Kelly's oldest), but would never have allowed Susie to be alone with him. No reason for this – just gut instinct. Philip heard some gossip from*

*Richard Jarrold a few months ago that Ed was known for a*
*cruel streak when he was younger – when they were 15 Ed*
*killed his own dog by stringing it up from a tree. Jarrold*
*said it was his way of trying to impress the other boys.*
*Seems very odd. It makes me think he's damaged, and so I*
*suspect is Kelly, but I can't help liking her. She has a sort of*
*guileless innocence.*

*Must stop speculating now. I must take note of what*
*Philip says – always remain rational. Only rely on*
*evidence!!*

'And did you discover any evidence?' Jenny asked.

'Nothing concrete,' Clare said. 'I know it's only hearsay,
but nevertheless . . .'

'These people you've mentioned—'

'Both gone,' Clare said. 'They were old at the time. Proper
village folk – born and bred here.'

'Not always the most reliable witnesses of fact,' Jenny
said, 'but I think you were aware of that.'

'I was more than aware of how people gossiped, of
course. Things get amplified in a place like this. Stories take
on lives of their own.' She opened a second notebook, turning to a page she had flagged. 'The trick is distinguishing all
that from the grains of truth.' She handed it to Jenny.

The entry was headed '*19 April, D+21*'.

*Most depressing conversation yet with DI Abbott this after-*
*noon. All of the four sightings that the investigation team*
*had deemed credible have proved otherwise. After three*
*weeks we are left with no witnesses and no forensic evi-*
*dence. Abbott says that the remoteness of our location*
*makes it unlikely that we are dealing with an opportunist.*
*He still feels a local man is the most likely culprit. Nearly*
*all have solid alibis, but only Ed Morgan's is unverifiable,*

*due to the fact he was supposedly working alone in wood-
land three miles from here at the time. He has no mobile
phone, so it's not possible to 'triangulate' his position from
the surrounding phone masts.*

*Abbott said that his team had been exploring another
theory suggested by a criminologist who's been drafted in
from the Met. He was reluctant to discuss it, but Philip
assured him that nothing could upset us any more than we
had been already. Apparently, several paedophile rings have
been broken in recent years in which children have been
taken 'to order', as he put it. A lot of money can change
hands. The fact that Susie disappeared in broad daylight
does suggest that if there was a witness – and Abbott thinks
it's highly likely – they've been silenced in some way. My
mind started to cloud at that point of the discussion (I've
learnt that there's a sort of natural defence that kicks in
when things become too distressing – which I suppose is
what has allowed me to function at all), but the gist was
that it's possible there was a wider conspiracy. It all
sounded too fantastical – a group of men coldly agreeing to
something so evil – but as Philip said to me after Abbott
had gone, history proves over and over that human beings
are capable of anything you can imagine, and worse. And
the more evil they are, the more plausible they are likely to
seem.*

*I can't sleep tonight even with pills. Too many unspeak-
able thoughts in my head. I tell myself to keep praying, but
it's hard. So hard.*

Jenny continued staring at the page, trying to imagine how
Clare must have felt as she wrote those words.

'Did anything come of this line of inquiry?'

'No evidence emerged. Although DS Abbott did assure us
they had interviewed every known offender they could find

who might have inside knowledge. There was a lot of money on offer for information, if you remember.'

'I do.' Jenny had a hazy recollection of the Ashtons posing with a businessman who had offered a six-figure reward. 'Can I assume you felt there was something in that line of inquiry?'

'I did. I still do.' Clare's voice seemed to gain in strength. There was a steeliness in her expression which paid no regard to the weakness of her body. 'Everything I've read about this type of abduction – and believe me, I have read everything – confirms that the impulsive criminal leaves a trail of evidence in his wake. Only those who have planned meticulously manage to escape detection.'

'And you think Ed Morgan was involved?'

'When the police failed to discover any evidence, I admit I came round to the view that Ed wasn't connected and that Susie may well have been taken by a complete stranger. In fact, that became my settled view and remained so until about six months ago.' Clare glanced off out of the kitchen window at a snow-covered cherry tree. 'I'm sorry.' She cleared her throat, raising an unsteady fist to her lips. 'Kelly said Layla was falling behind at school. Philip offered to coach her. She came here three times, then Philip said he was too busy with other commitments. It was a little embarrassing, really – I had arranged it and Kelly was disappointed. But looking back, I think something must have happened to make him recoil. He's usually so professional.'

'Such as?'

'There was no doubting Layla was sexualized. Provocative, even. And at only fourteen. I think she must have made Philip uncomfortable. As a teacher, he's highly sensitive to these things.'

'Did he say anything?'

'No.' She shook her head. 'He wouldn't have wanted to

worry me, and he certainly wouldn't have said anything to Kelly or Ed in case it prompted a reaction. Teachers are all guilty until proven innocent in these situations.'

'You think Layla Hart behaved inappropriately towards your husband when he was teaching her?'

'I'm sure of it. And a girl of her age would only behave like that towards a middle-aged man if it was a learned behaviour. It's a classic indicator of sexual abuse.'

'Wouldn't your husband have taken steps, contacted social services?'

'I think perhaps he now wishes he had.' Clare Ashton's face creased in anguish. 'He hasn't said a word to me, but I can tell – he's been deeply disturbed since the fire. It's almost as if—' She checked herself, but then continued: 'No, he's my husband, I should know. I think he feels responsible.'

Jenny tried to place what Clare had told her into a logical sequence. Everything she had said about Layla and her husband was pure guesswork, but a wife's instincts were powerful. A woman might know her partner better than he knew himself.

'I think what you're telling me, Mrs Ashton, is that you think Ed Morgan might have abused his stepdaughter and that your husband suspected the same.'

'Yes. I suppose I am.'

'Can I ask why you're raising this with me, and not first with him?'

'I was afraid of weakening if I consulted Philip. I'm so dependent on him, but I wanted to do the right thing.'

Jenny nodded. 'Of course. But have you any reason to think it was Ed? Do you know if there were other men who had regular access to Layla?'

'I wasn't aware of them having many visitors. I've seen Bob Bream visiting a few times.'

'I've met him.'

'He was very good to us. He and his wife organized a rota for people to cook for us in the weeks after Susie went. I shan't forget that. Kindness comes from unexpected places.' Clare looked suddenly distressed. 'I forgot to offer you any coffee, Mrs Cooper. What was I thinking?'

'I'm fine.' Jenny stopped her from struggling out of her chair. 'I should probably be going.' She glanced at the notebooks. 'Unless there's anything else you think I should know?'

Clare shook her head. During the course of their conversation, she had grown steadily more tired. Her face was the colour of old parchment. It felt inhuman to put more pressure on a woman so close to the end of her life, but Jenny had no option.

'Given what you've told me, I'll probably have to ask your husband to give evidence at my inquest. And one way or another, he's bound to know you've spoken to me.'

'I appreciate that, Mrs Cooper.' Somehow she managed to smile. 'And I'm really not quite as feeble as I look.'

As Jenny left Clare's cottage, snow had once again started to fall from a low, heavy sky. She scanned the common but saw no sign of Michael. Arriving at the Land Rover, she searched her coat pockets, then realized he must still have the keys. She checked her phone – a single bar of reception. She dialled his number. It was engaged. Faintly annoyed and getting colder by the second, she tried again. It was still busy. She couldn't stand still in the freezing wind, so for want of a better alternative, set off at a brisk walk towards the church, which stood some thirty yards away, at the far end of the common.

It was far harder going than she had anticipated. The snow was calf-deep and in the unsheltered expanse of the common the wind cut through her with a cruel sense of purpose. Jenny glanced over to where the burned-out house had stood and saw that since her first visit the site had been completely cleared. All the rubble and even the surrounding fences had been carted away and the entire plot levelled. The only sign that a home had stood there was a rectangle of bare earth that was fast disappearing under a thickening shroud of white. Soon there would be no trace left at all. The absence upset her. There seemed something indecent about the complete erasing of a family's life in so short a time.

Jenny carried her disquiet through the porch of the Norman church of St Mary and All Souls, unlatched the heavy iron-studded door, and entered its silent interior. It was a small building, no more than fifty feet from end to end, with plain stone pillars either side of the nave. At its eastern end stood a simple stone altar carved with a Celtic cross. The sandstone flags had been worn into hollows by centuries of human traffic and the rounded corners of the rough-hewn pews were rubbed smooth by generations of hands. Moving along the nave, she saw that the candles flickering in a small alcove in the chancel were illuminating a wooden Madonna and child. The craftsmanship was primitive, chisel marks showing through the flaking, centuries-old paint, but despite its crudeness and simplicity, the wood carver had managed to capture the enfolding softness of a nursing mother.

Jenny turned at the sound of footsteps and saw Helen Medway emerging from the open doorway to the vestry at the back of the church.

'Hello again, Mrs Cooper. I thought I saw your car.'

'I knew someone would.'

She came forward to join her, dressed well for a priest in the depths of winter, Jenny thought: knee-length leather boots over well-fitting jeans and an elegant belt buckled outside a waist-length, moss-green jumper.

'Not bad for six hundred, is she?' Helen said, nodding towards the statue. 'Somehow she survived Henry the Eighth and the Civil War. Twenty murderous Roundheads hacked at the font and the altar, defaced all the male saints, but didn't lay a finger on her. I suppose it must tell you something about the male psyche, though I'm not sure what.'

'I don't think I'd dare touch her either,' Jenny said.

'I always think she's part Christian, part pagan,' Helen said, looking at the figure with a more detached eye than Jenny had managed, 'as much a fertility symbol as a religious one.'

'Do you think she approves of you?' Jenny said, half jokingly.

'She does make me feel a little inadequate at times, I have to say. I never quite got round to motherhood, and then for some reason the fates pitched me into this parish.' She glanced at Jenny with a look that seemed to express several layers of bafflement. A sigh escaped her lips. 'I'm sure there's a reason.'

They stood gazing at the carved figure for a short while, Jenny feeling both comforted and challenged by the simple vision of perfection she presented.

'There's a leaflet at the back if you're interested,' Helen Medway said, abruptly retreating from her brief meditation, 'unless there's anything I can help you with.'

Jenny's mind, still preoccupied with thoughts of her own maternal failings, went temporarily blank, and it was only when Helen was halfway along the nave that a thought occurred to her.

'Sorry, if you have got a moment – ' She went after her. 'Your house – is it the one closest to where Kelly's stood?'

'Yes.'

'Did you hear anything on the night of the fire? I mean, before it started.'

'It's hard to say. My husband and I were getting ready for bed. I think there was a series of bangs, then it seemed like only moments later there were voices outside on the common and the house was on fire.'

'How many bangs?'

'Two or three.'

'No more?'

'Not as far as I recall. Spaced out a little, though. My husband thought it was an engine backfiring – Layla had friends round with cars and motorbikes; they'd often mess about late at night. Made us feel like terrible old curmudgeons for grumbling about it.' An anxious look crossed her face. 'Is it significant? Should we have done something?'

'No. There was nothing you could have done.' Jenny hesitated, instinctively cautious of revealing evidence ahead of her inquest, but deciding she could trust a priest. 'A shotgun was fired inside the house, though I'd be grateful if you'd keep that information to yourself.'

Now Helen Medway looked puzzled. 'Inside? No, what we heard was definitely outside, no doubt about it. These were loud, sharp bangs, not muffled. You say they were gunshots?'

'Possibly. I don't know,' Jenny answered truthfully, at the same time wondering who Ed Morgan could have been firing at *outside* the house? Could he have shot the girls in the open air and dragged their bodies back in before starting the fire?

'Ed Morgan shot the girls?' Helen Medway was incredulous.

'Are you sure you didn't hear voices?' Jenny pressed. 'Or screams?'

'No.' The priest shook her head emphatically. 'Nothing like that at all.' She looked at Jenny in disbelief. 'But he can't have done.' Her expression turned to one of incredulity. 'Why?'

It wasn't a question to which she expected an answer, and in any case Jenny couldn't have given one she believed to be truthful. 'I'll have to leave that question for my inquest. I'm afraid I'll have to ask both you and your husband to provide statements.'

'Of course,' Helen Medway answered, her face blanched with shock.

'Thank you.'

Jenny had made her way out of the church and was most of the way back along the path and nearly at the lane when Medway emerged from the church door and called after her.

'Mrs Cooper – hold on.'

Jenny halted under the bowed roof of the lychgate and sheltered from the worst of the wind. While she waited for her to catch up, she glanced out across the common, expecting to see Michael in the car, but there was still no sign of him. She hoped he hadn't got lost; in his current state of mind she wasn't sure he would be completely safe by himself.

'I hope you don't think I'm speaking out of turn,' she said, arriving flustered and out of breath, as if she had been swept up in a sudden rush of emotion, 'but all this seems so much more than coincidental, given what happened to Susie Ashton . . .'

Jenny said nothing, waiting for her to complete her train of thought without prompting.

'There are lots of theories, of course – behind closed doors, people talk of little else around here – but there's always been a lot of suspicion of the police's role. And to see the house swept away in a couple of days –' she gestured towards the empty plot where it had stood – 'it's almost as if they want to erase all memory for fear of . . .' she struggled to complete her sentence, 'for fear of being found out in some way.'

'What do you think they're trying to hide?' Jenny asked neutrally.

'I've no idea,' Helen said, 'but without wishing to sound paranoid, I do think they might have been watching the family recently.' She glanced nervously left and right, as if fearing they might be listened to.

'Tell me,' Jenny urged gently.

'Several times last autumn, always at weekends when they would all have been at home, I noticed a car parked just along here, as if it were calling at the church. I spotted a man inside. He must have parked there three or four times, but I saw his face twice. Dark hair, glasses. He was watching their house, I'm sure of it.'

'Did you challenge him?'

'No.'

'Could you describe the car?'

'Nondescript. It was a nothing colour, somewhere between green and brown. The sort you'd never notice if it were parked anywhere but here.'

'Did you mention it to anyone?'

'Only my husband. I can ask him if he ever made a note of the registration.'

Jenny searched her pockets. 'I haven't got a card. Look me up – if you can find it, email it to me.'

'I will.'

'You should get back inside before you freeze,' Jenny said.

Helen Medway nodded, but there was still something weighing on her mind. 'I shouldn't be,' she said guiltily, 'but I suppose I'm a little frightened.'

Jenny touched the priest on the arm, feeling the full irony of the moment as she offered her reassurance.

Helen Medway appreciated the gesture and gave a nod, as if to say she was satisfied she had done the right thing. 'Goodbye, Mrs Cooper, and thank you.' She turned, and clutching her frozen hands together, made her way back to the church.

A fresh blast of wind drove hard needles of icy snow into Jenny's already burning face. Michael had still failed to appear. Growing a little concerned, Jenny pulled out her phone and dialled his number. It rang once, then connected to an automated message informing her that his phone was un-available, which either meant he was without a signal or had switched it off. Determined not to indulge the irrational fears bubbling up in her mind, she set off towards the Land Rover, but after several yards found herself drawn towards the levelled patch of ground where Kelly and Ed's house had stood.

Jenny had never appreciated just how quickly and com-pletely all trace of a building could be erased. The footsteps she was leaving in an inch of fresh snow were near enough on the same spot where only three days ago Ed Morgan had carried out his slaughter. She had expected to feel something of the oppressive atmosphere she had felt while touring the ruins with DI Ryan, but all she experienced was a strange sense of absence, like returning home to an unexpectedly empty house. It was as if the memories had been stored in the fabric of the building itself. She noticed that the view from what would have been the front garden was clear across the common to the Ashtons' cottage. A person, even a small child standing in this spot, would have been visible. There was also an unobstructed line of sight to three other houses: the vicarage to the left of the Ashtons' and two fur-ther properties to its right, one of which was positioned on a rise set back some distance from the common. Other prop-erties could be seen from here, too, but each had trees or fences that kept them partially hidden.

Turning to face the hill behind her, Jenny recalled her headlights sweeping the treeline as she had left the site forty-eight hours before, and the illusion she had experienced of a figure darting between the shadows. Living among the forests of the Wye Valley, Jenny was more aware than most how they could play tricks on the mind. If you were in anything less than a robust mental state, fallen branches and stumps could easily become distorted human forms; shadows and hollows made hiding places for unseen predators. It wasn't hard to consider that Ed Morgan, unhinged for whatever reason, might have found himself shooting at phantoms in the night.

It was then that she spotted an incongruous dash of colour amongst the trees partway up the slope: specks of yellow and orange. Seized by curiosity, she set off towards it. Making her way up the bank, Jenny soon found herself scrambling on all fours as the gradient got steeper. She plunged her hands deep into the snow as she hauled herself up the incline. Finally arriving at the top, she found herself on a natural step in the hillside, where the ground flattened out before rising sharply again. There, at the foot of a young oak was a fresh bunch of hothouse tulips tied with black ribbon. A single word, '*Sorry*', was handwritten on a plain tag attached to them. Jenny stooped to examine them: the petals were frozen, but only powdered with snow, suggesting they had been placed there during the last few hours. She scoured the surrounding ground and spotted a trail of footprints leading off to her left. They belonged to a woman, or perhaps to a child, and were certainly no bigger than Jenny's. Leaving the flowers where they lay, she followed the prints across the level contour, then found herself on a path leading back down to the lane that ran along the side of the common. There the prints merged with several other sets travelling up and down the hill and became lost.

Jenny went left down the path. It made several sharp turns through a thick stand of birch trees and returned her to the lane approximately thirty yards from where the house had stood. Heading back across the common towards the Land Rover, she fetched out her phone and dialled Kelly Hart's number.

Kelly answered on the third ring with a cautious hello.

'Mrs Hart, it's Jenny Cooper.'

'I saw. Is it Robbie?'

'No. Sorry, I didn't mean to alarm you.'

'It's OK.' Kelly exhaled in relief.

'I'm at Blackstone Ley, Mrs Hart. Someone's left flowers near your house with a note. I just wanted to check that it wasn't you.'

'It wasn't me. What does it say?'

'*Sorry.*'

Kelly was silent for a moment, then said, 'Is there a name?'

'No name. Just the one word. I was wondering if you might have any idea.'

'No.'

Jenny could sense her distress. 'That's fine. I'm sorry if I upset you.'

'I haven't left this flat. I wish I could. I wish I had somewhere to go. I wish I had someone to see.'

Jenny felt helpless in the face of the unexpected plea and found herself with nothing to offer in return. 'I won't disturb you again unless I have to,' was all she could find to say. 'Thank you.' She rang off and glanced back at the empty plot, with the uneasy feeling that concealed somewhere amongst the trees on the hillside, someone was watching her.

'Jenny!'

She turned at the sound of Michael's voice. He was approaching from her right, on the far side of the common, and was waving to her. She waved back, but her relief at seeing him was clouded by the fact that he'd been gone nearly an hour and had frightened her.

'Where were you?' she demanded, when they met again beside the car.

'I followed a footpath over the hill and got a bit lost. I knew you'd be worried, but my blasted phone ran out of juice.'

'I kept trying you, but you were always engaged.'

'That was my boss. I thought he'd agreed to leave me alone this weekend. No such luck.' He unlocked the car and climbed into the driver's seat.

Jenny got in next to him, knowing there was bad news coming.

'Where to – home?' Michael said, avoiding the issue.

'Aren't you going to tell me?'

Michael sighed. 'He's pleading with me to fly to Zurich on New Year's Day. Some urgent shipments. We've still got tomorrow.'

'You could have said no.'

'Jenny, I can't afford to lose this job. No one else is going to employ a 47-year-old pilot, ex-RAF or not.'

'He needs you too badly to let you go. He only picks on you because he thinks you're a single man who has no one to upset by working through the holidays.' She gave him a stern look. 'He's wrong.'

'And you're right,' he conceded. 'You usually are.' He reached for her hand. Jenny let him take it. 'You're cold.'

She avoided his attempt to deflect her. 'There are a few things you're going to need help with, Michael.'

'I know.' He squeezed her fingers and kissed her on the cheek. 'This is the last time, OK?'

Jenny nodded, accepting that this time it was probably too late to undo what had already been done.

Michael started the engine and pulled away. 'I don't know

if it's what you've told me about this place, but I wouldn't be in any hurry to come back.'

'You didn't happen to pass a woman walking alone?' Jenny asked.

'No, I didn't see a woman, but there was a guy behaving a bit oddly up in those woods.' He nodded towards the hill.

'What do you mean, oddly?'

'I was going up the path, he was coming down. He spotted me, then veered off into the trees.'

'What sort of age?'

'Couldn't say, though he must have been fit. Vanished without a trace, in the time it took me to walk twenty yards. Weird thing, though – he left spots of blood in the snow.'

'Blood?'

Michael stared straight ahead, refusing to answer her.

'Michael—'

'Got you!' He laughed uproariously. 'I didn't see a soul.'

# FOURTEEN

JENNY STARED OUT OF HER kitchen window at the smothering of snow that had grown even deeper overnight. She tried to muster enthusiasm for the start of a new year, but struggled to rid herself of the feeling of loss that had descended the moment Michael had slipped out of the house several hours before dawn. She tried to console herself with the thought that nearly three unbroken days together had been a record – as had their avoidance of a single major argument during that time – but the dull feeling of emptiness refused to lift. In the past she had simply pressed on with her daily round, in the uncertain hope of seeing him again soon, but she knew that this time it was different. Something had changed. Michael hadn't raised the subject of living together again before he left, but Jenny knew that had been deliberate. He had handed the decision over to her.

Moving away from the window and warming her cold hands against the range, she realized how unsettled she was by the prospect of sharing every aspect of her life as well as her home. She had built high defensive walls around herself in the years since her divorce, and the prospect of having them torn down at a single stroke was leaving her feeling naked and exposed.

Equally, she accepted that it was a decision that wouldn't get any easier by postponing it. She forced herself to confront it. The answer seemed inevitable. If she was ever going to change, it would have to be now. She was too young to get stuck in a rut and to take no further risks. There, she had done it, and it had been almost painless. She was terrified, but the prospect of never changing was even worse.

Daunted, but also relieved that she had turned a corner, Jenny turned her back on the kitchen and retreated to her study, hoping to distract herself with the pile of reports that had remained unread on her desk over the weekend. She hadn't even settled in her chair when the phone rang.

It was DI Ryan, and he greeted her with his now customary apology for disturbing her out of hours. Jenny told him he needn't worry – he wasn't disturbing anything.

'Kelly Hart's been in touch,' Ryan said. 'She'd got herself worked up over something you told her yesterday – flowers laid at her house, with a note?'

'There is no house,' Jenny said, 'just scorched earth.'

'At least it keeps the cameras away.'

And the heat off Superintendent Abbott and his old colleagues, Jenny thought. She chose not to share her scepticism with Ryan. So far he'd proved a valuable ally, and she wanted to keep it that way.

'The flowers were laid in the woods on the bank behind the house. There was a note attached, saying *sorry*. No name, just the one word.'

'Did she have any idea who might have left them?'

'Didn't seem to. I'm no detective, but the footprints leading to them looked female. Though it's only what you'd expect – men don't touch flowers without a gun to the head.'

'Depends on the man,' Ryan said. He paused. 'Sorry if I'm making assumptions here, but from what she's said to me, I get the impression you haven't told her about what happened inside the house.'

'Do you think she's ready for it?'

'As she'll ever be. I always think it's better to hear the facts straight than drive yourself mad imagining things that didn't happen. If you want to tell me what you've got, I could share it with her.'

'No, it's OK. I've some more questions for her anyway. I should go and see her.'

'If you'd rather not face her alone, I could always come and hold your hand.'

'Won't your super have something to say about that? I thought this was no longer a police problem.'

'It's a holiday. He doesn't have to know.'

'You want to do it today?'

'You did say you weren't busy. How about this afternoon?'

There was no good reason Jenny could think of for putting it off, so she called Kelly and arranged to meet at her flat, together with DI Ryan, at noon. She had expected Kelly to ask her what the meeting was about, but she had responded with the passive acceptance of a woman resigned to whatever might be thrown at her. Despite this, the prospect of confronting her again in a few hours' time, and with such disturbing information, left Jenny too jumpy to settle at her desk, so instead she called the mortuary to see if anyone was on duty. She learned from a technician that Dr Hope was on her way in. It was the excuse she needed to get out of the house and away from her own company. Jenny grabbed her coat and headed for her car.

Michael had been the last to drive the Land Rover and had left the seat so far back Jenny could barely reach the pedals. As she reached down to adjust her position, her fingers closed around something cold and glassy. She brought up Michael's phone. It must have slipped from his trouser pocket under the seat. She went to stow it in the glovebox, but acting on an impulse that she realized was shameful even as she surrendered to it, she flicked to his call log to check if it really had been his boss who had kept him talking for so long the previous day. It contained only five entries, all of them unanswered incoming calls dialled that morning from the Bristol office of Michael's employers. She guessed he had been attempting to call his phone before taking off for Zurich. But why scrub out yesterday's records? And why not call her to find out if he had left the phone in the cottage.

Jenny scrolled through his contacts – of which there were very few, because Michael had only a handful of friends – and found two numbers with the '41' Swiss dialling code. The first was entered under 'Office – Zurich', the second under 'Menzingen'. She hesitated, doing battle with her conscience, then dialled the latter. After several, long continuous rings the phone was answered by a young woman: '*Hallo, Gasthoff Sonne.*'

Jenny rang off without replying. She knew very little German, but enough to know she had reached a hotel reception. She relaxed, remembering now that Michael had mentioned that he had found a guesthouse in a village called Menzingen a short drive from Zurich, where he could stay overnight in considerably more hospitable surroundings than those offered by the airport hotels.

Starting down the lane to Tintern, Jenny scolded herself. She'd only made up her mind to live with the man thirty minutes before, and she was already spying on him. She made a mental note to check that impulse. If he had issues to work on, so did she.

Jenny arrived at the Vale to find an almost empty car park dotted with grimy heaps of snow. Operating on a skeleton staff for the New Year holiday, the hospital complex was unnaturally empty. Bracing herself against the pitiless cold, she hurried the few short yards from her car to the door of the mortuary. As she waited to be buzzed through, she glanced up at the windows of the main hospital building – a blunt, six-storey concrete cube – and had the unwelcome thought that inside there would be a handful of patients who on any other day would live to see tomorrow, but who today would slip away for want of attention by the few overstretched staff unlucky enough to be on duty. New Year's Day was possibly the worst day of the year on which to be a hospital patient, a fact confirmed by the traffic jam of gurneys inside the mortuary's main corridor. At the far end, a hospital orderly was emerging from the subterranean passage which led to the hospital basement, wheeling in yet another. Jenny glanced away as she tripped past the new arrivals, no amount of exposure to the dead ever having inured her to the bleak sense of finality she felt on seeing the contours of a human body beneath a faded-green hospital sheet. She knocked on the swing doors of the autopsy room and pushed hastily through them.

Dr Jasmine Hope looked up from her work at the dissection bench with a mild, self-conscious smile. The body of a young woman with long black hair – Jenny glimpsed it briefly and felt her stomach turn over – lay opened from neck to navel on the table. Pathologists, in Jenny's observation, fell into two distinct categories: extroverts who gloried in a bloody gallows humour, and introverts too shy, or perhaps too painfully aware of the fragility of life, to tolerate working with living patients. Dr Hope, she believed, fell squarely into the latter category.

'Mrs Cooper.'

Her eyes darted uncertainly around the room, as if she were wishing someone might materialize to rescue her from this unexpected encounter.

'Hi. I spoke to your technician earlier this morning – about the case of Burden?'

'Oh, yes. Dr Kerr's case.'

'I understand there was some information for me.' Jenny realized she would have to push this along. 'Is there any chance you could look out the file?'

'The file. Certainly. Yes.' She set down her scalpel and reluctantly removed the bloody latex gloves from her hands. 'You come with me to the office?'

Jenny followed her across the corridor to the office, feeling the nausea which had stirred in the autopsy room steadily rising. The straight lines of the white walls began to swim in front of her eyes. She took a deep breath, telling herself it was purely a psychological reaction. *Pull yourself together, Jenny, you're a coroner, for goodness' sake. This is what you do.* For a moment, at least, the unpleasant sensation abated.

Dr Kerr's spartan office had felt confined when he was its sole occupant, but now that a second, smaller desk had been placed under the window, it was uncomfortably cramped. When both he and Dr Hope were working in it together, it would have made for an intimate atmosphere. Neither would have been able to draw breath without the other being aware of it. Dr Hope went to her colleague's computer, entered his confidential password and brought up the case notes for Daniel Burden.

'Would you like to see?'

Jenny stepped to the other side of the desk as Dr Hope opened the file containing the post-mortem report.

'Yes, this is it.'

She pointed to the very first line of the report:

Name of Deceased: **Daniel Burden (biological female; TG female to male)**
Age: **34 yrs 8 months**

'Mr Burden was born a female,' Dr Hope said. 'She changed her sex to male as a young adult.'

'I see,' Jenny said, surprised, but not shocked. Those who committed suicide invariably did so out of hopelessness or loneliness, and more usually a combination of the two. In the absence of a note, this information seemed to point to the answers her inquiry would be looking for.

Jenny scrolled down through the brief description of Burden's injuries. It was a familiar form of words, rendered in Dr Kerr's typically economical prose, that concluded in the sentence: *'Vertical lesions behind jawbone either side of neck and skull consistent with death by hanging.'* Then, in the *Comments* section at the foot of the report, he had written:

> *The deceased is a biological female who has undergone gender reassignment surgery. NHS records show that he was born Diana Francis Burden and underwent a bilateral mastectomy and hysterectomy followed by further genital reconstructive surgery aged 29 yrs. No evidence of drugs or alcohol present. Full toxicology tests to follow.*

Jenny remembered the shoes she had seen at Burden's flat. She had thought at the time that they had seemed unusually small for a man. The overly muscular body and prematurely balding scalp made sense, too: she wouldn't have been surprised to find that Burden had been taking more than the prescribed amount of testosterone. The male hormone, now relatively easy to manufacture and produced chiefly in laboratories in Pakistan, was widely (though illegally) available online. She had dealt with the suicides of a number of male bodybuilders who, besides having abused steroids, had in some cases many times the normal amount of testosterone in their bloodstreams. Aside from building muscle, testosterone could also induce violent and occasionally self-destructive urges.

Dr Hope opened a second file containing several photographs of Burden's remains taken prior to autopsy. The torso was that of a man, stocky and muscled, but the genitals remained those of a woman. The sight of a body caught somewhere in the space between male and female made Jenny feel strangely empty, as if she were momentarily experiencing some of the sense of displacement that must have engulfed him before he had taken his life.

'Is this what Dr Kerr wanted to talk to me about – the fact that he'd stopped short of full reconstruction?'

'I expect he was thinking of the family,' Dr Hope said, 'how much detail to include in the report.'

'I think perhaps he's being a little over-sensitive,' Jenny said. 'Tell him I'd like everything of relevance included. It's up to the family whether they choose to read it or not. I don't believe in holding relevant information back.'

Dr Hope nodded and clicked out of the file. 'I will. Is there anything else?'

Jenny considered whether she ought to view the body, if only to check that, post-autopsy, it had been restored to a state in which relatives could view it without undue distress (it took time and attention to disguise stitches around a skull devoid of hair). She decided that an email reminder would achieve the same end. She had no desire to see another corpse today. 'No. That's all. Thank you.' Jenny turned to the door and felt the return of the nausea, only this time it was even more acute. She held onto the back of a chair.

'Are you all right, Mrs Cooper?'

'It sometimes happens when I visit here,' Jenny said. 'It'll pass.'

Dr Hope gave an unexpected and sympathetic smile. 'Not only you. Here. Come with me.' She looped her arm through

Jenny's and led her out through the door. 'Don't look right. Keep your eyes on that exit sign up ahead.'

Jenny did as she said, touched by her thoughtfulness.

'You've known Andy Kerr a long time?' Dr Hope asked, as if to distract her from the line of corpses in the corridor.

'Nearly five years.'

'He's a good man, I think. I'd like to work here permanently if I can.'

'I'm sure he'd like that, too,' Jenny said, unable to resist a little matchmaking.

Quietly registering her comment, Dr Hope walked with her through the door at the end of the corridor and into the vestibule. 'You look pale,' she said as they parted. 'Maybe you should see your doctor?'

'On New Year's Day?'

'Then take it easy,' she chided gently. 'It's meant to be a holiday.'

'I'll do my best,' Jenny assured her, and stepped gratefully outside.

The cold air in her lungs had a miraculous healing effect. By the time she reached her car, the dizziness and nausea had all but left her. It was a relief to feel well again, but her sudden recovery confirmed Jenny's fear that the cause of her symptoms lay in her mind. Driving through a city whose inhabitants had yet to emerge from behind closed doors, she berated herself for the weakness that had allowed vestiges of her old illness to return. She had allowed herself to believe that the neuroses that had plagued her for so many years belonged firmly to her past, but the arrival of paranoid thoughts and psychosomatic nausea on the same morning seemed to be telling her that she wasn't quite as cured as she had thought.

She tried to apply logic in isolating the cause. Was it just her fear of over sharing her life with Michael, or was there something else, something that was nagging on a deeper level still? She searched and questioned, but the answer refused to reveal itself. Instead she was left with a vague and ominous feeling that she was failing to see something obvious. She was aware of its malevolent presence and had entered the cool of its shadow, yet for the moment, at least, whatever *it* was remained stubbornly out of sight and beyond her grasp.

'Perhaps I'm doomed always to be slightly crazy,' Jenny said out loud to herself, and then turned up the radio until she could no longer hear herself think.

# FIFTEEN

DI RYAN CLIMBED OUT OF his waiting car as Jenny pulled up opposite Kelly's flat. Joining him on the pavement, she noticed he was wearing a different but equally well-put-together outfit beneath his black ski jacket – cashmere sweater, designer jeans and tan leather boots. She felt like taking his picture to show Michael how it was done.

'Another nice day for it,' Ryan said dryly. 'I appreciate your coming.'

'Have you told her anything more?' Jenny asked. 'She didn't even ask me why we wanted to see her.'

Ryan shook his head. 'I thought it would probably be best if she heard it from you –' he hesitated, as if concerned that he was being presumptuous – 'unless you'd prefer me to do it.'

'You can be my wing-man,' Jenny said. 'I've broken plenty of bad news in this job, but I'll admit, never anything quite like this.'

'Me neither,' Ryan said. He turned to the block of flats with a look of grim resignation.

The safe apartment in which Kelly was being temporarily housed at police expense until the council found her somewhere permanent was on the second floor at the end of an L-shaped corridor. The building was eerily silent and anonymous, a place that it would be hard to call home. Kelly came to the door barefoot, dressed in a thigh-length white T-shirt over tracksuit bottoms, her thick black hair pushed back behind her ears. Jenny couldn't help but notice that even without make-up, and shattered with grief, she managed to be arrestingly beautiful. She mumbled a hello and took them along a short passageway. A cheap plain sofa, two matching chairs and a television were the only objects in a sitting room with bare white walls. There was nothing of Kelly in evidence, not a single book or magazine or even a box of Kleenex. She sat on one of the chairs, knees pressed together, her hands clutched anxiously on her lap. Her large eyes were fixed and staring, as if she were still frozen in shock.

'How are you feeling this morning?' Jenny said, as she sat on the other chair, leaving Ryan to occupy the sofa.

Kelly shrugged. 'Not feeling anything,' she said. 'It's kind of strange.'

'Have you seen a doctor?'

She shook her head. 'I don't want pills.' She pushed back the stray strands of hair that had fallen forwards over her face and looked Jenny in the eyes. 'I know you haven't come to tell me good news.'

'It's not about Robbie,' DI Ryan interjected. 'We're still looking.'

Kelly nodded, visibly relieved.

'I'd like to open an inquest next week,' Jenny said, 'but before that happens, I thought – well, DI Ryan and I both thought – that you ought to hear what we've discovered about what went on inside the house.'

Kelly became completely still. She gave a hint of a nod.

Jenny glanced at Ryan, who urged her on.

'There's no easy way of telling you this, Mrs Hart.' Jenny swallowed a lump that had formed in her throat and forced herself on. 'Both your daughters had fatal shotgun wounds to their bodies. It seems Ed then shot himself, probably after setting fire to the house.'

Kelly remained a statue. No emotion registered on her face.

Thrown by her lack of response, Jenny waited for a reaction, but Kelly remained an unreadable blank.

'Do you have any idea what might have caused him to do that?' Jenny asked.

There was a brief delay before Kelly slowly shook her head.

Jenny pressed on. 'The pathologist thinks Layla may have been several months pregnant.'

Finally a flicker, though of what, precisely, Jenny couldn't be sure.

'Did you know anything about that?' Jenny asked.

'No,' Kelly whispered. She closed her eyes, 'I'm not surprised. I mean, there were boys . . .'

'Wouldn't she have told you?'

Kelly looked away. Jenny hadn't intended to make her feel guilty, but she could see that was what she had done.

'What I mean is, can you think of any reason why she wouldn't have told you? If it was three months, surely she would have known?'

There followed an even longer silence. Jenny sensed that it was making Ryan uneasy, and she shot him a glance, urging him to trust her.

What felt like minutes, but was perhaps as little as thirty seconds, passed before Kelly said, 'I know what you're thinking, but it wasn't Ed's. No way.'

'It may be possible to do DNA tests,' Jenny said. 'We'll know shortly if that's possible.'

'It's nothing to do with Ed,' Kelly said emphatically. 'He wouldn't. He just wouldn't. No.'

Jenny studied Kelly's face and saw doubt. She was trying to convince herself and wasn't succeeding.

'Is there anyone Layla might have spoken to – a friend, perhaps?'

'You can ask Nicky, Nicky Brookes,' Kelly said. 'But I can tell you now, it wasn't Ed's.'

'Layla and Nicky – were they close?'

'They'd been at school together since they were little kids,' Kelly said. 'She'll know more about what Layla was up to than I could tell you.' She stared at her hands twisting on her lap. 'Too much of her father in her, that was her problem. Wouldn't be told. Didn't know when to stop.'

'Did Layla argue with Ed?'

Kelly shook her head. She was adamant. 'He was about the only one who could calm her down.' After a short pause, she glanced up. 'He was gentle. But you never met him, so how would you know?'

'You're right,' Jenny said, 'all I can do is ask questions and try to understand. I'll take your word that he was gentle at home, but his job at Fairmeadows Farm—'

'He didn't like it, we just needed the money. Said he learned to switch off and forget where he was.'

Jenny would like to have heard more on the subject, particularly Kelly's thoughts on how it was possible to spend eight hours a day shovelling carcasses into a grinder and come home emotionally intact, but these were details that could wait for the inquest. Now was the moment for the big issues, and one in particular that had weighed on her mind since her second meeting with Clare Ashton the previous morning.

'Do you mind if I ask you if Ed had any issues with depression or mood swings?' Jenny asked.

'Not really,' Kelly answered.

'You don't sound altogether sure.'

'He wasn't depressed, if that's what you mean. He didn't shout or lose his temper.'

'I was told he had problems as a teenager. A woman who used to live in the village once objected to his application for a shotgun licence.'

'I don't know anything about that.'

Her answer seemed spontaneous and Jenny believed her.

'Correct me if I'm wrong, but I get the impression Ed was the quiet, dependable type, who didn't talk about himself too much. He stood by while other people shouted at each other, but wouldn't get involved if he could help it.'

Kelly looked at Jenny in surprise, then turned to Ryan as if for an explanation for how her secrets had been unlocked.

'They're common traits in a certain type of man,' Jenny said. 'They avoid conflict, even though they might have experienced a lot of it in their early lives. They've learned from a young age to keep their emotions hidden.'

Kelly stared at her. It was the stare of a little girl, Jenny thought, and she wondered if that was what had been confusing her about Kelly: perhaps she was actually more naive than she had imagined. Perhaps she was one of nature's innocents, who had somehow managed to exist in the eternal present. The more she pursued this thought, the more it seemed to explain how Kelly could have survived into her mid-thirties and remained so outwardly untarnished by life. Her trick had been to remain a child inside a woman's body.

Jenny felt obliged to offer her an explanation in the hope it might provide some comfort: 'Sometimes men like that eventually erupt. No one can see it coming, least of all them. It doesn't have to be a big thing, something tiny or even insignificant can light the fuse.'

Kelly looked at her mistrustfully, though Jenny could see that she was thinking back, viewing Ed in a different light.

Ryan chipped in, unable to suppress his detective's

instincts. 'Did he ever get jealous of you working behind a bar, Kelly? You must have met a lot of men in your job, got a lot of attention – not always the kind you'd welcome.'

'If he was, he never said so. He never said a word about that.'

'But you'd have felt it if he'd been jealous, wouldn't you?' Ryan prompted. 'You don't live with someone and not sense their moods.'

Kelly lowered her gaze to the floor. 'Sometimes if I was late home he'd ask me where I'd been. That's all.'

Jenny intervened. 'I think perhaps this is a conversation to have when Mrs Hart is making her statement—'

Ryan ignored her. 'Did he have any reason to be jealous, Kelly?'

'No,' she retorted, a note of anger in her voice.

'I think that'll do now,' Jenny said. She changed the subject. 'I'm still not sure it's a good idea to be spending so much time alone, Mrs Hart. Have you got any friends nearby?'

'I don't want to see anyone.'

'What about Family Liaison?' Jenny asked Ryan.

'I've got their number,' Kelly said impatiently. 'I'm fine. Please. I prefer it this way.'

Jenny was reluctant to leave her, but if she insisted on being alone there was nothing she could do to stop her.

'I'm giving you my card,' Ryan said, and pressed one into Kelly's hand. 'I probably gave you one already, but I want you to keep this by the phone. Any time – you understand?'

She took it from him and whispered a thank you.

Jenny rose from her chair, and promising to be in touch the moment she had any more news, started to make her way out. She and Ryan were in the hallway when Kelly broke down.

'I just want it to be over,' she said between sobs. 'I don't care why he did it. What difference does it make? I'm never going to have them back. Please – I just want it to be over. Quickly.'

Jenny turned back to the sitting room, but Ryan put a restraining hand on her arm. 'Leave her. You've done your bit. I'll call Family Liaison and get someone to look in later.'

It went her against her every instinct, but Jenny forced herself to the door, exited with Ryan, and closed it behind her.

They made their way down to the sterile lobby in silence, both affected by the helplessness of Kelly's weeping, which had followed them all along the corridor and continued to echo in Jenny's ears.

'There was no other way,' Ryan said. 'Don't beat yourself up.'

'I'm not sure she really knew him,' Jenny said. 'And I'm not sure she wanted to – not after what happened with her husband.'

'You look washed out,' Ryan said. 'If there was anywhere decent round here, I'd offer to buy you lunch.'

'Thanks, but I think I'll go home and pour myself a drink,' Jenny said, 'try and enjoy a few hours' peace before all the madness starts again tomorrow.'

'Another time,' Ryan said. He opened the door and stood aside to let her through.

As they parted on the pavement, Jenny glanced involuntarily back at him and inadvertently caught him doing the same. Her face burned with embarrassment as she hurried across the road. What was she *thinking*?

She reached the safety of her car and avoided looking across at Ryan again as he pulled away. Plugging in her seatbelt, she noticed a message lighting up the screen of Michael's phone, which she had placed in the console between the seats. It announced a missed call from an unknown caller with a Swiss number. Hoping it was Michael, she called it back. After five long, single rings, it was a woman's voice that answered, in heavily accented English.

'Hello, Michael?'

'No,' Jenny stumbled. 'This is his partner, Jenny Cooper. Who is this, please?'

There was a pause, as if the woman had been caught off guard. 'This is Pascale Saltz speaking.'

'And you are?'

'Senior Account Manager for Luftracht Zugg. How may I help you?'

Luftracht Zugg. The name was familiar. Jenny recalled Michael having mentioned that his company had been sub-contracting from a Swiss freight company and presumed this was the one.

'He left his phone in the UK this morning. I saw your number and thought it might have been him trying to call.'

'I have not seen Mr Sherman today. I will let him know if I do.'

'Thank you.' Jenny rang off, annoyed with herself.

Looking at younger men one moment, raging with jealousy the next, her emotions were as erratic as a teenager's. She had a moment of panic: *God, what if I'm menopausal? I can't be, not yet!* She jerked down the vanity mirror and looked at herself. She saw a 46-year-old woman – still pretty, but fading – and as frightened of growing older as she was of being alone. It angered her that after years of establishing her independence she was finding herself growing more, not less insecure. Perhaps that was just the way life worked: the moment you were comfortable with one version of yourself, you were forced, kicking and screaming, into another.

She checked her reflection again. She was approaching

that time of life when she would have to cut her hair short, say goodbye to the lingering illusion of beauty and aim instead for graceful or elegant. Leaning in closer to the mirror, she examined her profile from both sides. Maybe she was being a little unkind to herself: with a bit of luck she could just about hold out for another year or two, maybe even three or four.

Jenny arrived home to find a message from Michael on the answerphone, giving her the number of his airport hotel in Zurich. Moments later she was speaking to another receptionist, who in perfect English wished her a happy New Year and connected her to Michael's room.

'Jenny, hi.' He sounded relieved to hear her voice. 'You caught me just in time – quick hop up to Hamburg this afternoon. They've got me criss-crossing Europe for the next three days.'

'I told you your job was safe.'

'I hope so. I hear you've been talking to my fancy woman?'

'Your *what*?'

'Pascale – she said you found my phone. You were a bit short with her.'

'I didn't know who she was.'

'I don't think anyone's ever been jealous over me before,' Michael said with a laugh. 'I'm flattered.'

'She sounded like she knew you.'

'She does. She's also about fifty-five and a grandmother.'

'I'm sorry. I don't know what's wrong with me.'

'You don't?'

'No. Not really.'

'Well, for a start we managed to spend thirty-six hours together without once mentioning – do I even have to say it?'

'No.'

'It's a pretty big thing to sweep under the carpet.'

'I'm not,' Jenny protested.

'Whatever you want to say, Jenny, I can take it. I just can't take you *not* saying it.'

She reached for the bottle of wine standing open on the counter and filled a glass. 'I needed some thinking time, that's all.'

'And to see me up close for a while? Check me out for bad habits?'

'Maybe.'

'How did I score?'

'Not bad at all.' She took a mouthful of Chianti and felt it slide into her empty stomach.

'I can hear you, Jenny. A bit early, isn't it?'

'It's a holiday.'

'Fair enough,' Michael said, 'but I wish I made you excited instead of nervous.'

'You do – except when I know you're flying through a blizzard somewhere over Europe.'

'Something's scaring you. I can tell.'

He waited for her to respond.

'What if it goes wrong?' Jenny said, surprising herself with her response. 'You've not been married like I have. I put fifteen years of my life into something that crumbled to dust. What if everything that feels so special now—'

'Hey,' Michael interrupted, 'I'm not asking you to marry me. I'm not. And to tell you the truth, if I could have found a less complicated woman I would have. I love you, Jenny, but I know I'm never going to own you.'

'When are you home?' Jenny asked, not wanting to pursue this conversation any further on the phone.

'The way things are going, maybe not till next week.'

'Well, bring a suitcase. We'll see where we go from there.'

# SIXTEEN

A GLASS OR TWO HAD unintentionally become five or six. The alcohol had made the remainder of New Year's Day pass in a pleasant haze and helped dissolve Jenny's worries over giving up her single life, but had left her with a headache and a sense of morning-after regret that not even two aspirin and three cups of coffee had managed to dislodge. Her commute into Bristol on the first working day of the year was as unforgiving as her hangover. The traffic was foul and she had no patience. After jousting with similarly irritable drivers all along the Hotwells Road, she arrived at the office frayed and short-tempered.

'Beat you to it, Mrs Cooper,' Alison announced gleefully as Jenny arrived, weighed down with a heavy briefcase.

It wasn't yet 8.30 and she was already at her desk, surrounded with paperwork. Across the room, a workman was standing on a stepladder doing something with wires in a junction box.

'This is Cal. He's from Dublin.' Alison nodded to the man up the ladder. He gave Jenny a good-natured smile. He was in his thirties, good-looking in a rough, unshaven sort of way, and Alison had evidently noticed.

'Fixing you a new cable from outside. It's all on us – it was our equipment down the street that blew it,' the man said. 'All froze up in this ice.'

'Thanks,' Jenny replied, not sure if she was meant to be grateful or annoyed. She turned to Alison: 'Have you got a moment?'

'He's not bad, is he?' Alison said as she closed the door of Jenny's office behind her.

Jenny gave a strained smile. 'I need you to have a look at Daniel Burden for me – the suicide in Henleaze. I called in at the mortuary yesterday – it turns out he was born a woman. There was no note, nothing of any particular help forwarded from the police, so I'll need to talk to a next of kin.'

'I can do that,' Alison said eagerly. 'I went on that training day last year, remember? I've still got all the ridiculous PC jargon they gave us written down somewhere.'

'I'd rather have that conversation myself, if you don't mind.'

'Don't trust me not to put my size eights in it?' Alison said.

'No, it's not that—'

Alison cut through her with a look. 'It's all right, Mrs Cooper. I can take it. If you'll be honest with me, I'll do the same with you.'

'All right,' Jenny said cautiously.

'Fine. Now we're getting somewhere. What else?'

Jenny summoned her few remaining shreds of patience. 'How did you get on with the CCTV from the petrol stations?'

'Watched nearly nine hours of the stuff. Didn't see Ed Morgan, though. I'll keep looking, but I'm not hopeful.'

'Thanks. It would be helpful to see him actually buying the diesel, but I've a feeling there'll be more than enough evidence stacking up against him. If you can track down a copy of his medical records, I'd be grateful.'

'Consider it done. Is that all? Only I've got a young

telephone engineer to ogle. I think I might ask him out for lunch and see if I get lucky.'

'I really don't think that's a good idea.'

Alison's face cracked into a mischievous smile. 'You'll have to sharpen up before your next inquest, Mrs Cooper – you're falling for it every time.'

Jenny strained to smile and rubbed her aching temples.

'And if you don't mind my saying, you're looking a bit off-colour. Not looking after yourself, are you? I've seen it before. It's not good for a coroner to get depressed. Look what happened to Mr Marshall.' Alison was referring to Jenny's predecessor as Severn Vale Coroner, a man who had slipped into despair and ended his life with a large measure of gin and a handful of sleeping pills. Alison had been fond of Harry – even a little in love – and had never quite forgiven him for the manner of his departure.

'I'd better get on,' Jenny said, eager to change the subject. 'I also need to speak with Nicky Brooks at Blackstone Ley. She was a friend of Layla Hart. Can you fix a time for me to see her?'

'Will do,' Alison said absently. She turned to go, but stopped short of the door and paused to gaze at the bookshelves that were still home to Harry Marshall's dusty collection of leather-bound law reports. 'I still sometimes forget that it's not him working in here. He fooled me completely. I think he even fooled himself.' She let out a lingering sigh. 'Coffee?'

'Yes, please.'

'Righto,' she answered brightly, and left the room humming to herself.

Jenny tried to settle to her work, while trying to blot out the constant stream of chatter between Alison and the telephone engineer on the other side of the door. She had to give her credit – the young man did seem to be enjoying her jokes. The coffee finally chased away the remnants of her headache and she began at long last to feel like herself again. Newly invigorated, she reviewed half a dozen files of deaths that had occurred since Christmas Eve, and was satisfied of cause of death and able to issue death certificates in five of them. The sixth would require more investigation: a nine-year-old girl who had died in the night following an asthma attack. Her single mother and younger brother had been present in the flat at the time, but the police report said that the mother had been drunk and insensible and had to be shaken awake by her five-year-old son to call an ambulance. Reading through the file, Jenny realized that, having heard the evidence, there was every chance an inquest jury would decide that the girl's death had been caused by the mother's gross negligence. Such a verdict would pave the way for a criminal charge of manslaughter and possibly a prison sentence. Jenny hated to be the one to pile more misery on top of tragedy, but she would have little choice. The most she could do to ease the family's suffering was to afford them a little time to grieve in peace. She scheduled the inquest for early February.

A sharp knock at her office door made her start. She checked the clock in the corner of her computer monitor and saw that it was just past midday. The morning had slipped past in what had felt like minutes.

Alison entered with a pile of fresh death reports. 'Bank holiday specials – four of them. Must have been a wild party.' She dropped them on the desk. 'There's a Mr Falco out here to see you. Says he's a solicitor. No appointment, but I told him I'd see if you could spare a minute.' She lowered her voice, but not sufficiently that it wouldn't carry through the semi-open door: 'Thinks he's a wee bit special.'

'I'll give him ten minutes. Did he say what it's about?'

'Strictly confidential, apparently. Shame he's not as discreet with his after-shave.'

Jenny pressed her finger to her lips in a vain attempt to make Alison keep her voice down.

'I don't think he's the sensitive type,' Alison said, failing to take the hint, and returned to reception, where she haughtily informed their visitor that the coroner would see him now.

Jenny did her best to conceal her embarrassment as a sharply suited man with collar-length black hair and more than a dash of the Mediterranean blood his name suggested came confidently through the door.

Jenny rose from her chair and offered her hand. 'Jenny Cooper. I don't believe we've met.' He enclosed it firmly in a fist decorated with two gold signet rings.

'We haven't. Louis Falco. Falco Associates.'

'I'm sure I've heard of you,' Jenny said, gesturing him to a seat. 'Criminal lawyers, aren't you?'

'Only when it pays,' Falco said, and settled into the seat on the opposite side of the desk.

Jenny noticed that his dark chalk stripe suit fitted too well to have been bought off the peg, and his well-cut shirt and tasteful silk tie hadn't been purchased in any of Bristol's department stores. Either he'd dressed up especially to meet her, or he wasn't the kind of criminal lawyer who spent too many nights on a duty shift at Broadmead police station.

'White-collar offences only,' Falco said, anticipating her next question. 'And definitely nothing involving bodily fluids.' He smiled. 'We also look after our clients' private affairs.'

Jenny responded with a neutral smile, refusing to appear impressed. She had met one or two Falcos before – the kind of lawyers who got a vicarious thrill from their clients' illicit activities, and more often than not picked up a few of their devious habits.

'What can I do for you, Mr Falco?'

'I presume our conversation won't go any further than these four walls?'

'Not unless what you're about to tell me contains admissible evidence.'

Falco gave a nod and glanced around the room, taking in the untidy stacks of papers piled either side of her desk and the two large filing cabinets with overflowing drawers.

Jenny felt herself bridle at what she assumed from his faint smile was his amusement at her unglamorous surroundings. 'You were saying, Mr Falco? I really don't have much time.'

'I had a client, a very good client,' Falco began obliquely. 'His name was Rozek. Jacob Rozek – sounds Jewish, but he wasn't. He was a Catholic, I'd even call him devout – he and his family used to worship at Our Lady of Ostrabrama on Cheltenham Road. That's where I first met him, in fact. Jacob was a first-class businessman. Arrived here ten years ago without a cent and built a portfolio of property worth £10 million.' He paused and gave her a questioning look. 'I thought you might have heard of him.'

Rozek. The name carried a dim significance.

'He went missing the week before Christmas. Set off for the gym in his Jaguar and never came home. Police found the car abandoned over at Barrow Gurney, about half a mile from the airport.'

'Yes, I do remember now – the local news. Weren't the police saying they thought he'd disappeared following some business problems?'

'That was their initial theory. But just before the weekend we had the result of forensics on the car. Blood and saliva spatters on the inside of the windows. Traces of urine and faecal matter on the driver's seat. No one's coming right out and saying it, but it all points to him having been – in the parlance – popped.' He pressed a finger to his temple. 'The spatter patterns suggest a bullet to the left side of the head. A low-velocity round designed not to make a mess. That takes a measure of foresight and sophistication.'

'It also involves bodily fluids.'

'I'll make an exception for Jacob. He was a good client.'

'It's a harrowing story, Mr Falco,' Jenny said, 'but Barrow Gurney comes under the jurisdiction of the Bristol Central Coroner's Office. It's outside my purview.'

'I'll level with you, Mrs Cooper,' Falco continued, appearing to disregard her point, 'Jacob Rozek probably did have enemies. The expatriate community to which he belonged has more than its fair share of rivalries, shall we say. He himself was under investigation for several alleged criminal offences – none of them of any material substance, but that's another matter.'

'As I was saying, very disturbing, I'm sure—'

'Burden,' Falco said, bringing Jenny up short. 'The police tell me that you're investigating the suicide of a man named Daniel Burden.'

'What about him?'

Sensing that he had her attention, Falco drew a slip of paper from his inside pocket and floated it across the desk. It contained a mobile number written in longhand.

'We have Mr Rozek's phone records,' he said. 'We can account for all the numbers he dialled in the last fortnight of his life, except for one. That one. We did our research and discovered that it was registered at an address rented by Mr Daniel Burden in Henleaze, though the account was in the name of a Miss Diana Francis. We don't believe that she exists.'

Daniel Burden had been born Diana Francis Burden, but Jenny decided not to entrust Falco with this information before she had delved a little deeper into Burden's case herself. She had a feeling it might be about to become interesting. 'I'll be talking to Mr Burden's next of kin shortly,' Jenny said. 'If you'd like me to, I'll raise it with him.'

'As far as I can establish, he was just some low-level official at the Newport passport office.'

'So I understand.'

'It would help me greatly to understand what his connection was with my client.'

'I'm sure the police will be interested, too,' Jenny said, although she already had her suspicions that Falco wasn't the kind who would be content to limit himself to the official channels.

'The bizarre thing is,' Falco said, 'the police say there was no phone found at the premises, not even a landline, which strikes me as odd. And you know what's even odder?'

Jenny smiled, playing along. 'Please tell.'

'My CID contact has had a look at the records for that number. It has never made a single outgoing call. Not one, in the entire eight months since it was registered.'

'That sounds like even more reason for the police to be interested,' Jenny said, picturing the pornographic images on Burden's computer, and wondering if they might hold some clue to a private life that she was beginning to suspect was more complicated than she had imagined.

'As one lawyer to another, Mrs Cooper, Mr Rozek's family don't have much faith in the police. In fact, they get the distinct impression that Jacob's murder – and we firmly believe that's what it was – isn't exactly top of their list of priorities.'

Jenny's tolerance for Falco's insinuations was running thin. 'I appreciate your concerns, but you know how the law works – if my inquiry into Burden's death throws up evidence relevant to a murder inquiry, I'll be forwarding it to the police, not to the victim's family.'

Falco pushed himself up from his chair and tugged at his

shirt cuffs. 'Trusting the upholders of the law is a wonderful ideal, Mrs Cooper, but in my experience the reality often falls short of expectations.' He glanced past her and out of the window, as if expecting to spot someone eavesdropping on them from the pavement outside. 'You'll have your opinions of me, I'm sure, but please take this much seriously: my client was murdered on December the 19th. Burden hanged himself four days later. As far as Rozek's family knew, there was no connection between them. But Jacob called him: he telephoned this nonentity of a civil servant, who uses a phone in the same way as a criminal.' Falco spread his palms in a gesture of sincerity. 'My simple advice to you is to be careful.'

He turned to leave.

'Do you know what kind of sex Mr Rozek was into?' Jenny asked, as Falco laid a hand on the door handle.

'If that's what Jacob had wanted, believe me, he could have had the prettiest girls in town. He was a good-looking guy. Thirty-eight years old and six feet tall, muscles popping out of his shirt.'

'Just a thought,' Jenny said, hoping to have planted a seed. 'Sometimes they're just the kind that look for a new challenge.'

'You didn't know Jacob,' Falco said gravely. 'And I'll forgive you for making that suggestion. He wouldn't have.'

He exited the office, leaving behind an odour of cigarettes and cologne that hung in the air like bad memories and made her feel queasy. Moments later, and almost without warning, Jenny felt a sudden return of the nausea that had gripped her the previous morning, but this time there was no beating it back. She rushed to the Ladies' and threw up.

# SEVENTEEN

'I SAID YOU WEREN'T LOOKING WELL, Mrs Cooper. It's a virus. Everyone's coming down with them at this time of year,' Alison insisted, pressing a cup of tea into Jenny's hands. 'You should be at home in bed.'

'I can't. I need to talk to Burden's brother—'

'You leave that to me. It's no trouble.'

Jenny couldn't deny that she felt too ill to focus on her mountain of paperwork, but giving up halfway through the first working day of the year would seem like a bad omen. Reluctantly, she settled on a compromise: she would leave Alison to take a statement from Burden's brother and to start the process of arranging an inquest into the deaths at Blackstone Ley, while she would take her work home, and if she felt strong enough, call in to talk to Nicky Brooks en route.

'You don't know when to stop,' Alison said reproachfully. 'You'll only make yourself worse.'

'Coming from you, that's rich,' Jenny answered. She started to load files into her briefcase, already having misgivings about leaving Alison to deal with a grieving relative alone.

'I couldn't help overhearing a little of your conversation with Mr Falco,' Alison confessed. 'Something about Burden and his client?'

'Maybe best to steer away from that this afternoon. Just

stick to the known facts and ask the other Mr Burden if he has any insights into his brother's state of mind.'

'Do I mention he might have been gay?'

'I don't recall saying that.'

'You hinted at it.'

'You really didn't miss much, then?'

'You know how voices travel in here.' Alison was un-apologetic. 'It's hardly something I can skirt around if he asks me what we know – not without lying to him, and I can't do that.'

Jenny weighed her options and realized that having Alison in possession of only half the facts was probably more dangerous than her knowing the full truth. She sucked in a deep breath as another wave of nausea consumed her.

'OK. I'll trust you with this as long as you try to be sensi-tive – it seems Daniel Burden was born female. He had some reassignment surgery in his twenties, but the process wasn't fully completed.'

'Really . . .?' Alison said, fishing for more.

'That's it. That's all I know.' Jenny's head was swimming. 'I'll call you later.' She hoisted her briefcase and made her way unsteadily from the office.

All the way up Whiteladies Road and over the top of Clifton Downs, Jenny clung to the steering wheel with white knuck-les, fearful that at any moment she might have to pull over, but as she broke out into the suburbs normal sensation gradually and miraculously returned. The speed and com-pleteness of her recovery was uncanny and only served to reinforce what she had concluded after her experience at the mortuary the previous day. She wasn't suffering from a winter virus. This was an entirely mental, not a physical disturbance. Once again she found herself searching for the reason, the trigger for this sudden and distressing reminder of her fallibility, and once again it eluded her. 'Fight it, Jenny,' she repeated to herself, but deep down she knew that railing against it wasn't the answer. There would be a reason for these episodes, and if her past experience was anything to go by, it would reveal itself only when it was good and ready.

Arriving at the corner of Blackstone Common, Jenny took the right fork that led to the Ashtons' cottage and the church beyond. But this time she travelled only a hundred yards along and pulled up behind a battered four-wheel-drive pick-up truck that was parked opposite the entrance to an unmade track. The decal on the side of the truck read: *Darren Brooks, Building Contractor.* The track was narrow and lay deep in snow, and deciding that it might prove too challenging even for the Land Rover, Jenny continued her journey on foot.

She followed a thin trail of footsteps along the track, around two steep bends and through an ancient apple orchard. Then she discovered the reason why Brooks's truck was parked out on the common: the house, a small, unlovely building built from rough-hewn lumps of the local grey-black stone, sat at the top of a steep bank that it would have been impossible to negotiate in anything less than a tractor. Jenny pressed on up the slope and arrived weak-kneed and out of breath at the top. Almost immediately she was assailed by the sound of furious barking. A black-and-tan pointer shot out from behind the house and ran straight at her. Instinctively she braced herself, ready to feel its bite, when a woman dressed in a thick cardigan flung open the back door. 'Dixie! Come away!' Her voice was sharp and commanding. 'Dixie! In!'

The dog stopped in its tracks, gave an ominous growl, and skulked head down back to the house.

'Sandra Brooks?' Jenny asked, her heart racing.

'Yes?' the woman answered coldly.

'Jenny Cooper. I'm the coroner investigating the deaths in the fire the other day. I visited your husband in hospital last week.' She drew closer to where Sandra Brooks stood guarding the entrance to her home. 'I understand your daughter Nicky was a friend of Layla Hart's. I was hoping I might speak to her. My officer should have called you.'

Sandra folded her arms defensively across her narrow, angular body as Jenny approached her. She would have been an attractive woman in her youth, with light blonde hair and china-blue eyes, but her skin had aged prematurely, the spiders' web of lines on her pale face telling a long story of disappointments and wrong turns. 'Speak to her about what?'

'About Layla and what was going on in her life. Kelly tells me they were close friends.' Jenny glanced beyond Sandra to the gloomy interior of the house.

'She doesn't know nothing about the fire.'

Jenny detected movement. A girl in a hooded sweater was standing in a doorway along the passage, peering out at her. The dog was sitting at her feet.

'I'd be happy to speak to the two of you together.'

'She already spoke to the police. They said they wouldn't trouble her no more.'

'I'm nothing to do with the police,' Jenny explained, aching to step out of the cold. 'I could have asked Nicky to come to my office in Bristol to make a formal statement, but I thought it might be easier this way.'

The hint of a threat gave Sandra Brooks pause. She glanced over her shoulder, then back at Jenny.

'I'll only be a few minutes,' Jenny said, deliberately softening her tone.'

Sandra Brooks called back to her daughter: 'Lock Dixie

out the back.' She gave Jenny a hard stare. 'Remember she's a kid, all right? She may not look it, but that's what she is.'

Jenny went with her down a cold hallway that smelt of mildew and into a room that served both as a kitchen and general living space. Several threadbare and mismatched armchairs were gathered around a coal stove. Washing was drying on a clothes horse suspended by a rope from the ceiling. Whatever Darren Brooks's skills were as a builder, he hadn't employed them in his own home: the floor was carpeted with taped-together oddments and the battered kitchen units could have been scavenged from a skip.

Nicky emerged through a latched door that led to a lean-to at the back at the house, letting in a gust of freezing air. She was as tall as Jenny, fuller-figured than her mother, and could easily have passed for eighteen. It was only her painful shyness and refusal to meet Jenny's gaze that gave her away as far younger. Jenny introduced herself and settled on the chair that was the least smothered with dog hair. Nicky nodded, unwilling to speak in more than a mumble, her eyes constantly seeking out her mother's.

Delivering the speech she reserved for people who had never encountered a coroner before, Jenny explained that she was nothing to do with the police and that her job was to find out the cause of Layla, Mandy and their stepfather's deaths. She couldn't be sure if Nicky had understood or not; when she wasn't looking at her mother, she kept her eyes fixed impassively on the flames licking the glass door of the stove.

Sandra reached for a packet of cheap cigarettes.

'Mum,' Nicky protested, 'not in the house.' They were the first words she had spoken.

'Won't hurt. Anyway, your dad's not here to complain.' Sandra lit one and sucked in the smoke with the urgency of a hardened addict.

'I've met with Kelly Hart a few times,' Jenny said to Nicky. 'I understand you've been friends with Layla since you were small.'

'Yeah,' Nicky mumbled, hiding her hands inside the baggy sleeves of her grey cotton sweater.

'Best friends?'

Nicky shrugged.

Sandra answered Jenny with a nod, smoke seeping out between her nicotine-stained teeth.

'You must have spent a lot of time together?'

Nicky shrugged again.

'She was always over at theirs or Layla was over here,' Sandra said, 'or else they were off out somewhere.' It was said with a note of disapproval, and Jenny felt Nicky draw even further into her shell.

'There are a couple of things in particular I'd like to ask you about, Nicky. I'd be really grateful if you'd be as honest as you can, OK?' Ignoring Nicky's sigh, Jenny persisted. 'Some time last autumn graffiti appeared on Layla's house. I expect you remember. Do you have any idea who put it there?' Jenny waited for an answer, and receiving none spoke a little more sternly: 'Nicky, this is important.'

'No, it's not.'

'Tell me.'

'It was just some boy Layla knew.'

'Which boy?'

'There were a bunch of them, from Bristol.'

'Why would they deface her house like that?'

Another evasive shrug.

'Tell her, Nicky,' Sandra said.

'They were taking liberties. Her stepdad had to get rid of them.'

Sandra gave her daughter a look to which she refused to respond. 'It was a bit more than that, wasn't it?'

Nicky turned her face even further away from Jenny.

Sandra drew on her cigarette and pushed her wispy hair back from her forehead. 'Ed told me he came home to find Layla and Nicky with four boys. They were videoing each other with their phones.' She glanced at Nicky, who was cringing with embarrassment. 'They were making the girls do things to them – you know. Mandy was upstairs somewhere scared half to death. Ed showed them his shotgun. He didn't tell the police, because he didn't want anyone to know. He thought one of them came back and did the graffiti.'

'Did he tell Kelly about this?'

'I'm not sure he did. She was at work. He felt responsible.'

'But he told you?'

'Didn't have much choice, did he?'

Jenny turned to Nicky, who had remained motionless throughout this exchange. 'Is that what happened, Nicky?'

'I never wanted to. It was Layla who went along with it. I just got dragged in.'

'I can believe that,' Sandra added, with an edge of bitterness.

'Did Layla tell you she was pregnant?' Jenny asked.

Nicky looked up at her in alarm. It was the first time she had made eye contact.

'She was three months pregnant when she died. Did she tell you who the father was?'

'She wasn't pregnant. No way. She can't have been. She would have told me.'

'The evidence isn't in doubt. Can you think of any reason why she might not have told you?'

Nicky shook her head, still refusing to believe it. Jenny studied her face closely and decided that her shock was real.

'Do you know who she might have had sex with? Could it have been one of these boys you were talking about?'

'No. She didn't do that with them. That was off limits.' A

note of uncertainty entered her voice. Sandra had heard it too, and cocked her head questioningly to one side, demanding to hear it all. Nicky wavered for a moment, then spat it out. 'She said she'd only ever been with one boy like that, and that was last summer.'

'Who?' Sandra asked, cutting in before Jenny.

'Is he going to be in trouble?' Nicky said.

'For Christ's sake, Nicky, just tell her,' Sandra snapped. 'It's not your job to protect him.'

Nicky lapsed into a stubborn silence.

'I will find out,' Jenny said calmly, 'one way or another.'

Nicky looked from Jenny to her mother and back again, and slowly seemed to accept that she was backed into a corner from which there was no escape.

'She said she'd done it with Simon Grant,' Nicky mumbled. 'She could have been making it up,' she added unconvincingly.

'Who is he?' Jenny asked.

'David and Emma Grant's son,' Sandra said with grim satisfaction. 'He's seventeen. Goes to some posh boys' boarding school. Kelly works up at their place. Layla must have gone up there with her in the holidays.'

'You're making her out to be a slut,' Nicky shot back at her mother. 'She wasn't. People got her all wrong. They thought she was putting out when she wasn't. She just got led along.'

'I'm sure you're right,' Jenny said, 'but sometimes there's a reason why girls behave like that.' She hesitated, trying to find a delicate way of putting her question, but there wasn't one. 'Nicky, did Layla ever mention if anything happened to her in the past?'

'What do you mean?'

'Did she ever give you any hint that she'd been abused by anyone?'

'No.' Nicky seemed puzzled at the suggestion.

'How did she get on with her stepfather?'

'Are you trying to say Ed did things to her? No way.' She shook her head in disgust.

'It's a question I have to ask.'

'No way. She loved him. There was nothing weird about Ed. You know when blokes are looking at you, you just do, but he wasn't like that. He wasn't.'

'All right,' Jenny said, trying not to appear disappointed with her answer. She pushed a little further. 'Layla had some extra help with her school work from your neighbour, Mr Ashton. Did she mention why that stopped?'

'Yeah. She said she didn't like going there. The place was weird.'

'The place or him?'

'I don't know. The whole thing with what happened to Susie and that. She didn't want to be there. She said it was creepy. I don't blame her.'

Jenny thought about raising the issue of Layla's allegedly having touched him, but decided against it. Ashton had a right to have his reputation safeguarded, and she had no illusions that anything she said to Nicky would remain private for long.

She switched back to Layla's relations with her stepfather. 'Tell me some more about Ed.'

'What do you want to know?'

'What was he like? How did he behave around you when you were at their house?'

'Normal. He always seemed pretty happy. You could have a laugh with him. He never got cross or nothing, even when Layla was answering him back.'

'Did they get on?'

'Fine. She could be a bit, you know, selfish sometimes.'

'How did things seem between him and Layla's mum? Did they get along?'

'Seemed to.'

'You didn't see them argue?'

'She was always pretty quiet, kept to herself. Layla wound her up now and then, but that's all.'

'It sounds like a happy family.'

Nicky glanced guiltily at her mother. 'Pretty much.'

Jenny sensed an atmosphere between them. She waited for one of them to respond. The tension grew thicker. Sandra sucked hard on the stub of her cigarette, yanked open the stove and tossed it into the fire.

'Is there something else?' Jenny prompted.

'Can I go now?' Nicky said, darting up from her chair.

Before Jenny could stop her, she hurried out of the room and ran upstairs with heavy, emotional footsteps.

Sandra, belligerently silent, snatched out another cigarette.

Jenny probed gently. 'Is this about Darren?'

Sandra looked back at her with eyes that wanted to cry but had learned not to.

'I was aware he had a history with Kelly,' Jenny said. 'They were together for a while—'

'Before she saw sense,' Sandra answered bitterly.

Jenny waited for her anger to fade. 'Do you want to tell me about it?'

'I wanted to move from here when we got back together. He wouldn't. It was because of her. He wouldn't admit it, but it was. We argued over Christmas. I told him I was going to leave. I was meant to be gone by now, but then all this happened.'

'I hope you don't my asking, but do you think anything might have reignited between them recently?'

'No chance. Look at her – she could have anyone. It's not

her fault. I've got nothing against Kelly – she's always been perfectly kind to me. Would have been far easier if she was a bitch. No, she wasn't interested in him.' Her face contorted in anger. 'And before you say it, that fire was nothing to do with me. The only person I was angry at was Darren.'

'Did Ed and Kelly know what was going on between the two of you?'

'Everyone knew Darren fancied Kelly. It's a running bloody joke. All I've ever had round here is pitying looks from people. I should have got out years ago, should never have let him come back to me. Don't know why I didn't leave. It's like there's something about this place that holds you . . . It's like a black bloody hole. A black hole of despair.'

Jenny hated having to cause her any more pain, but had to ask the question: 'Where was your husband when the fire broke out?'

'Here. In this room, working his way through a bottle of whiskey while I was shoving my clothes in a bag.'

'You're sure about that?'

'I was the one who saw it first – from the upstairs window. I called out to Nicky. She went and told him and he was straight out of the door. Anyway, he wanted to screw her, not kill her.'

'Was Ed jealous of him?'

'Not that he let on. But to be honest, he didn't give away much. He was one of those blokes – you wouldn't think twice about him, but looking back I suppose you could believe anything of him.'

'Why do you say that?'

'They say he hanged his own dog, when he was a kid. If you can do that, you can do anything.'

Jenny went from the Brookses' house into the fading light, with Sandra's unhappiness and Nicky's petulant grief trailing her like ghosts. She looked out over the tops of the orchards, whose centuries-old trees cast twisted, grotesque shadows in the gloom, and noticed that had Kelly's house still been standing, she would have been able to see it clearly from this spot. In fact, Darren Brooks could have stood at any window this side of his house and caught glimpses of her. And if Kelly had thought to raise her eyes, she might even have seen him looking down at her.

As Jenny descended into the dark channel between the tall hedgerows, it seemed impossible to her that Kelly would have been able to exist so close to her former lover without feeling the constant pressure of his unrequited desire. Ed, too, must have felt it. And however confident he had been of Kelly's loyalty, his former rival's persistent presence must have acted like the slow drip of poison. In low moments, when he and Kelly had exchanged cross words and her affection seemed to dim, there must always have been the lurking thought that the way was open for her to leave him for a man who loved her even more than he did. And from what she knew of Ed, he would have kept his slowly simmering jealousy to himself. If that was how it had happened, his road to madness would not have been a calculated or a malicious one, but rather a gradual and inexorable surrender to malignant imagination.

Troubled by these thoughts, Jenny picked up her pace, and for reasons every bit as irrational as those which might have afflicted Ed Morgan, she cast several anxious glances over her shoulder and made her way as quickly as she could to her car.

She was slotting the key into the ignition when Michael's phone, which was still on the console between the seats, gave two short buzzes. The screen sprang into life with a message announcing that there were three voicemails. Fighting the temptation to check them, Jenny proceeded to start the engine, but as she reached for the gear lever she found herself giving in yet again. She snatched up the phone and called the answering service. The first of the three messages was from a fellow pilot named Greg, who wanted some advice on a minor technical glitch with a plane Michael had been flying directly before him. The second was an instruction from his company's Bristol office about the collection of an airfreight container from Geneva. Jenny was wondering whether she ought to arrange to courier the phone to Michael overnight when the third message began. The voice belonged to a young woman and Jenny had heard it before. It was the receptionist from the Gasthoff Sonne in Menzingen.

'*Michael? Where are you?*' she said in heavily accented English. '*Pascale said you were in Zurich this week, staying at the Ibis, but you don't tell me.*' Her voice stuttered with emotion. '*You are avoiding me? Why? You could at least call.*' She stifled a sob. '*Call me, you bastard. Call me.*'

Jenny barely noticed the three sets of headlights approaching along the lane behind her, only becoming aware of the vehicles' presence as a police van and car drove past and pulled up a short distance ahead of her. She watched blankly as several uniformed officers unloaded three excited Labradors – sniffer dogs trained to detect cadavers – from the van. The unleashed dogs bounded in the snow before their handlers brought them to heel. A female officer who had climbed out of the following car carried a clear plastic evidence bag to the dog handlers. It appeared to contain an item of clothing made from red fabric. The handlers introduced each of the dogs in turn to its scent.

A car horn sounded. Jenny turned with a jerk of surprise and saw Ryan's car pulling up alongside. He jumped out and knocked on her window. Jenny lowered it in a daze.

'Back again, huh?' Ryan said.

'I've been talking to Sandra Brooks and her daughter.' Jenny struggled to maintain a pretence of normality. 'It was very helpful.'

'Someone found a kid's coat half buried under the snow. Kelly says it looks like Robbie's. It was at the edge of one of those Forestry tracks further down the lane there.' He nodded past the church, towards the turning to the lane that led eventually to the Forestry Commission depot. 'It's a long shot, but we'll see if the dogs can pick up a scent.' Ryan looked at her, detecting that something was amiss. 'Are you all right?'

'Just preoccupied. I've a lot to get through this week.'

Ryan's gaze dipped to her fist which was clenched tight around Michael's phone, then rose again to her eyes. 'Are you all right? You look like you're shaking.'

'Just cold.' Her fingers released their grip without her asking them to, and the phone clattered into the footwell. She scrambled for it, but in her haste struck her head on the rim of the steering wheel. 'Shit! Bloody thing!' She fished it out from between the pedals and slammed it into the glovebox. She turned to Ryan. 'I'd better go.'

'You're upset. Maybe you should wait a moment before driving.'

One of the dog-handlers called over that they were ready to set off.

Ryan answered that he would be right with them. He looked at Jenny with concern. 'If you don't mind my asking – is this a professional or a personal thing?'

'Personal.'

'Well, if you need to call someone . . .' He reached through the open window and touched her arm. 'You take care.'

'Thanks,' Jenny said. 'And you.'

# EIGHTEEN

JENNY TRIED AGAIN TO SWALLOW a mouthful of wine, but it tasted as sour as vinegar. She threw the rest of the glass into the sink in disgust. Everything had turned rotten in one afternoon, and now she couldn't even drink to dull the pain. Alone, and with no more tears left to shed, she wandered listlessly from room to room, her emotions veering wildly from fury to self-pity. How could he? How *could* he? It didn't matter that the girl who had left Michael the message had clearly been let down by him as well. It almost made it worse that he was as cowardly with the girls he picked up as he was with her. And if there had been one, she could be sure there had been more. Michael would insist they meant nothing to him, and he would probably mean it sincerely – what, after all, could be more meaningless and ultimately repellent than empty sex with someone you barely know? – but she would never again be able to trust him. And without trust, there was nothing. Jenny had become Michael's middle-aged fantasy, that was all – a comfortable berth to return to after each new foray. A woman to love and mother him but who could never excite him like the silky-skinned young girls who still came willingly to his hotel bed.

No wonder he had been behaving oddly. She suspected he had got out of his depth with this particular conquest and that she had fallen in love with him; made demands; pricked his conscience. He wasn't heartless – he could feel, all right; sometimes he could even cry like a child – he was just thoughtless. So ruled by a need to blot out all the pain of his past, with one young body after another, that he couldn't see the damage he was causing. Maybe there was a woman somewhere prepared to take him on occasional loan, but Jenny was now sure beyond doubt that it wasn't her.

No. She would rather see out her days alone than with a man who could never truly love her.

Along with this thought came a sudden sense of clarity. Over the course of the previous few days she had tried to convince herself that she could be part of a couple living under one roof again, but if she were honest, she had never completely surrendered herself to the idea. And now she knew why: she must have sensed his infidelity. She decided to act, to reclaim her dignity and let him know what she thought. She went through to her study, picked up the phone and dialled the number of Michael's hotel. She got through to the same helpful receptionist she had spoken to before, who put her through to his room. Jenny readied herself for the confrontation, but the phone went unanswered and connected to voicemail.

She kept it short, her voice steady and composed: 'Michael, your girlfriend – I assume that's what she is, or was – left a message on your phone. She was most upset to hear from Pascale that you're currently in Zurich and hadn't called her. There we are. That was all.'

She dropped the phone back on the hook and felt a weight lifting from her shoulders. The sensation was as strange as it was unexpected. She felt almost elated and invincible, like a victorious fighter. Holding onto the feeling, she went upstairs, stripped the sheets from her bed that had remained unchanged since Michael had left on New

Year's Day, and ran herself a deep bath to wash his memory away.

Jenny had feared that her giddy feeling of indomitability was too good to last. It had sustained her through the night, but by the time she pulled up outside her office in Jamaica Street the following morning, the nausea that had driven her away the previous afternoon was threatening to return. Meeting it with angry exasperation, she headed inside, determined not to weaken.

Marching down the hallway and shouldering open the door, she found Alison with the workman who had been there the previous morning.

'Mr Lafferty's back to check everything's in working order. That's his story, anyway.'

The man indulged her with a smile.

'Thank you, Mr Lafferty,' Jenny said curtly and continued on into her office.

'Don't mind her,' she heard Alison whisper. 'She takes a little while to warm up in the mornings. Never had that trouble myself.'

Jenny closed the door on them, deciding that she really would have to do something about Alison's behaviour. It would a mean a letter to her neurologist and all the emotional fallout and recriminations, but the alternative was risking a major professional embarrassment that she could ill afford.

Checking her emails, she ran her eyes down the list of thirty or more messages, but registered only one. It was from Michael and had been sent at 3 a.m. For that reason alone it would have been tempting to delete it unread, but after a moment's indecision she clicked it open. It was thankfully short:

Jenny, I'm sorry. There is no excuse so I won't insult you any more by attempting one. Yes, it happened just before Christmas – for the first and only time since I met you, I slept with someone else. The biggest mistake of my life. I feel sick with guilt and more certain than I have ever been that you are the only woman I could ever love.

For what it's worth now, I meant everything I said to you this weekend and I just can't imagine life without you. I've only myself to blame, but please believe me, Jenny – every word of this is true.

I love you.

I love you.

I love you.

Michael

Jenny stared at the screen knowing that the right response would be to fire back an email telling him to go to hell, but as her fingers reached for the keys they refused to obey. She realized that it wasn't only anger that she felt, but disappointment, and not only with Michael, but with herself. He had represented something of a fantasy to her, too: a tough pilot, a man who had flown fighter jets, whom she had allowed herself to believe wasn't afflicted by the usual human fears and weaknesses. A man who could make her feel safe. But he wasn't that at all. He was as fallible as she was.

Her struggle to formulate a reply was interrupted by Alison bursting in unannounced.

'Everything's working fine. Shouldn't be any more problems. He may have been cheeky, but he was cheap. Two hundred, cash.'

'You paid him in cash? Do we even have that much in the office?'

'I went to the ATM on the way in. You're always saying we need to save money.'

'Hold on – didn't he say this repair was being covered by his company? Something about frozen connections? Nothing to do with us?'

'Oh,' Alison said, deflated, 'he did say that, didn't he?'

Jenny sighed. The feeling of sickness that she had temporarily managed to face down was returning with a vengeance. 'Look, Alison, I'm very much aware that we haven't dealt properly with your medical situation. I've given it some thought, and I think I'll have to ask your neurologist for a report – just to make sure we all know where we stand.'

'I didn't have any problem dealing with Mr Burden after you'd gone yesterday.' She dropped the document she was holding onto the desk. 'I took his statement, and then I chased up the lab for the DNA results on Layla Hart.'

'Thank you,' Jenny said, feeling a twinge of guilt. 'Did they find anything?'

'Something and nothing. They got some usable samples from the tissue Dr Kerr sent over. It was too damaged to create a complete profile, but there was enough to compare with the sample we took from Ed Morgan after Susie Ashton went missing.'

'And?'

'He wasn't the father. Not even close. The full report will be with us tomorrow.'

Jenny slowly absorbed the implications of this news. Just because Ed wasn't the father didn't mean he hadn't behaved inappropriately with Layla, but it made the prospect of finding evidence to prove it close to impossible.

'Oh, well,' Jenny said, 'I suppose that's one small crumb of comfort for her mother. Tell me about your meeting with Mr Burden.'

'He couldn't have been any more ordinary. Works in the

back office of a builders' merchant down in Somerset. Married, two kids, boring car . . .'

'Does he have any idea what happened to his brother?'

'Not exactly, but when you hear his story you can start to join the dots. Both brothers were put into foster care when they were teenagers. Usual tale – violent dad, mum not coping. Tony – that's the older one – was sent to a family in Wells, who treated him like one of their own. Diana – as she then was – went from one family to the other and ended up in a home. Tony thinks she got into drugs while she was there and probably did what girls like that mostly do to pay for an expensive habit. She picked up a couple of juvenile convictions for possession, but somehow had the sense to join the Navy at seventeen and started to pull herself together. Her brother had no idea she had gender issues until she came out with it all in her early twenties. And once she'd made up her mind, that was it. She left the Navy, got a job in the civil service, and as far as he could tell, devoted her life to convincing the doctors she should be allowed the treatment. It took a few years, but she got there in the end.'

'Part of the way,' Jenny corrected her.

'I asked him about that. He said he thought *Daniel* had been putting money by to have the surgery done in the US. Apparently that's where you've got to go for the state-of-the-art procedures. That's the only reason he was holding out.'

'He sounds pretty together. Not like a man overwhelmed with despair.'

'That's what I thought,' Alison said. 'See?' She tapped her temple. 'Not so empty after all. Read on – I took it down word for word.'

Jenny turned to the second and final page of the statement, and found a paragraph in which Anthony Burden gave his thoughts on his brother's possible reasons for committing suicide:

> *All I can think of is that it was something to do with a relationship that went wrong. I know Dan had the occasional girlfriend, not that he introduced me to any of them, but there definitely was that side to his life and it was always women he was into. He'd changed sex, but his sexuality always remained the same. I've no idea why he would have been in touch with a Polish businessman. That makes no sense to me at all. I must have seen Dan five or six times in the last year, and there was no hint that he was unhappy. He used to spend a lot of time on his computer. Maybe you'll find something there.*

'I've asked CID to bring it over today,' Alison said. 'I've arranged to send it for data retrieval.'

'Thank you.'

'No need to sound surprised, Mrs Cooper. I've got more for you, too. I had a word with one of my old colleagues in CID and managed to get hold of Daniel Burden's bank details. I haven't got detailed statements through yet, but according to his account manager he had nearly fifty grand put away. I called his brother last night to ask if he knew how he came by it, and he didn't have a clue. He grossed just over thirty at the passport office, so it doesn't seem likely it all came out of his wages.'

'No,' Jenny agreed, now more confused than ever by Alison's many internal contradictions.

'I'd bet my house on it being drugs,' Alison said. 'Maybe not Class A, but steroids, hormones, all that kind of stuff. That's where all the smart money is these days. Back in the nineties it was heroin chic, now you've got to look like Arnold Schwarzenegger.'

Jenny recalled how clean and orderly Burden's flat had been. A considerate suicide. He hadn't left a note, which sometimes – but not always – was an indication that the deceased had felt too ashamed of something to commit the details to paper. But even so, those who couldn't bring themselves to write a note often inadvertently left a clue to the cause of their unhappiness. Burden's laptop had been set to a pornographic website, which was so obvious a signal that Jenny found herself wondering whether it might not have been intended to throw her or the police off the scent.

'There's little point speculating now,' Jenny said. 'Let's see what turns up.' She reached for the file she had opened on Burden's case and slotted his brother's statement in next to those of the police officers who had discovered the body. Tempting as it would have been to spend time delving into Burden's past, she needed to direct all her slender resources at the inquest she was opening in only five days' time. And daunting as the prospect was, she had little choice but to continue to rely on Alison's help. 'Do you think you could manage a trip out of the office to take a statement?' Jenny asked her.

'If you're sure I don't need a doctor's note.'

'You tell me.'

'I did a decent job with Burden's brother, didn't I?'

Jenny had to acknowledge that she had. She put her doubts to one side. 'Kelly Hart worked as a cleaner for a family called the Grants. Big house with a tennis court, just outside Blackstone Ley. Husband's a solicitor. And according to Nicky Brooks, their seventeen-year-old son slept with Layla last summer.'

'Nice to be eased back into the job gently,' Alison said. 'Good morning, madam, is it true your boy committed statutory rape?'

'You're right. I should go.' Jenny climbed out of her chair, but found herself grabbing the edge of the desk as the blood rushed from her head. Stars appeared in front of her eyes.

'Dizzy as well as sick?' Alison asked.

'It'll pass,' Jenny said. She made her way unsteadily to the door.

'These symptoms wouldn't be worse in the mornings, would they?'

Jenny stopped dead and looked back at her.

'It's not completely unknown at your age, Mrs Cooper,' Alison said. 'My mother had my youngest brother at forty-five.'

Jenny felt the floor buckling beneath her.

'I'm probably wrong, but I'd check if I were you – if only to put your mind at rest. I'll pop off to see the Grants now, shall I?' She went to the door ahead of Jenny and opened it for her. 'After you, Mrs Cooper.'

There was a chemist's shop in the small arcade that stood several doors along from Jenny's office, but she walked on past, too embarrassed to purchase a test kit over the counter from the assistant who knew her by name. She didn't believe for a moment that Alison could be correct in her diagnosis; it was unthinkable. She couldn't have arrived in her late forties only to find herself pregnant by a man who had cheated on her. Life couldn't be that unfair, not even hers. But however absurd, now the idea had been planted, she couldn't rest until she had discounted the possibility. She made her way down Park Street, crossed over College Green and went on past the cathedral to the new development at the harbourside. There she found a supermarket that served the residents of the neighbouring apartments. Moving between the aisles in comfortable anonymity, she sought out the pharmacy section, selected the most expensive product from the shelf and passed as quickly as she could through the self-service checkout. She emerged onto the street feeling like a shame-faced teenager, stuffed her secret purchase deep into her coat-pocket and turned back towards the office.

She had hardly gone ten yards when her phone rang. Dreading that it was Michael, she fetched it out, ready to switch it off immediately, but it was DI Ryan's name on the screen. Fighting the urge to dodge the conversation, she told herself to be strong and took the call.

'Hi. How did you get on with the search?'

'It was interesting, though not in the way we expected. Any chance of having a quick chat? I've just come from a meeting with colleagues at Broadmead. I could be at your office in ten minutes.'

Jenny stalled, not sure that she could survive a face-to-face meeting until she'd done her test.

Ryan persisted. 'Or we could meet up for a quick coffee somewhere. That might be best – I'd like to keep what I have to say strictly between ourselves for the time being.'

He didn't have to spell it out. Jenny knew that he meant he didn't altogether trust Alison with sensitive information, and she didn't blame him.

'OK, if we're quick,' Jenny said. 'I can meet you at No. 1 Harbourside in ten minutes.'

'I'll be right there.'

From her seat at the window, Jenny watched the gang of kids on the dockside throw snowballs onto the hard-frozen surface of the harbour, where they exploded amongst the other missiles that passers-by, excited at the novelty, had tossed onto the ice: tin cans, stones, several traffic cones, and a half-submerged shopping trolley, the back half of which jutted into the air at an incongruous angle.

'Is that one of Banksy's?'

Jenny looked up to see DI Ryan approaching with a cup of coffee. 'I did wave. You were lost in thought.'

'I must have been,' Jenny said, puzzled by how she had failed to see him. 'I don't think it's a sculpture, just a trolley some drunks threw in. It does look a little surreal, though.'

'One would be polemical,' Ryan said, pulling up a seat. 'I'd argue it would take two or more to make it surreal.'

'I see – I think.'

He gave an apologetic smile. 'I took a third-year module in the psychology of art. You're one of very few people to whom I've ever confessed that.'

'Is that the secret you wanted to tell me?'

'One of them.' He cast a subtle glance around the cafe tables and saw only a smattering of student and arty types. No one to cause him any concern. 'We didn't get anywhere with the coat, sadly. but something else turned up.' He brought a clear plastic bag with a tag attached. Inside was a mobile phone. 'It was jammed into a stack of felled timber on a forest track about a quarter of a mile down the road from Kelly's place.'

'Ed's?'

'Who else? It's got his Facebook on there, but no emails or texts, no contacts, nothing – they've been wiped. SIM's missing, too. It's as if he wanted it to be found, but only to wind us up some more.'

'He must have put it there before going back to the house,' Jenny said.

Ryan nodded. 'Had it all planned out.'

'Let's face it,' Jenny said, 'no one annihilates their family on a whim.'

'I guess not.' He nodded to the bag. 'You can keep it. I'll send you over a finder's statement later. How about you – anything useful at the Brookses' place?'

'What I mostly learned was that Darren Brooks has spent

the last ten years hoping Kelly would come running back to him.'

'We suspected that,' Ryan said, taking a sip of his coffee, 'but I doubt he got lucky. Kelly doesn't strike me as the kind to repeat her mistakes.'

'Is that an official psychological insight?'

'Just a gut feeling, taking account of her history.'

'She didn't exactly choose well with Ed.'

Ryan nodded. 'Point taken. But until he blew, Ed was a quiet, dependable type. I think that suited her. As she told us, she had enough going on with three kids without more excitement.'

Jenny noticed the careful way Ryan was holding his cup. He had gentle hands, not quite womanly, but almost. She kept expecting to come up against the tough side of his character that had attracted him to his profession, but she hadn't seen much evidence of it yet.

'Self-contained women drive men more crazy than any other kind,' Ryan said, as if thinking aloud, 'especially ones as attractive as Kelly. The less of herself she gives away, the more room there is to fill with fantasy – like a model in a magazine.'

'Freud?'

'And more than a little painful experience.' He finished his coffee and glanced at his stylish wristwatch. 'Much as I'd like to stay for another, I should be getting back to Gloucester. When's the inquest?'

'I was planning to make a start on Monday.'

They both got up from the table.

'Will you want me as a witness?' Ryan asked.

'I'll try not to trouble you unless I have to.' She lifted her coat from the back of her chair.

'So our paths may not cross for a while?'

'Who knows?' Jenny said.

'Would it be inappropriate of me to ask if you might be free for a drink one evening?'

Blind-sided by his question, Jenny looked away, finding herself unable to answer.

'Sorry – I didn't mean to embarrass you. It's just that you seem such an interesting person. And a little sad.' He calmly buttoned his coat. 'Good luck with the inquest. Any time.'

Jenny remained by the table as Ryan walked out of the cafe and disappeared along the quay. She caught her reflection in the glass: she barely recognized the bewildered, middle-aged face looking back at her. What would a good-looking young man like Ryan see in her? She looked so tired. She looked like her mother.

It was the strangest of days and surely couldn't get any stranger. Jenny pulled on her coat, thrust the bag containing Ed Morgan's phone in one pocket and felt her fingers tighten around the small cardboard package in the other. She threaded her way between the cafe tables and went through the door decorated with painted flowers.

Pregnancy tests had changed in twenty-three years. There were no ambiguous blue dots to interpret; a small digital display pronounced the result with unerring certainty: *Pregnant. 3+*. She had been pregnant for nearly a month, which meant it had happened during Michael's last overnight visit in early December. Jenny had been carrying his child while he cheated on her.

Now what? She didn't have an answer. She simply stared at the back of the cubicle door and sobbed.

# NINETEEN

It would all be dealt with in a little over forty-eight hours, Juliet Turner, Jenny's 32-year-old and, ironically, very pregnant GP, had told her. One dose of mifepristone today and a few hours in the antenatal ward on Saturday morning. Early stage termination was virtually a painless process, she had assured her, no worse than heavy period pains, but with the added benefit that they would only last for a few hours. Neither was there any need for embarrassment: she would be surprised to learn just how many women in their forties presented with the same dilemma. The consultation had been going well until Juliet had used that word: *dilemma*. Up to that moment Jenny hadn't been in any doubt. In truth, she had made her decision within half an hour of getting the result. There was no question of her interrupting her career to have a child who wouldn't be an independent adult until she was approaching her seventies. It wouldn't have been fair on either of them.

Jenny was equally adamant that she needed Michael out of her life, not lingering on the margins as an absent father to a child who would always harbour a secret fantasy of seeing them reconciled. If she needed any more reason, there was the fact that there always seemed to be something fated about the offspring of failed love affairs, as if their lives had been blighted by the unhappiness of their beginnings.

But Juliet's single word had caused her to question.

'Is that all right, Jenny?' Juliet said, insisting on using her Christian name. 'You won't have to be here long.'

'You mean I'd take the pill here?'

'In case of any unusual reaction, but it's not likely.' She sensed Jenny's reticence. 'Or at home if you'd prefer. Just as long as it's within the next hour or two.'

'I think I'd rather do that.'

Juliet gave an understanding smile. 'That's OK.'

*Please don't use that caring voice*, Jenny wanted to say, *it really doesn't make it any better*. But instead she smiled back and nodded politely as Juliet assured her that she could email whenever she liked with questions or concerns. Nothing was too much trouble. She even stood up from her chair, tottering under the weight of her swollen belly, to clasp Jenny's hand as she left.

'I know it's hard,' she said.

Juliet hadn't mentioned the father, not once, but she was doing it now, not in words, but in her sympathetic but ever-so-slightly pained expression. It seemed to carry the suggestion that, while it was Jenny's perfect right to go ahead as she intended, there really was no reason to hurry such a momentous decision, and perhaps it might be best to consider the father's wishes before rushing to action. It would, after all, be the considerate thing to do.

Jenny exited quickly through the waiting area, hoping not to see anyone who might recognize her, and emerged from the surgery to feel the cold slap of the wind on her face. In the time it took to walk the ten yards to her car, the anger that had seized her after the initial shock of yesterday morning gave way to a sadness that seemed to swallow her up. She should have been in the office half an hour ago, tackling her neglected cases and preparing for Monday's inquest – Alison would be tearing her hair out wondering where she had disappeared to – but none of that seemed to matter. Somehow, during her final moments with Juliet, the thing inside her had assumed an identity that was asserting itself; an identity beyond hers or Michael's. An individual presence whose voice, she sensed, needed to be heard.

It was a right turn out of the car park along the valley to Chepstow and the bridge, but Jenny found herself turning left and driving as if by instinct towards the place where she had already decided she wanted to make her decision. She threaded her way along eight miles of empty, ice-rutted lanes, passed through the tiny village of Penallt, and continued a mile further north along the narrow, undulating road to the church.

It was known as the Old Church because at some time early in its 700-year history, the name of the saint to whom it had been dedicated had been lost. Local tradition claimed it was St James, and that the church stood on an ancient pilgrimage route to his shrine in Compostela, northern Spain. But ever since she had first discovered this place, Jenny had never been able to conceive of it as being en route to anywhere. Set high on the corner of the hill overlooking the broad sweep of the Wye Valley, it was a final destination. Whoever had chosen its position must have felt as Jenny did each time she entered through its ancient lychgate and saw the countryside spread out before her: this was a place that stood midway between heaven and earth, in the midst of creation, but with the illusion of floating above it. There was an invisible reminder of hell here, too: the nameless structure owed its isolation to the fact that the community that had once thrived around it had been destroyed by the plague. There was nothing of life and death, no joys or horrors its walls hadn't witnessed.

Jenny pushed open the heavy oak door that was crudely carved with the year of its installation – 1539 – and entered the silent interior. A little sunlight penetrated the stained glass and pooled in the centre of the nave. She took a seat in a pew and tried to offer a prayer, but every phrase she attempted to form seemed stupidly and inappropriately childlike. Accepting that words were inadequate to the task, she instead sat in silence, letting her eyes wander along the ancient gravestones set in the floor that sloped downwards to the altar table. Slowly, and by imperceptible degrees, any sense of her own significance faded. The bodies buried beneath her feet and the names commemorated in the plaques on the walls became part of the same continuous and unbroken procession of life, none of them any more or less important than any other. A two-year-old infant, a ninety-year-old woman and a soldier killed in war had each been equally alive and were all equally dead.

She received no answer. There was no flash of light. But as she made her way back along the path, she paused by the dustbin at the edge of the graveyard and dropped the small package of pills she had brought with her from the doctor's surgery in amongst the dead flowers and crumpled cellophane.

# TWENTY

COURTROOMS AT BRISTOL'S SMALL STREET were in short supply after the holiday season, and even if Jenny had managed to twist arms and secure one in which to hold her inquest, the slender budget on which her office barely subsisted wouldn't have stretched to it. Instead, Alison had been through the *Yellow Pages* and at three days' notice hired the Oldbury Memorial Hall. The modest daily rate even included heating, which, given that the temperature had yet to nudge above freezing, meant they had secured a bargain.

Jenny had grown used to the sight of bemused-looking lawyers and even more confused jurors arriving at the humble buildings in remote locations in which she was forced to administer justice, and this morning was no exception. The village of Oldbury-on-Severn lay five miles to the west of Blackstone Ley as the crow flies, and was situated close to the windswept shore of the estuary. The Memorial Hall, built to commemorate the fallen of the Great War, stood on a quiet lane dotted with pretty stone houses whose gabled roofs remained blanketed with snow and were decorated with icicles.

Jenny arrived more than an hour before proceedings were scheduled to commence to find the road already lined with parked cars and Alison standing outside, swathed in a thick anorak, directing the new arrivals inside. As Jenny stepped through the gate and approached along the gritted path she realized that Alison was being bombarded with questions from a young female journalist; one who had a lot to learn about the rules of *sub judice*.

'You actually interviewed Ed Morgan personally?'

'Yes, I did.'

'I heard that for a while he was a suspect?'

'He was one of them.'

'So why didn't CID pursue him harder?'

'I wish I knew the answer.'

'Excuse me,' Jenny said, stepping between them. 'My officer won't be answering any more questions. And all you'll be reporting is the evidence in court.'

'Just doing my job,' the reporter shot back indignantly.

Jenny spared her a law lecture and gave her a look that said that was an end to it. The young woman stepped defiantly past her and pushed into the hall.

'What did you think you were doing?' Jenny asked.

'Hardly state secrets, Mrs Cooper.'

'Enough for a story.'

Alison looked puzzled, then confused. Then contrite. 'I'm sorry. We just got talking.'

'It's all right,' Jenny said. She touched Alison's arm. 'Just be careful.'

She turned to the door.

'Far end on the left,' Alison called after her. 'I left you some coffee.'

'Thank you.'

Jenny passed through the hall in which jurors and witnesses were gathering and followed Alison's directions to the committee room that would serve as her chambers during the inquest. It was a simple space lit by a single fluorescent light, which also served as a store for piles of wooden staging and spare furniture. A small trestle table with a fold-down chair stood in the centre of the remaining area of floor, and on it Alison had placed a Thermos flask and a cup and saucer. Her final act of thoughtfulness had been to tape several pieces of paper over the glass pane in the door, to lend her some privacy. No one could call it ostentatious, but as she unloaded her files and her battered copy of *Jervis on Coroners*, the textbook that never left her side at inquests, Jenny reminded herself that when it came to digging out the truth, a coroner's obscurity could be their greatest asset. She could ask questions that no judge sitting in ornate splendour would dare to. She had no senior colleagues looking over her shoulder. There was no network of court officials to inform on her. Her sole duty was to uncover the truth, however unappealing that might turn out to be.

The minutes counting down to a court session were always tense, and there had been a time not so long ago when Jenny would have needed a pill to calm her jangling nerves. She could safely say that she had now moved beyond chemical dependency, but she still felt her heart beat faster and noticed a tremor in her fingers. Skimming through her papers, she attempted to order her thoughts. Michael, the baby she was carrying and all her fears for the future were pushed to the margins of her consciousness, as she entered the tunnel of concentration from which she wouldn't emerge until her jury delivered a verdict.

She was disturbed after a short while by a knock at the door. She checked her watch: it was only quarter past nine, a full three-quarters of an hour before the session was due to start.

Alison entered unbidden. 'There's a solicitor to see you, Mrs Cooper. A Mr Lever. He said he's acting on behalf of the Grant family.'

'The Grants? Why have they got a lawyer? They're just witnesses.'

Alison had taken statements from both Emma Grant and her seventeen-year-old son, Simon, the previous week. Both had strongly rejected Nicky Brooks's allegation that Simon had had a sexual relationship with Layla and that he might be the father of her unborn child. Nevertheless, Jenny had decided that their denials needed to be tested in court. Harry Grant, Simon's father, had managed to make himself unavailable for a meeting, but to make sure he understood there was no avoiding her, Jenny had served him with a witness summons, too.

'I think that being witnesses is what it's about,' Alison said. 'They don't want anything to do with it.'

'I'm sure they don't. All right, show him in,' Jenny said reluctantly. 'I can give him five minutes.'

She got up and took another folding chair from the pile stacked against the wall, as Alison went back to fetch her visitor.

Jenny could tell from the brisk footsteps and impatient knock that he was a London lawyer. His puffy eyes told her he'd caught the 5.30 from Paddington to Bristol rather than spend a night away from the addictive hum of the city. His sour smile as he shook her hand told her it was a decision he was already regretting.

'Sam Lever. Heinemann Wade. I'm instructed by the Grant family.'

He was mid-height, suntanned and no more than forty years old. Jenny marked him down as an ambitious junior partner who'd been prevailed upon to do a personal favour for Harry Grant. After a Christmas probably spent on a Caribbean beach, he was, she imagined, feeling more than a little resentful at finding himself in a village hall in Gloucestershire.

'Good morning.' She gestured him to the uncomfortable chair and got straight to business. 'You want to tell me

Simon Grant and Emma Grant's evidence isn't relevant to my inquest. If it'll save you time, it's not an argument I'm prepared to entertain.'

Lever sighed. 'As far as I understand it, there is no evidence indicating anything other than that Mr Morgan set fire to his house and killed his stepdaughters. In which case, neither Harry or Emma Grant nor their son can possibly have anything to add. As I see it, the only purpose of calling them would be to suggest a sexual relationship between Simon and the dead girl, Layla Hart, which even if it were true, could have no possible bearing on the circumstances of the fire.' He paused briefly for breath. 'And we all know that if evidence is more prejudicial than probative, it is not admissible. Accusing Simon Grant of having sex with an underage girl could hardly be any more prejudicial, and it's proof of nothing.'

'And you assume I haven't carefully considered these factors, Mr Lever?'

'I assumed you had come to the wrong conclusion.'

Jenny gave a patient smile. 'Are you familiar with procedure in coroners' inquests?'

'I know I can go to the High Court and get these proceedings stayed while a judge determines the proper course.'

'Well, good luck. Is that all? I've a few things to attend to before we start.'

Lever looked at her with incredulity. 'This isn't a feint. I can have counsel before a judge in the Royal Courts before lunchtime.'

Jenny had lost count of the times she had been confronted with big-city lawyers who assumed that she would roll over at the first mention of the High Court. Often she would disabuse them with more grace then they deserved, but Lever had already riled her to the point where she could happily have reached over the desk and slapped him.

'Mr Lever, this is not a trial. It is an inquest, an inquiry into the facts surrounding and leading up to the deaths of three people. I have no idea what this inquiry will reveal or what evidence currently outside my knowledge may yet become relevant. I do know how much Mr Grant dislikes being in the public eye and I sympathize, but his son has been accused of, let's face it, a crime, and not only that, a crime that gives him a motive for having set fire to that house.'

Lever feigned outrage. 'This is preposterous. Morgan left a full confession.'

'A powerful point, which I'm sure the jury will consider carefully.'

'I've instructed my clients not to come to court today.'

'Then I'll simply issue warrants for their arrest.'

Lever's eyes widened in astonishment. 'You'll what? You can't—'

Jenny reached for her copy of *Jervis*. 'Would you like me to show you?' She started to turn to the relevant passage. She knew the reference by heart.

Lever issued another weary sigh and pushed a hand through his uniformly black hair. 'A DNA test, is that what you're after? If Simon agrees to one, can we avoid all this?'

Jenny folded her hands patiently on the desk in front of her.

'Where are we, Mr Lever?'

'I beg your pardon?'

'A simple enough question, surely.'

'Somewhere in Gloucestershire?' He smirked with his eyes.

'Can you be a little more specific?'

He shrugged. 'Oldbury?'

Jenny remained calm. 'We are in my chambers. And through that door is my court. And not once have you addressed me in the appropriate manner.'

'Appropriate—'

'I don't hear you.'

'What exactly do you—'

'I still don't hear you, Mr Lever.'

Lever looked at her blankly, then slowly the penny dropped. 'Oh, I see. *Ma'am.*' The word almost stuck in his throat.

'Thank you, Mr Lever. I will be asking Simon Grant if he would care to submit to a voluntary DNA test, but until we hear his evidence, I don't feel justified in compelling him to do so. If he thinks that a test would help clear things up quickly, that's a matter for him. I'll leave it with you.'

Lever pushed up from his chair.

'On reflection, I can grant you one thing, Mr Lever.'

He looked at her doubtfully.

'I'm prepared to treat Simon Grant as an interested party and allow you to cross-examine witnesses on his behalf.'

'I'll take my clients' instructions,' Lever said coldly, and left the room.

Jenny took a sip of coffee with a steady hand. She felt good. She was ready.


Alison knocked at one minute to ten. She entered wearing an immaculately pressed usher's gown over her dark suit and patent shoes. Confident and composed, she showed no outward sign of her recent trauma.

'We're all ready for you, Mrs Cooper.'

'And you?' Jenny asked.

'Just glad to be back.' Alison smiled. 'I won't let you down.' She turned smartly out of the door.

Jenny picked up her papers and followed her through the short connecting passageway to the main body of the hall. The heat rose in her chest. She took a deep breath.

Alison went ahead of her. 'All rise.'

Jenny stepped into the hall to be confronted by an unexpectedly large crowd. She estimated forty or fifty expectant faces looking back at her. Jurors, witnesses, lawyers and press could only account for half of their number. The rest had to be members of the public, curious to witness another chapter in the blighted history of Blackstone Ley.

As Jenny sat behind her table facing the assembled company, she noticed Kelly Hart on the far right of the front row of seats, accompanied by a young female police officer. Kelly was dressed plainly in jeans and a black roll-neck sweater, and showed no visible emotion. She was carrying herself with dignity, and seemed not to notice the heads in the rows behind craning to catch a glimpse of her. Jenny gave her a nod of encouragement and turned to the three lawyers sitting behind the desks ranged opposite hers. Sam Lever had swallowed his pride and decided that Simon Grant's best interests would be served by his taking a full part in the proceedings after all. Jenny guessed from his sulky expression that he had been forced to accept that the High Court wasn't going to save his clients from the embarrassment of giving evidence in public.

The silver-haired man to Lever's right stood and addressed her. The note Alison had left on her desk told her that he was Robert Newland QC. Jenny knew his reputation as a heavyweight prosecutor. Although he practised from chambers in London and plied his trade largely in the Old Bailey, Newland was a local man who made frequent forays to the Crown Courts in Bristol and Gloucester.

'Ma'am, I appear on the instruction of the Chief Constable of the Gloucestershire Constabulary.' He spoke with a trace of Gloucestershire accent that he no doubt felt lent him the common touch. He gestured to the woman sitting to his left. 'My learned friend Miss Palmer is appearing on behalf of Miss Kelly Hart, and Mr Lever is representing the interested party, Simon Grant.'

Katherine Palmer half rose from her seat. 'Good morning, ma'am.' In her mid-thirties, Palmer was an ambitious criminal barrister who had earned a name for herself in Bristol by securing a string of unlikely acquittals. One of the few women at the Bar with no qualms about defending men accused of sexual offences, she had a reputation for the skilful destruction of vulnerable witnesses. The Legal Aid Fund didn't pay lawyers to appear at inquests, so it was likely that Katherine Palmer was appearing without a fee. She clearly considered the cachet of being associated with such a high-profile and newsworthy case as sufficient reward in itself.

'Good morning, everyone.' Chiefly for Kelly Hart's benefit, Jenny struck a friendly, informal tone. 'Is there any reason why we shouldn't empanel a jury and make a start on the evidence?'

The lawyers raised no objection, so Jenny gave Alison her cue to call forward the four women and five men who had been summoned to do their duty. Each in turn swore an oath 'to diligently inquire on behalf of Our Sovereign Lady the Queen' and 'give a true verdict according to the evidence'. Seated in two rows of chairs to Jenny's left, at the side of the hall, the newly empanelled jurors wore expressions ranging from mild bewilderment to outright confusion. The job of a jury in a coroner's inquest was little understood, and it was now Jenny's task to explain it as simply as she could.

'Members of the jury,' she began, 'you have been called here today to perform a very solemn duty. 'On December the 27th, the bodies of three people were recovered from a house following a fire. They were Edward Morgan, aged thirty-five, and the daughters of his partner, Miss Kelly Hart. The girls were Layla Hart, aged fourteen, and her younger sister, Amanda, aged eleven. This inquest has one purpose: to determine the cause of those three deaths. This is not a trial. There are no competing cases for you to decide between. No one is being accused of any crime, although the evidence may disclose that a crime was committed. This is an inquiry called to ascertain the *truth*, and your role is to listen to all the evidence and, having considered it, to decide on the most appropriate verdict in each of the three cases. There are a number of possible verdicts open to you. Firstly, suicide, which means that the deceased deliberately took his or her own life. Secondly, accident, which I hope speaks for itself. Thirdly, misadventure, which means that the deceased knowingly undertook a risk that resulted directly in death. Fourthly, unlawful killing, which means the death was the result of a criminal act. Lastly, an open verdict, which is the verdict you would deliver if, having heard all the evidence, the cause of death still remains unclear.'

Having laid out the bare bones of their legal duties, Jenny spent the next fifteen minutes summarizing the known facts of the case. She told them that Kelly and Ed Morgan had been together nearly ten years and had a three-year-old son who remained missing and was presumed dead. She explained that Ed worked both as a forester and at Fairmeadows Farm, while Kelly had worked in the same Bristol pub for nearly seven years, travelling into the city each day by car. Although it hadn't been her conscious intention, the picture Jenny painted was of a hard-working family who had been quietly living their lives without incident until tragedy struck like lightning from a clear blue sky. On reflection, it was how she felt. She was as mystified by what had happened only eleven days before as the jurors clearly were: they hung on her every word. She concluded with a reminder that, no matter how tempting it was to jump to conclusions, they must strive at all times to keep open minds.

Jenny called the first witness. In the makeshift courtroom, the witness box was a small trestle table and chair positioned between Jenny's desk and the jury. Detective Sergeant Andy Millard had been given the job of representing Gloucester CID's investigation team. In his mid-forties, shaven-headed and heavily muscled, Millard had clearly been chosen as the detective least likely to speak out of turn, or indeed to say anything that wasn't in his script. He read the oath in a bass monotone, then proceeded to recount the dry facts of the fire and its aftermath, which he read out from his notebook.

Millard told the court that a 999 call had been made at 11.46 p.m. on 28 December by Mr Graham Medway, a near neighbour. Fire crew were scrambled from Thornbury and arrived at six minutes past midnight, by which time the building was consumed with flames. Shortly after their arrival, the propane tank at the side of the house exploded, causing further structural damage to the already partially destroyed building. The flames were quenched in a matter of minutes, but the intensity of the heat was such that there was no hope of finding any survivors inside.

The discovery of three sets of human remains in the rubble prompted the police to instigate a full-scale inquiry. A fire-investigation report was commissioned from an independent consultant who arrived early the next morning to take samples and survey the scene. Less than twenty-four hours later, it was confirmed that ashes and debris taken from what had been the living room and hallway of the house contained residual traces of diesel oil. Chemical markers added to the fuel at the refinery identified the diesel as having been supplied by a BP filling station.

The mother of the children inside, Kelly Hart, had arrived home after working an evening shift in The Berkeley, a pub on Queen's Road, central Bristol, at twenty past midnight.

At first she thought that all three of her children were inside the house. She was being comforted by officers when word arrived via the emergency-service operators that an anonymous caller had telephoned 999 to alert the police to a message that had appeared on Ed Morgan's Facebook timeline at 11.28 p.m. Millard reached into a folder he had brought with him to the witness box and produced a number of colour copies of a screenshot of Ed Morgan's final message. Alison distributed them to the three lawyers and the jury.

'*For Kelly,*' Millard quoted very deliberately. '*Robbie is gone but you will never find him. We are all at peace now, but you will be in living hell, which is all a whore like you deserves.*'

It was an obvious question, but Jenny had to ask it: 'Officer, how exactly did you interpret that message?'

'We took it to mean that some time prior to writing it, Mr Morgan had disposed of his three-year-old son, Robbie, in some way, and that either just before or just after writing it, he set fire to the house, intending to kill himself and his two stepdaughters. Subsequently, of course, gunshot wounds were found to all three bodies.'

'We'll get to those in a minute,' Jenny said. 'Tell me about the 999 call which tipped you off to this message. Do you have any idea who made it?'

'No. All we know is that it was made from a call box that stands approximately fifty yards from the house close to the church. The report we were handed said the caller was an adult male. No name.'

Jenny cast her mind back to her visits to Blackstone Ley and remembered an old red phone box, slightly on the lean, that was situated on the verge a short distance from the church.

'Were any fingerprints taken or attempts made to identify the caller?'

'No.'

'What about the message on Mr Morgan's Facebook page – have you established where it was written?'

'At the foot of the message it says it was uploaded by mobile. We assume that mobile was Mr Morgan's.'

Jenny turned to Alison, who was seated at a small table positioned at the side of the room. 'Can you please show Mr Morgan exhibit AM-1.'

Alison picked up the evidence bag DI Ryan had handed to Jenny the previous week and carried it to Detective Sergeant Millard.

'My inquiry was handed this phone last Thursday by one of your colleagues, Detective Inspector Ryan.'

'So I understand.'

'Can you tell us when and where it was found?'

'It was discovered on the 2nd of January. I was part of a five-man team searching for Robbie Morgan in woodland approximately a quarter of a mile from Mr Morgan's home. We were examining a pile of felled timber and spotted the phone jammed into the end of the stack. We sent it for data retrieval later the same day, but apart from the final message, there was nothing of interest.'

'Do you have a record of Mr Morgan's phone calls?'

'I do.' Millard reached into his folder and brought out a sheet of paper.

Alison took it from him and handed it to Jenny.

'He only made a couple of calls a week, mostly to his partner. He seems to have led a quiet life.'

Jenny ran her eyes down the list of numbers he had dialled during the previous three months and had to agree with Detective Sergeant Millard. Ed Morgan seemed to have used his phone only under sufferance. A glance at Kelly Hart told Jenny that she didn't disagree.

'How long would it take to walk from where the phone was found to the house?' Jenny asked.

'Five minutes. No more,' Millard replied with certainty. 'There was plenty of time for him to have left it there at 11.30 and gone back to the house to do what he did.'

'What do we know about his movements earlier in the evening?' Jenny asked.

'Ms Hart, his partner, left for work at approximately 5 p.m. She told us that she left Mr Morgan with the three children.'

'So we can assume, can we, that whatever happened to Robbie, happened at some time between five o'clock and 11.30?'

'Yes. But I'm afraid that as of yet we have no evidence confirming that Mr Morgan left the house, and no idea where he went. He had a pick-up truck, an old Ford Ranger, but it was parked next to the house and too damaged by the fire to yield any forensics.'

'Would you mind telling us what the current police theory is of what happened to Robbie Morgan?'

'It was high tide in the estuary at 10 p.m. If a body had gone into the water shortly afterwards, it could easily have been swept out to sea. Morgan had lived in the area all his life. He would have known that.'

'He also worked at a meat rendering plant—'

Millard stepped in quickly as Jenny had suspected he would. 'There is absolutely no evidence of Mr Morgan having visited the plant that evening. I can say that emphatically.'

Nevertheless, the jury had pricked up their ears, and several were now exchanging grim glances.

'Thank you, officer,' Jenny said, with what she intended as a disarming smile. She looked to the lawyers. 'Do any of you have any questions?'

Katherine Palmer was first to her feet. With her girlish, slender features, at first glance she couldn't have looked more unthreatening. But when she spoke, her tone was direct and uncompromising.

'There is absolutely no question, is there, Officer, that my client was anywhere in the vicinity of the house at the time the fire started?'

'None at all,' Millard said. 'Ms Hart left her place of work shortly after 11.30. The security cameras at the pub confirmed that.'

'In his final message, Mr Morgan describes my client as a "whore". Have you found any evidence that she was being, or had been, unfaithful to him?'

'No. We have not.'

'Then do you have any idea why he wrote that?'

Millard hesitated. He was being asked for an opinion. He was only comfortable with facts. He looked across briefly at Kelly Hart, who had dipped her head, hands folded on her lap. 'No,' he answered simply.

'Are you aware of the fact that most men who kill their families often do so having led unremarkable lives and without warning?'

'I am.'

'And that their acts of murder are often triggered by a threat, real or imagined, to their power or status as head of, and chief provider for, their family.'

'So I understand.'

'Then have you or your colleagues investigated this possibility?'

'We have. Neither of Morgan's jobs was particularly secure, but as far as we can tell he wasn't under any immediate danger of being laid off.'

'But the possibility might have been weighing on his mind?'

'I honestly couldn't say.'

'No further questions.' As she sat, Palmer smiled at the jury as if to say that her point had been proved entirely correct, and that Millard's refusal to answer exactly as she wished had merely been a misplaced display of tact on his part.

Robert Newland turned to Sam Lever, who gestured at him to go ahead. The QC stood and regarded Millard with a benign, patrician smile.

'For the avoidance of doubt, Detective Sergeant, are the police looking for anyone else in connection with the fire and the events immediately leading up to it?'

'No, we're not.'

'And you are continuing the search for Robbie Morgan?'

'We are.'

'And how far is the estuary from Blackstone Ley?'

'Two miles across country.'

'If I understand you correctly, Ed Morgan knew every corner of the surrounding country. He could have walked there and back in a little over an hour, even carrying the child's body.'

'Probably so.'

'One final question, officer – had Morgan ever come to the attention of the police before?'

'No. There was nothing on our files.'

'Thank you, officer.' Newland gave a satisfied smile and sat.

Jenny was about to release the detective from the witness box and move on to Dr Kerr's evidence when Sam Lever stood, checking a note he had made during Newland's cross-examination.

'If I may, ma'am, I do have a question for the witness.' In front of the jury, his manners were faultless.

'Go ahead, Mr Lever.'

'Officer, you were asked whether Mr Morgan had ever come to the attention of the police before. You said your files were empty.'

'So I believe.'

'But almost precisely ten years ago he was questioned in relation to the disappearance of a four-year-old child, Susie Ashton, who went missing from her home not 200 yards from Mr Morgan's front door.'

'Every man in the area was questioned. There was no evidence against him.'

Jenny glanced nervously at Alison, hoping that she was managing to disguise any feelings she had on the issue. Thankfully she remained a picture of calm.

'Mr Morgan was working for my client's parents at the time – Mr and Mrs Grant of Blackstone House Farm. Approximately three weeks after Susie Ashton's disappearance, Mr Grant dismissed him for stealing red diesel from the farm tank.'

'I'm afraid I know nothing about that.'

'That's odd, because Mr Grant reported the matter and was subsequently told in a phone call that there was insufficient evidence to proceed.'

'We have no record of that,' Millard answered defensively.

'I'm told diesel burns far slower than petrol,' Lever continued. 'It's waxy and viscous. Every farm worker knows that if you've got something awkward to burn – a pile of damp brash or even an animal carcass – you would always choose to lace it with diesel to get a steady fire going.'

Jenny interjected: 'And your point is, Mr Lever?'

Newland shot to his feet. 'I do hope Mr Lever isn't trying to make a connection between the present case and a completely unconnected incident from over ten years ago.'

'I have no idea if there's a connection or not,' Lever said. 'I'm simply making the point that Ed Morgan was a man who would have known more than a thing or two about burning.'

Lever's comment prompted a stifled sob from somewhere at the back of the hall. Jenny glanced up and saw that it had come from the frail figure of Clare Ashton, who was angled towards her husband with her face buried in his shoulder.

'Please be careful, Mr Lever,' Jenny warned.

'I will be extremely careful to interrogate the evidence, ma'am,' Lever said defiantly, 'no matter how uncomfortable for some that might be. That, I thought, was the purpose of these proceedings.' With a contemptuous glance at Detective Sergeant Millard, he dropped into his seat.

# TWENTY-ONE

WHILE DR KERR REPLACED MILLARD in the witness box, Jenny made a note of the theory which Palmer and Lever's cross-examinations had inadvertently suggested to her, and which seemed eminently plausible: Ed Morgan had killed his family, fearing that evidence was about to surface connecting him with Susie Ashton's disappearance. But what evidence, and where might it have come from? And if fear of exposure was the reason, why not admit it in his final message, rather than heap the blame on Kelly? The only explanation she could think of was that he had called her a whore in reference to what had occurred between her and Darren Brooks ten years before. Maybe there had been a painful period of overlap when she hadn't been fully committed to either of them? Distressing as it would be, these were questions that Kelly would have to answer when her turn finally came to give evidence.

Looking uncomfortable in his suit and tie, Dr Kerr betrayed more than a hint of nervousness as he read the words of the oath. In the six years Jenny had known him, he had never learned how to relax in front of a room full of people. He had once confessed to her that he would much rather be working alone in the mortuary at midnight than giving evidence in court.

Before leading him through his three post-mortem reports,

Jenny addressed the hall at large, though her words were intended for only one set of ears. 'Dr Kerr was the pathologist who examined the remains of Ed Morgan, Layla Hart and Amanda Hart. His findings are distressing and I will of course be obliged to take him through them in some detail. If anyone would like to step outside, please take this opportunity to do so.'

Her invitation was met with silence. She glanced at Kelly Hart and saw that she had no intention of leaving. Sitting upright and composed, she was determined to hear it all. She would feel she had no choice.

Taking the lead, Jenny took Dr Kerr through his findings. He started with Ed Morgan, describing the total incineration of his body tissue and the gunshot wound fired from close range that had left a six-centimetre hole in the back of his skull. At Jenny's request, Alison produced a large clear polythene bag containing what remained of the shotgun retrieved from the rubble of the house, and handed it to the jury. They passed it from one to another, some pausing to examine it, others barely able to give it a glance.

Next, Dr Kerr dealt with the damage to Ed Morgan's mouth. The upper right canine incisor was missing and there were cracks to the two teeth situated to its right: the lateral incisor and first premolar. The most likely cause of the trauma, he suggested, was the violent recoil from the gun as it discharged. He had managed to obtain dental records, but Ed Morgan hadn't been for a check-up for over five years. At the date of his last examination, the missing tooth had been present.

'Is a shotgun recoil really strong enough to knock out a tooth?' Jenny inquired.

'Certainly. Especially if it was already weakened or compromised in some way.'

'And your view is that this shot was fired by Mr Morgan himself.'

'In view of all the circumstances, it seems the most likely explanation. The barrel was twenty-nine inches, or if you prefer, seventy-three and a half centimetres long. If he had placed the end of the barrel inside his mouth, he would have been able to support the stock with his left hand and push the trigger back with the fingers or thumb of his right. And that leads me on to my last finding.' He was finally shedding his nerves. 'The two bones in the right forearm – the ulnar and radius – were both broken at the same point, approximately eleven centimetres from the wrist joint. Due to the fire damage it's impossible for me to say how those fractures might have occurred. In all likelihood he was struck by falling debris after death occurred, but I can't rule out the possibility that they were broken before death. If that was the case, I would have to say that the most likely explanation is that it was a defensive injury.' He raised his forearm as if to shield his forehead. 'If someone were to strike you with a blunt object, your reflex would be to absorb the impact just about here.' He gripped his forearm midway between elbow and wrist.

Jenny shot another glance at Kelly Hart. Her composure was holding, but only just.

'And if Mr Morgan's arm was broken before death, could he still have inflicted the gunshot wound on himself?' Jenny asked.

'It's possible. He would have to have held the gun in his left hand and possibly rested the butt on a table or shelf. He would have had no control over the fingers of his right hand.'

'Before I invite you to speculate further, Doctor, could you please tell us about the condition of the two girls' bodies?'

Tears formed in Kelly's eyes for the first time as he gave a detailed account of his findings. Dealing first with Layla, he told the jury that some of her tissues remained, thanks to the way in which the house had collapsed around her, saving her body from the most intense heat. Dissection of the lower abdomen had revealed beyond doubt that she was carrying a foetus of approximately fourteen weeks' gestation. Layla had also suffered a shotgun wound: it was ten centimetres wide and centred around the fourth thoracic vertebrae. In other words, she had been shot through the back. Mandy's body was a little more fire-damaged than her older sister's, and she had also been shot: at point-blank range through the centre of her chest.

With a little more prompting from Jenny, Dr Kerr drew together all of his findings to describe the most likely scenario. Assuming Ed Morgan had fired the fatal shots, he must of course have shot the two girls before turning the gun on himself. The position of Layla's body in the rubble suggested that she had been lying on the stairs or landing when the floor collapsed beneath her. Mandy had been somewhere around the threshold of her bedroom. So, having written his final message at 11.28 p.m., and assuming he had left his phone where it was later found, Ed Morgan would have arrived home some five or six minutes later. There may or may not have been a physical altercation in which his arm was broken, but it seemed Layla was shot in the back as she ran upstairs and Mandy was shot at the door to her bedroom. Given that Morgan's remains were found downstairs at the heart of the fire, it seemed likely that he shot the girls before setting light to the house, then shooting himself.

'If his arm had been broken, could he have fired the gun with his left hand?' Jenny asked.

'The gun weighs only six pounds, six ounces or 2.9 kilos,' Dr Kerr explained. 'I believe that a man as used to handling it as Mr Morgan was could indeed have shot it with his left hand, with the butt braced against his body.'

'And what about reloading?'

'Simple enough, even with one hand,' Dr Kerr answered.

He concluded his evidence with a report from a specialist ballistics laboratory that had examined the shotgun and some of the lead shot Dr Kerr had recovered from the three sets of remains. The gun had been fitted with a choke that allowed the shooter to narrow the aperture of the barrel to concentrate the shot in a smaller area, but the choke had been left fully open. The 10 cm wound in Layla's back suggested she was shot from a range of between five and a half and seven metres. The pellets recovered from Morgan and the two girls' bodies were identical: 2.79 mm birdshot, otherwise known as size 6.

A sombre silence settled over the courtroom as the pathologist's technical description of events in the house slowly translated into pictures of real events in the minds of his listeners. Seeing Kelly in distress, Jenny felt a sudden and overwhelming feeling of emptiness and grief on her behalf that, for a brief moment, held her so tightly in its grip she thought she might not be able to speak.

She drew in a breath and fought hard to compose herself. 'Thank you, Dr Kerr.' She turned to the lawyers and invited them to cross-examine.

Robert Newland QC was alone in taking up the offer. 'Dr Kerr, you have said that in all likelihood the impact from a large timber or falling piece of masonry is the most likely explanation for Mr Morgan's broken arm?'

'Yes.'

'You weren't able to test his body for alcohol, were you?'

'Obviously not.'

'But let's for the sake of argument say that he had consumed half a bottle of whiskey. Could that amount of alcohol numb the pain of a broken arm?'

'It could.'

Newland nodded and looked to the jury to ensure they had absorbed the point. 'That's all.'

'Actually, I do have a question.' Sam Lever rose wearily to his feet. 'Dr Kerr, how tall was Mr Morgan?'

'Six feet, three inches.'

'Sixteen stone or thereabouts?'

'Somewhere in that region.'

'Not an easy man to overpower.'

'No.'

Lever gave Jenny a pointed look. 'Thank you, Dr Kerr.'

Jenny glanced back over the notes she had made of DS Millard's and Dr Kerr's testimony and found herself unable to resist their conclusion that Ed Morgan had gone on a killing rampage. The only thing that was truly troubling her was why. What had sparked it? There had to be a reason. If there was a connection with the Susie Ashton disappearance, and if evidence was about to come to light, someone had to know about it.

'One final point, Dr Kerr,' Jenny said. 'We heard evidence earlier that hinted at the idea that Mr Morgan may have disposed of his son Robbie's remains by incineration. In your view, would it be possible to completely dispose of a body that way?'

'Up to a point.'

'Can you be more specific?'

'Well, let's say he used diesel oil and wood as the fuel. He could have disposed of all the tissue, but some bones and all the teeth would have remained intact, albeit in a weakened state. These would have to be ground down to render them into ashes.'

'How would you go about doing that?'

'The most obvious way would be with a mechanical grinder of some sort. Or if you didn't have one to hand, you might put the bones in a sack and beat them with a hammer.'

Jenny could see that Newland was on the edge of his seat, ready to object to her straying beyond the limits of her inquiry, but she had all the information she required. 'That's most helpful, Dr Kerr. You may step down.'

A witness. There had to have been a witness. If her theory was correct, someone must have seen something connecting Morgan to the disposal of Susie Ashton's remains. And whoever that person was, they must have somehow let him know that his secret was about to escape. She glanced over at Philip and Clare Ashton and saw from their grimly expectant expressions that they were having the same thought.

She was gripped by a feeling of excitement. *Step by step, Jenny. Stick to the facts. Impartial inquiry.* But she couldn't help herself. She skipped the next two names in her running order and instead called the Reverend Helen Medway to the witness box.

Helen Medway and her husband, an insurance broker who worked from offices in Bristol, had lived in Blackstone Ley for nearly ten years as near neighbours of Kelly Hart, Ed Morgan and their children. But despite their physical proximity, their paths had seldom crossed. To Helen's knowledge, no member of the family had ever attended the church. For the most part it had been an entirely peaceful and uneventful coexistence, interrupted only by the occasional visits paid by Layla's rowdy teenage friends. Even that had been nothing more than a minor irritation. Helen had almost been glad to see some more life in the village.

'What was your impression of Ed Morgan?' Jenny asked.

'Quiet. Self-contained.' Helen Medway thought some more. 'I suppose I always thought of him as a man who was content with his lot. I sometimes saw him working in the garden – he always seemed very relaxed, part of the landscape, if that's not too whimsical.'

'But is it fair to say he was the object of rumour amongst local people?'

'From time to time.'

Jenny ignored the warning look she was getting from Robert Newland. 'And those rumours were in relation to the disappearance of Susie Ashton?'

'Yes. It was all idle gossip, of course.'

'Why did the gossips focus on him, do you think?'

Helen Medway shifted awkwardly from foot to foot. 'Probably because people didn't feel they knew him. He was private. Enigmatic, almost. And of course he knew the country better than anyone else . . .' She hesitated.

Jenny completed her thought for her: 'So people thought that if anyone knew where to hide a body so it wouldn't be found, it was him.'

'I suppose that's right,' she answered guiltily.

'Do you think he knew people were having these thoughts?'

'I've no idea.'

Jenny glimpsed Kelly Hart from the corner of her eye and saw her give the tiniest shake of her head. She looked bewildered and hurt by the suggestion.

'Did anything you observed ever cause you to be suspicious of him?' Jenny asked cautiously.

'There was something last autumn, around the end of September,' Helen Medway answered hesitantly, 'though it may be wholly irrelevant . . .'

'Go on,' Jenny prompted.

'My husband and I both spotted a car parked on the verge between the church and Ed and Kelly's house. It appeared on about three or four occasions that we were aware of. Always on weekends.'

'How long was it there each time?'

'It's hard to say – an hour. Maybe more.'

'And was there someone inside it?'

'A man. He wore glasses and had dark hair. He appeared to be looking at their house.'

'What makes you say that?'

'On the second occasion I noticed the car, I confess I became suspicious. I was in the churchyard when it drew up in the lane. I didn't think the driver had seen me, so I watched him for a short while. There was no one with him, and he definitely seemed to be observing intently.'

Jenny caught a glimpse of Kelly's face. Her expression was of genuine puzzlement.

'A while later I walked past the car returning to my house,' Helen Medway continued. 'I could have been imagining it, but the driver appeared to look away as I passed by, as if he didn't want me to see his face.'

'You didn't talk to him?'

'No.'

'Do you know what make of car it was?'

'My husband saw it once or twice and thought it might be a Vauxhall. All I can tell you is that it was a dirty greenish colour and rather small.'

'You didn't make a note of the registration?'

'No. I've probably made the whole thing sound rather more sinister than it was. For all I know he could simply have been waiting for someone. Perhaps even one of the family.'

Another glance at Kelly told Jenny that wasn't the case.

'Do you know if they were home at the times when this vehicle appeared?'

'As far as I recall, each time it was on a Saturday or a

Sunday afternoon. There was usually someone home.' Worried that she had overstepped the mark, Helen Medway backtracked further, 'Really, it may be nothing. I've no idea.'

'Of course.' Jenny gave a reassuring smile. 'And have you seen the car or the man inside it since?'

'No. No, I haven't.'

'If I can take you now to the night of the fire, can you please tell us what you saw or heard?'

'Graham and I – that's my husband – we were getting ready for bed. He was in the bathroom when I heard several bangs – two or three, I think. They sounded almost like fire-crackers or an exhaust backfiring. I thought it was probably something to do with Layla and her friends – it usually was.'

'Did your husband hear them?'

'No, I don't think so. He usually had the radio on. It was so unremarkable I didn't even bother to mention it. It was about ten or fifteen minutes later and we were already in bed when we heard voices out on the common. Graham went to the window – that's when he saw the flames coming from the house.'

'And whose were the voices?'

'About a dozen of our neighbours were already in front of the burning building, but the heat was so intense there was nothing anyone could do except wait for the fire brigade. It was really quite horrendous. We both went out, but we were nothing more than helpless spectators.'

'These bangs you heard – did they sound as if they had come from the burning house?'

'I couldn't say, but they were very loud, very sharp. But if it was gunshots we heard, I'd swear they were fired out in the lane, not inside the house.'

'But you don't know they were gunshots?'

'No.'

'So they could have been caused by the fire?'

'Quite possibly.'

Jenny saw any prospect of Helen Medway's evidence providing the revelation she was hoping for fall away. Instead, it had presented her with even more loose ends.

'We know there were three gunshots fired inside the house, and in all likelihood they were several seconds apart. Could that have been what you heard?'

'No, I don't think so. These were very close together – hardly a second between them.'

Jenny nodded and offered the witness to the lawyers. All three shook their heads. Nothing she had said threatened to alter anything they had already heard.

Jenny thanked the priest for her help and told her she was free to go. She glanced at the clock. The morning was nearly at an end.

'Before we rise for lunch, could we please hear briefly from Detective Sergeant Millard. There's something I'd like to clarify.'

Millard shuffled out from his seat, looking decidedly put out to be called upon again.

'You remain under oath,' Jenny reminded him.

Millard gave a taciturn nod, exchanging a glance with Newland, whom Jenny sensed was warning him to be on his guard.

'Officer, discounting the fact that Ed Morgan didn't appear on your files, are you able to tell us if Mr Morgan had been the subject of any police interest in recent months?'

'He had not,' Millard replied.

'So you can be certain that whoever it was in the car we have just heard described, it wasn't a police officer.'

'Yes. He was not under investigation.'

Jenny studied him closely, but he had a face that was impossible to read.

'To your knowledge, is there still a substantial reward on

offer for information that would solve the Susie Ashton case?'

DS Millard glanced over to Philip Ashton who nodded in confirmation. 'I believe there is.'

'I see. That's all, Officer.'

With that, Jenny called the lunch adjournment. Whether he had been telling the whole truth she couldn't be certain, but she left the hall with the feeling that she had touched on the beginnings of something. The question was where to look next.

While Alison shepherded the jury and remaining witnesses to the pub along the lane for their lunch, Jenny sat alone in the cramped committee room, struggling to eat a sandwich snatched from a convenience-store shelf early that morning. The brief surge of elation she had experienced an hour earlier, when she had thought she was on the cusp of a breakthrough, had bled away, leaving her with a feeling of anticlimax and frustration. She had several witnesses yet to call, but her gut told her that the only one likely to offer genuine insight was Kelly Hart. The challenge would be finding a way to dig beneath the surface. If anyone had known the inner workings of Ed Morgan's mind it was her, but in their conversations to date, Kelly had left Jenny with the impression that she had felt so comfortable with Ed almost because she had remained unaware of his complexities. Again, Kelly struck her as like a child in that respect: trusting and unquestioning, too unknowing to look for deeper layers.

Jenny sifted through the papers on her desk and uncovered the booklet of post-mortem photographs Dr Kerr had appended to his report, photos that Jenny had deemed it unnecessary that the jury see. It had been the right decision. They were images that once seen would never be deleted from the mind. Spurred into action, she started to sketch out her theory in a fresh legal pad. It centred on Ed having disposed of both Susie Ashton and Freddie's bodies by similar means: he would have cremated them somewhere out of the way, or possibly even somewhere in plain sight, then disposed of the remaining fragments of teeth and bone in a manner he considered foolproof. She quickly concluded that he would either have ground up the bone fragments himself and disposed of them in the woods or in the estuary, or put them through the grinders at Fairmeadows Farm. On balance, the former seemed more likely than the latter, if only because the chances of being seen were so much smaller. For her theory to work, someone would have to have seen him behaving suspiciously. Could it have been the man Helen Medway had seen in the car? And if it was, what was he doing? Trying to get a clear view of Ed, perhaps? Trying to connect his face with one glimpsed through trees ten years before?

The watcher in the car quickly took on a story of his own. He'd passed Ed in the woods ten years before, perhaps even seen him scattering ashes, but thought nothing of it. Nearly a decade later a memory had stirred. He'd gone to the internet, seen Ed's picture and begun to wonder. His recollection was imperfect, not enough to guarantee a conviction and the reward that would come with it, but if he had isolated the guilty man there were ways of working on him. Perhaps he had contacted him, threatening to go to the police if he didn't pay up. That could easily have pushed Ed over the edge.

And here was another thought, a really devilish one: what if the watcher wasn't a witness, but had been part of the original investigation? A police officer who thought he could put the squeeze on Ed – the one that got away – and thereby boost his retirement fund. It wasn't too ridiculous.

An even darker possibility suggested itself. What if the police-canteen rumours had been true and Ed had been part of a paedophile ring? After the Susie Ashton case he had cut free and kept his head down, but ten years later one of his old contacts had come back to haunt him.

Now even further into the pit: the watcher had appeared in late September. Exactly three months before the fire, and at exactly the time Layla had become pregnant.

Jenny shuddered. Her increasingly bleak train of thought had left her with an unsettled feeling, as if the room had been invaded by a bad spirit. The image of the levelled, snow-covered site where the house had stood returned to her, and with it the sense that had been with her that afternoon when the police had been so eager to demolish the burned-out house: something important had been erased. She pulled out her phone and called up the thirty seconds of video footage she taken before the great clawed machine had moved in. The picture was dark, almost sepia. It scanned over ghostly, soot-stained walls and charred timbers; a child's swing and upended toys in the garden. But it was something else that caught her eye: in the far background of a sweeping shot of the garden she noticed a section of wire hanging loose from the high fence surrounding the property. She froze the frame and zoomed in, but the image grew more ambiguous the larger and grainier it became.

With thirty minutes to go before the afternoon session, Jenny felt the need for fresh air. Slipping out of her shoes and into her boots, she left the hall and took a short walk along the lane. The freezing air sharpened her senses and helped reorder her thoughts. A plan started to form. She would use the witnesses to build a chronological picture of Ed Morgan's life and hope that, bit by bit, incidental pieces of evidence would come together in a way that would help her and the jury glimpse inside his mind. All she required was patience and a little faith. Answers would come. They always did.

She had managed to walk for nearly a mile out and back along the lane, and was nearing the end of the return leg when she saw a police car double-parked outside the hall. An officer in uniform was talking to Alison at the gate. Jenny quickened her step, knowing instinctively that something was wrong. Alison's grave expression as she approached confirmed her fears.

'What's happened?' Jenny asked.

'It's Nicky Brooks,' Alison said. She glanced at the constable, who gave a solemn, confirmatory nod. 'She's dead.'

# TWENTY-TWO

THE CONSTABLE HAD ONLY SKETCHY details. Nicky Brooks's mother, Sandra, had discovered her daughter's body in her bedroom at home earlier that morning. She appeared to have taken her own life. He thought she had hanged herself, but couldn't be sure; he had heard rumours amongst his colleagues that she had been found kneeling on the floor.

Jenny hurried past the jurors and witnesses gathering in the hall and shut the office door. She dialled DI Ryan's number, clasping her phone in trembling fingers.

'Jenny. You heard about Nicky Brooks?'

'When? . . . How?'

'I'm just about to speak to her mother. Can I call you later?'

'I need to know how she died. I'm in the middle of my inquest – she was meant to be appearing as a witness tomorrow.'

'I know—'

'Was it suicide?'

'Looks like it.'

'Did she leave a note?'

'If she did, no one's told me.'

Jenny struggled to think clearly. She felt sick and appalled, and confused. All the pieces so carefully arranged in her mind had been thrown into disarray. 'Look, I'm going to need some answers. She was a key witness – the most important after Kelly. Maybe even more so, I don't know.'

'And you expect me to do what, exactly – conclude a fatal-incident investigation in four hours flat?'

'Shit . . . Shit!' Jenny slammed her clenched fist against her forehead. Her chest tightened. She could hardly breathe.

'Jenny? What are you doing? Stop it.'

'She was *fourteen*.'

'This is not your fault. You're the coroner, not her social worker.'

'What the hell has been going on? You can't tell me there isn't something your super's trying to hide.'

'You know how it is. He's trying to stop a bad smell, and save his pension while he's at it.'

'Smell of what?'

'Look, now's not the time, OK? Let me get some details. Believe me, we both want the same thing . . . Jenny? Are you still there?'

She switched off her phone without giving him an answer.

Maintaining a veneer of outward calm had taken all of Jenny's effort as she reported the news of Nicky Brooks's death to a subdued courtroom, and announced that the inquest would be suspended while police investigated the circumstances. The only blessing had been that Kelly Hart had already been informed outside the hall, and to save her from the attention of the press, had been whisked back to her flat in a police car. Of all the stunned and appalled expressions she had registered on the faces looking back at her, it was those of Clare and Philip Ashton that had scored themselves deepest. Horror wasn't nearly an adequate word to describe the emotion which had frozen both their faces. It had taken Jenny until the hall had emptied to realize just what the thought must have been that was passing through their minds: Nicky Brooks, Layla Hart and Susie Ashton were all the same age, and they lived within a quarter of a mile of one another. Now all three were dead.

Alison had been full of wild speculation as she stacked away the chairs and folded up the trestles. As far as she was concerned, Nicky's death was vindication of her darkest theories about Ed Morgan's involvement with powerful and predatory paedophiles. She was convinced that Layla and Nicky must have numbered amongst their victims, and possibly Mandy, and perhaps even Susie Ashton, too. The fact that Nicky died the day before she was due to give evidence proved it beyond all doubt: the people who had abused her had so damaged her mind that she had taken her own life rather than expose them in court.

'Please, please, don't repeat any of this,' Jenny had implored her. 'Not even to your friends or family. The press will be scavenging for anything they can get hold of.'

'You think I don't know that, Mrs Cooper?' Alison had answered, as if the very idea of her breathing a word was preposterous.

'You know how they operate. Just don't trust anyone.'

'I could say the same to you, Mrs Cooper. You haven't exactly got form for staying out of trouble yourself.'

Jenny had taken Alison's parting shot on the chin, and left without telling her where she was going.

Jenny pushed through the swing doors to the autopsy room to find Dr Kerr and Dr Hope working together on a body that lay fully opened on the table. It was Nicky's. She tried to avert her eyes, but was too late. She inwardly groaned. The tragedy of another young life lost bore down on her like a great weight.

'Mrs Cooper. Aren't you meant to be holding an inquest?' Dr Kerr stepped forward, apparently surprised to see her.

'The police haven't told you who she is?'

He shrugged. 'Name and age. That's all.'

'She was meant to be giving evidence tomorrow. She was Layla Hart's best friend, not to mention her neighbour.'

'Ah.' He exchanged a glance with Jasmine Hope, who for the moment had laid her scalpel aside. 'I thought the officers who brought her in seemed a little tense.'

'What did they say? Was it Ryan?'

'He was one of them.' Dr Kerr glanced again at his colleague.

'What? What is it?' Jenny asked, sensing there was something he wasn't telling her. He seemed torn.

'Tell her, Andy,' Dr Hope urged.

'I had a call from Superintendent Abbott asking if I could report my findings to him before I forwarded them to you.'

'What did you say to him?'

'He didn't really give me a chance. It was more of an order than a request.'

'One he's not entitled to give. Do I need to remind you of the law?'

'That's not necessary.' Dr Hope answered for him. They had become quite a double act since the last time she had seen them together.

'Sam Abbott was on the team that failed to solve the Susie Ashton disappearance ten years ago,' Jenny said. 'His worst fear is all of this having something to do with that. It's not your job or mine to stop his nightmares coming true.'

Dr Kerr nodded. He wasn't a man who enjoyed conflict, but it couldn't be helped.

Jenny forced herself to take a proper look and moved forward to the table. She saw the lesion caused by the ligature at once: an ugly narrow groove travelling virtually horizontally across the neck approximately two inches beneath the chin. Nicky's swollen face bore all the classic signs she had come to recognize from asphyxiations: the lips were blue, the eyes wide open and bulging; there were traces of blood-stained froth beneath the nostrils.

'The police provided photographs of the body *in situ*,' Dr Hope said. She pointed to a brown A4 envelope sitting on the bench at the side of the lab.

It was the last thing Jenny wanted to see, but she had no choice. She steeled herself and picked up the envelope. A welcome sense of unreality descended as she drew out the contents.

A dozen or so photographs covered the scene from every angle. Unlike the downstairs rooms Jenny had been in, Nicky's bedroom was tidy and well kept. She was kneeling at the foot of her bed, dressed in knickers and an overlong white T-shirt. A length of orange nylon string was tied tightly around her neck. The end was tied to a pipe that travelled down the wall behind her to a radiator. Her head was slumped forward, her hair covering her face. Her fists were tightly clenched and in the area around her knees the beige carpet was stained with a liquid that Jenny presumed was urine.

It wasn't a sight she had witnessed before, but it was something she had read about. In recent years there had been clusters of teenage suicides in which the victims, who had often communicated with each other online, had used this technique. They called it 'rocking yourself to sleep'. A little forward pressure, then a little more. It was reputedly a far less traumatic end than suspension from above.

'Have you got a time of death?' Jenny asked.

'We estimate 9.30 this morning, give or take half an hour.'

'A strange time,' Jenny said. Most suicides took place at night; very few in the morning hours of daylight. 'Any sign of drugs or alcohol?'

'The bloods results will be back any minute,' Dr Kerr

said, 'but I doubt it. The stomach was empty. Doesn't look as if she had consumed anything since yesterday evening.'

Jenny slotted the photographs back in the envelope. 'You're satisfied it's suicide?'

Dr Kerr nodded.

'Has the mother formally ID'd her yet?'

'No, they brought the father down,' Dr Kerr said. 'He's a patient in the hospital.'

'I know,' Jenny said bleakly. 'I probably ought to pay him a visit.'

He was standing upright, dressed in a towelling robe and pyjamas and staring out of the day-room window at the snow-covered roofs of the nearby business park. Jenny closed the door behind her, shutting out the noise of the busy corridor.

'Mr Brooks?'

He half turned his shaved head. Large patches of his face were badly scabbed and blistered, but it was no longer enclosed in dressings. His forearms and hands remained tightly wrapped in bandages from which only his fingertips protruded.

'I'm so sorry.'

He turned his gaze back to the window.

She gave him a moment. 'Do you know what happened?'

'Sandra drove out to the shops this morning. When she came back, she called Nicky down for her breakfast. She didn't answer.'

'Do you have any idea why she did it?'

He shook his head, then dipped it towards his chest as if the effort of holding it upright was too much. 'Excuse me.' He lowered himself stiffly into a chair, grimacing at the pain in his arms. He hauled them onto his lap like wooden appendages and stared, unfocused, at the opposite wall. 'If there's something you want to ask, just get it over with.'

'Could Nicky have known something about Ed Morgan? Could he have been involved with other people, people who might have put pressure on her?'

He swivelled his eyes towards her. 'What do you mean?'

There was no gentle way of putting it. 'You must know the rumours as well as I do.'

'You mean Ed got himself a beautiful woman to cover up what he was really into?'

'I hadn't quite thought of it that way, but yes – what do you think?'

'Never known a man live a quieter life,' Brooks said in scarcely more than a whisper. 'Could never understand what it was held them together.'

Jenny pressed a little harder. 'You were never suspicious?'

He reflected for a moment. 'You'd wonder about him. Spent a lot of time alone. Never spoke a word more than he had to—'

'Wonder what?'

'What went on in his head . . . What Kelly saw in him.'

'Nicky told me she didn't mind his company.'

'She liked Ed. Had more problem with me than she did with him. Never got angry, she said. "Peaceful", she called him.'

'Did you and your wife truly know your daughter, Mr Brooks?'

'I thought we did.'

Brooks's face creased with pain. Jenny had pushed him as far as she humanely could.

'I'm sorry for your loss, Mr Brooks. I really am.' She turned to go.

As she laid a hand on the door, he said: 'You still think I started that fire?'

'No,' Jenny said quietly, and left him alone to grieve.

'It's as I thought – no alcohol, no drugs. She did it with a clear head.' Dr Kerr had stepped outside the autopsy room to save Jenny the ordeal of seeing Nicky's body a second time. 'She knew what she was doing. I suspect she'd been thinking about it for a while, probably researching online.'

'No other signs of violence? Previous injuries?'

'Nothing of note. And no evidence of sexual interference. No abrasions or lesions. She was having her period. The tampon was still in place.'

Jenny swallowed against the feeling of nausea that had returned during the course of the afternoon, in a milder echo of what she had experienced the week before. There was no doubting she had grown more squeamish. The very smells and sounds of the mortuary set her on edge. It was probably nature's way of encouraging her to withdraw from danger to make a safe nest somewhere. There was little chance of that.

'Have you talked to the police yet?'

'Just about to. Do I pretend we haven't spoken?'

'Who will it be – Ryan? He's all right.'

'You trust that man? I don't.'

Dr Kerr's bluntness took Jenny by surprise. He was normally polite about detectives, deferential even.

'Any particular reason?'

'The way he dresses, for one thing. All front and no back, as my mother would have said.'

'I'll let you into a secret, Andy – women quite like that nowadays. Ask Jasmine.'

Jenny felt her phone vibrate in her coat pocket. She pulled it out and saw that it was Alison calling.

'She feels the same way,' Dr Kerr said, refusing to lighten up.

'Well, if he gives you any grief, let me know.' Jenny gave him a smile and headed out along the corridor. She switched her attention to the call. 'Alison, hi.'

'Where are you? I thought you'd be back at the office.' Alison sounded indignant.

'I called in at the mortuary.'

'And you didn't think I could be trusted to know that?'

'It's not that, I just—'

Alison cut her off: 'I've had Family Liaison chasing us. They don't know what to tell Kelly Hart about the inquest.'

'I'd better call in and talk to her on my way back.'

'In that case, there's something you might want to ask her. I've got an email from Bob Bream here – Ed Morgan's boss at the Forestry. He says his office supplied Ed's shotgun shells and only ever ordered size 4. They're a heavier gauge, apparently – 3.3 mm. He says Ed preferred them for shooting small stuff and that when he hunted deer he did it with a rifle, not a shotgun.'

'OK, I'll try her with it.'

'Oh, and DI Ryan's after you, too.'

'What does he want?'

'Didn't say, but I can guess. His super will want to know when you're going to get your inquest over with.'

'That rather depends, doesn't it?'

'Bummer of a job he's been landed with, poor fella,' Alison said dryly. 'He must be wondering who's next.'

Jenny recognized the black Toyota parked outside Kelly's block as Ryan's. She touched the bonnet as she passed by – it was warm. She guessed he'd been tipped off to her visit by Family Liaison, which must have meant that special lines of communication had been set up so that the whole team could keep tabs on her. They really were becoming paranoid.

It was Kelly's voice on the intercom, but Ryan who came to the front door of the flat. He stepped out onto the landing as she approached, looking flustered.

'Might want to give her a moment. She's upset.' He stood in front of the entrance, keeping Jenny outside.

'Who was it told you I'd be here?' Jenny asked. 'Not that it particularly matters, but if the police feel the need to watch my every move it doesn't exactly inspire trust.'

'No one,' Ryan said, feigning innocence. 'I just came by to ask a few questions.' He was a bad liar. 'You've suspended the inquest?'

'For the time being.'

He nodded, with that thoughtful, enigmatic look of his. He turned and called back through the door. 'Are you all right to see us now, Kelly?'

Her answered travelled faintly back along the hall. 'Yeah. I'm OK.'

'I think it's finally beginning to sink in,' Ryan said as he stepped aside to let Jenny in. 'It had to happen some time.'

She was sitting at the small kitchen table clutching a Kleenex, and didn't look up as Jenny said hello. The atmosphere in the room was thick with emotion. After eleven days of keeping it inside her, the dam had finally burst.

'Do you mind if I sit down?' Jenny asked.

Kelly shrugged.

Jenny sat opposite her. Ryan leaned against the kitchen counter, not wanting to crowd her.

'I've had to suspend the inquest while we find out what happened to Nicky,' Jenny said. 'It looks like suicide, but even so, seeing as she was such an important witness, I have to know her reasons.' Kelly nodded, but Jenny couldn't be sure if she had understood or not. 'Nicky gave a statement last week saying she was at your house earlier on the evening of the fire. She said she left about eight. She was probably the last person to see them all alive. You understand how important that is?'

'Yeah,' Kelly whispered. She swept back the hair that had fallen across her face, revealing an expression that seemed tormented with questions. Jenny could see that she was replaying the events of the evening, trying to slot them all together.

'Do you mind if I ask a few questions about Nicky?' Jenny said.

'Sure.'

Jenny took her legal pad from her bag, ignoring Ryan's frown.

'Nicky wasn't at the house when you left for work?'

'No. She must have come round after.'

'She said she was at your house most days during the school holidays.'

'That's right.'

'But what she didn't say was how things were between her and Layla.'

Kelly didn't respond immediately. Jenny let the question hang.

'How do you mean?' Kelly said eventually.

'Fourteen's a turbulent age, especially for girls. All sorts of emotions swirling around. Did they get on? Did they ever argue?'

'Sometimes, I suppose.'

'Over what?'

Kelly shrugged. 'This and that. Nothing in particular.'

Jenny tried another tack. 'How did they communicate when they weren't together – were they always messaging on their phones?'

Kelly nodded. 'It's what all kids do, isn't it?'

Jenny glanced at Ryan. 'Any sign of Nicky's phone?'

'Yeah. We think we found it – in the woodstove down-stairs.'

'She put it there?'

'The mother didn't. At least, she says she didn't.'

Jenny turned back to Kelly and saw that this information seemed to have rocked her even further off her moorings.

'Have you any idea what she might have been hiding?' Jenny asked. 'Do you know if Nicky had anything to be ashamed of?'

'She and Kelly would argue,' Kelly said distantly. 'Some-times it got ugly. Doors slamming, shouting, calling each other names . . . Then five minutes later they'd be best friends again.'

'What were these arguments about?' Jenny asked.

'I never paid much attention.'

Jenny didn't believe her, but knew that now wasn't the right moment to set herself up as an antagonist. She needed to preserve Kelly's trust.

'Sandra Brooks told me about an incident last year with the four boys over at your house. She wasn't sure if Ed had ever told you.'

'He didn't. Layla told me. She felt guilty. Scared herself, I think.'

'Did that cause any bad feeling between them? Nicky told me it was Layla who was leading the way.'

'She would've, wouldn't she?'

'What was Layla's version?'

'I think they were as bad as each other.'

'Look, Kelly, I don't want to make connections where there aren't any, but it does sound like one of those incidents that could have had a lasting effect on both of them. It doesn't take a lot to upset a young mind.'

'No. They didn't care about those boys.'

Something in Kelly's tone told Jenny she was getting close to something.

'What happened with them, exactly?' Ryan asked.

Jenny held up a hand. 'Hold on. Kelly, are you saying there *was* something they cared about?'

Kelly's perfect features creased with emotion. Her eyes filled with tears that spilled silently down her cheeks, skirted her lips and dripped onto the table.

'What is it?' Jenny prompted.

'Simon Grant . . . Nicky was jealous. Wouldn't let Layla go near him.'

'And they argued about him?'

Kelly nodded, wiping away more tears.

Jenny tried to remember what it had felt like to be a fourteen-year-old girl, overwhelmed with volcanic emotions that were constantly searching for an object on which to focus. 'Do you think it was a big enough thing between them to have made Nicky kill herself?'

'I heard them yelling at each other a few days before Christmas,' Kelly said. 'Nicky was saying Layla would have to choose between their friendship and Simon. It was stupid – don't think he was that interested in either of them.'

'But he did have sex with Layla.'

Kelly sighed in a way that only a mother could. 'Sometimes dealing with Layla was like dealing with a crazy person. You didn't know what she was going to do from one minute to the next. Nor did she. Nicky wasn't like that. She was more serious, stuck with things. Like her dad, I suppose.'

Jenny felt the muscles in her throat tighten, the physical sensation of dread preceding the thought that followed it. 'Nicky didn't know about the gunshots. All she knew was that there had been a fire. Do you think it's possible that

Nicky thought Layla might have started the fire? . . . And that she had somehow pushed her to it?'

Kelly looked at Ryan with wide, startled eyes, then at Jenny. She didn't need to say a word.

'I'd better talk to Simon Grant,' Jenny said. 'Let's not jump to any conclusions.'

She made a note in her legal pad and slotted it back into her briefcase. Her limbs felt suddenly weak. The thought of Nicky killing herself over a mistaken sense of guilt had landed like a sickening blow and left her reeling.

She willed herself to remain composed. 'I'm sorry, Kelly – it may take a few days for the police to finish their inquiries and for me to have all the evidence we need to continue with the inquest. I'll move as quickly as I can. It can't be helped.'

Jenny stood up from the table on legs that were reluctant to support her weight. She wanted badly to leave and be alone with her thoughts, but could see that Ryan wanted another private word. She was almost at the door when she belatedly remembered what Alison had told her on the phone. 'There's something else I meant to ask you – you don't happen to know where Ed got his shotgun shells from?'

Kelly searched her memory but could bring nothing to mind.

'Do you recall him going out and buying them, or did he get them from work?'

Kelly shook her head. 'I couldn't really tell you. I know he kept all that stuff out the back.'

'Did he have two locked cabinets?' Ryan asked. 'One for the gun, and one for the shot?'

'I think so,' Kelly answered uncertainly.

'Get in touch if you remember,' Jenny said. 'It would be useful to know.'

'Ha. I almost said I'll ask Layla.' Kelly looked up with a tragic expression that made Jenny want to hold her in her arms.

Ryan handed her another Kleenex. 'I'll be right back,' he said gently. 'I just need a quick word with Mrs Cooper.'

Ryan followed Jenny out of the flat and into the corridor, pulling the door almost fully closed behind them. 'Who were the boys you were talking about?'

'Acquaintances of Layla's. Four lads from Bristol, according to Nicky. Ed came home one day last October and found her and Layla down on their knees – all being recorded for posterity, of course. Apparently Ed waved his shotgun at them and they made themselves scarce. The graffiti on the wall outside appeared shortly afterwards.'

Ryan nodded, slowly assimilating this information into what he already knew. 'And what's this about the shells?'

'The shot found in all three bodies was size 6. Bob Bream got in touch with my officer after hearing the evidence to say that he supplied Ed with his shells, and they were always size 4. I think that means they're heavier.'

'Four is a larger gauge,' Ryan said.

'Do you think it's significant?'

'Ed knew his guns.' Worry lines creased his forehead. 'Mind if I talk to Bream?'

'I can't stop you.'

He looked at her with an expression of concern. 'Can you sit tight for a couple of days while I follow this up?'

'You're having some dark thoughts, aren't you?'

'Thoughts can be deceptive, but still – mind how you go.'

He stepped back into the flat and closed the door.

# TWENTY-THREE

JENNY SHOULDERED OPEN THE DOOR of her office, hoping for some time alone to regroup and plan her next moves, but it wasn't to be: she had guests waiting. Sitting in the cramped waiting area in reception was Sam Lever with a smartly dressed woman and a gum-chewing teenage boy with hair falling over his eyes. She knew at once that they were Emma Grant and her son, Simon.

'I tried to get of hold of you, Mrs Cooper,' Alison said wearily.

'My phone's out of battery.'

'Always is,' Alison muttered.

Sam Lever rose to his feet. 'Mrs Cooper. I've taken the liberty of bringing Simon and Mrs Grant along. If you wouldn't mind, he'd like to make some amendments to his statement.' Lever's tone was markedly more conciliatory than it had been during their clash at court.

'Good afternoon, Mrs Cooper. Emma Grant.' Mrs Grant stood up and stepped forward to introduce herself. She was about fifty, but slim and fit, with unfussy, well-cut hair. Her handshake was powerful, like a man's; a horsewoman, Jenny guessed. 'I must apologize for this morning's misunderstanding—'

'I stressed to Mr Lever that a summons to an inquest

can't be ignored, Mrs Grant,' Jenny said, wanting to force the point home. 'It's a serious matter.'

'It's all right –' Lever stepped in to head off excuses that would only embarrass him and his clients further – 'Mrs Cooper and I have resolved that issue.'

Jenny resisted the urge to slap Lever down again with a reminder that his attempt to seek special treatment for the Grant family could have landed them all with a charge of contempt and the prospect of being arrested and brought to court in the back of a police car. She would allow him his dignity and offer him one more chance. He might even deserve it.

'I won't be a moment.' Jenny headed into her office, wanting to clear her desk of any stray documents before inviting them in. The first thing lawyers learned in practice was how to read upside down.

As she closed the door she heard Mrs Grant hiss in exasperation at her son: 'For goodness' sake! What do you look like? Get rid of that gum.'

Jenny felt a pang of sympathy for her. She could only imagine the tension in the Grant household since they'd received their summonses to appear in court. Few things could have held more horror for a woman like Emma Grant than having her family's dirty linen washed in front of friends and neighbours at a public inquest.

Simon Grant had combed his hair and spat out his gum by the time he followed Lever and his mother into the office. The three of them settled in an uneasy semicircle on chairs arranged on the opposite side of the desk, with Lever to Jenny's left and Mrs Grant in the middle.

'How can I help you?' Jenny asked briskly, hoping to convey that she would like their meeting to be over quickly.

Lever glanced at Simon and Mrs Grant. 'As I mentioned, Simon would like to amend his statement.'

'Amend or materially alter?' Jenny asked.

'I'm not sure that's an altogether helpful distinction,' Lever said. 'The fact is he was very distressed by the news of what happened to Layla and Mandy Hart last week.'

'We have all been,' Emma Grant added. 'It's quite horrifying. Incomprehensible—'

'And the distress affected his recollection?' Jenny said.

Simon Grant looked away, his face reddening with embarrassment.

'If he's reluctant to tell me certain things, how much harder must it be to tell you?' Emma Grant said. 'He's only seventeen, Mrs Cooper, only *just* seventeen, and frankly with a lot of growing up left to do.'

Jenny was beginning to understand what had happened. Having been told that his clients were coming to court whether they liked it or not, Lever would have gone into damage-limitation mode and insisted that they tell him everything. He would also have emphasized that lying under oath was an offence which always landed the offender in prison. In which case it was far safer to confess any untruths already spoken in the coroner's office than to be exposed in open court.

'I'll be frank with you, Mrs Cooper,' Lever said. 'I have explained to Simon that he doesn't have to say anything that may incriminate him, but I've also told him that, in this instance, it would be better for all concerned, not least Kelly Hart, if he simply told the truth. I spoke to Gloucester CID. They're not interested in pressing any charges against him.'

'You mean for having sex with a minor?'

'Yes,' Lever answered.

Mrs Grant plunged her hands deep into her lap and closed her eyes, consumed with shame.

'All right,' Jenny said, deciding there was little to be gained by making the family's suffering any worse, 'I'm pre-

pared to disregard his previous statement and start again.'
She tapped some keys on her computer and brought up the
pro forma witness statement. 'Simon, I trust Mr Lever has
explained to you that if you include anything in your statement that's untrue, you will be prosecuted.'

'Yes,' he answered cagily. 'Is there any chance I can do this
without Mum in the room?'

Mrs Grant opened her mouth to object, but Lever got in
first: 'I think that's an excellent idea. Why don't you wait
outside, Mrs Grant?'

She looked from the lawyer to her son and back again;
then, as if accepting that events had spiralled beyond her
control, she rose quickly and left, touching her son's shoulder as she went.

'OK,' Jenny said, 'you talk, I'll type.'

With a little initial prompting from Lever, Simon began to
tell his story. He couldn't bring himself to look Jenny in the
eye and directed his mumbled narrative to the floor, but it
had a ring of truth, and as Jenny transcribed it, she could
think of no good reason to disbelieve him.

He told her that he had been at boarding school in Shrop-
shire – the one that his father had attended – since he was
eight years old. His long holidays were spent at the family
home in Blackstone Ley. Kelly Hart had worked as a cleaner
at the house two half-days a week for as long as he could
remember. The previous summer holiday, Kelly had started
bringing Layla along, ostensibly to help out, though Simon
suspected the real reason was to keep Layla out of trouble.
Layla would sometimes boast to him about her friends in
Bristol – older teenage boys she had met online – and the
different ways she contrived to slip away from home and get
herself into the city. Despite being only fourteen, she acted
and behaved like a girl several years older. She was street-
wise and savvy. She knew where she could go to get served

alcohol, and where to buy party drugs, and she talked as if she had already had several serious boyfriends.

The first time they had sex was by 'accident'. It was a Friday night at the start of September. Simon had been out with a group of friends his own age in the nearby town of Thornbury when Layla approached him in the street outside the pub. It was midnight and she was looking for a lift home. Simon let her share his taxi, but during the journey she made a move on him. He was almost as drunk as she was, and inevitably one thing led to another. They had sex in the corner of the churchyard near her house – her idea. They did it again several times before he left again for school. On one occasion it happened in his bedroom at home while Kelly was downstairs cleaning.

'I sort of forgot how old she was,' Simon said. 'I know lots of girls my age who aren't as mature as she was.'

Jenny spotted Lever smiling to himself as his client delivered the line.

They hadn't seen each other again until the second week of December, when he was back home from school. He'd bumped into her again in the same pub in Thornbury. This time she was with her friend Nicky Brooks, who was as drunk and flirtatious as she was. The three of them caught a taxi home, which he paid for, but Nicky had made sure nothing happened between him and Layla. A couple of days later, Layla texted him saying she'd like to meet up again. They had met in the afternoon and gone back to his house while his parents were out. Afterwards, Layla asked him for money, claiming she needed it to buy Christmas presents for her family. He gave her £30. Then she helped herself to a bottle of his father's gin. She seemed to know every corner of the house and everything in it.

'I sort of realized then that she was totally out of control,' Simon said. 'It was like she only came round because she thought she could get stuff. Then I thought maybe Layla was something to do with Mum's car getting stolen—'

'Hold on.' Jenny paused from typing. 'What happened with the car?'

'It was back in October time. It was stolen off the drive one night – nothing special, it's a VW Polo. About two weeks later, Mum realized the spare keys had gone missing.'

'It's the first I've heard,' Lever said. 'Do you want me to fetch Mrs Grant?'

'It can wait. Did you see Layla again?' Jenny asked.

'No.' She texted a couple of times, but I ignored it. 'Nicky texted as well, but I ignored her, too.'

'What did Nicky want?'

'It was just dumb remarks, trying to get me to message back.'

'She was flirting with you?'

He shrugged. 'I s'pose.'

'Did you see Nicky again?'

'No. It was just the messages.'

Jenny glanced back over the two pages she had typed. 'You had sex with Layla in early September, and not again until the second week of last month.'

'Yeah,' Simon grunted.

'You're quite sure?'

'Why would I lie about that?'

'Did you know she was pregnant?'

'No. Not till all this. Not surprised, though. I don't think I was the only one she went with.'

Jenny recorded his words, prepared to accept that, given all she had learned about Layla, he was probably right.

Simon had nothing to add to what he had already told Alison concerning his whereabouts on the night of the fire. He had been at home with his parents, watching a film on television until shortly after midnight. They had dimly heard the sound of sirens, but didn't learn what had happened until the following morning, when a policeman knocked on their door to ask if they had seen anything suspicious.

Jenny had one last question: 'Did Layla or Nicky ever talk about what happened to Susie Ashton?'

'No,' Simon said, seemingly confused by the non sequitur. 'I never heard them mention her.'

'Can I assume a DNA test won't now be necessary,' Simon Lever said, as Jenny printed off three copies of the statement. 'He's admitted they had sex. He didn't know she was pregnant, and even if he had known, he was aware that he was only one of several potential fathers. What could possibly be gained from it?'

Jenny had to concede that he had a point. Now that Simon had admitted having sex with Layla on several occasions more than two months apart, and there was evidence that Layla had engaged in sexual activity with other boys, there was no extra insight she or her jury could gain from knowing for certain whether or not he was the biological father of her child.

'Point taken,' Jenny said.

Simon and Lever exchanged a look of profound relief.

Leaving them to check the statement through before Simon signed, Jenny went into reception to speak to Mrs Grant, who looked up in alarm, as if fearing Simon had made a dreadful admission she knew nothing about.

'I've left him reading his statement,' Jenny said. 'He mentioned that you had a car stolen last October – a set of keys went missing from your house.'

'That's right.'

'And you suspected Layla?'

'She was the only person who had been in the house who I thought—' She stopped herself. 'It doesn't seem right to be saying this now.'

'But at the time, you thought she was capable of stealing?'

'Well, if I'm honest,' she glanced across at Alison as if fearing her judgement, 'well, yes. She was a nice girl, but at the same time, sort of feral. If I thought she was coming with Kelly, I'd always make sure there was nothing valuable lying about.'

'And you remembered her stepfather stealing diesel from you,' Alison chimed in from behind her desk, a judgemental note in her voice.

'I suppose there was that,' Emma Grant said.

'What did the police say?' Jenny asked.

'They never found the car. I didn't tell them about the keys – I didn't want Kelly to get in any trouble. I thought she had enough on her plate.' She glanced anxiously towards the partially open door to Jenny's office. 'Will there be a DNA test?'

'No. I don't think that'll be necessary.'

'Oh. Good.' Mrs Grant sighed with relief. It was one less social stigma to worry about.

Jenny sensed Alison bridle. She had taken against Mrs Grant – she had always harboured a special loathing for women she considered pampered – and was making a bad job of disguising the fact.

'Why don't you come through,' Jenny said, motioning Mrs Grant to follow her into her office.

As Jenny turned, she shot Alison a look warning her to behave. Alison rolled her eyes and stabbed her fingers noisily into her computer keyboard.

Jenny had had her office to herself for only a few minutes after Lever and the Grants had left, and was beginning to marshal her thoughts, when Alison burst in unannounced and dropped a sheaf of papers on her desk.

'Ed Morgan's bank statements and every debit-card

payment in the last three years. As far as I can see he didn't buy any shotgun shells. In fact, he didn't buy much of anything outside of groceries and fuel. He couldn't afford to – he hardly made three hundred a week.'

Jenny glanced through the list of everyday transactions and found herself losing heart. As soon as she thought she glimpsed daylight through the fog, it seemed to close in again. The most likely explanation for the three deaths in the fire still remained an argument between Layla and Ed having set off a violent chain reaction, but the question mark over the ammunition opened the door to frightening possibilities that Jenny could only guess at.

Alison seemed to read Jenny's thoughts more clearly than she was experiencing them: 'Feral,' she said. 'She'd probably think the same of any girl who doesn't have two plums in her mouth, but still, it does make you wonder if she really was damaged. You worked with abused kids, Mrs Cooper – you know how they behave.'

Jenny had to agree. Layla could have been a textbook case: sexually precocious, reckless, drifting into petty crime. In her former career in child protection, she had dealt with girls removed from sexually abusive situations at a very young age, who, after ten years of stable family life with adoptive parents, would nevertheless exhibit much of the behaviour you would expect from those who had continued to be abused. It had often seemed to Jenny that if harm was done early enough, it became woven into the fabric of the being.

'Nicky Brooks, too, judging from what that lad told you,' Alison said. 'If you start to look at it that way, it all begins to make sense, doesn't it?'

'I'm not sure it does. Not really.'

'Put yourself in Ed Morgan's shoes. He would have felt

like he owned those girls. Then when Layla started going her own way, sleeping with other boys . . .'

'And what if it wasn't him, if someone else fired the gun?' It was the first time Jenny had truly allowed herself to consider the possibility.

'You'll drive yourself mad, Mrs Cooper. I should just stick to the evidence, if I were you, see where it takes you. You're looking better, by the way.'

Alison's sudden change of tack took Jenny by surprise. 'Do I? I'm not sure I feel it.'

'Negative, was it?'

'I beg your pardon?'

'The test.'

Caught off guard, Jenny struggled to find a ready response.

'I thought that was it,' Alison said, nodding wisely. 'What'll you do? Or have you already—?'

'No!' Jenny surprised herself with the abruptness of her denial. She felt her face flush with the heat of emotion. 'Can we talk about this some other time?' She turned to her computer and tried to focus on a batch of newly arrived emails. 'What's happening with the Daniel Burden case?'

'Seeing as we're delayed for a few days, I thought we might slip in an inquest this Thursday. Did I tell you Mr Falco is representing the family?'

'Falco?' It took Jenny a moment to put the name together with the flamboyant solicitor who had paid her a visit the previous week. 'When did he get in on the act?' The details of their conversation filtered back to her. 'He came here fishing for information about Burden. He said he had a rich client who disappeared before Christmas who had been in contact with him.'

'I had an email this morning. The client was Jacob Rozek – a villain. Falco's got it into his head he was murdered.'

Jenny pushed her fingers through her hair, overwhelmed at the thought of opening yet another can of worms. 'One thing at a time. Rewind. I'd like you to check with the police about Emma Grant's car – see what the crime report says and if they had any leads. Then I'd like you to find out the names and addresses of all the registered shotgun owners in and around Blackstone Ley.'

'I can give you the answer to that already,' Alison said. 'There are a couple of farmers who've got licences, and then there's Darren Brooks. I thought Harry Grant might have a gun, but he let his licence lapse three years ago.'

'Brooks owns a shotgun? When did you find this out?'

'When you were over at Kelly Hart's. You didn't think I was going to sit here waiting for orders?'

Jenny pictured the view from the Brookses' house across the common. She had imagined Darren Brooks gazing out with jealous longing, slowly dying from the inside. Now she placed a gun in his hands, her imagination began to tell a more dramatic and bloody story: two armed men facing off. Darren staking his claim to Kelly. Shots fired outside the house. Ed trying to talk him down. Darren forcing his way in, shooting Ed first, then the witnesses.

'Mrs Cooper? Are you there?' Alison waved a hand in front of Jenny's face.

Jenny snapped out of her daydream. 'I need to make a house call. I think it might be best if we do this one together.'

According to the gauge on Jenny's dashboard it was seven degrees below freezing. Stepping out into the premature night on Blackstone Common, it felt colder still. With only the weak and flickering beam from a key-ring torch to light their way, Jenny and Alison staggered along the track to the Brookses' house through the hard-frozen snow. Plunging deeper into inky, unfamiliar darkness, Alison's bursts of chatter soon dried up and they walked in silence, each nursing their own private fears.

Alison's breathing grew heavy as they climbed the steep bank to the house. Several times she lost her footing and stumbled, but she refused Jenny's attempts to help her.

They had reached the top of the rise when Jenny remembered the dog, *the bloody dog*. Scanning the snow-covered yard with the feeble torch, she spotted a spade planted in a pile of snow, which had been used to scrape a path around the house. She took hold of it, and walked ahead of Alison to the back door. Wisely, the dog chose not to show itself. Nor was there any sound of barking when Jenny rapped on the door.

She had knocked a second time before Sandra came to the door and peered out bleary-eyed from behind the security chain.

'It's me, Mrs Brooks. Jenny Cooper. The coroner. And this is my officer, Mrs Trent.'

'What do you want?' She smelt strongly of alcohol and slurred her words.

'We've a couple of questions, that's all.' Jenny became aware that she was still holding the spade. 'I don't see your dog.'

'Haven't seen him since this morning.' She blinked in the exaggerated way of the profoundly drunk and fumbled with the chain until it came free. She stepped back clumsily, leaning on the wall for support as she pulled open the door.

'Are you all right, Mrs Brooks?' Alison said. 'You've had a difficult day.'

Not bothering – or perhaps unable – to respond, Sandra managed to turn around and weave her way towards the kitchen. Jenny and Alison followed close behind, ready to catch her if she fell.

Sandra flopped into one of the chairs by the woodstove

and concentrated all her attention on pulling a cigarette from a packet. A clutch of scorch marks on her cardigan suggested it had become a dangerous habit. An empty half-bottle of vodka lay on the floor alongside a cheap bottle of lemonade. Dirty dishes and unwashed mugs were stacked on the counter. The carpet was covered with dirty footprints. The room bore all the traces of having had a small army of police officers pass through it earlier in the day. Typically, none of them had thought to clean up.

Alison insisted on remaining standing, letting Jenny have the remaining chair. They watched in silent suspense as Sandra struggled with a lighter and finally put a flame to her cigarette.

'No one here with you?' Jenny asked.

'Don't want no one,' Sandra said, her head rocking unsteadily on her neck.

'Have you seen your husband?'

'Fuck him.'

Tempting as it was to talk to her about Nicky, Jenny knew it wasn't the moment, not even to offer condolences.

'The reason I'm here, Mrs Brooks, is that I understand your husband is licensed to own a shotgun.'

Sandra let out a laugh. 'You think he did it? He'd never have the guts.'

Alison spoke for the first time: 'Do you know where he keeps his ammunition, Mrs Brooks?'

'Cupboard out there.' She flipped a hand towards the door behind her chair.

Alison excused herself and went to have a look.

'She's wasting her time,' Sandra said, smoke leaching out of her mouth as she spoke. 'He was here. Drunk. Useless.' She let out a bitter laugh. 'Feeling sorry for himself, as usual. Be easier for me if it had been him.'

Jenny wondered what could hold together two people who were so unhappy with each other.

'Is that it?' Sandra said.

'For now. Unless there's anything you want to tell me.'

'Like what?' She spat out the two words like an accusation.

'That's up to you.'

Sandra held her in an unsteady gaze as the sound of Alison rummaging through a cupboard travelled through the partially open door. Moments later she reappeared holding an old shoebox.

'Think I found them.' She opened the lid and brought out an open paper packet containing red cylindrical cartridges. 'Double-aught buckshot. Four dozen of them, and several empty wrappers for the same. What does your husband shoot, Mrs Brooks?'

'Bambi.' She smiled. 'Poor little Bambi.'

'That's venison he's got out there in the freezer, is it?'

'Can't stand the stuff. Tough as boot leather.'

'No size 4,' Alison said to Jenny. 'This shot is the other end of the scale. Shoot a bird with this, there'd be nothing left of it.'

'I told you – he was here. In that chair. Snoring like a pig.' Sandra aimed the cigarette for her lips, but dropped it down her front, leaving a trail of ash. 'Shit.' It rolled off her lap and landed on the floor out of her reach.

Alison passed Jenny the shoebox and picked it up. 'Maybe it's time you went to bed, Mrs Brooks. You don't want to have an accident.'

Sandra swiped the cigarette from Alison's hand.

'Come on,' Alison said,

She leaned in to help her out of her chair, but Sandra shrunk away from her. 'Leave me alone. I'm staying here.'

Jenny threw Alison a glance urging her to back off. Drunk

or not, she could understand Sandra not wanting to sleep alone in a room that adjoined the one in which her daughter had taken her own life only hours before. 'Why don't we find you a blanket, at least?'

As Jenny stood, Sandra shot out a hand and gripped her tightly around the wrist. 'It wasn't my fault. None of this was my fault. I was the one trying to keep a home going here. Not that either of them cared.' Tears spilled down her lined and sunken cheeks. 'She didn't tell you the truth. She didn't tell you—'

'Didn't tell me what, Sandra?' Jenny said gently.

'She was there all evening – at Ed's. She'd got hold of some booze and was upstairs drinking it with Layla in her room. Ed found them. He wanted to drive her home but she yelled at him. They had a stand-up row – all three of them. Then Nicky ran out of the house.' Sandra's tears turned into uncontrolled sobs. 'She told me she was too frightened to walk back here by herself in the dark and she'd left her phone inside. She went and hid in the bus shelter and must have passed out. She came round and saw the place in flames . . . She said she was standing there looking at it, wondering what the hell to do, and then he fired at her—'

'Nicky told you that Ed Morgan shot at her?'

Sandra's fingers dug harder into Jenny's flesh. 'Twice. He fired at her twice. He tried to kill her. She ran off into the woods.'

'Why didn't she tell me this?'

'She didn't tell me till yesterday, not all of it. She thought it was her fault. She thought it had all blown up because of her. She thought the whole bloody thing was her fault.' Sandra screwed up her eyes and spoke through clenched teeth. 'I tried telling her there was no excuse for what he did. I tried – ' She shook her head and let it loll onto her chest as she sobbed.

Jenny sent Alison in search of bedclothes and stayed with her. Sandra clung on to her hand like a child as she wept. Jenny didn't try to speak; there was nothing she could find to say.

Within minutes of unburdening herself, Sandra fell deeply asleep. Alison loaded the stove with logs and trimmed it so it would last the night, while Jenny covered Sandra with a blanket and found a bucket, which she placed next to her chair. Having made her as safe and comfortable as they could, Jenny ventured up the stairs and found Nicky's bedroom. It was just as it had been in the photographs: the tidiest room in the house. There was something incongruous about the make-up and bottles of nail polish arranged neatly on the dressing table, the folded underwear and carefully rolled tights in her chest of drawers. It was the opposite of what she would have expected from an emotional, self-destructive teenager. But Jenny reminded herself that those flirting with death often behaved this way; it was a form of compensation.

Jenny stood for a moment close to the spot where Nicky had died, hoping for an insight into what exactly had happened here this morning, but all she felt was an unnatural stillness and a cold draught from the ill-fitting sash window. Feeling like an intruder, she checked the single drawer of the dressing table. Inside was yet more make-up, hair elastics and hair brushes, and in amongst them she spotted a small reel of black ribbon. Jenny fetched it out and saw that it was identical to the ribbon that had been tied around the flowers left in the woods above the razed house. It must have been Nicky who had left them, along with the tag saying 'Sorry'. Jenny placed the reel back in the drawer and pushed it shut. She swept her eyes once more around the room and still wasn't convinced that regret alone was enough for Nicky to have taken her own life.

'She'll not be fit to give evidence for a few days,' Alison said as they closed the back door of the house after them.

'I think I'll give her until next week. She and her husband can both give evidence. They might even know more about Nicky than they realize.'

'You mean my theory about Ed?' Alison said darkly.

'She was a complicated girl, I know that much. Who wouldn't be, growing up with her parents?'

They lapsed into silence as they started down the steep slope towards the track, their concentration taken up with remaining upright. They were a little over halfway down when there was a sudden and alarming scuffling noise to their right. Alison spun around as a startled fox leapt out from the foot of the hedge, and bolted down the hill.

Alison held the torch beam on the hedge. 'What's that? There's something in there, look.' She moved closer, shining the light into a gap between the hawthorns from which the fox had emerged. 'It's a dog. A dead dog.'

'Black and tan,' Jenny said. 'It's the one that lived here.' She took the torch from Alison's hand and crouched down. The dog was curled on the ground in the heart of the hedge, having crawled in through what looked like a badger run. One of its rear legs was broken and sticking out at an unnatural angle, the fur wet with saliva where the fox had been pulling at it.

'It must have crawled in there to die,' Alison said. 'They do that. It's an instinct. Maybe it got hit on the road and gave up the ghost before it reached home?'

'Maybe.' Jenny stepped back. 'I'll call Sandra in the morning.'

'It doesn't feel right, does it?' Alison said. 'It's too much of a coincidence.' Alison glanced anxiously left and right. 'There's something wrong with this place.' She snatched the torch from Jenny's hand and shone it down the track. 'Who is it? Who's there?'

'No one,' Jenny said, as confused as she was disconcerted by Alison's panic.

'How do you know? They could be just down there, just out of sight, waiting for us with a loaded shotgun.'

'Stop it.'

'One man, four girls and a dog – I'm not imagining that.'

'So what are you going to do, stand here all night?'

Alison drew in a shuddering breath. 'There's something here. Something evil. I felt it the moment we stepped out of the car.'

Jenny looped her arm through Alison's and pressed it hard against her body. 'Let's go.' She set off down the slope, dragging her along with her.

'You can't ignore what's staring you in the face, Mrs Cooper. I'm telling you now, there'll be more—'

Jenny snapped, 'Alison, will you please shut up!'

'Nicky won't be the last.'

'Shut up!'

'It's all the ones who *know*. And the closer we get, the more *we* know.'

Jenny stopped walking. They were at the foot of the slope now. The darkness around them was complete. 'Alison, what's this about? Are you deliberately trying to frighten me?'

Alison was quiet for several seconds. So quiet and so still she almost seemed to have disappeared. Then, abruptly, she said, 'Why the burning? Why would Ed do that? It's not like he was trying to cover his tracks.'

'I thought you always suspected him.'

'He was a hunter. He wouldn't have missed Nicky if he'd fired at her. He'd have shot her down and dragged her into the house, along with the others. No, there's someone else. A man who likes little girls and can't handle a gun. He's here. I can smell him.'

'Let's talk about this tomorrow, shall we?'

'But if your number's up, it's up, I suppose.' Alison unhooked her arm from Jenny's and strode on along the track towards the lane. 'Chilly, isn't it?' she said conversationally. 'Can you believe they're forecasting more snow for the morning?'

# TWENTY-FOUR

THE STRANGENESS OF HER LATEST visit to Blackstone Ley had left Jenny craving a dose of normality. She found it in the brightly lit aisles of the supermarket in Chepstow where she stopped off on her way home. She wandered aimlessly filling a trolley and listening to snatches of her fellow shoppers' reassuringly banal conversations. Alison's erratic behaviour had disturbed her. It wasn't so much her oddness she found it hard to cope with as her sudden shifts in mood. Alison had seemed so competent and in control of herself whilst they were dealing with Sandra Brooks, but almost in an instant she had seemed to lose all rational sense. Thinking back over the evening, Jenny pinpointed the moment at which she had shown the first signs: it had been when Jenny had asked her if she would like to come with her to look at Nicky's bedroom. She had come halfway up the stairs, then recoiled, inventing an excuse to hurry back to the kitchen. Her reaction had been like that of a child frightened of seeing a ghost. It was ironic: the Alison she remembered from before her accident was utterly contemptuous of superstition and flights of imagination. Jenny had always been the one beset by irrational fears.

Unhinged as she had been on the walk back to the common, Alison had, however, raised a question that had been worrying away in the back of Jenny's mind for some

259

time: *why the burning?* Why indeed? She had always thought of it as Ed's way of inflicting maximum damage on Kelly, or perhaps of erasing memories of whatever he might have done within those four walls. It had made sense when she had thought of the killings as something which he had been planning, but what Sandra had told them about Nicky and Layla getting drunk and it sparking a row seemed to suggest a more spontaneous eruption. But then there were the shotgun cartridges. The wrong size. That really troubled her. And the fact that Bob Bream had been the one who alerted her troubled her even more: in the back of her mind she had held him as a suspect, but why then would he alert her to a detail that she would otherwise have missed?

A day that had started with relative certainty had ended with chaos. Nothing fitted any more. In all likelihood she would reconvene her inquest the following week, hear the evidence and reach no conclusion at all. With that dispiriting thought, Jenny unloaded her groceries at the checkout and turned her thoughts to what she might cook for dinner. She had a craving for something – eggs, that was it. She would have a Spanish omelette, a little Parmesan cheese on top, and a few glasses of Rioja. And then she remembered: she was pregnant, for God's sake. She wasn't meant to drink.

That as well. Pregnant. Somehow she had gone almost twelve hours scarcely giving it a thought. A flood of emotions she had kept squashed down all day rushed up and consumed her. For a moment she thought she might cry, humiliate herself in public and have to rush out, abandoning her shopping at the till. She reached out and took a chocolate bar from the shelf beside the till. And then she took another.

Jenny slipped her feet into a pair of comfortable boots, pulled on a lambswool sweater and jeans and cocooned herself in the kitchen. Listening to familiar voices on the radio, she sliced potatoes, cracked the eggs and heated oil in a pan. Now and then she would dip her fingers into a bowl of olives and sip from a glass of sparkling water she had dosed with an inch of white wine. Cooking the omelette over a slow heat, getting it just so, she slipped into a hazy state of contentment, the kind that was only possible when she had no looming deadline and no one to please but herself.

The peace was too good to last. She was eating her dinner in front of the TV when the phone rang. Telling herself to ignore it didn't work. Wondering who it was would only make her fret; nowadays no one called you on your landline unless it was urgent or they had something to sell. She set her tray aside and crossed the room to pick up the receiver. An instinct told her to brace herself for bad news. For some reason she expected to hear a policeman's voice.

She was wrong. It was Michael.

'Jenny?'

'What do you want?'

'Sorry to disturb you. Is now a good time?'

'For what?' Jenny said sharply, refusing to be lulled by his conciliatory tone.

He took a moment to respond. 'I tried to call you earlier – at the office.'

'When?'

'You were busy apparently – in a meeting. I spoke to Alison.'

'And?'

'I asked her how you were. She said you might be pregnant.'

Jenny was speechless.

'Not very discreet of her, I know, but I think she told me out of concern. She's very fond of you.'

'She had no right.'

'Is it true? Are you?'

'Michael, this is none of your business. And it's none of Alison's, either.'

'I was with that girl for two nights. Two nights, Jenny. I'm sorry. It was stupid. It was beyond stupid, it was the most hurtful, self-destructive thing I have ever done. She holds no interest for me. I want nothing more to do with her. I will never see her again. I promise. I *promise*. Please don't shut me out, Jenny. Not now. Please.'

'Begging doesn't make it any better, Michael.'

'I'm trying to be truthful. I love you, Jenny, and I know now that I must have left my phone behind because I needed you to know. Honestly, I'm not trying to be anything other than the man I am. I want a life with you. I want it more than anything I've ever wanted. Nothing else matters.'

'Nice speech. About two months too late. Goodbye.'

'You don't mean that.'

'Try me.'

'Then why are you keeping it?'

'What?'

'If you want me out of your life, why are you keeping my child?'

Jenny felt a surge of fury. 'You don't know what I'm doing!'

'You haven't told me otherwise. How many times do I have to say it to make you believe me, Jenny? I love you. I love you. I'm sorry . . . I want to see you.'

'Michael, I've asked you to leave me alone.'

'Please—'

There was nothing more to be said. Jenny cut him off, then pulled the phone lead from the socket.

She went back to her dinner and ate it with a determined calm that came of knowing that there was no doubt left in her mind. His pleading words hadn't touched her. The most she could say she felt for him right now was pity. And as for the child she was carrying, he had no claim. No, his presence in her life was over, and she was fine with that. And as for Alison, they would have to talk in the morning.

Determined not to let Michael spoil her evening, Jenny went to make herself some coffee and tidy up the kitchen. Then she would treat herself to one of her favourite films; one that didn't feature guns or expanses of female flesh. She thought of *Annie Hall*, but decided the humour was a little too neurotic. She wanted to be lulled and reassured. She wanted hope. She settled on *A Room With a View*. Watching alone, she could weep all she liked. She loaded the dishwasher and wiped down the counter, escaping into a fantasy of an innocence she had never experienced for herself. She pictured herself as the character Lucy, turning her face to the warm sun and gazing on the world through pure, unsullied eyes.

Leaving her pot of decaf to brew on top of the range, she went to fetch the second of the two bars of chocolate from the fridge, when she spotted something at the foot of the back door. Some sort of liquid had seeped under the sill and formed a reddish brown pool on the quarry tiles. More curious than alarmed, Jenny flicked on the outside light and opened the door. The halogen lamp lit up the snow-covered garden like a floodlight. Travelling in a straight line the full length of the lawn to the stream at its end was a bright crimson trail. Jenny looked down at her feet and saw a heap of liver and kidneys dumped on the step.

Her reaction was immediate and instinctive. She slammed the door, closed the bolts, then rushed through to the living room and reconnected the phone. She dialled the switchboard at Gloucester police station and demanded to be patched through to DI Ryan.

\*

'You can put that down now, Jenny.' Ryan looked at her nervously as he stepped through the door. 'I drew a firearm.' He pulled open his waist-length coat, revealing a shoulder holster. 'Special dispensation – just for you.'

Jenny looked at the barbeque knife in her fist and realized that she had been gripping it so tightly that she had lost nearly all sensation above her wrist. She had been standing in the hallway for the full hour it had taken Ryan to arrive. It was the only place in the house with several lines of sight and from which, if the worst were to happen, she stood any chance of escape. She prised her fingers away from the handle and set it down on the windowsill.

'Any signs of break-in?'

'Not that I can see.'

Ryan pushed open the door to her study, then glanced into the sitting room.

'Have you checked everywhere?'

'There's a spare room upstairs. I haven't dared,' Jenny admitted.

Ryan took off up the stairs, drawing his gun as he did so.

Jenny massaged the blood back into her numb hand as he went gun-first into the spare bedroom.

'All clear,' he called out.

He repeated the same drill with the bathroom and Jenny's bedroom. There was no sign of an intruder.

He came down, slotting the gun back into the holster. 'Stay here while I check out the back. Have you got a torch?'

Jenny pulled open the small boot cupboard under the stairs and found the million-candle flashlight that Michael had bought for her after an October storm had left her without power for five days. She hadn't used it since.

'Won't be a moment.' Ryan smiled. He seemed almost

amused, as if it were all a great game. 'You look like you could do with a drink.'

Jenny stayed behind the hall door as he went through the living room to the kitchen. She heard him slowly open the back door – a long moment of silence – then close it after him. It felt like an age until she heard him come back inside again. She waited to hear him bolt the door before going through to join him.

'Was there anything there?'

'As a matter of fact there was,' he said casually. 'A pig's head. I dragged it out of the stream and left it out the back here. Hope you don't mind. I took a picture on my phone if you want to see it.'

'No thanks. A *pig's head*?' She dropped into a chair feeling an unaccountable mixture of horror and relief that it wasn't something worse.

'We'll get forensics to look at what was left on the step, but I'm pretty sure it came out of a pig, too,' Ryan said. 'Have you got anything stronger than coffee?'

Jenny nodded to the solitary bottle of red wine on the rack. 'Help yourself. I won't.'

'You're sure? You look terrible.'

'I feel it.'

Ryan fetched a glass from the cupboard. 'Any ideas?'

'How long have you got?'

'As long as you like. Unless you want to go elsewhere, I don't think I ought to leave you here alone tonight.' He undid the screw top and poured out a quarter of the bottle. 'Pig's head, slaughterhouse, Ed Morgan. Someone taking serious issue with your inquiry. I don't know—'

'It seems rather obvious.'

'It is. That's probably the idea. But how do you feel?'

'How do you think?'

'Tell me.'

'Scared.'

'Of what?'

'I don't know.' Jenny gave an irritated shrug. 'Everything.'

'There you go. Mission accomplished.' He took a mouthful of wine. 'Did Fairmeadows Farm come up this morning?'

'In passing.'

'If that's where Ed got rid of Robbie's remains, there's no way we'll ever find out. Not a chance. So many carcasses pass through that place you've more chance of finding a peanut in the Pacific. So, in a sense, the guys who own it just have to sit this all out. Except I hear they're in competition with several other rendering plants down in Somerset and Wiltshire. It's a cut-throat business,' he smiled, 'literally. And by all accounts it doesn't tend to attract the most sensitive souls.'

'I have animal parts in my garden because a competitor of Fairmeadows Farm is trying to discredit them?'

'You know how much that business turned over last year? Eight million, three-hundred and fifty thousand. That's a large slice of pie. Easily worth the price of a hog's head and a bucket of guts. You get scared, call in the police, and we're meant to jump to the obvious conclusion. Instead of poking around, we shut the place down and start fishing for DNA we'll never find, because we'll look negligent if we don't.'

Jenny wanted to believe him, but remained wary.

'What's your theory?' Ryan asked, sensing that he had failed to convince her.

'My officer thinks we have a third party involved. Someone who, perhaps even in association with Ed Morgan, was involved with the disappearance of Susie Ashton, and now all of this.'

'Give me one piece of evidence.'

'The shotgun cartridges.'

Ryan was sceptical. 'Ed's had a shotgun for nearly twenty

years. Who knows what he had rattling round his gun cupboard? He might even have thought he was being humane – smaller shot, less mess. And don't forget, Bob Bream's a relation – never underestimate the fear of family stigma, especially out here.'

'I don't know . . .' Jenny told him about her visit to Sandra Brooks, beginning with her story about Nicky having been shot at by Ed Morgan and ending with the discovery of the dead dog.

Ryan listened patiently, sipping his wine until she had finished downloading. 'Jenny? Look at me.'

She was tired, and even the effort of lifting her head felt like an effort.

'Ed Morgan was a family annihilator. It's the ugliest crime there is. No one wants to believe it's possible, because if human beings can slaughter their own children it means there really is such a thing as evil. Nicky was fourteen and full of raging hormones. She got caught up in the whole psychodrama.' He laid a hand on her shoulder. 'Don't torment yourself. There is no one else.'

Jenny was too exhausted to contradict him. She got up from the table. 'Look, you really don't have to stay. I can call the local police. I'm sure they'll put a man outside if I ask them nicely.'

'No need – I brought my overnight kit. And besides, I could do with another drink.'

'I thought you said there was nothing to worry about?'

'I'd like you to sleep easy, that's all. It seems to me you're carrying a lot for one pair of shoulders.' He smiled. 'All right if I take the sofa?'

It was mildly disconcerting, climbing into bed knowing that Ryan was downstairs. Despite the fact that he was a detective performing his professional duty, his presence felt somehow illicit. She might have been imagining it, but when they had said goodnight she thought she had seen him look at her in the way he had done at the cafe in Bristol, as if he were holding on to the slender hope that she might reconsider his offer. But still, there was nothing wrong with indulging a little escapist fantasy. What *would* she do if he tapped on her door? Pretend she hadn't heard? Pull back the covers and pat the sheet? Was Ryan downstairs wondering the same thing? He probably was, which was what made it fun.

*Grow up, Jenny*. She laughed at herself – more in despair than with fondness – then rolled over and tried to sleep.

# TWENTY-FIVE

RYAN WAS ALREADY DRINKING COFFEE and making phone calls by the time Jenny came downstairs shortly after seven. 'Hold on a moment, she's right here.' He spoke to Jenny: 'Where did you say the dead dog was?'

'Partway up the steep track by the house, in the hedge. Why? Who is that?'

Ryan returned to the call and poured her a cup of coffee. 'Did you get that? . . . Yesterday morning, apparently . . . Thanks. Let me know.' He dropped the phone onto the counter. 'Thought I'd put your mind at rest. One of our dog team is going over to take a look.'

'Maybe they can check on Sandra while they're at it.'

'They will. Her husband was in touch last night from hospital – he's not happy with the post-mortem findings. Doesn't believe Nicky would have known how to kill herself that way. We're sending Family Liaison over with a laptop – they'll show him how a five-second search would have left her spoiled for choice. Would you mind if I make some toast before I hit the road?'

'Help yourself.'

'What about you?'

'No thanks. I can't stop thinking about that pig's head outside my door.'

He slotted several slices of bread into the toaster, moving

about the kitchen as contentedly as if it were his own. 'Have you got anything to put on it?'

Jenny pointed to a cupboard. 'Take your pick.'

He looked up at a shelf filled with jars. 'You buy all this for yourself? I have a jar of peanut butter and some cobwebs.'

'I'm not always alone.'

'You said.' Ryan sorted through the jars and pulled out some marmalade. 'What does he do?'

'He's a pilot,' Jenny said, hoping he might change the subject.

'What kind of planes?'

'Cargo, mostly.' She sighed, deciding to come clean. Lying to him only felt like lying to herself. 'Actually, we broke up recently.'

'Sorry to hear that.'

'So's he.'

'Your call?'

Jenny gave him a look.

'I know. Too many questions – my mother always said it was my biggest fault, which means it must be true.' He poured himself some more coffee while he waited for the toast. The conversation between them lulled. 'Fun day ahead?'

'Prepping for another inquest. A man who hanged himself just before Christmas. I say a man, but in fact he'd been born female.'

'I bet you sometimes wish you'd been an accountant.'

'Not often, but right now compiling a tax return does feel like an attractive option.'

Ryan smiled as the toaster popped. He carried his breakfast to the table, making himself comfortable.

'I don't suppose you've ever heard of a man called Jacob Rozek?' Jenny said.

'Uh-huh. I know Rozek. Set up quite an operation. Even had girls working for him over in Gloucester. A real entrepreneur. Went missing before Christmas.'

'I heard he was in the property business.'

'He was, he just didn't pay much attention to building regs. He'd buy a house, split it up, and fill it up with lucky girls from his homeland. Did one of them turn up in the morgue? Or was it him?'

'Neither. His lawyer pitched up in my office. He said Rozek was murdered. "Popped", was the word he used. In the driver's seat of his Jaguar, out near Bristol airport.'

'That wouldn't surprise me. But that's a bit off your beat, isn't it?'

'Why wouldn't it surprise you?' Jenny said, ignoring his question.

'Running whores and slaughtering the competition isn't often a recipe for a long life.' Ryan persisted with his question: 'What's your connection?'

'It seems Rozek might have been in touch with my suicide shortly before he died.'

Ryan nodded while chewing thoughtfully on his toast.

'What was his line of business – the suicide?'

'He worked at the passport office.'

'Really?' He shook his head as if at an unexpected coincidence. 'Who's the lawyer?'

'His name's Falco.'

'I know. Dresses like a gangster trying to be a businessman. Wears cologne. Jesus, Jenny, are you sure you want to get involved with Polish mafia wars on top of everything else?'

'It's just a suicide—'

'Yeah, of a transgender passport-office worker who was in touch with one of Bristol's biggest criminals. Just your everyday suicide. Have CID made these connections yet?'

'I don't believe so.' He had made her feel foolish and she wasn't sure why.

'Well, for what it's worth, my advice is to keep Rozek and his friends out of your inquiry. It's a hornet's nest. Leave them to people able to defend themselves.' Ryan swallowed the last quarter of toast, his expression becoming more serious as he thought some more about what she had told him.

'What is it?'

'Fairmeadows Farm. Half of their workers are Polish. Casuals who work for cash. No questions asked. I don't know what you've strayed into, but it doesn't take a lot to start joining the dots. What was this guy's name, the suicide? I'll ask around.'

'Burden. Daniel Burden.'

Ryan brought out his phone and keyed in a note of the name. 'I can't let you stay here alone while you're caught up with all of this. I'll call in on the local plod on my way to Gloucester, sort something out for you.'

'Should I be scared?'

'Probably. But I get the feeling nothing I can say will make any difference.' He carried his plate to the sink. 'Thanks for breakfast. I'd better go and shovel up some kidneys.'

'Jenny, it's Simon.'

The crisp, public-school vowels ringing out from her car speakers could hardly have belonged to anyone else. Formerly a Director in the Ministry of Justice, Simon Moreton had managed to get himself seconded to the still-new office of the Chief Coroner situated in the Royal Courts of Justice, where he continued to perform his former role as none-too-subtle enforcer of the party line.

'You're up early. I feel privileged,' Jenny answered with a trace of sarcasm.

She came to a halt at the foot of her lane and turned right through the village of Tintern. The ruins of the abbey rose out of a ghostly dawn. As Alison had promised, more snow was starting to fall. Jenny could hardly believe it.

'Only for you, Jenny. Now listen, I've been following your family-annihilation case with interest—'

'I'd be disappointed if you hadn't.'

'Can I assume from your light-hearted tone that you don't know the reason for my call?'

'You want to take me for lunch.'

'Alas, not today.'

'You're sounding me out for Deputy Chief Coroner.'

'I never knew you harboured such ambitions. Hmm. How interesting.'

'No good. You'll have to put me out of my misery.'

'You're leaking.'

'I beg your pardon?'

'Your office is leaking. Badly. Are you a user of the social media?'

'Not if I can help it.'

'Very wise. It's a pity that your recently returned officer, Mrs Trent, doesn't share the same lack of interest. Her musings haven't quite gone viral, but they're enough to have the Chief choking on his cornflakes.'

Jenny had a bad feeling. 'What happened?'

'Apparently a young man named Simon Grant made the fourteen-year-old victim pregnant and is being treated as a murder suspect. I've already taken the precaution of contacting Superintendent Abbott – the police have no suspects apart from the dead man Morgan.'

'I know nothing about this.' Jenny felt cold pricks of perspiration on her neck.

'There's more. Not only was Simon Grant having sex with Layla Hart, he was also intimately involved with one

Nicky Brooks, who yesterday took her own life. There's no direct allegation, but the implication is clear enough.'

'Really, I don't understand—'

'You haven't heard the best bit yet; the tour de force. I quote from Mrs Trent's Facebook page: "At the time of Susie Ashton's disappearance, Simon Grant was a seven-year-old boy who attended the same primary school in the nearby town of Thornbury. This placed him and his family in daily contact with the four-year-old Susie." Thankfully it stops at innuendo, but that's enough for the libel courts. I'd say that was an easy seven figures for Harry Grant if he chooses to take that route.'

Jenny felt weak. She had barely pulled herself together after her conversation with Ryan. 'I don't know what to say.'

'You don't have to say anything, Jenny. But you will have to do something. I appreciate your long association with Mrs Trent, but this really is nothing less than gross misconduct.'

'She's been ill.'

'Quite so. And I understand you've been more than generous to her. I presume she's had a full medical assessment?'

'Not yet,' Jenny confessed.

Moreton let out a long-suffering sigh that was only partly tinged with affection.

'Well, if we leave aside the issue of your judgement, it does at least offer you a gentler exit route than might otherwise have been the case.'

Jenny felt her nausea return: a hard, unrelenting sensation that swept through her body and left her helpless in its grip.

'Can I presume you'll have this sorted out in the next hour or two?' Moreton pressed.

'Yes,' Jenny answered weakly.

'Then with a little luck the Chief might never know,' Moreton said. 'Make sure she takes it down. Immediately.'

'I will.'

'Keep me posted. And perhaps we should arrange that lunch. I'd like that. '

Jenny pulled up outside the office as the snow shower was turning into the predicted storm. The street was deserted. Weeks of relentless cold seemed finally to have brought the city to a complete halt.

Jenny shivered as she walked along the hallway towards the office. Her footsteps seemed to ring off the walls. She felt like an executioner as she turned the brass handle and stepped inside.

Alison was craning forward at her desk watching CCTV footage on her computer. The room was warm and damp and smelt of the gas fire and the breakfast roll Alison had heated in the microwave.

'I told you they'd forecast snow,' Alison said with a note of triumph. 'A few more days like this, we'll be up to our necks. I've never known anything like it.' She nodded to the screen. 'This is the BP station on Gloucester Road. I thought I had Ed, but it wasn't him. Have you ever done this? It's like watching paint dry. I could hardly sleep at all last night – I kept thinking, why? Why the burning? Why go to the bother of killing everyone twice? And all that business with Nicky being shot at – Sandra said the house was *already* in flames. I can't make sense of it.'

There was something manic in Alison's manner. Her eyes were wide and staring as if she'd been peering at the screen for hours. Her hair was slightly askew. Jenny counted three empty mugs on her desk next to the pile of DVDs she was working through.

'What time did you come in?'

'I'm not sure. Five-ish. I wanted to beat the weather. Couldn't face another day stuck at home.'

Jenny pulled off her coat. 'Alison, can you do something for me, please – bring up your Facebook page?'

'*What?*'

'Your Facebook page.'

'Any particular reason?'

'I had a call from Simon Moreton on the way in. He'd seen something on it.'

'Moreton? What was he doing looking me up?'

'I imagine he was tipped off.'

The colour drained from Alison's face. She hurriedly closed the window on which the video was playing and brought up the internet browser. Moments later they were both looking at her timeline. There were three offending entries in total, each made shortly before midnight. They had been 'liked' more than 200 times. Jenny watched the counter register two more approvals in the space of a few seconds.

Alison stared at it in disbelief. 'I didn't write this. I didn't. I was in bed by half past ten. Ask Paul, he'll tell you.'

'You had better delete them.'

Alison clicked edit and delete, and in moments the three entries had vanished, although she continued to stare at the screen as if doubting they had ever existed.

'Is it possible you got out of bed?' Jenny asked, treading carefully.

'No. I'd remember. Surely I would.'

'Do you forget things?'

Alison looked at her blankly with the same suddenly confused expression Jenny had seen the other day.

'Where do you keep the computer at home?' Jenny asked.

'I use an iPad. I was reading on it.'

'Then what?'

'I have it next to the bed, but I didn't touch it again. I'm certain . . .'

But she wasn't. Jenny could see it. The phone rang. Alison snatched up the receiver before Jenny could reach it.

'Coroner's Office.' Her face fell. 'Yes, of course. I'll get her for you now.'

She cupped her hand over the mouthpiece and spoke in a flat, expressionless voice. 'Mr Lever for you, Mrs Cooper.'

Jenny walked through to her office and closed the door behind her. She spoke as quietly as she could into the phone, aware that Alison would be listening out for every word.

'I presume you know what this is about, Mrs Cooper,' Lever began.

'I do. And it's been dealt with.'

She heard a click of computer keys at the other end of the line. 'That's a start. But you'll appreciate there will be further consequences. As your officer is legally your agent, my clients will be holding you, or at least your office, responsible for this libel.'

'You'll appreciate that, as sympathetic as I am, I really shouldn't discuss this any further.'

'There will be a court application made today requiring you and Mrs Trent to desist from disseminating any further opinion or information. You'll understand it's likely to be a formality. But perhaps you could explain to her that once the order is made, she will find herself in grave trouble if anything of this nature were to happen again.'

As Lever issued his threat Jenny had another doom-laden realization: it would be no excuse that Alison had suffered a serious injury. The only reason she had access to sensitive evidence and was able to discuss it was that Jenny had allowed her back to work when by any objective standard she wasn't fit.

'Is there anything you wish to say, Mrs Cooper,' Lever was relishing their unexpected reversal of fortunes, 'before I issue proceedings?'

'No. There's nothing more.'

Jenny set down the phone and returned to Alison to find her already pulling on her coat and stuffing the DVDs into a briefcase.

'You don't have to say anything, Mrs Cooper. I've left you the file for Thursday's inquest. Everything should be in order. Court five at 10 a.m.'

'I think perhaps a report from Mrs Trent's neurologist—'

'Yes. That would be the proper thing to do.' Her voice was brittle, as if at any moment she might break down. 'Of course it would.' She buckled her briefcase and went to the door. Unable to bring herself to look at her, Alison said, 'I'm sorry, Mrs Cooper. I've let you down. At least it won't happen again.'

Before Jenny could find any words of comfort, she was on her way out of the building.

Moreton was nothing if not thorough. Alison had been gone no more than ten minutes when he called again to check on progress. Satisfied that the offending messages had been taken down and that Alison's career as a coroner's officer was effectively over, he informed Jenny that he would be taking personal control of negotiations with Harry Grant and his lawyers. All he required from Jenny was a signed statement setting out what had happened. Jenny knew that he was doing her a favour – if he had chosen to, Moreton could have laid the blame for what had happened equally at her feet, for having allowed Alison to come back at all – but it was hard to see it that way. She had tried to be generous to a woman to whom she probably owed both her life and her son's, but Moreton wasn't interested in sentimental justifications, only in keeping the lid firmly screwed down and ensuring that Jenny knew she was now under scrutiny. *Close* scrutiny.

'You'll be stressed, Jenny,' he said, 'which isn't an ideal state in which to be conducting a delicate inquest. Consider me a helpmeet – there to assist if you're unsure of your judgement. You'll survive. We've weathered worse together.'

Moreton's niceness did little to sugar the bitter pill of having to write Alison a letter informing her that her misconduct would be reviewed in light of a detailed medical examination. If she preferred not to endure this ordeal, she was free to tender her resignation on the understanding that an *ex gratia* payment would be offered as a gesture of goodwill. Signing her name on the hard copy, Jenny was reminded of a phrase her father used to utter – 'there is no such thing as a weak and generous man' – and realized that until that moment, she had never understood what he had meant.

Turning to the carefully prepared file Alison had left for her, Jenny struggled to believe that it had been put together by the same woman who had blurted out her secrets to Michael and taken to the internet with wild and inappropriate allegations. She had become two entirely separate beings: one rational, one mentally incontinent. Jenny had to remind herself of what the neurologist had told her the previous autumn: the part of Alison's brain that controlled social responses had been badly damaged. She wouldn't have appreciated the consequences of what she was writing. The fact that she could pass as remotely normal was a minor miracle.

Forcing herself on, Jenny reviewed the short list of witnesses she would call in her inquest into Daniel Burden's death. There was DI Ballantyne, Dr Hope the pathologist, Burden's brother and a man called Kenyon who was Burden's line manager at the passport office. True to her word, Alison had sent the laptop recovered from his flat to a data-retrieval expert. His report was short but interesting. The concluding paragraph read:

Aside from the recent history on the internet browser and that associated with factory-installed software, this machine was clean of data. The hard drive ('C') was checked for signs of data deletion but none was found. This indicates that this machine has not been used, or more likely, that the owner operated largely with a plug-in hard drive which has been disconnected from the machine. Signs of wear on the high-speed USB port on the right-hand side of the casing corroborates this supposition.

What is of interest is that the machine has a 64-bit operating system and 20 GB of RAM. This is far in excess of the capacity of most personal computers and might even be considered 'specialist'. This would lead me to suspect that it may have been used to run a program(s) requiring an unusually large amount of processing power. The absence of data on the C drive suggests a user with more than the usual degree of computing knowledge and skill.

Extensive searches on the IP address of this machine failed to find any trace of its online activity. This may suggest that it has been used via a proxy server, meaning, in layman's terms, that the user disguised his identity while accessing the internet.

Dr James Fletcher
Doward Data Systems

Daniel Burden was a computer buff who had learned to cover his tracks. There was nothing too surprising in that. What was more intriguing was the prospect that whatever he had been hiding might prove to be the key to understanding his suicide. Pornography was the obvious inference, but as far as Jenny knew, you didn't need a particularly powerful computer for that. She turned a page in the file and found another document attached to an exchange of emails

Alison had conducted with a computer shop in central Bristol. It was a copy of an invoice dated the previous July, for a MacBook Pro and a 10-terabyte hard drive. She had no idea how much data that could store, but she knew it was a lot. Enough to support a process being conducted on an industrial scale. Longing for one straightforward case to cross her desk, she opened a legal pad and started writing questions.

Jenny had worked at her desk for five hours straight until hunger got the better of her. She was heading out along the snow-covered pavement to a cafe on Park Street when a familiar black Toyota turned the corner into Jamaica Street. Ryan spotted her and called out as he pulled up across the street.

'Jenny – got a moment?'

'If I don't get some lunch, I'm going to drop.'

'Room for another?'

'If you're quick.'

She waited impatiently, stamping her feet while he backed into a space.

He emerged from the car wearing yet another coat: mid-length, dark blue with leather pocket-trim and a black upturned collar. The fabric was thick and expensive. If she hadn't suspected he was fishing for it, she would have paid him a compliment.

'Are you all right?' Ryan said as he joined her. 'You've had staff problems.'

'Who told you that?'

'We were briefed. A member of the public saw something online and tipped off the team looking for Robbie Morgan.'

'It makes you wonder how anyone keeps a secret nowadays.'

'How much trouble are you in?' Ryan asked.

'Enough,' Jenny said, and turned the corner onto the main road.

She and Ryan both ordered a large paper cup of soup with a crusty roll. The cafe was crammed with people having the same idea, and the only seats they could find were high stools at the end of a counter by the kitchen door.

'Are you OK to talk here?' Ryan said.

Jenny glanced at the diners nearest them. Most of them were students from the university and caught up in their own conversations. She couldn't spot any obvious journalists or criminals.

'Go ahead.'

'Three things. Firstly, there'll be a police presence outside your house for the next few days. The DCI over at Chepstow was happy to oblige – says he's a friend of yours.'

Jenny smiled. 'Our paths have crossed.'

'Secondly, we've had a look at the dog from the Brookses' place. The vet says it has four broken ribs, a broken jaw and suffered pulmonary haemorrhage. The most likely explanation is that it was hit by a car.'

'Are there any less obvious alternatives?'

'It ran into someone who really hates dogs. Seriously, they spoke to Sandra and she thinks the animal might have got scared off when all the police and the ambulance arrived. She can't remember clearly. Obviously.' He gave her his reassuring look. 'So that's one thing you can strike off your list of worries.'

'Thanks. What's the third?'

'Actually there's four. Number three is that the animal body parts dumped outside your house are not going to yield any forensics.'

'Because?'

'Abbott's not prepared to pay for it and you haven't formally reported a crime to your local force. Whether you want to take that step is up to you.'

'It sounds as if you're suggesting there's a reason I shouldn't?'

Ryan wiped his mouth a napkin. 'That's number five. Do you know anyone who drives a blue Saab saloon? The vehicle's about ten years old.'

'Yes. Michael. My ex. Why?'

'Your neighbour at the foot of the lane saw the car drive up in the direction of your place late yesterday afternoon. About thirty minutes later it came down again.'

Jenny set down her soup, frightened that she would spill it. 'Michael? . . . No. Why would he do that?'

'How did things end between you?'

Jenny tried to hold her focus through a confusion of emotions. 'He wanted to move in with me, but I found out he'd been cheating while he was abroad. I wouldn't forgive him. He spoke to Alison, my officer, *ex*-officer, and she told him – ' She paused, frightened she might cry. 'She told him she thought I was pregnant.'

Ryan looked at her sympathetically. 'And are you? . . . I mean, does he know one way or the other?'

Jenny nodded. 'He called me last night. He wants to be forgiven. He was pleading with me.'

'Your life really isn't simple, is it?'

Jenny laughed, but it came out halfway to a sob. Tears trickled down her cheeks. Just what she didn't want to happen. She pressed a napkin to her face, willing herself to be strong.

'Don't worry about it,' Ryan said.

She felt his hand on her arm. He squeezed her lightly. A welcome gesture of comfort.

'I still don't see why he would,' Jenny said.

'A man will do all sorts of things if he's desperate enough.

Look at Ed. My guess is he thought you'd pick up the phone and beg him to come and protect you.' Still holding her arm, Ryan added, 'He knows about your case, right? About Ed's connection with Fairmeadows Farm?'

'I think I mentioned it.'

'Then it starts to make sense. Call it a romantic gesture. Well, a passionate one, at least.'

Jenny tried to imagine Michael dumping a pig's head at the end of her garden. It didn't compute.

'I'll be honest with you – the neighbour knew who it was. I checked him out. He flew fighter jets in combat – Bosnia, Iraq and Afghanistan.'

Jenny nodded.

'So when you've blown that many people up, what he did doesn't seem quite so bad, does it? At least from his point of view.'

She pictured Michael at the roadblock the previous week. His malevolent silence as the policeman had walked towards the car. Then remembered waking that same night to find him standing naked at the foot at the bed, freezing cold as if he'd been there for hours. It must have been the therapy she had pushed him into: drawing the poison to the surface. She couldn't help blaming herself.

Taking his hand from her arm, Ryan looked at her sincerely. 'Anything more I can do, I'm all yours.'

'Thank you,' Jenny said. And wished he'd stayed touching her a little longer.

# TWENTY-SIX

JENNY ENTERED THROUGH A DOOR in the wood panelling and stepped onto a raised dais to take her seat in the judge's chair. The courtroom was small, windowless and over-heated, giving it a stuffy, claustrophobic feel, but she didn't plan on being here long. In an inquest without a significant conflict of evidence, there was no need for a jury. If she kept up the pace she could expect to hear all the witnesses before the end of the morning and to deliver a verdict that after-noon. She was already virtually certain what that verdict would be.

She had been provided with an usher, an elderly part-timer called Dennis, who was already comfortably seated at the side of the court reading his newspaper. She had no doubt that in a few minutes he would be fast asleep.

Besides the three witnesses and a quietly dignified man in a plain suit and tie, who Jenny assumed to be the dead man's brother, Anthony Burden, the only other persons present were Louis Falco and, seated along from him on the advocates' bench, a young female lawyer whose name didn't appear on Jenny's note of legal representatives.

Falco rose to make introductions. Large gold cufflinks glinted at the end of his suit sleeves and his glossy hair shone with oil, but in a nod to the sobriety of the occasion he wore a black silk tie. He could have been a drug dealer at a funeral.

'Good morning, ma'am. I represent Anthony Burden, the brother and next of kin of the deceased, Daniel Burden, and my friend, Miss Clara Lawson, is, I understand, keeping a watching brief on behalf of the deceased's employers, the Home Office.'

'Only a watching brief, Miss Lawson? You have no wish to examine any witnesses?'

The young woman stood up nervously. She was slight, with mousy hair and cheap, dark-rimmed glasses. Jenny suspected she was an in-house lawyer at the Passport Service, sent to keep an eye for no reason other than that one of their employees was giving evidence. 'No, ma'am. Just a watching brief.'

'Very well,' Jenny said. 'Shall we proceed?'

'There is one matter,' Falco said. 'A witness I should like to call later this morning.'

'If the evidence is relevant, I've no objection, Mr Falco. What is the witness's name and connection with the deceased?'

Falco cast a sideways glance at DI Ballantyne, who was seated in the row behind him. The detective looked as sour and hung-over as the last time Jenny had seen him, at Burden's flat. 'Perhaps we could call him Mr Smith – at least for the time being.' Jenny became aware that she could easily grow impatient with Falco. 'He's a man with certain, shall we say, "underworld" connections. If he's able to be heard – and I think you would find him very useful, ma'am – I would request that the gallery be cleared and that he be allowed to give evidence without his true identity being made public.'

Jenny looked at Anthony Burden and saw that he was as bemused by Falco's request as she was.

'Have you spoken to your client about this potential witness, Mr Falco? I get the impression you may have surprised him.'

'Events have moved rather quickly, ma'am. I don't yet have Mr Smith's full statement, but I will, of course, keep my client fully informed.'

DI Ballantyne scowled moodily at Falco's neck, viewing him, no doubt, as indivisible from the criminals from whom he made his living.

Jenny tried to be patient. It was too early in the day to lose her temper, and experience had taught her that once lost it would be hard to regain.

'All right, Mr Falco, here's what we'll do. As and when your witness is ready to testify, you can tell me in chambers why I should grant the conditions you request, and we'll take it from there.'

'I'm obliged, ma'am,' Falco answered with exaggerated politeness, and, ignoring the look he was receiving from Anthony Burden, sat down.

Jenny formally opened the inquest and reminded those assembled that Daniel Robert Burden was thirty-five years old and had been born Diana Burden, before starting the process of gender reassignment in his late twenties. He was unmarried, lived alone, and worked as a civil servant for the Home Office's Passport Service at their offices in Newport, South Wales. He had lost both his parents and had only one sibling. Described so succinctly, Daniel Burden's sounded a miserably lonely and unfulfilled life.

DI Ballantyne gave evidence on behalf of the Bristol and Avon police and was in a hurry to get it over with. Some police officers appearing at inquests took the trouble to consider the feelings of any relatives present; Ballantyne wasn't among their number. He described with brutal bluntness how he had been called to the first-floor flat in Henleaze when neighbours had been alerted by a foul smell. Burden's body was hanging from the pull-up bars of a mini-gym by a length of nylon tow rope. There was no note, and nothing to indicate his state of mind other than a pornographic video which was open on the browser of his laptop computer. His personal affairs were in good order and he had a little over £50,000 in a Barclays deposit account. His monthly salary after tax was £1,952.

'Inspector, was there any sign of forced entry to the property?' Jenny asked.

'None.'

'Any evidence of drugs or excessive alcohol use?'

'No.'

'Was there any indication or sexual activity proximate to the time of death?'

'Apart from what was on the computer, none,' Ballantyne said, tucking his notebook back into his jacket. His eyes flicked impatiently to the clock on the side wall.

'The £50,000 in his bank account – are you able to say where that came from?'

'No.'

'"No" it's impossible to say, or "no" you haven't in-quired?' Jenny asked patiently.

'The money has accumulated over the last two years, all cash deposits in the region of £1,000 to £2,000.'

'Was there any evidence in the flat of how he might have come by extra money?'

'No, ma'am. Your guess is as good as mine.'

'All right, Inspector. I sense Mr Falco may have a question for you.'

Falco stood and gave Ballantyne a smile that suggested an eventful history between them. As he did so, the door at the rear of the court creaked open. Jenny glanced up to see Alison enter. Alison proffered a smile that contained no hint of bitterness, took a seat in the back row and produced a notebook and pen.

'Are you familiar with a businessman by the name of Jacob Rozek, Inspector?' Falco asked.

'I've heard the name. Though I'm not sure that the Rozek I'm thinking of was exactly legitimate.'

'Success does tend to breed suspicion,' Falco said, 'and envy too, of course. But I digress. Are you aware that he disappeared on December the 19th of last year?'

'I fail to see the relevance,' Ballantyne grunted, appealing to Jenny.

'Get to your point quickly, Mr Falco,' Jenny interjected. 'Answer the question, please, Inspector.'

Ballantyne gave a bad-tempered sigh. 'Yes, I know Rozek disappeared, and yes, I'm aware that my colleagues are investigating the possibility that he was murdered. What of it?'

'Did you find any mobile phones in Mr Burden's flat?'

'Not as I recall.'

'Doesn't that strike you as odd?'

'Unusual, but not exactly "odd". Not in the sense I imagine you're implying.'

Falco consulted some papers on his desk. 'There's no sign of him making a monthly payment, I'll grant you, but he did have a mobile number that his brother was aware of. I have it written down here. It turns out to have been a pay as you go registered in the name of a Miss Diana Francis. You may know that Daniel Burden was born Diana Francis Burden. So far, so good, but my client has searched his brother's flat, and his car, and he can't find it. Now, in my book, when you add all that up, it becomes odd.'

'I think we read from different books.'

'We have a missing phone, Inspector. So either Mr Burden disposed of it before he died, or you or your officers took it and won't admit the fact.'

'Why would we do that?' Ballantyne growled.

'Let me give you a possibility – when Rozek disappeared, your colleagues naturally went through his phone records. One of the numbers he had dialled was registered to a Miss Diana Francis. Rozek called that number only once – on December the 11th, eight days before his disappearance. Am I getting warmer?'

'There's no jury to impress,' Jenny reminded Falco. 'All that interests me are the facts.'

'Inspector, Mr Burden worked at the passport office, approving applications. Mr Rozek was a businessman from Poland who had begun to attract the attention of some of your colleagues – actually, some of your *undercover* colleagues – who I'm reliably informed have been passing themselves off as criminals in the human-trafficking and prostitution business.'

'I thought that was Mr Rozek's line of country,' Ballantyne said, his temper hanging by a thread.

Believing that he had Ballantyne cornered, Falco goaded him with a tolerant smile. 'Inspector, for reasons irrelevant to this inquest, Mr Rozek may well have felt the need to acquire an alternate identity. Mr Burden approved passports for a living and was making regular cash deposits at the bank. The connection is obvious. Now, what I'd like to know from you is whether you took Mr Burden's phone because he was someone already of interest to you, or merely because you checked his number and found that it connected him with Mr Rozek.'

Ballantyne responded with a hard stare. 'I told you, we didn't find a phone.'

Falco met Ballantyne's gaze. The humour that had played about his eyes during their previous exchange had vanished. 'Was Mr Burden working as an informer to the police,

Inspector? Was he what you would nowadays call a "covert human-intelligence source"?'

'I have no idea what you're talking about,' Ballantyne said.

'Did Mr Burden tip you off that Mr Rozek was seeking a passport under an assumed name?'

'Ditto.'

'These are proper questions, Inspector,' Jenny said, beginning to feel unsettled by Falco's suggestions. 'Please treat them seriously.'

DI Ballantyne looked at Falco in the way he might look at a suspect across an interview-room table. 'No. Daniel Burden did not inform CID that Mr Rozek was seeking a false identity.'

'I'm nearly finished, Inspector,' Falco said. 'Are you aware that, in the course of the last twelve months, no fewer than five Polish men, all with substantial assets, have disappeared from this city without trace?'

'Their pictures are on the wall in the station: two pimps, two drug dealers and Jacob Rozek, who, I believe, had numerous interests, not just confined to drugs and prostitution.'

Ignoring the slur, Falco pressed on. 'Would you concede that five missing men suggests something distinctly odd?'

'Criminals kill each other all the time, Mr Falco. You of all people should know that.'

Falco didn't flinch. 'Mindful of the oath you have sworn, to tell the *whole* truth, Inspector Ballantyne, is there anything further about Daniel Burden that you haven't yet shared with the court?'

'Not a thing,' Ballantyne shot back.

'If you were aware, for example, that Daniel Burden's role as a police informer had somehow leaked and that his life had thereby been placed at risk, you would disclose the fact?'

Ballantyne answered through gritted teeth. 'I am fully aware of my obligations to the court.'

Falco gave a hint of a smile. 'I'm sure the court will note your reply.' He gave an exaggerated nod to the bench and sat.

'Thank you, Inspector,' Jenny said. 'You may stand down.'

Ballantyne left the witness box and headed for the exit, but as he neared the door he seemed to undergo a change of heart and found a place in the back row, across the aisle from Alison.

Alison glanced at Jenny with raised eyebrows. She seemed to be telling her that Falco's line of questioning might not have been entirely fanciful. Jenny took a large mouthful of water and a deep breath, then called for Dr Jasmine Hope.

Dr Hope was quiet, but unexpectedly confident and sure of herself as she entered the witness box and commenced her evidence. Grateful to be on uncontested territory, Jenny led her swiftly through the details of the post-mortem. Dr Hope was adamant that Burden had died from asphyxiation due to strangulation, and that all the surrounding circumstances led to the conclusion that he had been standing on the office chair which lay on its side several feet from where the body was found hanging. Further unequivocal evidence was provided by the vertical orientation of the rope lesions around the neck and the fact that blood had pooled in the lower extremities. The death did not show any of the characteristics of accidental autoerotic asphyxiation, not least because the deceased was fully clothed, and in any event, such accidental deaths were nearly always associated with biological males. In short, it was beyond all doubt that Daniel Burden had intended to kill himself and that he had succeeded.

'Are you happy with Dr Hope's evidence?' Jenny asked Falco, when she had finished her questioning.

Falco leant his hands on the desk and pushed himself upright. 'No, ma'am, sadly I am not.'

Jenny exchanged a further glance with Alison and invited Falco to proceed.

'Dr Hope, did you measure the length of the rope from where it was knotted at Mr Burden's neck to where it was attached to the bars above him?'

'Give me a moment.' Dr Hope sifted through the notes she had brought with her to the witness box, then after several seconds of fruitless searching shook her head. 'No, I'm afraid I didn't.'

'Can I assume, then, you that you did not measure the length of his arms?'

Dr Hope cast Jenny an uncertain glance. 'It wasn't really necessary.'

Jenny guessed what was coming next and kicked herself for not having thought of it before post-mortem. The prospect of a quick and tidy end to proceedings by mid-afternoon was fast becoming a distant hope.

Falco picked up the booklet of photographs issued by the police photographer. 'In the absence of hard evidence, I suppose we'll have to make do with some educated guesswork. Could you look at the photographs of the body *in situ*, please.'

Dr Hope opened her own copy of the booklet.

'Mr Burden was five feet, three inches tall. His feet look to be a little over a foot, perhaps eighteen inches, off the ground. Would you agree?'

'Yes. About that.'

'Look at the gap between the top of his head and the bar – what would you say that is?'

Dr Hope studied the photograph hard. 'Slightly less than one foot.'

'Meaning he could have reached up and grabbed those bars to save himself, had he wanted to. He wouldn't have died straight away, would he? His neck wasn't broken. He would have been conscious for some seconds, perhaps thirty seconds, or even a minute or longer?'

'It's possible.' Dr Hope said hesitantly.

'Did you examine his wrists and arms for signs of restraint?'

'There were no visible marks,' Dr Hope said.

'No *visible* marks,' Falco repeated. 'Hmm. All right. I'm going to paint you a picture, and you tell me if it could be consistent with what you see on this photograph.' He paused to glance at Anthony Burden, who reluctantly nodded his agreement for Falco to proceed. 'Let's say Mr Burden was not alone at the time of his death. There was someone, or more than one person, present. They fastened his wrists together, perhaps with something soft that wouldn't mark, like a rag then duct tape, attached the rope to the bars and made him stand on the chair. Then maybe they asked him some questions, and when they were finished, kicked away the chair and waited for him to die. Then they removed the restraints to make it look like suicide.'

Anthony Burden stared clench-jawed into space, waiting for Dr Hope's answer.

'It's possible,' Dr Hope said hesitantly.

Falco raised his voice, and jabbed his finger in the air. 'Doctor, on this evidence you cannot be sure whether Daniel Burden committed suicide or was murdered, can you?'

'No,' Dr Hope conceded.

Falco dropped back into his seat with a defiant, upwards tilt of his chin.

Jenny had no more questions for Dr Hope. Letting her go,

she told her that it was no reflection on her professional abilities that she hadn't taken the measurements suggested by Mr Falco. Her job as a pathologist was to determine the physical cause of death, which was precisely what she had done. As she left the witness box, Jenny saw DI Ballantyne's stony expression show a flicker of doubt. His wasn't the studied calm of a man executing a cover-up; she sensed that Falco's cross-examination had made him question what, until now, he had thought to be certainties.

Gordon Kenyon wore a brown suit that hung limply off his bony frame, together with a brown-and-cream checked tie that almost matched. He was pale and balding with eyes permanently fixed in the expression of someone who had spent a lifetime staring at a computer screen. What he lacked in charisma he made up for in precision, answering each question after a short, considered pause and with the unadorned exactness of a robot.

Kenyon told the court that he had been a Home Office employee for twenty-seven years and a senior approvals officer at the Newport office of the Passport Service for the previous six. During that period he had seen Daniel Burden rise from a minor role in data entry to the position he had held for the previous two years.

'Mr Burden's principal task was to process and approve passport applications, is that correct?'

'Yes, ma'am,' Kenyon answered.

'Did he perform it well?'

'His record was entirely satisfactory.'

'His job, as I understand it, required him to perform personal interviews with passport applicants.'

'Correct.'

'And would it have been possible for him to have abused that position – to create passports using false identities?'

'Difficult but not impossible,' Kenyon replied perfunctorily.

'For an adult to acquire a new UK passport it would require an identity already to have been established to a high degree of authenticity. There is almost no way of achieving it from scratch.'

'If not from scratch, how would you do it?'

'The most obvious way is to collude with someone who is willing to give up a passport they already hold legitimately – a serving prisoner, for example. The passport is reported lost, a replacement is sought but a new photograph substituted. Even so, every approval Mr Burden made would have been subject to random review. We now employ facial-recognition software that would detect any change in personal appearance.' He smiled. 'It really is close to impossible to cheat the system without running a huge risk. If an officer were caught, it would mean years in prison.'

'Have any of Mr Burden's approvals ever been questioned?' Jenny asked.

'No. I have never had cause to question his honesty or competence.'

'I appreciate your assistance, Mr Kenyon.' Jenny addressed Falco: 'Do you have any questions for this witness?'

'Only a couple,' Falco said. 'Mr Kenyon, did you socialize with Daniel Burden?'

'I did not.'

'You surprise me. Were you aware of his having friends amongst his colleagues?'

Kenyon frowned as he considered the question. Personal relationships seemed outside his area of expertise. 'I would say that Mr Burden kept personal and professional life largely separate. I was not aware of him socializing with colleagues.'

'In other words, he kept a low profile?'

'Yes.'

'Were you aware of him having another source of income besides his salary?'

'No.'

'So the man you knew was diligent, private, and socially disconnected from his colleagues.'

Kenyon thought about his answer. 'Yes. That would seem a fair assessment.'

'One last matter, Mr Kenyon – would you mind checking something for me when you're back in the office? Did Mr Burden approve a replacement passport for a Mr Lech Weil some time in December? That's W-E-I-L.'

Kenyon's eyes flitted to the lawyer, Clara Lawson, as if he had been caught out in some way. 'Yes. Certainly. May I ask the significance?'

'Weil was dead at the time his passport was issued,' Falco said casually.

He offered no further questions, but had succeeded in raising issues Jenny would now struggle to ignore. Burden had had proven contact with a criminal, had been depositing unaccounted-for sums of cash into his bank account and was in a position – albeit at substantial risk – to provide false passports. What's more, he had a motive to behave dishonestly: he was seeking specialist surgery that would cost tens of thousands of pounds.

Jenny asked Kenyon one final question of her own: 'Have you reviewed Mr Burden's caseload since his death, and if so, has it revealed anything irregular?'

'Yes, we have, and no, it hasn't,' Kenyon answered at once. 'In fact, if I may say so, I find the suggestion that he was behaving dishonestly laughable. It did not happen.'

Coming from Kenyon these were strong words, and Jenny silently thanked him for them. A little of her uncertainty fell away.

Jenny hadn't planned on calling Anthony Burden to give

evidence unless having heard the evidence he wished to add something to the written statement he had already given. Falco consulted with him and informed Jenny that he had nothing further to contribute. In Burden's confused expression Jenny saw that he still knew as much and as little about his sister-turned-brother as he had done before his untimely death.

'Well, Mr Falco, I now have all the evidence I wished to call. Are you still proposing to ask me to hear another witness?'

Jenny saw DI Ballantyne crane forward to hear Falco's response. He didn't want to miss a word.

'Ma'am, might I address you in chambers?'

Jenny was in two minds. Although she had earlier extended the offer of a private meeting, she had an instinctive dislike of off-the-record conversations with lawyers. But on the other hand, she suspected that Falco was pushing at a door that she ought, if possible, to look behind. This was the very last opportunity to uncover the whole truth. If she were simply to call a halt now and return an open verdict, the file on Daniel Burden's death would remain closed forever.

She avoided looking at Anthony Burden, not wanting her decision to be an emotional one. The coroner's duty was not to the family of the deceased but to the truth, no matter how uncomfortable or distressing that might be. It was Ryan's words that she heard repeating in her mind, or rather a phrase: 'the Polish mafia'. She had no doubt that Falco was plugged into its heart, and that he would not have gone to all the trouble of contacting Anthony Burden and appearing at an inquest (without a fee, Jenny presumed) unless he had a very good reason.

'Very well, Mr Falco, as long as you're brief.'

Clara Lawson stirred from her silence and rose timidly to her feet. 'Ma'am – will I be permitted to be present?'

'Your client is not a party to these proceedings, Miss Lawson,' Jenny explained, forgiving her inexperience, 'so no, you are not permitted to be present.'

Jenny stood. As she had predicted, the elderly usher had fallen into a doze and failed to notice. It was Alison's voice that sounded around the court: 'All rise.'

Falco took several minutes to arrive. When he did, he tugged nervously at his cuffs as he took a seat opposite Jenny in the small, functional office that had been allocated to her in the corridor behind the court.

'Well, Mr Falco?'

'I mentioned a potential witness, ma'am. I've just been making some inquiries. It seems that during the last hour Bristol CID have persuaded magistrates to issue a warrant for his arrest.'

'On what charge?'

'Living on the proceeds of immoral earnings. That's what I've heard. It does seem rather convenient.'

'And his relationship to this case?'

'He has information about the activities of certain individuals he believes to be undercover police officers.'

'I'm afraid you'll have to be more specific, Mr Falco,' Jenny said.

'You may find this a little shocking, ma'am, but he suggests that two men – formerly Polish police officers, now members of our local constabulary – have been operating in the city undercover for some years, posing as drug dealers and pimps. He suggests they may have "gone native". In fact, he claims they have disappeared and killed people.'

'Including Mr Burden?'

'Yes.' Falco fidgeted with his gold cufflinks. 'And Mr Rozek'.

Jenny realized now that Falco was frightened. Sitting close to him in the confined space, she felt some of his apprehension transferring to her.

'I'm prepared to hear his evidence, but I can't prevent him from being arrested if there's a warrant.'

Falco rubbed the heels of his palms together as he tried to think of a way through. 'Ma'am, may I assume that if he were to give evidence in court, you would agree to him doing so *in camera*? – on the basis that you would have to protect the identities of any undercover officers he might name.'

'In those circumstances, I probably would.'

'Then would it make any difference if his testimony were also to be given via a video link?'

'This is a man knowingly evading arrest, and you want me to hear his evidence in an empty courtroom and over a video link, without his disclosing his whereabouts? That's an interesting proposition, Mr Falco. Exactly how much weight do you think any evidence he gives under those conditions might carry?'

'You have to consider the interests of justice, ma'am. Would they be better served by *not* hearing him?'

'If those were the terms, yes.'

Falco fell into a troubled silence, as if he were wrestling with a dilemma.

'Ma'am, what if I were to tell you that this witness is called Tomasz Zaleski, and that he works at Fairmeadows Farm? I believe that, by unhappy coincidence, he was a colleague of one Edward Morgan.'

Jenny felt a crawling sensation along her spine as she recalled the unassuming young man she had spoken to at the end of her visit to the rendering plant.

'As you may surmise, there are several reasons why Mr Zaleski is inclined to keep his head down at present,' Falco said.

Jenny weighed her options. Falco's terms were out of the question. Evidence could only be given via a video link if there were a good reason for a witness not attending court in person. Seeking to avoid arrest on a lawful warrant didn't qualify.

However, there was also a danger that refusing to hear what might prove to be definitive evidence would amount to a denial of justice.

'Would you step outside for a moment, Mr Falco, I need to consider.'

Falco did as she asked.

Ten minutes later Jenny had arrived at a decision that, at a push, she felt able to square with the law and her ethics, and made phone calls to settle arrangements. She called Falco back in and, without inviting him to sit, told him that she would be reconvening her inquest at 5 p.m. that afternoon in a first-floor conference room at Chandos House, Queen Square. The session was to be held *in camera*. If Mr Zaleski wanted to give evidence, this was his one and only opportunity. Mr Anthony Burden was, of course, welcome to attend.

'And if Zaleski won't take the risk?' Falco said.

'If there's any truth in what you've told me, the more people who hear his story, the safer he'll be.'

Falco nodded. 'I'll see what I can do.'

Unsettled by her encounter with Falco, Jenny adjourned proceedings until the following morning and headed out of the building via the judges' entrance. Once again, everything she had assumed about events at Blackstone Ley had been called into question, leaving her feeling even more uncertain and alone. She wanted to talk to Ryan, to ask him if he thought there was any truth in what Falco had told her, and whether she was right to be scared; was it even safe to meet

Zaleski? But she knew that calling Ryan was out of the question, at least until the afternoon was over. He was a police officer, after all, and given what she had just heard, she could trust him only up to a point.

As she went out into the chill wind, a figure stepped out from the wall to the side of the doorway and accosted her. Jenny spun round in alarm, a shot of adrenalin coursing into her veins.

'It's me, Mrs Cooper.' Alison pulled down the hood of her anorak and revealed herself. 'Sorry. I didn't mean to scare you.'

Jenny caught her breath. Her heart was pounding out of control.

'I hope I didn't make you uncomfortable, turning up in court – I just needed to keep an eye on things. To see what might turn up. I didn't post those messages on the internet, Mrs Cooper,' Alison said with total conviction. 'I may be brain-damaged, but I've still got most of my marbles. I don't have any enemies I can think of, and my ex has got himself a new girlfriend, so I can only think that someone's trying to isolate you. Weaken your resources. Make you lose confidence.' She looked at Jenny with concern. 'I know you can't tell me what Mr Falco said, but I can see it's shocked you.'

'I'm OK,' Jenny lied. 'And I really don't think you should be worrying about this right now.'

'I'm going through the CCTV footage for you – cutting together pictures of everyone who bought diesel in a jerrycan from each of those four stations. Call it clerical assistance.'

'I'm grateful. But Alison, you know I can't—'

'Remember that bent solicitor named McAvoy, who crossed your path a few years ago?'

The name brought Jenny up short. McAvoy had swept through her life like an intoxicating demon. 'What about him?'

'Back when I was in CID, a snout once told me he followed a three-stage strategy for seeing off people who were becoming a problem for his clients: I-I-D: isolate, intimidate, and if that doesn't work, destroy.'

Jenny's unease grew deeper.

'So don't forget, Mrs Cooper, you're not alone. Whoever is responsible for this isn't even at stage one.'

Alison pulled up her hood and trudged off determinedly through the snow.

# TWENTY-SEVEN

THE CONFERENCE ROOM IN Chandos House was on the second floor of the elegant early Victorian building, with a view across the formal gardens that occupied the centre of the square. The decor was spare and elegant, the room dominated by a vast mahogany table that smelt of beeswax polish. Jenny had seated herself facing the door with her back to the fireplace, and positioned the stenographer at the far end, where she sat filing her nails while they waited. Proceedings in court had been tape recorded, but Jenny had wanted the stenographer present to emphasize the formality of the occasion. She needed both Falco and his witness to understand that the hired space was no less a courtroom than the one she had presided over that morning.

Jenny and the stenographer sat in silence as the antique carriage clock on the mantel ticked towards five o'clock and quietly chimed the hour. There had been no communication from Falco since their earlier meeting. After another ten minutes the stenographer gave her an expectant look. Jenny had promised her the job would last an hour at most. She was the right age to have a child at school. She would probably have made arrangements that would be difficult for her to alter.

'We'll give him another five minutes,' Jenny said, secretly hoping that she would soon be on the way home, with the danger having passed.

The clock sounded a single chime on the quarter hour. The stenographer was readying to pack away when they heard voices on the stairwell and a cautious knock at the door.

Jenny exhaled. 'Come in.'

Falco entered first. He was wearing a fedora hat and a scarf that obscured most of his face. Tomasz Zaleski followed, dressed in a tatty green parka and a baseball cap.

'Good afternoon, gentlemen. I'd almost given up on you.'

Falco took off his coat and reminded Tomasz to remove his cap. 'My apologies, ma'am. There were complications.'

He didn't elaborate, and, aware that, as requested, the stenographer had already started to record their words verbatim, Jenny didn't ask him to.

'Are we expecting Mr Burden?' Jenny inquired.

'Family commitments,' Falco said. 'I promised him a full report.'

The men settled into chairs opposite Jenny. Tomasz (she thought of him by his Christian name) was pale and unshaven with the hunted look of a man on the run, but the soft blue eyes Jenny remembered from their meeting at Fairmeadows retained their trusting, childlike quality. She felt instinctively sorry for him. He didn't look tough enough to be caught up with the world of Jacob Rozek and organized crime.

Jenny formally opened the proceedings by informing Tomasz that he was in the Severn Vale District Coroner's Court and that she had agreed to Mr Falco's suggestion that she hear any evidence he may have of relevance to the death of Daniel Burden. At Falco's prompting, Tomasz replied that he understood. Jenny directed him to a card sitting alongside a Bible on the table in front of him. Very solemnly, Tomasz took the Bible in his right hand and read the words of the oath like he meant it.

'Seeing as we have no written statement, I'm happy to let you begin, Mr Falco,' Jenny said.

Falco poured glasses of mineral water for both him and his witness as he took him through the formalities of confirming his name, age and address. Jenny noticed a faint tremor in Falco's hand.

'And your principal occupation, Mr Zaleski?' he said.

'I'm a processing operative at Fairmeadows Farm,' Tomasz answered, stumbling a little over the long words.

'And you have had another job alongside it?'

'Yes. I used to work sometimes for Mr Rozek. Jacob Rozek.'

'In what capacity?'

Tomasz looked at him, not understanding the question.

'What work did you do for Mr Rozek?'

'Painting. Painting and decorating.'

'Where?'

'His properties. He has houses all over the city. Buy, sell, you know. Each one, a team of guys come and turn it into flats. Carpenter, plasterer, plumber, then me.'

'Is that the only work you did for him?'

'Yes.' Tomasz said the word insistently, as if he had been accused of lying.

'And what did Mr Rozek do with these properties once you had worked on them.'

'He rented them.'

'To whom?'

'Sometimes to different people, sometimes to two guys who took the whole building. And then they rent the flats to their own people.'

Falco shot Jenny a glance, reading her thoughts. 'If I could continue for a moment, ma'am?'

She nodded.

'Who were these men?'

Tomasz made his hands into a single fist on the table and stared at it, the muscles of his arms tensing.

'Are you able to tell us their names, Mr Zaleski?' Falco nudged.

'Aron Janick and Danek Mazur,' Tomasz said.

They paused for a moment while Falco spelled the names out for the stenographer. Tomasz continued to stare at his hands. Jenny sensed he'd crossed a Rubicon and knew there was no way back.

'Where were these men from?' Falco asked.

'Krakow. They have the accent,' Tomasz said. 'A lot of people from Krakow come to Bristol. They don't speak English. They trust guys like this who get them somewhere to live.'

'Did you meet them?'

He shrugged. 'A few times.'

'What is the nature of their business, Mr Zaleski?'

'They put girls in the flats. Prostitutes. They're pimps. They sell drugs.'

'You know that for a fact?'

'Yes. Sometimes I did a day's work for them, too. Fix up a flat when a girl moves out.'

'Describe these men for me – their characters.'

'They can be nice, you know, give you cigarettes, talk about home. Then the next minute they're crazy – shouting at girls, hitting them. Like animals. Everyone's afraid of them, even Mr Rozek.'

'Tell the coroner what you told me about Jacob Rozek, Mr Zaleski.'

Tomasz stalled. He shook his head. Falco allowed him a moment, but still he didn't speak.

'Does any of this have any bearing on Mr Burden?' Jenny asked.

'In a moment, ma'am – if Mr Zaleski feels able.'

Tomasz blew out and shook his head like a man afraid to take a dangerous leap.

'Come on,' Falco urged in a whisper.

The stenographer glanced Jenny's way. Jenny nodded at her to note every word and aside.

'OK,' Tomasz began. 'It was last year, a few months ago. I was in a house in Redland. I heard them beat up a girl who owed them money. They broke her arm. I took her to the hospital after they'd gone. She was frightened. She told me that Janick said to her next time she didn't pay they would get rid of her at the "farm", like they had done to a guy who owed them money – Lech Weil. They told her they had friends there who'd grind her up, turn her into sausage meat.'

'Did the name Lech Weil mean anything to you?'

Tomasz nodded. 'He was Mr Rozek's cousin. He had a taxi company. He went missing last July.'

'What did you do with this information?'

'I called Mr Rozek. He wouldn't speak on the phone. He asked me to come to his office. I went the next day, told him everything about Janick and Mazur.' Tomasz paused and cast Jenny a nervous glance.

'Carry on, Mr Zaleski.'

'He told me there was nothing he could do. He said these guys were working for the police and no one could touch them. He told me his cousin refused to give them money and they killed him. He knew it was them who killed Lech. He told me just stay out of their way, they're dangerous. I'd never seen him look scared, but that night he was. Real scared.'

'Do you know why he was scared?'

'Afterwards, I heard some of the other guys talking when we were working in one of Mr Rozek's properties. They said he was having problems with these two – they were hurting his business. Some guys had heard the story they were police, but most just thought they were gangsters.'

'How does this connect with Mr Burden?' Jenny asked.

'A few days later – it was a Friday night – Mr Rozek called me and asked would I pick something up for him. I had to go to his office first and collect a package, what do you call it? – a Jiffy bag. He gave me an address in Henleaze: 15 Janus Avenue. He told me to speak to Daniel – he had something for me to bring back. I went to the flat. A short guy came to the door. He took the package, gave me an envelope for Mr Rozek. That was it.'

'What size was this envelope?' Falco asked.

'Small,' Tomasz said, and placed his forefingers six inches apart on the table.

'Passport size?'

'Yes. Could be.'

'Was anyone watching you?'

Tomasz shrugged. 'I don't know. I wasn't looking.'

'Do you remember the date this happened?'

'November 29th.'

'Did you see Mr Rozek again?' Falco asked.

'No. I never did.' Tomasz shook his head. 'His wife called me on December the 20th and said the police found his car empty. She asked if I had heard anything. I told her about the night he was scared. That's all. I never told her about the package. That was his business.'

Falco sat back in his chair. 'That's it, ma'am, although there is one piece of documentary evidence I would like to offer the court, if that's appropriate.'

'I'll decide on relevance, Mr Falco.'

He reached into the slim leather document case he had brought with him and took out a single sheet which he offered across the desk. It was a printout of a Ryanair e-ticket. It was in the name of Mr Lech Weil and was for a one-way flight from Bristol International to Warsaw at 15.35 on 19 December: the day Rozek had vanished.

'I finally persuaded the airline to release their records. It took a little persuasion,' Falco said with ironic understatement.

'Let me put your case together, Mr Falco: you are suggesting to me that Mr Rozek paid Mr Burden for a false passport using the identity of his dead cousin, Mr Lech Weil. That he bought a ticket for Warsaw in Weil's name, but was intercepted and murdered en route, possibly by Janick and Mazur, who were criminals, or police officers *acting criminally*, who then disposed of his body with the help of contacts they had at Fairmeadows Farm.'

'That's about the length of it, ma'am. I am as appalled as I'm sure you are.'

'Are you suggesting a motive?'

'They occupy three of Mr Rozek's properties. They haven't paid rent since December the 1st.'

'And their connection with Burden? I'm not sure I follow.'

'Say Mr Rozek didn't die in his car, but was shot and merely injured. Perhaps before he died they found his passport and asked him how he came by it.'

Jenny was struggling to picture the scene in the North Somerset village: a dying, blood-soaked man being interrogated at gunpoint by rogue undercover detectives. But then when she put it alongside what had happened at Blackstone Ley, it no longer seemed so incredible. Anything *could* happen. Anywhere.

'Do you have any evidence – as opposed to rumour – that these two are officers?'

'I did think of phoning the Chief Constable, ma'am, but on reflection I decided he might be more inclined to talk to Her Majesty's Coroner.' He gave a grim smile.

The clock on the mantel chimed six. 'Thank you, Mr Falco. We'll resume tomorrow morning.' Jenny turned to the stenographer. 'That'll be all. If you would be kind enough to email me the transcript before you go.'

As the stenographer gratefully packed her things into a

case, Jenny gave Falco a look inviting him to wait for her to leave. Moments later, the transcript appeared attached to an email on Jenny's phone and the stenographer was hurrying on her way.

Jenny leaned forward and addressed Tomasz. 'This is off the record now, Mr Zaleski, and it's nothing to do with this case. I'm talking about Ed Morgan. Are you telling me that he could have been connected with the disposal of human remains at Fairmeadows Farm?'

Tomasz met her eye. 'I told you already, Ed was a nice guy. He wouldn't do that, not without a gun in his face. But he could have seen something.' Jenny's phone vibrated once on the desk, alerting her to a text message. She glanced sideways at the screen. It read: *Advise excuse yourself now. Simon.*

Jenny slipped the phone into her pocket. 'I'm sorry. I need to make a personal call. Could you perhaps think about that a little more deeply, Mr Zaleski. Dates, names – anything I should be following up. Do excuse me a moment.'

Ignoring Falco's uncertain glance, Jenny stepped around the table and exited through the door. Out on the landing, she heard voices travelling up the four flights of stairs from the lobby. One of them belonged to the stenographer; the other voices were male and seemed to be questioning her. A sign pointed upstairs to the Ladies'. She followed it and arrived on the upper landing as several sets of footsteps travelled quickly up from the ground floor. She pressed herself against the wall, out of sight from the entrance to the conference room, as several detectives bundled inside. She heard Falco's voice raised in outraged protest as he and Tomasz were informed that they were under arrest. Falco continued to threaten that he would sue them all for false arrest as they were taken downstairs. There wasn't a word from Tomasz, who went as meekly as a lamb.

\*

The black government Jaguar was idling on the opposite side of the darkened street outside the building. The tinted rear window lowered as Jenny stepped outside, revealing Simon Moreton's face.

He smiled as if in congratulation. 'Well done, Jenny,' he called across the road, 'you took the hint for once. Spot of early dinner? With all your excitement, I managed to miss lunch.'

The driver climbed out of the front and opened the back door facing the pavement. He stood patiently, waiting for her to cross over and climb in. It was no use resisting. Moreton hadn't travelled from London only to leave without making his point. He would have his pound of flesh one way or another.

She slid onto the warm leather seat and in a petulant act of defiance refused to fasten her seatbelt.

'At your own risk,' Moreton said. He switched off the tablet computer on which he had been reading the transcript of Zaleski's evidence. The stenographer must have emailed it to him from the lobby. 'I thought The Avon Gorge Hotel. It seems like a night for comfort food.'

He patted her wrist and the car moved silently away.

The hotel was a large, stucco building on Sion Hill, close to the edge of the gorge. The restaurant, quiet this early in the evening, looked over to the Clifton Suspension Bridge. Lit up against a moonless night, it seemed to hover in black space. Lulled by the first sips of wine from the single glass she would allow herself, Jenny gazed past Simon Moreton as he inspected the menu, and watched the disembodied headlights pass to and fro across the gorge. Moreton was looking even fitter and slimmer than the last time Jenny had seen him some six months before. He had to be fifty-five, but his dark hair showed only the faintest traces of grey and there was no sign of a bulge above his belt.

'Beef Wellington with roast potatoes,' Moreton exclaimed with satisfaction. 'Just the thing. Can I tempt you to join me, or would you prefer "traditional fish pie"?'

'That'll do.'

'Excellent.' He raised his glass, 'To all that's solid and dependable,' and clinked it against Jenny's. He took a large mouthful of rich Bordeaux and rolled it around his tongue. 'My God, that's good.' He swallowed and smiled at her across the table, which was just large enough not to be awkwardly intimate. 'How could life be any sweeter?' He beamed at her, and summoned the waiter to take their order.

When they were alone again, Moreton leant forward a little, crossing the invisible threshold between them. 'The Chief doesn't know about this, all right? And I'm more than happy for it to stay that way.'

'I'm not sure what I've done wrong,' Jenny said. 'I weighed what the interests of justice required and decided I needed to hear Zaleski's evidence. I'm glad I did. It's shocking. And I certainly made no attempt to help him evade arrest.'

Moreton gave a sympathetic nod of the kind a psychiatrist might give to a delusional patient.

'What?' Jenny demanded.

'Aren't you interested to know how I came to be here? It seems only fair I should tell you.'

'I imagine DI Ballantyne has something to do with it.'

'He played his part, but I confess Mr Falco has been of interest to the police more than usual in the weeks since his client Mr Rozek's death.'

'He's been under surveillance? Why? What's he meant to have done?'

'Rozek was a notorious criminal, Jenny. You were so

locked on to the scent that you didn't step back and do your research. He and his Polish friends have been slaughtering each other for the last eighteen months. It's what happens when criminal gangs have saturated the local market – they contest the turf.'

'Their rivalries don't interest me. All I'm concerned with—'

'Hold on,' Moreton interrupted, 'hear me out. What you probably don't know is that at the time of his death Rozek was under pressure. He'd been smart enough to keep at arm's length from the prostitution and people-trafficking, so they were looking at tax fraud. All they needed was to convict him of one offence and, hey presto, all his ill-gotten gains would have been up for grabs as proceeds of crime. He would have found himself in court, having to prove that every pound of his fortune was acquired legitimately. Being dead doesn't get him off the hook, it's just passed the problem to his wife. Mr Falco is fighting tooth and nail to save their swag, Jenny. The Rozeks are his livelihood. He's a desperate man.'

'What are you alleging – that Falco paid Zaleski to give false evidence this afternoon?'

'Well done! We'll make a coroner of you yet. From what the police tell me, Zaleski did do the odd job for Mr Rozek, but Janick and Mazur aren't undercover officers any more than you or I. It's a fantasy. A story made up by Falco to muddy the waters and cause terminal embarrassment to the agencies trying to steal his clients' assets – *first you kill him, then you rob him!* What a headline he could have made from that! He thought he could scare the police off.'

'How do I know any of this is true?'

'You have my word,' Moreton said, wounded by her insinuation. 'Scout's honour.'

'I wish that were enough.'

'Jenny, step back for a moment and listen. You may be interested to know that a Mr Lech Weil was indeed "disappeared" last year. And I am reliably informed that Mr Burden did indeed issue a replacement passport in his name last December. In fact, there's every reason to believe Mr Falco introduced Rozek to Burden – he's a well-connected man. And unlike you, he knows how to think like a criminal, and with the alacrity of an opportunist. He seized on Burden's suicide and set about spinning you a tale. You were meant to deliver a verdict to strengthen his arm – *Coroner rules man murdered by undercover cops!* You might almost call him an artist – the way he reeled you in with the Ed Morgan connection was really quite a master stroke. And the theatre!'

'What do you mean?'

'There was no warrant for Zaleski. It was a fiction.' Moreton fetched out his phone. 'I have an email from the Chief Constable, no less. Would you like to see it?'

'No, thank you. Then why was he arrested?'

'For conspiring to pervert the course of justice, obviously. Along with Falco. He won't be at court tomorrow.'

Moreton sat triumphantly back in his chair. Jenny stared self-consciously into her glass, unable to share in his delight.

'Word reached me of your domestic incident,' Moreton said. 'I think this ought to allay your anxiety on that front, too. Another of Zaleski's odd jobs, I suspect.' He took an appreciative sip of wine. 'I'm sorry, Jenny, I feel like I'm telling my daughter there's no such thing as Santa Claus. A trusting nature is an attractive quality, but you have to learn – in our business, people are seldom what they seem.'

'Your version is as good as Zaleski's,' Jenny said, 'and you have a motive.'

Moreton gave an amused smile. 'Do tell.'

'Tidy it all up with as little mess as possible. Prevent a

public outcry at murdered criminals entering the food chain.'

'I mean this in the nicest possible way, but wherever there's a hint of the unexplained, people instinctively suspect witchcraft. It takes a cool and rational mind to stick to brutal logic.'

'I'm hysterical and irrational, am I? I thought I was doing rather well.'

'You are a little. But fortunately you've also had flashes of brilliance. That's what I've always admired about you.'

He smiled with his eyes: the look that always came when he was hoping for her to return the compliment and let him feel a frisson between them.

She glanced away, then turned back a little and met his gaze for a moment. She allowed him just a hint of promise: enough to feed his ego and let him travel back to London imagining the night they might have had if he had allowed himself to slip the shackles of marriage and respectability. It was a harmless enough dance, and Jenny indulged it because no matter how infuriating he managed to be, she always felt rather sorry for him. He'd lived life by proxy, all his thrills vicarious and his fantasies unfulfilled. He craved excitement, but could only glimpse it through her.

'Shall we draw a line, Jenny? Mark this one down to experience and enjoy the evening.'

'Simon, what exactly are you asking me to do?'

'Stop ghost-hunting. There are no phantoms in these shadows. Trust me for once, and move on.' He raised his glass: 'To sunnier times.'

'To sunnier times,' Jenny echoed without conviction.

They drank their toast and Jenny let Moreton briefly brush his ankle against hers.

# TWENTY-EIGHT

Jenny entered the court and took her seat at a minute past ten. It was an intimate gathering consisting of the usher, Anthony Burden, DI Ballantyne and Clara Lawson, the young lawyer keeping a watching brief for the Home Office. Ballantyne wore a look of quiet satisfaction, but Anthony Burden appeared gravely troubled in a way he hadn't the previous day. Jenny wished there was more she could have done for him, but every avenue had been choked off.

Earlier that morning she had received two emails. The first confirmed that both Louis Falco and Tomasz Zaleski had been charged with conspiracy to pervert the course of justice, and that in due course Jenny would be contacted as a witness. The second was from Daniel Burden's superior, Gordon Kenyon, stating that Burden had indeed approved a passport in the name of Lech Weil, but that all the supporting documents were in order. The discrepancies between the photograph of Mr Weil on his previous passport and on the photograph submitted had been judged 'within acceptable tolerances'. That being so, no evidence existed that Burden had been criminally involved with Rozek.

Jenny didn't trust Kenyon's assurance, and she found it hard to believe that Burden hadn't been abusing his position to make money on the side, but all she had was circumstantial evidence that proved nothing.

Jenny addressed Anthony Burden: 'Mr Burden, before I deliver my findings is there anything you would like to say?'

He shook his head in a way which told Jenny he'd had enough of looking into the murky corners of his brother's life.

'Very well. I have considered the evidence we heard yesterday and have arrived at the conclusion that there is insufficient evidence available to precisely determine the cause of and circumstances of Daniel Burden's death. With some reluctance, I am therefore obliged to return an open verdict.'

She offered Anthony Burden a look of sympathy, but all she read on his face was relief that the ordeal was over. As soon as she rose from her chair, he turned and headed out of the courtroom. DI Ballantyne cast him a philosophical glance: 'You wouldn't want to know if I told you,' it seemed to say. And Jenny thought he would probably be right.

It was a long shot, but Jenny needed to try, if only to convince herself that she had exhausted every avenue. Loose ends left her feeling listless and dissatisfied, and worse – as if she had failed in her job.

She called him from her office as soon as she arrived back from court. Ryan answered his phone against the sound of fast-moving traffic.

'Jenny, hi.' He sounded awkward.

'Not a good moment?'

'I'm at Gordano service station. Someone thought they spotted a white male with Robbie Morgan. It's bullshit, but it doesn't save us from having to trawl through hours of CCTV footage.'

'Any chance we could meet later? I'd like to sound you out over a couple of things.'

He lowered his voice. 'I'm here with colleagues. Then I've

a meeting with the Chief back at Gloucester. I'm tied up till mid-afternoon.'

Jenny looked at the files stacking up on her desk. There were ten or more awaiting her urgent attention, but she knew she wouldn't be able to concentrate on any of them until she had shared her fears with Ryan.

'What if I were to come over, meet you in Gloucester?'

'Hold on a moment.' Jenny heard him press his hand over the phone, while one of the others in his team talked about uploading camera footage to a laptop. 'Sorry about that,' Ryan said after a lengthy exchange. She could hear that he was walking away from his colleagues now. 'Do you know a place called Vinings at Gloucester docks? I can be there at four.'

'I'll find it.'

'I heard about Falco,' Ryan said. 'I can't say I was surprised.'

'I'm not sure I know what to believe.'

'You can tell me all about it later,' Ryan said. He paused. 'Hey, it'll all be fine. I promise.'

Jenny wished she could believe him.

She rang off and stared across the empty room at the closed door, feeling shocked at herself. Her exchange with Ryan had been so casual, so natural, so intimate. How had that happened? She placed a hand instinctively over her belly, as if to remind herself there was another life in there, one that had nothing to do with him. Was she really so frightened of being alone that she couldn't even go days without the reassurance of there being a man somewhere close by she could lean on? She was forced to accept there was more than a grain of truth in that, and being pregnant only made it worse. Whatever was happening with her hormones was making her feel permanently exposed and unnaturally sensitive. These were just the sort of feminine weaknesses she had spent her entire career privately despising in other women – the kind who would sob in the Ladies' after a difficult meeting – but here she was, feeling tearful and lonely and wishing someone could make it all go away.

*Pull out of it, Jenny. What are you thinking?* She tried, but it was no good. Her erratic emotions were winning. She brushed away angry tears and went to fetch some coffee.

Jenny arrived outside the restaurant at Gloucester docks to find it closed. A handwritten sign in the window said it wouldn't open again until the evening. The slender trade on a freezing January afternoon clearly wasn't worth the candle. Jenny huddled into the doorway, sheltering from the cutting wind, and tried to stay warm by stamping her feet. Dim lights flickered in the windows of several barges tethered in what until a fortnight ago would have been the still waters of the dock. Now it was an open expanse of snow-covered ice inches thick, and the inhabitants of the boats were marooned. The unrelenting cold was beginning to feel like a curse that would never lift.

It was nearly a quarter past before Ryan jogged towards her along the narrow path cleared in the snow, a briefcase under his arm and breathing clouds of steam.

'Sorry, Jenny – the meeting ran on.' He caught his breath and looked at the unlit windows of the restaurant. 'They're closed? What's wrong with them?'

'Looks like the whole place is,' Jenny said. 'I saw a pub around the corner that didn't look too rough.'

'It is. Trust me.' He scanned up and down the docks but there was little sign of life. 'My flat's just across there. It's not pretty, but it's warm.' He pointed across to the far side of the docks at a modern apartment building.

'Fine. Let's go.' She was desperate to get inside and out of the cold.

'I heard your friend Mr Falco got bail this afternoon,' Ryan said, as they set off across the cobbles, 'but the Polish guy's still in custody. Judge didn't trust him not to disappear.'

'Is that canteen gossip or did you make a call?'

'Jack Ballantyne's an old friend. I did a favour for him once.'

'Sounds mysterious.'

Ryan smiled. 'Got to have a little mystery in this job. There's not much glamour in it, that's for sure.'

They arrived at the brightly lit entrance to an apartment building on the far side of the frozen dock. Ryan punched in an access code and the door clicked open. Stepping through into a stark white hallway that still smelt of paint and fresh plaster, Jenny abandoned any fantasies she had harboured about leaving her home in the country. Even the potted palm was plastic. The building had all the charm of a shopping mall. They travelled up four floors in a shiny, slow-moving lift that felt as if it wasn't moving at all. In the confined space, Jenny became acutely aware of the scent of Ryan's clothes, his hair, his skin; being pregnant was sharpening her sense of smell to an almost painful degree. Her senses, like her emotions, felt overloaded.

'Are you claustrophobic?' Ryan said as they crept upwards.

'Horribly.'

'Me, too. Any second now.'

They came to a gentle halt. The doors opened, bringing more smells: new carpet and varnished skirting boards. Jenny followed Ryan along the passage to a door at the end of the corridor. He unlocked it and stepped inside. The lights came on without him having to flick a switch, revealing a spacious studio room with floor-to-ceiling French doors that opened onto a balcony overlooking the docks. It was minimalist, but pleasant: two large tan sofas and a TV at one end, and a fitted kitchen in light-coloured wood at the other. An open staircase led up to a mezzanine, shielded from view by panels of smoked glass, that served as a bedroom.

Ryan shrugged off his coat and took Jenny's to hang in the closet behind the door. 'More of a hotel room than a home, but it does me. Can I get you something to drink?'

'Tea, if you've got it.'

'You're in luck.'

Jenny went to look at the view over the city while Ryan fetched their drinks. The illuminated spire of Gloucester Cathedral rose over the rooftops. In the far distance, traffic wound up the hill to the Birdlip Ridge and the Cotswolds beyond. The street-level Gloucester she knew was one of scuffed and neglected Victorian buildings interspersed with 1960s concrete; rustic accents alongside Punjabi, Latvian and Jamaican patois; a once-charming place that was losing the war against becoming another down-at-heel provincial city. But viewed from this vantage point it came close to being beautiful, the streets melding together into something that made coherent sense.

'I spend hours doing that,' Ryan said. 'I call it my eagle's nest. Milk?'

'Just a drop.'

He came alongside and handed her a cup.

'How did you get on at the service station?' Jenny asked.

'Didn't amount to anything,' Ryan said dismissively. 'A small blond boy with a man in the corner of the car park – could have been anyone. Picked something up on one of the cameras, but Kelly was adamant it wasn't her boy.'

'Mind if I have a look?'

'If you like.' From his briefcase Ryan pulled a laptop, which he proceeded to set up on the coffee table between the two sofas. 'Are you going to tell me what's on your mind?'

'Falco's story was all about two undercover detectives. He said they were originally from Poland, drafted in to penetrate the Polish criminal gangs in Bristol. Does that sound far-fetched to you?'

'I remember the Met tried something similar with the Jamaican Yardies back in the nineties. As I recall, it all went swimmingly, until they forgot whose side they were on and started to kill people.'

'Do you think it could have happened again, or was it just where Falco got the idea?'

'I've not heard anything along those lines.'

'And if you had?' Jenny challenged.

'Good question. Would I tell you?' He gave her a playfully enigmatic look. 'I shouldn't, but I probably would. Off the record, of course.'

'Can these sorts of operations remain entirely confidential, even within the police?'

'All sorts of things remain confidential inside the police. Detectives aren't even allowed their own informers any more – they're all handled by the source unit.'

'And those kind of secrets really hold?'

'We're detectives. We like secrets. They make us feel powerful.'

'I can't tell if you're joking.'

'Tell you what – give me these guys' names and I'll check them out for you.'

'How?'

Ryan smiled. 'You'll have to trust me.'

Jenny sighed. His flippancy wasn't helping. 'Tomasz Zaleski said he thought the bodies of the criminals who've disappeared might have ended up at Fairmeadows Farm. He was hinting that Ed Morgan had witnessed something, or even got involved. Look, I'll admit it – what he said frightened me. What if it's true? What if Ed was murdered by these people and they were the ones who dumped a pig's head outside my house?' Her voice rose half an octave. 'What then? Are they going to stop there? How crazy are they? And if any of this is true, why the hell would the police protect them?'

'They wouldn't,' Ryan replied calmly. 'If these two have anything to do with CID, they won't be walking the streets any longer than it takes to pick them up.' He started tapping on the computer as he logged on to the police intranet. 'What are their names?'

'Aron Janick and Danek Mazur.' She spelled them out letter by letter as he typed.

Ryan waited a moment for results to scroll up. He shook his head. 'No sign of them on our database, but that's not saying a lot. I'll dig a bit deeper in the morning for you. But if you want my opinion, undercover detectives, even stupid ones, would have more nous than to intimidate a coroner. Think about it, Jenny – you're undercover, you've gone rogue, you've killed a man. You're going to make damn sure someone else takes the blame and you keep a low profile. You do nothing to draw attention to yourself.'

'You're assuming rationality,' Jenny said.

'Even psychopaths have a certain amount.'

Jenny was still far from convinced.

Ryan remained patient. 'It's not a convincing story, Jenny. It sounds like something a lawyer would make up. They're so proud of their own supposed intelligence, they never credit criminals with any. It takes real brains to make a living breaking the law, believe me.'

Jenny sat on the corner of the sofa, deep feelings of unease refusing to leave her.

'You let yourself get frightened, Jenny. I'm not surprised.'

'With good reason. My officer's been suspended. There were inappropriate messages on her Facebook account. She claims it was hacked.'

'Now you're looking for evidence to fuel your irrational fears. You're letting yourself get trapped inside it – you've got to step back.'

Jenny looked at him, hardly noticing that he had his hand on her arm.

'I spent yesterday evening being told to be rational. I'm trying, but my problem is there is a rational explanation that sits with Falco's story: Janick and Mazur did exactly what he said; the police figured that out, and they're working like crazy to cover their tracks.'

'And that would make me part of it. I don't enjoy seeing you like this. To be honest, it's painful.' He squeezed her arm, then took his hand away. 'Do you want to see this footage?'

Jenny nodded and moved a little closer to him so that she could see the screen.

Ryan opened a video file. The picture was in colour but low resolution. The field of view covered an area of car park away from the service-station building, close to an area with picnic tables that in normal weather would have been grass.

'This is it now.' He pointed to a vehicle that partially entered the frame and pulled into a space at the lower-left corner of the screen. A man dressed in a black ski jacket and baseball cap climbed out of the driver's door and took a small child dressed in a red coat from the back seat. He carried the child to the gutter and leant over from the waist. It wasn't altogether clear what was happening, but Jenny assumed the child was having a pee. The man stood for a long moment, gazing away from the camera, then leant over again, before helping the child back into the car.

'Looks like the kid was taking a leak,' Ryan said.

Jenny kept watching as the car reversed out of the space. It was blue and only the rear half of it was visible, but something about it – or was it something about the man? – troubled her.

'I want to see it again,' Jenny said.

Ryan played the footage a second time. The man's face remained frustratingly obscured beneath the rim of his cap. Jenny briefly convinced herself that nevertheless there was something familiar about him – the motion of his arm as he wiped the back of his hand across his mouth while he waited for the boy, perhaps – but just as quickly she told herself she was imagining things. Seeing ghosts again.

'It's a phenomenon,' Ryan said. 'People will be sighting him up and down the country for the next six months, then they'll forget about it. If it was female child, it would last twelve months, or so the experts tell me.'

He brought down the lid of his laptop and slowly pressed it shut. 'So, is that what you needed – reassurance that Polish undercover cops aren't going to murder you in your bed?'

'Something like that.'

She was quiet for a moment, and aware of Ryan's body only inches from hers. Close enough that she could feel his heat. Both of them responded to the same instinct to let the silence continue; to see what might emerge from it. As five seconds moved towards ten, Jenny felt the tension rise; neither making a move, both staring straight ahead, both of them old and self-aware enough to be thinking of consequences. Ryan broke the spell and touched his leg against hers.

'Are you all right? You're quiet.'

Jenny looked at him and wondered if she had imagined the last half-minute. She thought he looked rather beautiful. Young and untravelled. Skin taut across his jaw; deep eyes that were soulful despite his efforts to remain businesslike. She silently chided herself for even entertaining the idea that they might – She stopped herself from even having the thought. The moment of temptation was over, and she had emerged unscathed. They had both done the right and decent thing. She was able to trust herself.

'I'm OK,' Jenny said purposefully. 'I'm going to try to take on board what you said. See if it helps.'

For a brief moment Ryan looked as if he were hovering on the edge of moving forward to kiss her, but he pulled back from the brink. 'I hope so.' He stood up from the sofa, placing himself outside touching distance. But as he stepped away Jenny felt the tug of an invisible force field that was pulling them back together.

'I ought to go,' Jenny said.

She moved towards the cupboard where Ryan had hung her coat, passing close by him.

'Hey,' he said softly.

She glanced back. He took a step towards her and folded his arms around her, embracing her in a hug.

'I'm here, all right?' he said. 'It may be unprofessional of me, but I care about you – I mean, I care about *you*.'

'That's kind,' Jenny said, not knowing how else to respond, and felt her hands come up from her sides and loop around his upper back. From there it felt only natural to rest her cheek against his shoulder as he stroked the back of her head. Jenny stepped back from their gentle embrace with a warm smile, letting him know that he had given her something precious.

Jenny fetched out her coat and pulled it on, telling herself it was time to change the mood. There was still an outside possibility she might have to call Ryan as a witness to her resumed inquest the following week, which was another very good reason she was glad to have held back.

'I'm starting again Monday morning,' Jenny said. 'You'll let me know if anything more turns up at your end.'

'Apart from my team that's still meant to be looking for Robbie, we're all done,' Ryan said. 'My boss is more than satisfied that Nicky Brooks took her own life, so that's another file you'll find on your desk tomorrow morning.'

She had tried not to think about Nicky. Four days on from her death, Jenny was feeling the tragedy of it more acutely, not less, as if she were somehow bound up with her. 'What *do* you think Ed did with Robbie?' Jenny asked. 'He didn't have a lot of time that evening. He couldn't have taken him far.'

'He planned it,' Ryan said. 'He'd have had something worked out.'

A thought jumped into Jenny's mind for the first time, and in the same instant, she realized that she had hardly thought about Robbie in isolation from his half-sisters. 'It's almost as if in making him disappear he was mirroring what happened to Susie Ashton – the idea that not knowing is worse than knowing.'

Ryan seemed taken with the thought. 'That has a certain logic. He'd seen it all play out for the last ten years.'

Jenny's mind raced on. 'What if Ed did have a hand in Susie's disappearance? And what if the rumours about a paedophile ring were right and he wasn't acting alone? Robbie might even still be alive.'

'You know what you've just done?' Ryan said. 'You've displaced all that anxiety you came with onto something else. You've got to check this tendency, Jenny. You'll drive yourself crazy.'

She felt a rush of energy as some mental blockage seemed to fall away. Half-formed thoughts and ideas that had sub-consciously disturbed her for days burst into fullness. 'No. Listen. Ed knew Layla and Mandy carried the baggage of the past. He knew Kelly would get over them somehow. But Robbie was theirs. He was pure; born into happiness. The *only* pure thing Kelly had ever had. So what's the worst he could do? It's not killing him. It's allowing him to live, but a life of horror; a life that'll make him inhuman and pervert everything he was to her.'

Ryan raised his eyebrows. 'You've got a dark imagination.'

'Or what if Ed knew what happened to Susie Ashton and was on the brink of revealing it as his own child approached that age? You should be trawling his history for all his associates, not just following leads from the public.'

'I'll pass on your thoughts. Meanwhile, I recommend a large drink when you get home.'

'Damn!'

'What now?'

'The car on the video you just showed me – could it have been a VW?'

'Possibly. Why?'

'A VW Polo belonging to Emma Grant was stolen from her house last November.'

'Now you really are losing it.'

'I'd like to check,' Jenny said. 'And maybe you could get me a copy of that footage and of any pictures of Robbie you might have.'

'He's dead, Jenny.'

'You can believe that if you like, but I've seen no evidence to prove it. And part of a coroner's job – the bit that most people forget about – is to try to keep more people from dying.'

He looked at her with concern. 'You seem a little manic.'

'It feels like waking up. Call me. I'll be waiting.' She gave Ryan another brief hug and let herself out.

*

329

Jenny allowed herself one drink, but it did little to calm her frenetic thoughts. It wasn't until late in the evening, after she had been working for several hours in her study, that her lids finally started to droop and she began to think about hauling herself upstairs to bed.

She had tidied her notes and was about to switch off the hall light and turn in when she heard heavy footsteps approach the front door. There were three evenly spaced knocks, a signal that it was the constable who had been posted outside in a squad car.

Jenny opened the door to the young man in uniform who looked suspiciously as if he had just been roused from a deep sleep.

'You've got a visitor, Mrs Cooper. A Mrs Trent. I told her to stay in her car.' He nodded towards a small hatchback parked in the lane.

Jenny glanced at her watch: it was a quarter to midnight. 'All right. Tell her to come in.'

As the policeman turned and went back down the path to fetch her, Jenny asked herself what on earth Alison could want that couldn't wait until the morning. But when she appeared it was clear that the time was the last thing on her mind. She marched up the path clutching a briefcase, filled with a sense of purpose.

'I've got something for you, Mrs Cooper. I thought you'd want to know immediately.'

Jenny didn't bother protesting. She took Alison through to the kitchen – the only room in the house that was still warm this late in the evening – and tried her best to remain patient.

Alison was bursting with excitement as she emptied papers and iPad onto the kitchen table. 'You know I'm actually grateful to Simon Moreton,' Alison said. 'I wouldn't have had time to do any of this if I'd been caught up with other things.'

Jenny surveyed the unpromising mess between them. 'Is this about your Facebook account?'

'Oh, far better than that, Mrs Cooper. Much more significant.' She could hardly contain herself. 'You remember Reverend Medway's evidence about the man watching Kelly Hart's house? I think I've found out who it is.'

'You have?' Jenny said sceptically.

'Daniel Burden.' Alison's eyes gleamed as she revelled in Jenny's surprise. 'I've been going through his bank statements and credit-card bills and wondering how the police could have failed to be interested.' From amongst the papers she extracted a printout. 'Last September he bought a camera online – state of the art, along with a tripod. Eight hundred and fifty-three pounds. I don't suppose you saw any sign of it at his flat?'

'No, but it doesn't mean it wasn't there. Is this important?'

'Not by itself. But when you look at this –' She brought out a credit-card bill and pointed to an item she had double underlined in red.

Jenny looked at the item. It was a single purchase of a little over £3,000. 'Idenco Ltd. What's that?'

'They make software. Very clever software that they sell to the Home Office and Border Agency. In fact, they sell it all around the world.' Alison was enjoying holding her in suspense. 'Can you guess what kind?'

'I have no idea.'

'Facial recognition!' She grabbed another document from amidst the heap and handed it across to Jenny. 'That's the spec. Not only can you use it to identify faces from your own database, it'll also trawl the entire internet and look for any photograph that resembles a picture of someone you've uploaded. Read what it says – if I were to ask it to look at a picture of you taken today, it claims it could pick you out from a 1980 school photograph.'

'How?'

'It measures the distance between various features and then it does some clever maths. Oh, and there's something about 3D in there too. It's not perfect, but governments wouldn't be buying it unless it was some use.'

Jenny skimmed through the explanation of the technical wizardry that allowed a computer program to compare every photograph on the internet with a template. Illustrated examples showed photographs of a range of current celebrities alongside recovered photographs of them going back to their late teens: entire pictorial histories assembled in minutes, listed alongside the web addresses of the sites from which each image was harvested.

'When did you find all this out?' Jenny asked, still trying to piece together what it could mean.

'Over the last few days,' Alison said. 'But then when I sat in court and heard that fellow Kenyon talking it really got me thinking.' Alison leaned forward over the table, invading her space. She looked a little unhinged: she hadn't brushed her hair for a long while and it had fallen away from her temple, revealing the flattened area of skin covering the titanium plate. Jenny reminded herself to treat what she said carefully. 'All that business about checking newly approved passports at random with software like this. Like I said, it isn't 100 per cent accurate, so if you can get a picture which is sufficiently close, or *manipulate* one so that it's close enough to pass the test, then you've something valuable. You see, most passport officials are more interested in what their computers say than the evidence of their own eyes. As long as you look roughly like your picture and the passport scans OK, you're home free.'

Jenny tried to follow her logic. 'So Burden could have used all this equipment and software to help him create passports for criminal customers?'

'You're not as dim as you look, Mrs Cooper.' Alison grinned. 'Oh, did I mention that you need a powerful computer to run this software? – you won't do it on your home PC. That's why he had something bespoke, and the separate hard drive to keep it tucked away out of sight. Come to think of it, he would most likely have kept it all in a cubbyhole somewhere. I wonder . . .'

Jenny scanned the growing pile of evidence in front of her. She had to give Alison credit, it was mounting up to proof that Burden really was in the forgery business. Just a pity she hadn't had it twenty-four hours earlier at court. Something still jarred with her. Then she realized what it was: the dates.

'He'd been banking money for more than two years, but he only assembled all this early last autumn—'

'See? I told you!' Alison smiled with a glee Jenny hadn't seen since before her accident. 'I wondered that, too. He spent over five thousand – that's a serious investment. So I checked all his statements again. I found something that got me excited.' She turned to a second item underlined on the credit-card statement. 'Twenty-five pounds, seventy-five pence, to Europcar. The only time you get charged such a small amount by a car-rental company is when they claw it back for fuel or a stain on the upholstery. There's no other payment to Europcar, so I guessed he might have settled in cash.' From the bottom of the assorted papers, Alison produced three sheets clipped together. 'You have a very old friend of mine from Bristol CID to thank for this,' Alison said. 'He came with me to their office. Daniel Burden hired the cheapest car on their list for three separate weekends last September and October. A Kia Picanto. I took a picture of it.' Alison produced her phone and called up an image of a small, unremarkable car in a sickly colour somewhere between green and very dark yellow. 'The colour's called Lemongrass. I'd call it bile.'

Jenny stared at the rental documents with a growing sense of disbelief. It was there in black and white: Daniel Burden had hired the vehicle in his own name and given his address at 15 Janus Avenue, Henleaze.

'I told you I wasn't a complete fruitcake,' Alison said. 'True, I sometimes forget to stop myself breaking wind in polite company, but I figure if you can train a toddler not to, I'm not beyond all hope.'

Jenny looked up from the papers that were trembling slightly in her hands and had the disconcerting feeling that she was looking at the world through distorting mirrors. Her mind was churning but not gaining any traction, like wheels spinning fruitlessly on ice. She had no idea what any of this *meant*.

'I can see you're confused. I was, until I drove there on my way over,' Alison said confidently. 'Reverend Medway said he parked just along the church on the verge. True, you could have seen Kelly's place from there, but if you were to turn around and look out of the back window – or point a camera that way – you're looking straight at the Ashtons' cottage. And that would be the clever thing to do, wouldn't it – park the opposite way to the direction you're looking in?'

'Why the Ashtons'?' Part of the answer arrived in Jenny's mind before Alison delivered it. 'The £100,000 reward.'

'There's a motive for a man who needs money. But he must have suspected Philip Ashton for some reason, and maybe had a photograph somewhere that he was trying to get a comparison with.'

Jenny was struggling to keep up.

'Look,' Alison said impatiently, 'I remember how attractive Clare Ashton was. You wouldn't see it now, but she was beautiful. Doll-like. *Innocent*, as if she couldn't see the bad in people. He always seemed so rigid and awkward next to her. He had this sort of pent-up-ness you knew was there even before it all happened. You know the kind.'

Jenny thought of her ex-husband, a man who was capable of losing his temper at a stray crumb on the kitchen counter. 'I know.'

'It came back to me – one of the theories in the canteen was that Philip Ashton was the culprit. All that tension came from his being a paedophile posing as a concerned school teacher. His alibi was always that he'd been at work when his daughter went missing. But what if he had come home early? He'd have known how to get to the house without being seen.'

'How could Burden hope to prove any of that?'

'What would a guilty, intelligent man like Ashton do to give himself an escape route? What if he'd got himself a passport in a false name, planning to do a bunk if the heat ever got too much? Who would know? No one, not until this technology comes along and you can pick a face out from a virtual line-up of several billion.'

'That's a lot of theory and not much evidence.'

'Well, think about this. What if Burden was building a circumstantial case? What if he got just enough evidence that he thought he could squeeze Ashton's balls without involving the police? See where I'm going?' Alison held Jenny in an unblinking gaze. 'Then he's cornered. Burden knows the house has got to be worth four hundred thousand and Clare's not long for this world, so he holds all the cards – he's going to be rich. What does Ashton do about it? He kills Burden and sets up Ed Morgan. Tries to solve it all at once.'

'And hacks into Morgan's Facebook account while he's at it?'

'It's not hard to extract a man's password when you've got a shotgun in his face.'

Jenny shook her head. Now she was hopelessly confused by yet another plausible theory that had never occurred to her. 'I don't know . . .'

'Two tragedies, ten years and fifty yards apart, and one dodgy suicide sitting halfway between them. You tell me which is the coincidence.' Alison scooped up the papers scattered across the desk. 'Either you go to the police with all this or I do. Personally, I think it would be more convincing coming from you, seeing as your brain hasn't got a chunk out of it.' She fetched one more item from a side pocket of her briefcase – a DVD in a blank cover. 'I promised you I'd stitch together the footage of people filling fuel cans. There's about thirty of them. None of them looks like Ed, though, or Ashton for that matter. Probably had a stash in the shed.' Alison got up from the table. 'I'll bet that bugger hacked into my account as well. And he manages to look so respectable.' She gave a contemptuous grunt and headed for the door. 'I'll leave you to it, Mrs Cooper. Sleep tight, mind the bugs don't bite.'

Jenny called after her. 'Alison – you'll promise me you won't do anything rash?'

She turned at the door. 'I keep telling you, Mrs Cooper – I'm as rational as you are.' Then she smiled again. 'So God help us both.'

# TWENTY-NINE

JENNY COULDN'T SLEEP. She went to fetch a pill but stopped herself as her fingers closed around the foil, reminding herself that she was pregnant. 'Seek doctor's advice before taking', the packet said. *Pregnant*. She slammed the drawer shut, rammed her feet into a pair of slipper socks and trudged downstairs, with a distant memory that twenty-three years ago warm milk had helped.

It didn't. Sitting at the kitchen table, trying and failing to ignore the pile of evidence Alison had left behind her, she felt herself more painfully alert with each passing second. Something inside her had shifted that afternoon. She had felt it happen at Ryan's flat and the process had only accelerated since Alison's arrival. The overwhelming feeling of tragedy that had enveloped her each time she thought of Blackstone Ley had been replaced by one of urgency. Her entire body felt restless and sprung, as if it were responding to some subconscious impulse to act, to *do* something. Four lives had ended; five if she counted Burden; six if she accepted that Ed had killed Robbie – but nothing felt complete or concluded or anywhere near explained.

She had to be rational. Logical. Methodical. That would mean taking Alison's evidence to Ryan, but her instincts told her the police would be reluctant to act. They had dragged their heels since the very first day, hoping that if they looked the other way long enough it would all go away and leave them untainted. If they continued to take that line, her only option would be to threaten to drag senior officers into court, and then it would get ugly. Moreton would reappear to remind her that, even if he didn't have grounds to remove her, he could make life intolerable – move her to some far-flung corner of the country, perhaps, the usual method for dealing with stubbornly independent coroners – and there would be no future for Alison.

Trying not to let herself be sidetracked by empty politics, she fetched her laptop from the study and brought it back to the warmth of the kitchen. She slotted in the DVD Alison had left and started to watch a procession of grainy clips of surveillance footage from four BP stations. After fifteen minutes of viewing men filling petrol cans, the tiredness finally began to steal over her. Twenty minutes in, she was struggling to keep her eyes open. The rest would have to wait till morning. She was about to press pause when yet another clip from the Gloucester Road forecourt in Bristol started to play. An indistinct figure in a baseball cap and dark anorak appeared on foot from the left of the screen, just as a driver who had been filling a van headed inside to pay. The man in the cap disappeared behind the van for no more than thirty seconds, then walked off the way he had come, making no attempt to pay. Jenny scrolled back five seconds and replayed it. There was no moment when his face was visible, no way of gauging the thief's age other than to observe that he still moved easily, with no sign of middle-aged stiffness; but the moment before he left the frame, Jenny saw him bring up his left arm and wipe the back of his hand across his mouth. She spun round in her chair and grabbed the phone from the counter.

'Jenny?' Ryan groaned. 'What time is it?'

'Nearly 3 a.m. You promised you'd email me the footage you showed me. Where is it?'

'Are you kidding me?'

'I need it. Now.'

'Look, hold on.' He was slowly coming to life. 'I'm not even sure I should have shown it to you.'

'Well, you did, and it's become part of my inquiry. You can consider this a formal request. I'll put it in writing and copy your super right now if you like.'

'No. My God.' A mild note of panic entered his voice. 'Is this how you normally do business?'

'I'm serious, Gabriel.'

'You know I think that's the first time you've called me that. I call you Jenny, but you haven't used my name once.'

'Well, I'm asking you to be an angel, to climb down off your bed and send it to me now.'

'Can I ask why?'

'The man with the boy – I think I've seen him somewhere else.'

'Huh.' Ryan had meant to sound dismissive, but couldn't hide his surprise. 'Where?'

'On film. Helping himself to a can of diesel. Why don't I trade you? You send me yours, and I'll send you mine.'

'Do you know how unreliable this sort of footage is?'

'Now you're talking like a policeman who's trying to build a case. I'm a coroner looking for the truth, remember? Two very different things, *Gabriel*.'

'It's Gabe. People call me Gabe.'

Jenny starting typing an email headed *Request for production of evidence*. 'Are you out of bed yet? I can't hear you moving.'

'I'm putting on underwear.'

'Well, hurry up.'

Jenny rang off, finished the three-sentence email, and sent

it to Ryan from her official address. She waited impatiently for his reply, playing and replaying the footage of the diesel thief in between checking her inbox. She was about to call him back when it started arriving, a zipped video file attached to an email reading '*For your eyes only. Gabe.*'

Jenny opened Ryan's file in a separate window and scrolled forward to the moment where the man wiped his mouth. She looked at the two pictures side by side. It was definitely the same man; the same gesture. He was slim in the legs and, looking at him from several angles, she got the impression that he was physically fit. Alert. Cunning.

She returned Ryan's favour and emailed her footage over to him. She knew what would happen next. He would see the similarity and try to stall her until he'd consulted his super in the morning. But the same instinct that had brought her this far told her she couldn't wait that long. She had to move.

Give her ten minutes to collect herself, it seemed only decent. As she left the motorway at Cribbs Causeway and headed into Bristol, Jenny switched on her phone, which she had deliberately kept switched off since leaving home. It was shortly before 3.45 a.m. Kelly's phone was on, but Jenny counted ten rings and still she hadn't answered. It clicked to the answer service. Jenny tried again, guessing Kelly might respond if she gained the impression it was an emergency. She was right. Several rings in, her startled voice came on the line.

'Mrs Cooper? What's happened?'

'I need to show you something – some footage. I'm going to be at your flat in ten minutes.'

'Now? Really?' She sounded distressed.

'I'm afraid it can't wait. You'll see why. I'm sorry about this.'

'OK,' Kelly answered sharply, 'whatever you want.' She rang off.

She sounded angry, and rightly so. Jenny suspected that her night wasn't about to get any better.

Kelly answered her door in a rumpled cotton nightdress, with shadows under her sad eyes, but she still managed to look beautiful, even at four o'clock in the morning. Jenny followed her through to the sitting room, the flat feeling a little more lived-in than it had before. There was a faint smell of the previous evening's cooking in the air. Jenny noticed an empty wine bottle on the carpet next to the sofa.

'I'll be quick,' Jenny said, pulling her laptop out of her shoulder bag. 'I know you were shown some footage of a man with a child at service station earlier today.'

'It wasn't Robbie,' Kelly said. She was looking at Jenny suspiciously, bare arms folded across her chest. 'I know my own child. Robbie had black hair like mine.'

'All right, but I want you to look at it again. I want you to look at the man.'

Jenny opened the file Ryan had sent her and played the footage full-screen. This time she kept half an eye on Kelly, studying her face as she watched.

Kelly shrugged without emotion. 'That's what they showed me.'

'Now look at this.'

Jenny brought up the clip from the filling station and rolled the footage. This time Kelly's pupils widened in surprise, her eyes tracking the faceless figure in the cap as he crossed the forecourt. She scratched her neck and shifted a little, her tension showing in a subtle hollowing of her cheeks. The figure reappeared.

'Watch what he does now,' Jenny said. 'Look.'

Kelly eyes stayed on him as he wiped his mouth.

'That's all,' Jenny said. 'What do you think?'

'About what?' Kelly said. She seemed a little dazed.

'It's the same man. He stole diesel from a BP filling station on the Gloucester Road on December the 26th. It was a BP station. It was one of only three within twenty miles of your home. You remember the evidence about markers in fuel—'

'Robbie's dead,' Kelly said flatly and still without feeling. 'Ed killed him. He said so. He's dead.' She looked away and wiped a palm across her eyes as tears pricked them. 'It's not him. It can't be.'

'Look at it again, Kelly. Forget can and can't.'

Kelly shook her head.

'*Please*,' Jenny insisted. She switched back to the images from the service station. 'Look at the child. I know it's hazy. I know the hair's the wrong colour.'

Frightened and tearful, Kelly forced herself to turn back to the screen.

The child was visible for no more than five seconds in total, and only as a fleeting blur, but Jenny knew that if it had been her son, if there had been even the slightest possibility, she would have known. She paused the image at the point at which the man returned the child to the car.

'I can't say. I can't—' Kelly said.

'Can you say it *isn't* him?'

Kelly's gaze flicked from the screen to Jenny and back again. She didn't say a word, but she didn't have to. Jenny knew the answer.

'This is more difficult that I can ever imagine, I know,' Jenny said, 'but try to come at this with an open mind. Have you any idea who this man might be?'

'No.' She began to shake her head. 'You can't even see him.'

'I expect that's deliberate. So let's think this through. He's in good shape, not too old, and if he has anything at all to do with what's happened in your life this last ten days, he'll either know you, or he'll have known Ed.'

Kelly looked at her blankly, from a place of confusion.

Jenny pushed further. 'Have you ever seen anyone near your home who resembles him?'

'I can't . . .' She faltered. Jenny could see her mind shifting gears. She had a lot of preconceptions to shed before she could answer such a question with any certainty. 'I'm not sure. I don't think so. He doesn't look like anyone who lives around there.'

'Let's go through your neighbours. Helen Medway's husband.'

'No, he's in his fifties. Sort of fat.'

'I'd say Darren Brooks, except he's still in the burns unit.'

'That's not Darren.' She was adamant.

'Philip Ashton.'

Kelly fell still and looked back at the screen. Jenny left her alone with her thoughts for a short while.

'Have you ever seen him do that thing with his hand?'

'Maybe.' Her answer was uncertain, but her changing expressions seemed to indicate a history of warring emotions.

'You worked for him and his wife. Tell me about him.'

Kelly brought a hand up to her face. 'What has he said?'

'His wife told me that Layla behaved inappropriately towards him when he was giving her the extra help with her schoolwork you arranged for her. He said he didn't like to tell you what had happened – he thought you had enough on your plate. But I think he described her as "sexually precocious".'

'Philip said that?'

'That's apparently what he told her,' Jenny proceeded tactfully. 'It can't be entirely untrue, though, can it?'

'Yeah, but coming from him.' Kelly's mouth narrowed in anger.

Jenny felt her pulse quicken. She'd touched a nerve. The cracks in Kelly's mask were finally starting to show. 'What about him, Kelly? Tell me.'

'I don't want all this. I told you at the beginning – I just want it over. I don't want all this.'

Jenny knew she must tread carefully. Tempting as it was to tell her about Daniel Burden, she couldn't afford to put thoughts into her mind. She needed whatever Kelly was holding inside her to come out uncontaminated.

'Kelly, please forgive me for saying this, but if there's even the slightest chance that that was your son, don't you think you should tell me anything at all that might give us a lead to him?'

'It wasn't my fault. I felt sorry for him.' She clung on to her knees and rocked to and fro, her eyes tight shut. 'He offered me money. I needed it.'

'Money for what?'

'To have sex with me, of course! What do you think?'

'Just you?'

'Yes! And he said he'd help Layla with her schoolwork. When you've got nothing, you do what you have to. Sell whatever you've got.'

'Did Ed know?'

'No. No way. No one knew. No one. It only happened a few times. Five or six. That's all. When Clare was upstairs having a nap. And then he'd want to talk . . .'

Kelly's face burned with resentment. 'His sick wife is upstairs and he's telling me that she never knew how to "make love", how she'd always been frightened of her body, frightened of life, and that's why she'd got ill. Not because she lost her child, but because she'd never had it in her to live in the first place. Just a lot of clever crap to excuse himself. He saw me in the house and wanted a piece. Most men do. Just how it is. You get used to it. They all try it once, even Harry Grant. I slapped his face. He never bothered me again.'

'Did Ashton talk to you about his daughter?'

'He said something weird once about her disappearance being his punishment.'

'Punishment for what?'

'Marrying Clare. Not having the guts to be himself. All that shit men come out with when they realize their lives are going nowhere.'

Jenny paused to take stock. All that Kelly had told her was surprising, but not shocking, and certainly not incriminating. She had come expecting her to say the man in the footage was Ashton. That was what she had wanted. But Kelly hadn't come anywhere close to saying so. With the heavy sense that her luck had run out, Jenny had a final roll of the dice: 'Have you any reason to think that Philip Ashton is a violent man?'

'I can't take this, Mrs Cooper. You're messing with my head. I *know* who killed my kids. And so do the police.'

'You didn't answer me.'

Kelly locked eyes with her. 'You're taking me to places I don't want to go. You're going to make me say all this in court. Why should I? I'm the one who's lost her family.'

'I asked you to forgive me, and I'm going to ask you again. Think of what's most important to you, and try to answer my question truthfully.'

'And then you'll leave me alone?'

'Yes.'

Kelly went into herself for a long moment. Jenny could see the buried pain slowly forcing its way to the surface.

Just as she thought Kelly was going to keep whatever it was locked up inside her, she spoke: 'He liked to put his hands around my throat. He said it was like nothing else.'

'He did this against your will?'

'The first time.' More tears travelled down her face and touched her full, red lips. A beautiful, fragile, weeping angel. 'Now are you going to tell me it's all my fault?'

'No, Kelly,' Jenny said. 'None of this is your fault.'

Jenny had to give Ryan credit where it was due – as soon as he had got her email with Kelly's hastily written statement attached, he'd swung into action. He'd even done her the courtesy of keeping her in the loop as the calls went to and fro between him and Superintendent Abbott. It was the prospect of the man in the cap being Ashton that had done it. No matter how much Abbott and the officers above him wanted to stay out of the limelight, they couldn't afford to allow a coroner to unmask a killer who'd been right under their noses for ten years.

At shortly before 7 a.m., and still wired, Jenny drove through the predawn darkness into Blackstone Ley and pulled up on the common, twenty yards short of the Ashtons' house. Several lights were on inside. She caught a glimpse of Philip at an upstairs window in a sports vest. It was hard to tell, but it looked as if he had been doing an exercise routine. She tried to imagine the scene: Clare wasting to nothing, while he pumped out press-ups like a man possessed.

She had been waiting no more than five minutes when two sets of headlights reflected off her rear-view mirror. An unmarked car passed her and pulled up outside the house. Ryan's Toyota followed behind. He tucked in in front of Jenny. She climbed out to meet him and felt something unexpected: the air was humid and mild against her skin. The snow underfoot no longer had a hard crust.

'You really don't want to sleep tonight, do you?' Ryan said, as he climbed out of his car.

'I thought I should talk to Clare after he's gone,' Jenny said. 'She deserves an explanation.'

'You're a social worker now?'

'She's been helpful. And she's ill.'

'Maybe I'll hang back and come with you,' Ryan said. 'You've touched my conscience.' He was trying to sound ironic, but Jenny suspected he meant it. 'Give us a moment to get it done.'

Jenny waited by her car as Ryan and two detective constables went to the door of the cottage and rapped the knocker. Ashton took a while to answer. He was dressed in a white shirt and tie and looked surprised to have visitors. She saw him stiffen as Ryan explained that, while he wasn't under arrest, they would appreciate his cooperation in assisting their inquiries at the police station. Ashton turned back into the house, followed by all three detectives. A short while later he emerged wearing a coat and carrying a briefcase, and went with the two detective constables to their car.

He glanced briefly and disinterestedly at Jenny as he climbed in. He was every inch the respectable school teacher. She couldn't begin to imagine him with Kelly, less still with his hands clasped around her delicate neck.

Ryan came out onto the doorstep and gestured her over.

'She's upset,' Ryan said as she approached.

'What did you expect?'

Jenny went ahead of him and found Clare in the kitchen. She was leaning against the counter, her emaciated frame swathed in a thick, quilted dressing gown from which her wrists and neck protruded like gnarled sticks.

'What do you want with him?' She spat the words accusingly at both of them. 'He's done nothing wrong. What are you thinking of?'

Ryan stepped forward. 'Mrs Cooper would like to explain, but before she does, would you mind if I had a little

347

look around? We can wait and get a warrant if you wish, but it might be easier this way.'

'Help yourself,' Clare said contemptuously.

'I'm grateful. Your husband doesn't happen to own a shotgun, does he?'

'What do you think?'

Ryan nodded, walked past them both, unbolted the back door and went outside.

'Would you like to sit down, Mrs Ashton?' Jenny said.

'No, I would not.'

She clung on to the countertop with a determination that told Jenny she would rather die where she stood than be patronized.

'A number of pieces of circumstantial evidence emerged,' Jenny began. 'I had no option but to forward them to the police.' She brought out the laptop that had been with her all night and set it down. 'There's a man we need to identify. Would you mind taking a look?'

'It won't be him.'

Jenny flipped the lid and opened the video files as Ryan reappeared through the back door with a plastic petrol can. He unscrewed the lid and sniffed. 'Does your car run on diesel, Mrs Ashton?'

'What of it?'

'Where does your husband tend to fill up?'

'I have no idea.'

Ryan shot Jenny a glance and went through to the hallway and up the stairs.

'This was taken on December the 26th – Boxing Day,' Jenny said, and rolled the footage from the filling station. 'Do you recognize that man?'

'What, *him*? No. Is this meant to be Philip? Are you joking? He doesn't dress like that. Anyway, he was with me that day.'

'All day? He goes out running, doesn't he?'

'I'm telling you, it's not him.'

Jenny wasn't convinced by her answer. She opened the second clip. 'This was taken the day before yesterday. It looks like the same man. He makes the same gesture. Watch carefully – the way he wipes his hand over his mouth.'

'Philip was at school. He was working.'

'Which is where?'

'Westbury.'

Westbury-on-Trym was a suburb over on the east side of the city and only a short drive from Gordano. Jenny logged the fact but kept it to herself and returned the laptop to her bag.

'You must have more than this,' Clare said, now clinging on with both hands. 'You can't tell me there isn't something else.' She staggered slightly.

'I really think you ought to sit down, Mrs Ashton.'

'Tell me, for God's sake! Do you honestly think anything you have to say can make me feel any worse?'

Jenny drew in a breath. She had come to tell the truth and now she had to deliver it. 'Kelly Hart has given a statement. She says your husband had sex with her. She says it happened here, in this house while he was working, and that he paid her . . .' Jenny ground to a halt. It felt unspeakably cruel.

'Go on,' Clare said coldly. Her face was stone.

'She says he was violent. He would put his hands around her throat.'

Clare's face curled into a cruel smile. 'She's lying to you.'

'I'm only repeating what she told me. I felt I had to.'

'And even if it were true, what would it prove?'

'A tendency, a possible motive.'

'He was going to wait for me to die, then scoop her up in his arms? Is that what you thought?' Clare gave a short, derisive laugh. 'And what did Kelly tell you about the child in that film you just showed me? Let me guess – she said it wasn't Robbie.' Clare took a step away from the counter and aimed a bony finger at Jenny's chest. Her eyes lit up with fury. 'She's lying again. She dotes on that child. Even I can tell it's him. You've found your killer, Mrs Cooper, but it's not my husband. Do you honestly think a woman who has been through all I have wouldn't know if she was married to a monster? How dare you even *think* it!'

Clare lashed out, catching Jenny entirely by surprise. Sharp nails dug into her left cheek and clung into the flesh. 'How *dare* you!'

Ryan came running at the sound of Jenny's cry of surprise. 'Mrs Ashton!'

Clare released her grip and took two unsteady steps backwards. Then without warning, her legs gave way beneath her body and she collapsed to the floor, where she lay in a contorted heap, gasping for air like a landed fish.

Ryan immediately crouched at her side and started to manoeuvre her into the recovery position. 'It's all right. You'll be OK.' He remained calm, reacting to the crisis as if he had done this many times before. He glanced up at Jenny and winced at the welts on her face. 'Sorry. Shouldn't have left you.'

'She said it's Robbie.'

'I heard. Best call her an ambulance.'

# THIRTY

Jenny opened her eyes and found herself staring at an unfamiliar white ceiling in a room with the shades drawn. She was gripped by the panic of having no idea where she was or how she had got there. Her mind went through the desperate process of grasping for points of reference. She was on a sofa beneath a duvet. She felt her bare legs against each other and became aware that she was dressed only in her underwear and a T-shirt. There was a sharp pain beneath her left eye. Daylight slanted between the nearly closed slats of blinds covering a large window. The sound of a door opening.

She pushed up on her elbows, still hopelessly confused, as Ryan entered. A wave of relief passed through her as she remembered.

'Did I wake you? I didn't know if you'd still be here.'

'What time is it?'

Ryan glanced at his watch as he wandered over. 'Nearly two. You must have needed it.' He took off his blue coat and draped it over the coffee table, before crossing to the window to open the blinds a touch.

Jenny sank back on the pillow and replayed the sequence of events that had brought her here. Clare had lapsed in and out of consciousness on the kitchen floor while they waited nearly half an hour for an ambulance. They had both thought she might die, but the paramedics arrived with oxygen that seemed to pull her back from the brink. Ryan had been nervous of letting Jenny drive home exhausted and with one eye nearly swollen shut, and she had reluctantly agreed to let him drive them both to his apartment in her car. She remembered him bathing her scratched face and finding her a T-shirt, and that was about it. She must have gone out like a light.

'How are you feeling? The eye looks better.' He perched on the arm of the other sofa. 'I think you'll survive.'

'Do we know if she did?'

'I called the hospital on the way back. She's "stable", whatever that means. But I get the impression she's a very sick woman.'

Jenny blotted out an image of Clare curled up on the floor, nothing more than skin and bone and fury. 'How was the interview?'

'All of Ashton's movements are accounted for on Wednesday – he was in a staff meeting with fifteen others when the footage was shot at Gordano. It's not him on either of those tapes.'

'What does he say about Kelly?'

'Denies it all. Her word against his.'

'Do you believe him?'

'I'm keeping an open mind.'

'Why would she make something like that up? I don't understand.'

'Kelly puts on a good show, but I'm not sure that, right now, she knows which way is up. How would any of us feel in her shoes? I can't begin to imagine.'

'Burden? Did he say anything about Burden?'

Ryan shook his head. 'Never heard of him. And we pulled Ashton's file from ten years ago. There was never any real question of him being a suspect. He'd just finished taking an after-school athletics class when his wife raised the alarm – twenty kids all confirmed the fact. It was a good theory, but his hands are clean, Jenny. I believe that.'

Jenny felt a weight of responsibility descend on her as if she had done something terribly wrong.

Ryan saw it in her face and reached for her hand. 'I know what you're thinking, but you did the right thing. We showed him the footage of the man and the child. He couldn't say it wasn't Robbie. We've released it to the media. Hopefully we'll get a lead on the man at Gordano, but whether we can be *sure* he's the diesel thief, I can't say yet. We've got experts on the case comparing the images to see if they match.'

'So where does that leave us? Burden must have gone to Blackstone Ley for a reason.'

'I agree. And so does my super. We're having another look at the Polish angle. We're going over to meet with Ballan-tyne and his colleagues early this afternoon. My best guess is that Ed was in on some sort of scam with the Poles up at Fairmeadows. Maybe that's what tipped him over the edge. No one can deny those guys seem to have fingers in a lot of pies.' Ryan smiled flatly.

Jenny wasn't in the mood for jokes. 'Do you still believe Robbie's dead?'

'Yes,' Ryan said quietly. 'There's nothing reliable to prove otherwise. I think Clare said what she did because it was all she had left. It was her only means to land a blow.'

Jenny closed her eyes and felt all the muscles in her face clench with tension. Ten hours ago she had been so sure she had made the breakthrough, now all she could hear was Simon Moreton's warning to stick to brutal logic. But wasn't that what she had done? How exactly had she behaved irra-tionally? Moreton's superior voice echoed back to her again:

*Stop ghost-hunting. There are no phantoms in these shadows. Trust me.*

'You've done all you can, Jenny. You've got to let yourself off the hook. You're asking too much of yourself.'

'I wish I could believe you.'

'You have to.'

Ryan leaned a little closer and touched her arm that lay crossed over her chest outside the duvet. She took it as an innocent gesture, but as his hand lingered against her skin she opened her eyes and saw that she had misunderstood. His fingers traced along the back of her wrist, then travelled up the inside of her arm to the sensitive crook of her elbow. He bent closer. Jenny froze as she felt his lips touch hers. He kissed her tenderly, then pulled back as if having surprised himself.

'I thought if I didn't now, I never would,' he said, as if explaining to himself as much as to her. 'Are you angry?'

'No.'

His fingers sought out hers, his touch igniting sparks all over her body.

'I'll tell you what,' he said in almost a whisper, 'I've a couple of calls to make. Why don't I see to them now and leave you to think for a moment.' He kissed her lightly on the forehead, untangled their fingers, then took his phone from his coat pocket and stepped out of the French doors onto the balcony.

Jenny sat up, catching her breath. She felt giddy, irresponsible and on fire all at once. If he had lingered a moment longer, she wouldn't have been able to stop herself. It would have been easy; there would have no choice to make, but the bastard had been so decent he'd thrown the decision back on her. She pushed her hair away from her face and caught a glimpse of her reflection in the window: no make-up, crumpled T-shirt and yes, even in this light, crow's-feet. Was she really what he wanted? *To hell with it*. She was a free agent; if that's where it was going, what was the harm?

Self-conscious now, waiting for him and planning what she'd say, she nervously smoothed the creases in the T-shirt. She felt something tickle her cheek. She reached up and found the source of the irritation: a single thick black hair, ten inches long. She held it against the white cotton duvet, making sure it wasn't one of hers. No, it wasn't. Her hair was chestnut: this was raven black. She dropped it to the floor, reached forward and examined the collar of Ryan's coat. There was another, caught against the soft fabric. The same thick, black hair. She glanced to the window and through the narrow gaps in the slats of the blind saw Ryan with his back to her, leaning against the railing of the balcony as he discussed meeting times with a colleague. Jenny brought the coat to her face and smelt the cloth. A subtle trace of perfume, perhaps? She couldn't be sure. She glanced up and saw Ryan dialling another number, still facing away from her. Relaxed. Easy in himself. Keeping one eye on him, she dipped a hand into his outer coat pocket. She felt a slender leather wallet and some keys. She extracted the wallet, and hiding her hands beneath the coffee table, opened it out. There were three credit and debit cards in one side and a driver's licence behind a transparent window in the other. Jenny had to read it twice. The name printed on the front of the licence was *John Wheelock*. The address beneath was that of Ryan's apartment. She looked at each of the three bank cards in turn. The first was in the name of Gabriel Ryan, the second and third both in the name of Wheelock. She checked the pocket behind the card slots and along with two ten-pound notes there was a single condom and another empty foil wrapper.

Feeling a little sick, she slotted the wallet back into the coat and grabbed her clothes that were folded over the far end of the sofa. She ripped off the borrowed T-shirt and dressed as hurriedly as she could. She was pulling on her jacket and stepping into her shoes as Ryan came back in from the balcony.

'I checked my missed calls,' Jenny lied, 'I'm meant to be somewhere.'

'Oh.' He looked hurt. 'Can I see you over the weekend?'

'I'll call you later,' Jenny said.

Ryan moved towards her, wanting to kiss her. 'No. You mustn't start that again,' Jenny said. She kissed her fingers and touched his cheek with them, making him smile. 'Save it.'

She hurried to the cupboard behind the door and fetched her coat. As she pulled it on, she noticed a half-drunk bottle of red wine on the kitchen counter. The picture on the label was of a rearing horse.

'Bye. Thank you.' She flashed Ryan a smile and let herself out.

She walk towards the lift expecting him at any moment to come after her, but thankfully he remained inside. As the doors closed and she headed down to the ground, she remembered where she had seen the image of a rearing horse before: it was on the empty bottle of wine Jenny had spotted at Kelly's flat the previous night.

There was a point at which circumstantial evidence became enough to prove a case, and as far as Jenny was concerned, she had reached it.

'You've got to be kidding me.' Louis Falco sounded drunk or high, or both. The sounds in the background were of a bar filled with professional types with middle-class accents excited to have cut loose early on this gloomy Friday afternoon. 'You get me arrested and charged, and now you want to *meet*?'

'It wasn't me who got you arrested.' She hustled her way across two lanes of traffic and made the exit for the M32 with only yards to spare.

'You and Ballantyne aren't friends?' he said sarcastically.

'If you think I'm in the pocket of CID you didn't do your research, Mr Falco.'

'Those two guys were cops. I'd put money on it. Not that anyone's going to admit it. They've probably wiped the files and thrown the pair of them on the first plane to Poland.' Jenny heard the ice rattle in a glass as he took a drink. 'Do you have any idea how much security I had to lodge for bail? Eighty fucking grand!'

'Where do I find you?'

'You're not joking, are you?' He laughed, highly amused. 'When?'

'Fifteen minutes.'

'I'm afraid you won't find me at my best, Mrs Cooper.'

'That makes two of us.'

'The Sugar Club. Denmark Street,' he slurred. 'I'm in the basement.'

The bar was less than a quarter-mile from Jenny's office, in the warren of old streets that back in slaving days had been the city's commercial centre. The former warehouses that had once been stacked to the rafters with hemp sacks of tobacco and sugar had been turned into apartments and trendy bars. The Sugar Club was in an old Georgian town-house sandwiched improbably between two such buildings. There was nothing to announce its presence except a discreet sign above the bell push.

Jenny entered a hallway panelled in dark oak, dimly lit by a brass candelabra.

The smell of cigar smoke drifted down from an upstairs lounge. A pretty female receptionist greeted her from behind the desk. She smiled when Jenny said she was a guest of Mr Falco, in a way that suggested he was a resident character.

A winding flight of stone steps led down to a large cellar consisting of several connecting rooms with vaulted brick ceilings. Drinkers sat around tables fashioned from upturned barrels or propped up a bar crafted from old ships' timbers. It had a warm, fusty, subterranean smell and the cliquey atmosphere of a place where the regulars were all familiar with each other. The arrival of a new and unfamiliar face in their midst drew several inquisitive glances. Falco emerged from a shadowy alcove and gestured her over with an exaggerated wave of his hand. There was no doubting he was drunk, and when she sat on the stool opposite she smelt the alcohol coming off him in powerful waves.

'I bought champagne,' he said with an ironic smile. He had an open bottle of Moët in an ice bucket and two glasses waiting. 'Can I tempt you?'

'Just a little,' Jenny said.

'That's always a good place to begin.' He filled both their glasses. 'Even the very wicked start out with the best of intentions.' He handed her a glass. 'Your health, and my freedom.' He clinked his glass against Jenny's, gave a lopsided smile and swallowed two-thirds of his measure in a single mouthful.

Jenny took a sip and savoured the taste. Pregnant or not, she was looking forward to the feeling of lightness that would start to arrive at any moment.

'Can I assume you're not here to offer your commiserations?' Falco said.

'I don't know what went on between you and Tomasz Zaleski, but I have been told there was no warrant for his arrest.'

'Did you honestly think he would have given that evidence in open court? The poor guy's not even safe in jail. He's had to go on seg' with all the nonces.'

'I sympathize. They must be poor company after pimps, prostitutes and gangsters.'

'You're a harsh woman. Jacob Rozek was clean. The man didn't even have points on his driving licence.'

'Let's not get bogged down in recriminations. Maybe we can help each other,' Jenny said.

'What can you possibly offer me?' Falco said.

'Mitigation, perhaps? You're going to need someone with clean hands to speak to your character.'

'And why would you do that?'

'You might have information that could help me.'

The mists began to clear from Falco's bloodshot eyes. She had his interest.

'There's a detective inspector from Gloucester called Gabriel Ryan. He knows you. I was wondering if you know him.'

Falco gave a guarded nod. 'I know Ryan.'

'That's all you've got?'

'What do you want to know?'

'Who he is. What he gets up to.'

Falco poured himself more champagne, in no hurry now he felt he held the cards.

'I'd appreciate a little more than mitigation, Mrs Cooper. I'm looking at losing my whole livelihood. And I do sincerely believe that Jacob Rozek was murdered, and also that the police have zero interest in apprehending his killers, only in seizing his assets.'

'We'll call it a gentleman's agreement,' Jenny said. 'You help me out, I'll do what I can.'

'I guess that's all you can do. But I will hold you to it, Mrs Cooper – I presume your name's upstairs in the guest book.'

Jenny couldn't argue with that, and as she sipped her champagne, she wondered how she could have been so stupid as to sign her own name. Moreton was right: over twenty years in the law and she still hadn't learned to be cunning.

'So tell me how you know Ryan,' Jenny said.

'Some of my clients have had dealings with him. Gloucester and Bristol CID ran a joint source unit for several years before they all fell out with each other. Ryan was part of it. Worked out of Broadmead. He had a reputation for charming wives and girlfriends into passing information on their other halves. Quite the gigolo.'

Jenny felt the muscles of her jaw tense in anger. 'Really. That is interesting.' She took a larger mouthful of champagne. 'So his job was handling informers?'

'Until the unit broke up. That was about two years ago. What I heard was that Bristol had started to resent their country cousins moving in on their turf, and in Ryan's case, doing the job better than they were.'

'And since then he's been in Gloucester CID?'

Falco sucked air sharply through his teeth. 'Now we're getting sensitive. I have to be very, very careful that my answer to that question doesn't come back to haunt me.'

Jenny was intrigued. 'All right. I didn't hear it from you.'

Falco cast a careful glance around the neighbouring tables and leant forward. 'My information is that he took over witness protection. Gloucestershire's a good place to hide people. Put them out in the sticks where no one can find them, fix them up with a new identity.' He fixed her with a look. 'You see why I'm concerned?'

Jenny nodded, trying to hide the fact that her stomach had just turned over and the room was spinning in front of her eyes.

Falco was too smart not to register her surprise. 'Where

have your paths crossed? I might be able to help some more. As long as you remember to return the favour.'

Jenny told herself to be cautious. He was a shark. Don't give him everything. Just enough.

'Kelly Hart.'

'What about her?'

'She came from London ten years ago with two daughters. She was married to a villain called Molyneux.'

'How do you know that?'

'Ryan told me. Which given what you've just said doesn't make a lot of sense. Why would he tell me her story if it was meant to be a secret?'

'Double bluff? Throw you off the scent.'

'I think he might be sleeping with her.'

Falco laughed. 'That's sick, even for a detective. Jesus.'

'It's true. I suppose it could have been going on for a while. Her partner called her a whore in his final note.'

'I read she works up the road from here behind a bar. It's not exactly a low-profile occupation – perhaps he's running her as an informer? Or –' his face lit up with delight as he presented another possibility – 'she could have been informing on Ed Morgan and whatever he was into up at Fairmeadows. Maybe he rumbled her and took it out on the kids.' He rubbed his hands together. 'Now we are talking. This is dynamite. Might even keep me out of jail if I'm allowed a credit. I'm presuming the police have kept you entirely in the dark over this?'

'Yes. I'm afraid they have.'

'So what do you want to do? Fuck it, what have I got to lose? I'll swear a statement for you. I'll go in the witness box at your inquest and give you Ryan's life story. I might even be able to dredge up some of his old girlfriends. Embarrass the shit out of him. How does that sound?'

'Good,' Jenny said. 'Perfect.' She decided to keep what she

had learned about Burden to herself. She was happy to have
Falco working for her, but she didn't trust him an inch. She
raised her glass. 'To truth.'

Falco slapped a hand onto the table. 'Amen.'

# THIRTY-ONE

Jenny emerged from the underground bar to find rain falling from the blackening sky and to a chorus of indignant bleeps from her phone. In the absence of a signal she had missed three calls from Ryan and one from Michael. *Michael?* As if life wasn't complicated enough. He was the very last person she felt like dealing with. Heading off along the street, she began to text him a message reminding him that he was no longer welcome in her life, but as she kicked through the melting slush she lost heart. She hadn't the energy to be angry. All she wanted was to be left alone to think and plan what she would do next. On top of having to cope with the fact that she had nearly allowed herself to be seduced by a duplicitous detective who hadn't even had the grace to tell her his real name, she now had to wrestle with the possibility that Kelly Hart wasn't who she appeared to be either.

If Falco was to be believed – and that was a big *if* – Kelly was likely either to have spent ten years in hiding, having been a court witness to serious crime, or else she was a police informer who happened to be sleeping with her handler. Either possibility meant that her reconvened inquest on Monday would be full of excitement, to say the least. There was no way the police could emerge from it well, and little chance of Ryan keeping his job if Kelly admitted to sleeping with him. No wonder he had been trying to call her. From the very first moment he had appeared at her gate, his tactic must have been to keep her close, to build an emotional bond, just as he had with his female informers. Except in this case it was to obscure her thinking, rather than to tease out the truth.

It was going to be her pleasure to make sure he got exactly what he deserved. First thing on Monday morning he would find himself in the witness box answering her summons. She would make sure he had no inkling that Falco was coming next, and let him lie and lie, feeding him all the rope he needed to hang himself. And when he was done she would bring on Falco, then Ryan's past informers, and then Kelly. And finally she would bring Ryan back to the witness box and watch him dance as the noose tightened around his sorry neck.

Propelled by a stream of angry, cathartic fantasies, she made her way back to the office, making plans to issue summonses not only to Ryan, but to Superintendent Abbott and the Chief Constable, too. She wanted the world to hear precisely why it was that the most important piece of evidence in her case had been wilfully withheld from her. And if they were no-shows this time there would be no parley with Simon Moreton, just warrants for their arrest, with the press primed and ready to capture their walks of shame. She slotted the key into the lock, feeling the headiness from the champagne overtaken by a much more powerful intoxicant: she was going to be revenged.

She pushed open the door to see Alison at the top of a stepladder in the corner of the room. Alison pressed a hand to her chest and exhaled in relief.

'It's you, Mrs Cooper. I thought you were *him*.'

Jenny came inside and closed the door behind her. The computer on Alison's desk was switched on and the drawers were open.

'What are you doing?' Jenny asked, preparing herself to discover that Alison had completely lost her mind.

'The telephone engineer – Lafferty. You remember him – the good-looking Irish boy.' She was coming excitedly down the steps with something in her hand. The front of the grey telephone junction-box high on the wall was hanging from a single screw, exposing the knot of multicoloured wires inside. 'It was him!'

'Him, what?' Jenny said dubiously.

Reaching the ground, Alison held a small black object two inches square in her palm. A short length of cable was extending from it, at the end of which was a phone jack. 'It's a bug. It was wired into the phone line. We used to use them in CID. A bit bigger in those days, but the same idea. It's got a SIM card inside, like a mini phone. All you have to do is dial in, and you can listen in on phone calls and hear everything going on in this room.'

Jenny took it from her and turned it over in her hands. It certainly looked suspicious. 'Is it working now?'

'No. There's no power to it. I thought he was taking a long time. He must have been stalling, just waiting for an opportunity to be in here by himself when I popped out.'

'Hold on.' Jenny tried to reorganize her thoughts and bring the phone engineer to mind. He had hardly made an impression on her. She could picture his face – boyish, covered in light-brown stubble – but mostly she remembered cringing as Alison clumsily flirted with him while she was trying to work. 'Start from the beginning. What led you to this?'

'Those Facebook messages, of course. I told you they were nothing to do with me. The only machines I use are this one and the iPad at home. Paul can barely send an email, so it stood to reason something had happened here. Then I remembered Lafferty – all those hours he spent here. And just before he finished, I'd gone out for sandwiches and left him alone in here for fifteen minutes.' Alison went behind her desk and angled her computer monitor so Jenny could see it, too. 'Look.' She brought up the program menu. 'I had an anti-spyware program. It's gone. Deleted. You know what that means? He could have installed a keystroke tracker. Everything I write, every key I press gets secretly emailed to him.'

'Have you found any evidence?'

'I wouldn't be able to. You need a geek for that. But that's the only explanation – there's no other way, Mrs Cooper.'

'Wow,' Jenny said, unable to dislodge the suspicion that Alison might just have spent the last few days constructing an elaborate ruse to get her job back. 'Do we have his credentials? Can we check him out?'

'I've tried BT. They've never heard of a Lafferty in the Bristol team. I know what you're thinking – you can try them yourself. Here's the maintenance-depot number.' She found a scrap of paper on her desk and pressed it into Jenny's hand. 'You call them. Calum Lafferty. They'll also tell you there was never any problem with frozen bloody connections. It was just more bullshit.' Her cheeks flushed deep red. 'Pardon me, Mrs Cooper. I'm furious. I could wring his neck.'

'Excuse me a moment. You understand.'

'Of course,' Alison said, failing to disguise her hurt at being mistrusted. 'I'll make us some tea, shall I?'

Jenny went through to her office and in a state of stillness that felt like the eerie quiet before the storm, dialled the local number Alison had given her. She got through to a helpful depot manager who confirmed that he had no one called Lafferty working for him in Bristol. Nor had there been any reports of faults in Jamaica Street since the previous year. It seemed Alison was telling the truth. Setting down the receiver, Jenny attempted to absorb the implications. It was becoming close to impossible not to conclude that Falco was on to something, and that the tragedy at Blackstone Ley was inextricably connected with violent criminals happy to slaughter innocent children to protect their interests.

'You look ill, Mrs Cooper,' Alison said, as she appeared with mugs of tea. 'Still feeling queasy?'

'You were right,' Jenny said. 'There is no Lafferty.'

'I've got a theory,' Alison said, her eyes widening with excitement. 'It's all about Blackstone Ley. Gloucester CID were terrified of us solving Susie Ashton's murder and making them look like idiots, so they've done this to keep tabs. It's a wrecking operation.'

'There are some things I ought to tell you,' Jenny said, 'if only because I'm not sure I should be only one who knows them.'

They looked at each other in silence.

'Do you think it's safe to talk in here?' Alison said.

'For all the difference it's going to make, I really don't care.'

It was a relief to at last be able to share all that had happened in the last few days. Jenny didn't hold back. She started with the attempt to intimidate her at her home, moved through all the twists and turns with Falco and the hapless Tomasz Zaleski, and told the story of her association with Ryan, from the first time he turned up at her house until her discovery that he was going under a false name, and Falco's revelation that he had moved from handling informers to hiding witnesses in the countryside. Finally, she shared what had happened with Philip and Clare Ashton, and Clare's claim that the child in the video was Robbie Morgan. It felt to her as improbable as it sounded. She had laid it all out, end to end, but the different parts failed to add up to a whole.

When Jenny had finished, Alison looked momentarily perplexed, and then, like a parting of clouds, a smile appeared. 'Now I think I know where Burden must fit in.'

'Then you're ahead of me,' Jenny said.

'Passports. Every time Ryan put a witness on his programme he would have to have arranged a new identity. Birth certificate, national-insurance number, driver's licence and passport. I'll bet you Burden had access to those files. Think what they must be worth in the wrong hands.'

'Yes. *Yes*.' the idea gained traction in Jenny's mind, and began to manoeuvre into place like a piece in some complex three-dimensional puzzle. Except that an awkward corner refused to fit: 'But if Burden was looking at Kelly, why would Ryan tell me she'd been married to a criminal? Surely that breaks the first rule of his job.'

'Has she told you her story herself?'

Jenny had to admit that she'd never asked her to delve deep into her past.

'Then I'm with Falco on the double bluff. You said Ryan studied psychology – he's probably trying to play some mind trick on you.'

'I wouldn't be surprised.'

Alison scratched the flattened part of her forehead, her face creased up in concentration. 'Burden's starting to make sense, though – the fancy computer and the facial-recognition software. If he was being asked to assist in creating a new identity, the police wouldn't disclose the original one – only a handful of officers would be trusted with that information. But what he does have is photographs . . .'

Jenny completed her thought for her: 'And he'd got himself the wherewithal to uncover the original identities from photographs alone.'

Alison slurped her tea noisily, pulling more unusual faces as further connections formed in her brain. 'DI Ballantyne's lot won't know about the hard drive Burden had, and they certainly hadn't put him in Blackstone Ley. And Burden wasn't stupid – he wouldn't have left that thing lying around for a burglar to lift, and he wouldn't have put it anywhere obvious, either.' She lowered her voice to a whisper and leant across the desk with a sense of pressing urgency. 'You need to get over to his place before someone else does, Mrs Cooper?'

'Me? I wouldn't know where to start.'

'Then what you need is someone who knows their way around. An ex-detective, perhaps?'

They made their way to Janus Avenue in separate cars. Alison went ahead, intending to call past her flat en route, in order to collect her 'search kit'. She took off with the enthusiasm of a child impatient for an adventure, already making plans for how she would improve office security after her return to work. Jenny didn't have the heart to remind her that no matter what, Moreton would still insist that she take a medical that she stood almost no chance of passing. Another of life's many injustices. Sometimes Jenny longed to be like those who could sail through each day in a state of callous detachment. How easy it must be to live without empathy.

As if on cue the phone rang; it was Ryan's name on the screen. She let it go unanswered, waiting to see if he would leave a message. He did, sounding for once as if his emotions were getting the better of him: 'This is a message for Mrs Cooper. It's 5.20 p.m. I need to speak to you urgently. Kelly Hart isn't at her flat and she isn't answering her phone. I need to know if she has communicated with you and I'm concerned for her safety. Please call me.'

If he was telling the truth, Kelly was either in trouble or

had decided to put herself out of Ryan's reach. She had seemed genuinely distraught when she gave her statement about Philip Ashton. It had felt to Jenny like a moment in which she had started to confront the burden of having lived her life as a continual object of men's fantasies. It stood to reason she would be avoiding Ryan. If she stood any chance of being free, she would have to begin by getting out from under his control.

Jenny switched on her mobile phone and checked for new messages. There was nothing from Kelly, but Michael had called again, also leaving a message. Gritting her teeth, she dialled in to hear what he had to say. His sounded deadly serious: 'Jenny, I've now had two calls from a fellow called Ryan, who claims he's a detective. It seems he's trying to track you down. He sounds a complete arsehole, but I got the impression he thinks you might be in some danger. Can you at least let me know if you're all right?'

Jenny sighed and texted him back. 'I'm fine. And yes, he is.'

As she went to slot the phone back in her pocket, Michael texted back – he must have responded instantly. 'Good. I'm here. M.'

Alison was already waiting on the pavement outside 15 Janus Avenue, between the grubby heaps of melting snow, a small rucksack slung over her shoulder. A short, irritable man wearing a camel-coloured coat climbed out from a white Mercedes as Jenny approached.

'This is Mr Hoskins – the owner,' Alison explained as Jenny joined them.

'I thought the police had already searched that flat,' Hoskins said, not troubling himself to say hello.

'I'm the coroner, Mr Hoskins. My inquiry is quite independent of the police.' She handed him one of her business cards.

He gave it a cursory glance, unimpressed. 'His brother's coming to clear the place out tomorrow. Couldn't it wait till then?'

'No,' Jenny answered coolly. 'I won't need to detain you – just as long as you can let us in.'

'And leave you alone to wreck the place? You must be joking.' He stomped bad-temperedly to the front door.

Hoskins stood with his arms crossed indignantly over his belly as Alison and Jenny began their search of the four rooms, which seemed to have remained untouched since Jenny's initial visit. Jenny went into the bedroom to look through the cupboards and drawers, while Alison went into the bathroom.

'What are you looking for anyway?' Hoskins demanded.

'If you don't mind, I'd rather not say,' Jenny said.

'Not drugs, is it? That's all I need. Have you any idea how hard it is to let a flat where someone's topped themselves? You can't hide a damn thing these days – it's all on the bloody internet.' He called through to Alison. 'Hey! What do you think you're doing?'

'Unscrewing the bath panel. I'll put it back.'

'Damn right you will.'

Jenny resisted the urge to slap Hoskins down, reasoning that sooner or later Alison was bound to oblige, and set about searching Daniel Burden's meticulously organized bedroom. He may have become a man, but no man Jenny had ever met kept his belongings as neatly. Right down to his socks and underwear, everything was ironed and folded. She went through a chest of drawers, searched the wardrobe and under the bed, but didn't find so much as a stray button. The habits he had learned in the Navy had clearly stayed with him: his sense of wellbeing seemed to have been intimately linked with external order. It was the same in the kitchen. Everything in its place; utensils and crockery gleaming. No superfluous items and scarcely a personal touch. After inspecting one spotless cupboard after another, Jenny couldn't help but feel that Burden's obsession with tidiness was more than just a habit: it was as if he'd been consciously trying to erase all traces of himself. The rented flat was merely a space he occupied; a temporary way-station on his journey to becoming his true self.

Having drawn a blank, Jenny joined Alison in the sitting room, where she was down on her hands and knees behind the sofa, which she had pulled away from the wall.

'I hope you know what you're doing,' Hoskins said. 'This isn't going to take much longer, is it? I've got to be somewhere.'

'Please?' Jenny said, as she stepped past him. She was rapidly becoming impatient.

He snorted and turned into the hall.

Jenny tried not to look at the mini-gym from which Burden's body had been hanging, and turned her back to it. 'I can't see anything that looks like a hard drive.' Jenny said.

'You wouldn't have,' Alison said confidently.

'Oh?'

'This is the only partition wall in the place. It's going to be in here. Yes!'

Jenny looked behind the sofa and saw that Alison had removed a small plastic cap that sat at the bottom of a double electric socket.

'USB port,' Alison said triumphantly. 'It's behind here. I can see where he's patched the plaster. Pass the hammer would you? It's in the bag.'

Jenny glanced to the doorway. Hoskins had stepped into the bathroom. She fetched the heavy club hammer from Alison's rucksack and handed it over.

'He's going to love this,' Alison said, and swung it hard into the wall.

There was a hurried toilet flush and Hoskins emerged red-faced from the bathroom, tugging at his zip. 'What the hell do you think you're doing?'

'Smashing a hole in the wall – what does it look like?' Alison said from amidst a cloud of dust.

Hoskins's cheeks puffed up like red balloons as with another big swing the several fist-sized holes she had made became one large one. 'Now, listen here—'

'Got it!' Alison reached through the hole she had punched through the plasterboard and brought out a small black box with two cables attached.

Jenny couldn't help herself: 'Don't worry, Mr Hoskins, by the time we move the sofa back you won't even notice it's there.'

When Jenny had finally calmed the irate landlord down and packed him off with a promise to make good the damage, Jenny resolved that her first priority must be to get the contents of the hard drive copied and safely uploaded to an online storage facility as soon as possible. It wasn't safe to take it to the office, and Jenny was feeling superstitious enough not to attempt to drive it all the way home across the Severn Bridge and along the twisting roads of the Wye Valley without having secured the data first. Opting for safety in anonymity, they drove the short distance to the McDonald's restaurant at Stoke Gifford. It wasn't glamorous, but it had free Wi-Fi, and by running Jenny's laptop on battery and using its power lead to get the hard drive up and running, Alison was able to hook them together with a USB connector she had picked up at Burden's flat. While Jenny filled her aching stomach with a tasteless portion of fries, Alison managed to access the contents.

A list of several hundred files scrolled up the screen. It was immediately apparent that this was the repository of Burden's entire digital life. A glance at the file names revealed that here was stored everything from emails to games to favourite music and movies.

Jenny felt briefly overwhelmed at the extent of the material, but Alison quickly homed in on a file named *Idencofit* and clicked it open. The program was huge and took several minutes to load. Once running, Alison navigated her way through to a sub-file that Jenny was sure she would never have found by herself, which contained the details of the most recent searches. Two rows of thumbnail photographs came up. Of the twenty or so images, six were headshots of Kelly. The first was a plain passport photograph of the type taken in a pay-booth. The rest had clearly been cropped out of pictures taken in several different locations. Two looked as if they may have been taken outside the house at Blackstone Ley, and one image showing Kelly in a low-cut blouse with an array of bottles behind her appeared to have been captured in the bar where she worked.

Alison clicked on the passport photograph, selected the 'matches' option from the pop-up menu and a split second later the stored results appeared on the screen.

Jenny froze, her cup halfway to her mouth. Tens of photographs spilled onto the screen, all of different sizes; all harvested from the internet. Every last one was from a newspaper or magazine and they all featured one of two shots. The first was a posed school portrait of a beautiful, olive-skinned schoolgirl in neat blue blazer, and the second was of the same girl a year or two older, sandwiched between two much larger female police officers.

Alison clicked on the clearest rendering of the second picture and opted to visit the web page from which it was drawn. Another window opened, displaying an archive article from the *Gibraltar Chronicle*, dated 13 April 1998. The headline above the picture declared: 'GIB GIRL NOT GUILTY OF MURDER'.

Jenny's eyes skimmed over the text below:

15-year-old Malia Sanders, who, along with 17-year-old Liam Doyle of Queensway Road, had been standing trial charged with the murders of 11-year-old Gabriella Vallejo and her younger sister Amelia, 9, walked free today, after Mr Justice Davies instructed the jury to return a verdict of not guilty in her case, shortly after proceedings commenced.

The bodies of Gabriella and Amelia Vallejo were discovered by their parents, floating in the pool at their home in Europa Road in early January. Miss Sanders, a student at Eastside School, was frequently employed by the family as a babysitter. At the time of their deaths, Doyle was working part-time as a pool cleaner. The court today heard evidence from pathologist Professor Rex Ferris that both girls showed signs of having been sexually assaulted and violently asphyxiated.

The case against Doyle continues.

'That's Kelly,' Alison said, stating the obvious. 'From Gibraltar. That must be where she gets her looks from. Two girls.' The symmetry between the events of Kelly's past and present seemed almost too horrible to remark upon. The food lying in Jenny's stomach had turned to acid. 'Fifteen years old. They would have been allowed to publish her photograph because she was found innocent. See if you can find a picture of Doyle . . .'

Alison brought up a search engine and entered his name. Amongst the many irrelevant references to different Liam Doyles, numerous reports of his conviction for double murder were returned. She worked through them all, but none carried a photograph. Being technically a juvenile at the time of his sentence, he had been legally protected from having his image published, and back at the dawn of the internet such rules, which nowadays were routinely flouted, were capable of being enforced.

'There. Look. She turned Queen's evidence against him.' Jenny pointed to a passage in a report of Doyle's trial, which stated that Malia Sanders, as she then was, had been a principal witness for the prosecution. She had told the court that while working as a regular babysitter for the two girls, she had become friendly with Doyle, who worked for the pool-maintenance company. They soon fell into a sexual relationship which Sanders described as 'intense and passionate'. On the night the girls died, she claimed Doyle had plied her with marijuana and alcohol and that she fell asleep on the sofa and later woke to find Doyle gone and the girls dead. Panicking, she fled the scene before their parents returned.

Doyle gave no evidence in his defence. Instead his barrister argued that the prosecution had constructed only a flimsy circumstantial case, which could apply equally to Malia Sanders, whom he described as a 'devious and calculating young woman, hiding behind an innocent, doe-eyed exterior.' The jury did not agree with him. Doyle was found guilty on a majority verdict and given a mandatory life sentence with a recommendation that he serve at least fifteen years.

'Sounds to me like she was in it up to her neck,' Alison said. 'No wonder they fixed her up with a new identity. There was no way she could have stayed in a small place like that.'

Oblivious to the noise and clatter of the fast-food restaurant going on around her, Jenny clicked back to the images of the young Malia and stared at her perfect and ever-so-slightly melancholic face. She was truly mesmerizing, though not in an obvious way; hers was a beauty that drew you closer and closer in, inviting you to seek her out; a dark well drawing you into its depths. Jenny recalled Darren Brooks's words – *Once in a man's lifetime he'll fall for a woman who is not of this earth* – and for the first time she began to understand. There was indeed something darkly and diabolically enchanting about Malia Sanders, something that could touch even someone like her, who had never regarded another woman in that way.

'What would Burden have wanted from her?' Jenny said, thinking aloud. 'She doesn't have money – she lived in a council house.'

'You can ask her at the inquest, can't you?' Alison said. 'You won't be so afraid of hurting her feelings now we know who she is. Do you think Ed knew? Or do you think Burden *told* him?' Alison turned to her, wide-eyed. 'And Susie Ashton. What about Susie Ashton?'

Jenny had begun to have the same thought. Wherever Kelly went, death seemed to go with her.

# THIRTY-TWO

'Jenny? Where the hell have you been?'

'Here and there.'

'Kelly's gone from her flat. I can't find her anywhere. Has she called you?'

'All things considered, I'm not sure I'd tell you if she had.'

'What are you talking about?' Ryan strained to sound patient.

'An officer running witness protection sleeping with his charge only days after she's lost her family. Call me a prude, but it doesn't feel quite seemly, let alone ethical.'

She was met with silence. Unable to trust herself not to fly into a dangerous rage, she had pulled over into a layby used by overnighting truckers, just a short distance beyond the Severn Bridge. She watched the passing traffic and tried to remain calm as she waited for Ryan – she couldn't think of him as 'John Wheelock' – to respond. But the silence stretched on. She had obviously surprised him. Floored him.

'Well, look, I appreciate she's an attractive woman, and I know you've a weakness for them, which you've even managed to turn to your professional advantage, but there is a time to draw the line, *John*.' Still no sign of life. 'And I can also see why you and your super have been so keen to get it all swept up so quickly. You were meant to be looking after her, keeping that ugly past from coming back to bite her.

That didn't go very well, did it? I haven't got all the pieces, but I'm getting there. I'm even prepared to bet it was you who put the pig's head outside my house, just so you could cosy up a little closer.'

'Who told you?'

'I had a little help from someone who knows you by reputation, but mostly I put it together myself. You can expect a summons, of course. Maybe you and your super can share a ride.'

'You have no proof that anything improper has occurred between me and Kelly.'

Jenny waited while a big articulated truck rumbled past.

'We'll leave that for court, shall we?'

'If you're hiding her, Jenny, you're being very irresponsible. You can't even look after yourself, let alone her as well. Forget about me, think about her safety. Haven't enough people died already?'

'Who exactly do you think is going to kill her? Let's see – what about Philip Ashton? Does he know?'

'Stop it, Jenny. You're being stupid.'

'As a matter of interest, how do you pronounce Wheelock – is it "we" or "wheel"?'

'We.'

'Wheelock. It's not a bad name, more distinctive than Ryan.'

'I meant it,' Ryan said. He almost sounded sincere.

'Nice try, but a little too late. See you on Monday.'


A full day of warmer air had largely dissolved the snow that had smothered the hedgerows and verges in the bottom of the valley, but as Jenny turned left and climbed the steep lane to Melin Bach, the signs of thaw were fewer and the temperature gauge on the Land Rover dipped back below zero. The overhanging trees, still stooped and weighed down with icicles formed during the melt, seemed to claw at her as she wove her way up, reminding her that there was a long way to go before she would see bright skies again.

The police car parked in the lane outside the house was a welcome sight. She flashed her headlights as she approached, and the driver signalled back. She would make sure to offer him a warm drink as soon as she had got her laptop and the hard drive safely inside. She pulled onto the old cart track at the side of the house and hoisted her laptop bag from the passenger seat. She was wearing the wrong shoes for the dash across the slush to the front door, but getting her feet wet now wouldn't hurt. In a few minutes she'd be under a warm shower for the first time in thirty-six hours. She couldn't wait.

The nervous energy that had sustained her throughout the day bled out of her limbs as she crossed the threshold and entered the welcome sanctuary of the cottage. She sloughed off her coat, dumped her bag in her study and went through to the kitchen in search of something to keep her going while she decided what she might cook for dinner. It felt like days since she had eaten properly. She was halfway through an apple and coming round to the idea of lasagne when there was a tap at the back door. She hoped it was the shy young constable wanting to use the bathroom and not his older colleague, who never lost an opportunity to regale her with the soap opera of his troubled marriage.

'Hold on.' She swallowed her mouthful and unbolted the stable door, preparing to be friendly but brisk.

The first thing Jenny saw was the ends of the two shiny, sawn-off barrels pointed straight at her chest. She took a step back and froze as she took in the figure casually holding the shotgun in front of him. He was mid-height, dressed in a black, waist-length anorak and had the brim of a black baseball cap pulled down low over his eyes. She recognized him at once: the telephone engineer, Lafferty.

'Hello again,' he said with a smile that, if it hadn't been offered from behind a shotgun, would have been pleasantly friendly. He poked his head inside the door and glanced left and right. 'Why don't you take a seat over there.' He nodded towards the kitchen table.

Jenny did as he asked, her legs turning to jelly. Her heart was pounding so fast she could barely catch her breath. Her vision faded at the margins.

Lafferty stepped inside and swung the door shut with his elbow. Keeping the gun on her, he drew the blind fully down over the window behind the sink. Jenny noticed that his boots and ankles were covered in wet snow and that he was wearing disposable latex gloves.

'Nice and snug in here,' Lafferty said, and leaned back against the rail along the front of the range, warming himself while he kept the shotgun cocked under his arm, a finger lightly touching the dual triggers.

Jenny focused all her effort on trying not to scream or faint. The two barrels hovered less than eighteen inches from her head.

'Sorry to spring a visit on you, but things have been getting a little bit tighter than I'd hoped. You've been busy; managed to catch me on film. I tried to think of everything, but it all gets so complicated. The best laid plans and all that.'

From the corner of her eye Jenny saw Lafferty bring up his arm and wipe the back of his hand across his mouth. He smacked his lips and swallowed, the tension of the moment making him produce too much saliva.

'I didn't set out to involve you in any of this, you understand, but no one thought you'd be poking around so much. Not even the police. Then I looked you up and, of course, the alarm bells started to ring. You're quite a terrier, aren't you? You never give up.'

Jenny managed to find her voice. 'What do you want?'

'What have you told the police?'

'Nothing.'

'Why should I believe that?'

'It's not in my interests. I haven't been able to trust them.'

'Is that so?' He shook his head gently from side to side, as if finding it hard to believe her. 'What's going to happen now, Mrs Cooper – do you mind if I call you Jenny? – is you're going to tell me what you know, so that we can work out where we stand.' He moved the barrels a little closer to her head. 'Off you go.'

She was too frightened to play games. At that moment, she would have done anything to get that gun away from her. 'I know who Kelly is. Her real name's Malia Sanders. She was a witness in a murder trial seventeen years ago. Two young girls were killed. She was placed on witness protection, moved to London, then to Gloucestershire . . .' She paused as the very obvious last piece of the puzzle snapped into place.

'Go on.'

'You're Liam Doyle, aren't you?'

'Very good.' He smiled, showing rows of even teeth. 'That was my name. They gave me a new one when they let me go: Patrick Gaddon. I've tried to get used to it, but somehow it's not me. I liked Cal Lafferty – it was my grandfather's name – but I guess that's no good to me now, either. Much more of this, I won't know who I am.' The smile left his face. 'How'd you find out?'

Jenny stalled, tempted to lie. He sensed it in her and touched the cold metal of the gun against her temple, making her stomach spasm. She could only think of him as Doyle the murderer.

'Tell me,' he demanded.

'A man called Daniel Burden, he worked at the passport office—'

'I know who he is,' Doyle interrupted. 'He was dead before Christmas. You must have found something I didn't. What?' He pressed the barrel of the shotgun into the side of Jenny's head. 'It's no time to go quiet on me, Jenny. You wouldn't want me to start getting ugly, would you?'

'There was a hard drive buried in the wall at his flat. He had software – the kind that trawls the internet for faces. He'd been researching Kelly's past.'

'Her name's *Malia*.'

'Sorry. Yes, Malia.'

'He was a devious little bastard. Still, it's thanks to him we found each other again. When he didn't get any change out of her, he came looking for me. I promised him a hundred grand if he told me where I could find her. Told him I'd inherited property. Dumb fucker.' He laughed. 'Greed makes people stupid, doesn't it? Prison's full of them. Clever guys who could've been living like pigs in shit if they'd only known when to stop.'

An image of Burden's hanging body flashed before Jenny's eyes, the overturned chair on the floor next to it. Now she saw Doyle with his gun trained on him, making him climb onto the chair and tie the rope. She had no doubt he'd killed Nicky too; clubbed the dog with the butt of that gun and strolled into her bedroom with a length of twine. He was the figure she must have seen outside the burning house when she came round from her drunken stupor. It was Doyle who had slaughtered Ed and the girls, then taken shots at Nicky as she ran off into the night.

Jenny felt something in Doyle's demeanour shift, as if his curiosity had suddenly become exhausted and his attention had switched focus. He snatched the phone from its cradle on the counter and placed it in her trembling hands.

'I'm going to need you to pull yourself together, Jenny. I know DI Ryan's looking for Kelly, so you're going to call him and tell him that she's let you know she's safe and sound and'll be at court on Monday. If he asks you any questions, just tell him he'll have to save them for next week.'

'What if he asks about you?'

'Unless you intend to tell me different, he knows nothing about me. And I aim to keep it that way. Have you got his number?'

'On my mobile.' She reached for her jacket pocket.

'Uh-huh.' Doyle reached his hand in and brought out the phone. 'Where do I find it?'

'In my contacts.'

She watched him clumsily navigating around the phone, stabbing at the screen with his thumb. His awkwardness with it suggested he hadn't been out of prison long. 'This it?' He held it in front of her face.

She nodded and dialled Ryan's number into the landline. Doyle switched her mobile off and put it in his coat pocket.

'Put it on speaker so I can hear.' Doyle stepped back a pace and angled the gun towards the floor, taking the pressure off her while she made the call.

Ryan answered on the second ring. Jenny could hear at once that he was travelling in his car.

He had seen her number and got in first. 'Jenny, I need to speak to you—'

'I've something to tell you,' Jenny said, talking over him. Her heart was beating at more than twice its normal speed, making it almost impossible to speak calmly. She forced herself on. 'I know where Kelly is and I'll be keeping her safe until she comes to court on Monday.'

'You've got her with *you*?'

'It doesn't matter where she is, and I'm certainly not prepared to let you speak to her before she testifies. I'd ask you to respect my wishes and leave her to grieve in peace.'

'Jenny, no matter what's passed between us, I am good at my job and nothing I have done contributed to what Ed Morgan did. I'm prepared to accept that it's possible he found out about her past, but I swear to you, I did everything to protect her.'

'I've said all I have to say.'

'You can tell me to my face. I'm on my way over.'

Doyle leant forward, pushing Jenny roughly out of the way and pressed the red button to end the call.

'What does he mean, "what's passed between us"?' Doyle asked, levelling the gun back at her.

'He tried to seduce me,' Jenny said, her humiliation complete.

'Don't tell me you turned him down, Jenny – a good-looking guy like that? He tried it with Malia, too. Poor fella must be wondering what's wrong with him.' Doyle leered at her from under the brim of his cap. 'I've often wondered what it'd be like with an older woman. What do you say?'

Jenny felt her entire body go numb. Doyle's stubbled face cracked into a smile. 'Joking. I'm attached. Besides, time's a bit short if you're expecting visitors.' He nudged the barrel of the gun under her shoulder. 'Get up.'

Jenny obeyed.

'This is what happens next. We're going to go to your car and you're going to drive us away, nice and gently, so that policeman outside doesn't get excited. Where are your keys?'

'In my coat. It's in the hall.'

Doyle opened the kitchen door a touch and looked through to the living room. Jenny hadn't yet drawn the curtains and if the constable in the car outside had glanced to his right, he would have a clear line of vision into the house. 'All right. Go and fetch it.'

Jenny moved towards the door.

'Be good,' Doyle said casually as she stepped past.

Jenny crossed the sitting room, opened the door to the front hall and reached her coat from the peg. Her eyes moved instinctively to the front door: the big brass key was in the deadlock and both heavy bolts pulled shut. There was no escape. She turned back to the kitchen, pulling on her coat. Glancing to the window, she saw a light on in the police car outside. She could see the young constable quite clearly: he was turning the pages of a magazine.

Keeping the gun trained on her, Doyle moved to the back door and opened it. 'After you. You'll get in the front, I'll hop in the back. I want you to back out onto the road and turn left up the hill.'

Jenny stepped outside into the frigid night and followed the frozen path that led along the back of the house and behind a hedge that would shield them entirely from the constable's view. She prayed he wouldn't choose that moment to leave his car and patrol the house, in no doubt that Doyle would shoot him dead.

She walked quickly to the car, Doyle no more than two paces behind her. She popped the locks and slid into the driver's seat. Doyle climbed in behind her, ducking down.

'Go.'

Jenny started the engine and forced her foot down on the clutch. The car moved off jerkily as she backed into the lane, its rear bumper coming to within several feet of the police car. As she crunched the lever into first she glanced in her mirror and saw the driver's door open and the constable start to climb out. She jammed her foot on the throttle, almost stalling as she pulled away.

Doyle cursed loudly as he sat up and poked the gun between the two front seats. 'The fuck was that?'

'I'm sorry. I'm not used to driving with one of those in my back.' The car lurched again as Jenny shifted into third.

'You won't have to for long,' Doyle said. 'In a little while you'll see a blue VW parked at the side of the road. There's a track just beyond it. I want you to pull into it.'

Jenny drove in silence, wondering what came next. Doyle had wanted her to stall Ryan and keep the police from looking for Kelly over the weekend, which made her think he was trying to buy her some time to slip away.

She chanced her arm. 'Are you and Malia planning on starting a new life together?'

'It's already started,' Doyle said, 'just like I always promised her. She never wanted to turn against me. It was me who told her to save herself. I knew our day would come.'

'How are you going to get away without being found?' It was a bold question, but she was beginning to feel that she didn't have a lot to lose.

'We've got it covered,' Doyle said. 'There.' He pointed to a blue VW hatchback parked in a small lay-by at the side of the lane. Just beyond it was an open gate at the end of a track she had occasionally walked along. It led through a copse and into a sloping field used for summer grazing.

'Through that gate and keep going until I tell you to stop.'

Jenny had a very dark feeling as she shifted into four-wheel drive and slowed to turn into the track.

'Don't stop,' Doyle urged, and jabbed her shoulder with the gun.

Turning into the narrow track and moving through the untouched snow, Jenny became aware of the sound of his breathing: it grew slower and heavier, and more menacing.

'Stop there.'

Jenny came to a halt and pulled on the handbrake. They were out of sight of the road now and the Land Rover could probably remain here for several days before it was noticed.

'Lower the windows,' Doyle ordered sharply.

Jenny did as he asked, sensing another shift in his energy. They had climbed a further 200 feet since Melin Bach and the air was several degrees cooler still. Within seconds, the inside of the car had turned into an ice box.

'Hand me the key.'

Pulling the key from the ignition and handing it back between the seats, Jenny was aware of a feeling of unreality, as if she were withdrawing from her body and looking down on herself from above. She heard Doyle fetch something from his pocket and the sound of him removing the lid from a container of some sort.

'I forgot water. You'll have to do your best.'

He flicked on the overhead light in the back and shoved a small white container forward to her. She dimly made out the words 'Elavil (amitryptyline)' on the label. The generic name of the anti-depressant drug was all too familiar to her. She had read it many times on the post-mortem reports of women – it was always women – who had taken their own lives. A dozen or so pills and she'd be unconscious. In the freezing car she wouldn't stand a chance.

'Start swallowing,' Doyle barked, 'unless you'd prefer me to make a mess of you.'

Jenny reached into the container with fingers that no longer felt like her own, and pressed a pill to her lips. She swallowed, then hooked out another.

'How are you going to clear passport control?' Jenny said, no longer fearing that she had anything to lose. 'Ryan will have put out an alert for her. It doesn't matter what the name on the passport says, there are cameras on every desk that will pick her out immediately.' She was busking now, asserting as facts things she had no understanding of, but again, what did she stand to lose? 'And if Robbie's with you it's even more certain you'll be picked up. You don't leave the country with a child without its face being checked against the database. You'll be stuck in the UK with your pictures in all the newspapers and your images picked up almost every time you go outdoors.'

'Shut up and swallow,' Doyle hissed.

'If you really want to get away, you'll need a much better plan than that.'

'I said swallow!' He thrust the barrel hard into her ribs.

'I know how you can do it,' Jenny said, through teeth clenched against the pain. She steeled herself for another blow. 'My boyfriend's a pilot. Light aircraft. He can get you out of the country unnoticed.'

Doyle fell silent. She could sense him brooding, thinking through his options.

'How would that work?'

'I'll call him and get him to arrange a plane tonight. He can take you to the continent, drop you off at one of the private airfields he knows in France. He can get you a car at the other end, whatever you need. If you give me my phone, I'll look him up for you right now – show you I'm not bluffing.'

She could feel Doyle's anger at having lost the initiative, but she could equally sense his interest. She believed he wanted to live; her very worst fear had been that he was beyond caring. Wanting to live was good, something she could trade on. He was psychotic, but not suicidal.

'I think we both want the same thing, Mr Doyle – to be with the people we love and out of harm's way. Give me the phone. Let me show you.'

Grudgingly, Doyle retrieved her phone and passed it forward. The time it took to switch on and boot up felt like an age. Jenny silently prayed that when it did finally come to life there would be a signal. Her prayer was answered: one bar, then a second. Not much, but enough. She clicked on the web browser and typed in his name: Flight Lieutenant Michael Sherman. An agonizing wait, then slowly Michael's image appeared on his company website, posing in front of a Cessna. The paragraph of biography beneath made it sound as if he had liberated Bosnia, Afghanistan and Iraq single-handed.

Jenny handed the phone back to Doyle. 'That's him. He'll do it if he knows I'm safe.'

'Yeah?' Doyle said distrustfully. 'What guarantee do I have of that?'

'I'm carrying his child,' Jenny said.

'That's sweet,' Doyle said. 'Though I'd say you were a little old for that.' He thought briefly about her offer, then handed back the phone. 'Call him. It has to be tonight. No tricks. No police. Any problems,' he touched her cheek with the gun, 'you know what happens.'

Jenny found the last text Michael had sent her and dialled the number. There was an agonizing time-lag as she waited for it to connect, and an even longer wait for him to answer. Jenny pictured him looking at the screen and weighing whether he could face talking to her. *Please, Michael! Please!*

She had imagined wrong. He answered breathlessly, as if he had run from the other side of the house. 'Jenny. Thank God. Are you all right?'

'Yes,' Jenny said, painfully aware of the thinness of her voice. 'I need you to do a favour for me.'

'You don't sound all right. Where are you?'

'Michael, listen. Just tell me whether you can do this – yes or no. I need you to take two friends of mine and their child to France, tonight – to one of those private landing strips you were always flying to. They need to travel urgently. I'll come with them to the airfield and you take them from there. Can you do that for me?'

Michael answered without hesitating, switching spontaneously into professional mode. 'Of course. I can book a Cessna out of Bristol. What time would they like to leave?'

Jenny turned to Doyle. 'He can fly you from Bristol. What time?'

'Tell him an hour.'

'An hour?' Jenny said.

'I can do that – just,' Michael said. 'Tell them I can put them down near Rouen. There's a field there, a couple of kilometres out of town.'

'One more thing,' Jenny said, 'this is a private arrangement. No one's to know. We can't afford any hitches. Of any kind.' She glanced at Doyle. 'Or you won't be seeing me again.' Jenny added. 'Is that clear?'

'I'll be there in an hour,' Michael said. 'You know where to go.'

When she had ended the call, Doyle took the phone from her and ordered her to sit tight. He climbed out of the back, came round to the driver's door and made her step outside.

'Stand against the car.'

She leant against the rear door, telling herself it would be OK. He wouldn't kill her here. She had given him an escape route. Keeping the gun pressed to her stomach, Doyle pulled a pair of thick cable ties from his jacket pocket, looped them both around her outstretched wrists, then pulled them tight to make handcuffs that cut into her flesh. Next he pushed her into the back seat and put ties around her ankles, trussing her up like a bird.

'Now shut your mouth,' Doyle said, and smacked the tip of the shotgun barrel against the bridge of her nose.

Streaming tears, Jenny crumpled against the door and silently sobbed.

Indifferent to her pain, Doyle climbed into the front, rested the gun against the passenger seat and backed out of the track. He turned left on the lane and drove with reckless speed towards the road at the top of the hill that would take them down the side of the valley to Chepstow.

Slumped in the back seat, her nose clogged with blood, and losing all feeling beyond the tight bands around her wrists and ankles, Jenny could do nothing except close her eyes and continue to pray. Her only consolation was that the two pills she had swallowed had left her feeling strangely disembodied, a spectator to her own nightmare.

Doyle drove on in determined silence, following a route through the back roads that he must have carefully memorized. He emerged on the fringes of Chepstow and headed for the bridge, moderating his speed now he was amongst traffic. It a was a small mercy and Jenny clung to it.

Ten minutes later he was turning off the motorway into the grey, rundown streets of Patchway on the outer fringes of Bristol. Jenny lost her bearings as he turned off the main road and threaded through an estate of ugly, pre-fabricated houses interspersed with low-rise blocks of even more dismal flats. He pulled up into the small car park outside a particularly brutal, concrete-sided building. He tucked the gun under his coat and disappeared inside, leaving Jenny imprisoned in the car. A short while after he'd left her, a group of hooded teenagers wandered past. Jenny struggled with all her strength against the urge to beat her bound hands against the glass and cry out for help, knowing that if Doyle appeared he wouldn't think twice about shooting at them then killing her. That was why he had left her there, of course: it was a test to see if he could trust her.

The youths drifted out of sight. Several more minutes passed before Doyle emerged from the building, lugging a holdall. Kelly came after him wearing her pink anorak with the hood pulled up. Clinging to her front with his arms looped around her neck was a small child in a blue snowsuit: it was Robbie. Doyle slung the holdall into the passenger seat and put the sawn-off shotgun on top. Kelly came around to the opposite side of the back seat and climbed in with Robbie, who looked as if he had been dragged unwillingly from his bed.

'Hi,' Kelly said matter-of-factly, then turned her gaze out of the window as Doyle got behind the wheel.

Robbie peered warily at Jenny from beneath his bleached-blond fringe, then buried his face in his mother's coat. Kelly wrapped a protective arm around him and stroked his back. By the time they had turned out of the car park and reached the end of the street, Robbie had his thumb in his mouth and was drifting back to sleep.

They travelled in silence towards the airport, passing unnoticed through the late-evening traffic. Jenny kept her eyes front or angled away from Kelly, but from occasional sideways glimpses saw that she was cradling the sleeping Robbie's head as lovingly as any other mother would. She exuded an aura of tranquillity that seemed also to have settled on Doyle. Neither spoke to the other, but Jenny sensed that they didn't have to; it was as if they had a complete understanding that transcended the normal modes of communication.

They were less than half a mile from the turn-off to the main passenger terminal when Doyle spoke for the first time since leaving Patchway.

'Where to?'

Jenny told him to continue onwards to the next roundabout. From there she directed him along the unsigned road that led to a parking area next to a cluster of buildings that housed airport administration and the offices of the smaller freight and private-charter airlines. Among the handful of cars parked outside at this late hour, Jenny spotted Michael's Saab. He was here. She instructed Doyle to drive close to the gate in the wire perimeter fence, through which they would have to pass on foot in order to reach the aircraft. As they drew nearer, she could see that Michael was already waiting on their side of the gate.

'That's him,' Jenny said. 'Straight ahead.'

She felt Doyle's tension rise as they came to a halt and reversed into a space no more than thirty feet from where Michael stood.

'Tell him to come over,' Doyle said, and wound down Jenny's window.

Jenny called over to him. 'Michael, could you come here, please?'

Doyle lowered the front passenger window and reached for his gun as Michael approached at an unhurried pace.

Michael glanced first at Jenny, registering her damaged face, then turned his gaze to Doyle, giving every impression of not having noticed the gun pointing at him.

'Good evening,' Michael said. 'I've managed to secure a six-seater Cessna. I've registered a flight to Rouen, but we can stop short and land at a field next to a village that lies just outside the city. Would that suit you?'

'We'll need transport.'

'Of course. I can phone through and book a taxi into town while we're in the air. That's probably best. I do it all the time.'

Jenny couldn't help but admire his calm. He even managed to smile.

Michael nodded towards the gun. 'If you're planning to bring that with you, I'd suggest you put it in the bag for now.'

'Go back to the gate,' Doyle said.

Michael cast another glance at Jenny then went back the way he had come.

Doyle produced a small pocket knife and reached back between the seats. 'Give me your hands.'

Jenny held out her wrists. He cut them loose, then reached down and did the same to her ankles. The blood rushed painfully back into her hands and feet.

'We all go together. You carry the bag.'

Following his instructions, Jenny climbed out of the car and fetched the holdall from the passenger seat. Doyle motioned for Kelly to go first, Robbie clinging to her waist with his legs, his face still buried deep in her chest. Jenny followed several paces behind, with Doyle bringing up the rear. He had the gun in his right hand concealed under the flap of his coat. They passed through the gate without incident, then Doyle gestured for Michael to lead off at the front of the procession where he could see him.

Michael took them around the front of the building then struck out across an open expanse of tarmac that was only dimly lit by lights buried in the ground, towards a small hangar. A single-engine aircraft stood outside it, a single set of steps set out beneath its open door. A nervous flier at the best of times, Jenny prepared herself for the ordeal that lay ahead. She knew enough to understand that a night flight in winter was hazardous, and that trying to land on an unlit airstrip in the pitch black was close to impossible. Then there was the question of what happened once they were on the ground. A feeling of dread swept over her as she imagined what Doyle would be planning: two barrels – one shot for her and one for Michael. And if his previous actions were anything to go by, he'd set fire to the plane and leave them to burn up in the wreckage while he and Kelly vanished into the night. It would take accident investigators days to figure out what had happened.

They were less than ten yards from the aircraft, and beads

of sweat were running down Jenny's neck, when she noticed Michael glance left. She instinctively did the same and saw a figure stepping quickly out from the unlit interior of the hangar. It was Ryan, and he was holding a pistol.

'Step away from her, Doyle.' He was forty feet away and closing quickly.

Doyle reacted instantly, jamming the gun into Jenny's spine. 'Stop there or I'll kill her.'

'Go ahead,' Ryan said, quickening his pace. He was now less than thirty feet away and still coming.

'Ryan! Stop!' Michael shouted.

'I'll kill her!' Doyle yelled.

Jenny saw a flash from the muzzle of Ryan's gun, and in the same moment Michael hauled Kelly and Robbie aside and rushed towards Doyle. As time seemed to slow to a fraction of its normal speed, all Jenny could feel was rage at Ryan for being so thoughtless and letting it end like this.

He kept coming. Fifteen feet. Another flash. Ten.

Jenny braced herself for the blast she knew would blow her into the air, but in a split second she felt the hard muzzle of the gun sweep up past her shoulder, and a burst of intense heat against her cheek accompanied by an explosion that felt as if it had cracked her head in two, as Doyle fired. He swung right towards Michael and fired again, but this time the shot went harmlessly into the sky, as Michael rammed into him shoulder-first and sent him sprawling to the ground.

Jenny staggered sideways and fell as Doyle scrambled to his knees. Michael grabbed the shotgun before he could reach it and bludgeoned the butt into Doyle's disbelieving face. He made a sound somewhere between a short low groan and a grunt, and slumped like a slaughtered bull.

Michael straightened, tossed the gun aside, and went to Ryan, who was lying front-down on the tarmac. As he stooped down to turn him over, he stopped abruptly and stepped back.

'What is it?' Jenny said.

'He doesn't have a face,' Michael answered quietly.

Jenny looked off to her right as she registered this news and saw Kelly running into the darkness, dragging Robbie behind her. In the far distance, several sirens started up.

'You must have told him I called,' Jenny said.

'Of course. But I thought he'd bring the cavalry, not come alone.'

She felt strangely ambivalent. Ryan hadn't cared if she lived or died. He'd just been trying to get a clean shot at Doyle. He was obsessed. This was his last chance to keep Kelly for himself, and he'd thrown his life at it.

Michael leant down and helped her to her feet.

She turned in the direction of the approaching sirens. Three sets of headlights were speeding across the airfield. Kelly stopped running and stood paralysed as they raced towards her.

'I thought I'd lost you,' Michael said.

Jenny reached for his hand and closed her fingers around it. 'You should be so lucky.'

# THIRTY-THREE

THE VOICE ON THE TELEPHONE the previous evening had been so faint and strained that Jenny had assumed it belonged to someone old and confused who had dialled her number by mistake. She had been about to put down the receiver when she caught the word 'Philip' and realized that it was Clare Ashton speaking, and that she was asking Jenny to come and visit her. It didn't feel decent to refuse, and she arranged to call in on her way to the office.

Leaving Melin Bach as dawn broke, Jenny took some comfort from the fact that the rhythms of nature were as comfortingly dependable as human life was unpredictable. In the two weeks since the night at the airport, the garden had become a carpet of snowdrops that carried a distant promise of spring, and the sun, which since before Christmas had travelled too low in the sky to touch her crook of the valley, had reappeared above Barbadoes Hill to ripen buds and stir the crows. Meanwhile, far from certain that she was doing the right thing, Jenny had found it in herself to give Michael another chance. But the Gods still had one more hand to play and only three days later she had found herself back in the doctor's surgery with stomach cramps, to be told what in her heart already knew: she wasn't going to be a mother again. It was nothing she had done, she was assured, it was just that at her age the odds were stacked against her. Jenny had expected Michael to sulk, at least a little, but surprising her again, he had told her that he loved her for who she was, and not for what she might give him. Whether or not he meant it from the depths of his being, she couldn't say – such intentions could only be tested against time and fate – but in her quiet moments she dared to think that they really might grow old together.

The same could not be said of Kelly Hart and Liam Doyle, who were both being held on remand on multiple charges of murder by joint enterprise. Jenny's inquest had been stalled while DI Ballantyne and his colleagues were given charge of fresh investigations into the deaths at Blackstone Ley as well as those of Daniel Burden and DI Ryan. Initially, Kelly and Doyle had resolutely refused to answer any of the detectives' questions, but Daniel Burden's hard drive began to yield evidence that led to an email address Doyle had been using, which in turn led to another belonging to Kelly. The forensic case had begun to mount, too: Dr Kerr confirmed that Doyle had shot Ryan with size-4 shot identical to that found in the bodies at Blackstone Ley, and the Home Office laboratory had ascertained that fragments of his DNA had been detected on Nicky Brooks's body.

It had been at the beginning of the previous October that the former teenage lovers had made contact for the first time in seventeen years, and it was largely as Doyle had described it. Having failed to find a way of extracting money from Kelly, Daniel Burden had discovered Doyle's whereabouts, following his release from prison, using the computers and facial-recognition software at his office. It had been almost too easy. Doyle's original image remained on the Home Office database and threw up a match with a photograph in a passport recently issued in the name of Patrick Brennan.

But Burden's cunning met its match in Doyle, who had seemed to understand instinctively that a blackmailer is by definition a coward, whose greed is a fatal weakness. Reeling Burden in by elaborate promises of money raised against inherited properties, he extracted Kelly's whereabouts and surprised her one autumn evening by walking into her bar and ordering a drink.

Jenny hadn't yet seen the emails that had passed between them, but the snatches Ballantyne had shared with her had been chilling. It seemed they revealed that the 15-year-old Malia Sanders, as Kelly then was, had been the instigator of the killings of Gabriella and Amelia Vallejo, spurring Doyle on and rewarding him with sex. When they became reacquainted, whatever had possessed them all those years ago had surged up from its hiding place to consume them both again. It had been Kelly's fantasy to leave her troublesome family behind and start again where they had left off. It was she who had dreamed up the plan for the fire and taken Ed's phone from him in order that Doyle could forge his final message.

Ballantyne's theory was that it was all about primitive power: a woman who can make a man kill – especially when the victims were beautiful young girls on the cusp of maturity – has exercised the ultimate control. He saw her as a human iteration of a queen bee or a she-wolf who savaged her female young. For him it also explained why Kelly had insisted Doyle keep Robbie alive: unlike her daughters, Robbie posed no sexual threat, but was quite the opposite – another willing male to manipulate and control. Jenny was only partially convinced by Ballantyne's cod psychology. However you dressed it up, a spark of evil had jumped between the two and ignited something so perverted that Kelly had been willing to sacrifice her own daughters and the man who had devoted himself to them, not to mention Nicky Brooks and the hapless Daniel Burden, just to feel the thrill again. In a strange way, Jenny found Doyle's motivation far easier to understand than Kelly's: 'Ask any killer, they'll all tell you it puts sex and drugs in the shade,' Ballantyne had pronounced at their last meeting, 'and the more innocent the victim, the sweeter the taste.'

Ryan had been an unexpected snag in Kelly's plan to reinvent herself. Like Darren Brooks before him, he had allowed himself to become captivated to the point of losing his reason. As far as Ballantyne could work out, Ryan's relationship with Kelly had only become physical in the past few months. Recent messages on his phone between him and Kelly showed that at first he had been terrified that somehow Ed Morgan had got wind of their affair, but she had assured him that it wasn't the case, and indulged his fantasy that when the inquest was over she and he might start a life together.

Ryan had had no inkling that Doyle had reappeared, nor it seemed had Kelly let him in on her problems with Burden. It would have made her too dependent on him, Ballantyne thought, and would have risked Ed finding out the truth about her past, should Ryan have judged the threat great enough to move her or change her identity once again. Kelly had never wanted that. Perhaps this was proof that a small, decent part of her had been concerned to protect her daughters and Ed from the trauma of having to cope with who and what she had once been, but Jenny thought it unlikely. Beautiful. Evil. Empty. These were the three words she returned to every time she thought of Kelly, with the emphasis on the last. There was a black space where her humanity should have been. Just as a violent man might beat his way through life with his fists, Kelly had learned to caress and seduce.

Jenny had to admit to having felt a certain cruel satisfaction when, as these facts came to light, Simon Moreton had appeared with his tail between his legs to offer an apology and the congratulations of the Chief Coroner. He had clearly hoped to escape back to London after a few soothing words offered over lunch on expenses, but Jenny had refused to let him off lightly. To his credit, he had behaved honourably. He accepted Jenny's word that it must have been Doyle who, attempting to isolate Jenny further, had hacked into Alison's Facebook account, and they struck a deal to allow her to come back to work part-time. He also listened to what Jenny told him about the help Falco had given her. He promised to have discreet words with the CPS, and soon afterwards the charges against Falco and Tomasz Zaleski were quietly dropped. The prospect of Falco being free to return to the bosom of the organized-crime fraternity troubled Jenny's conscience a touch, but she consoled herself with the thought that for every Falco that fell by the wayside there was always another ready to take his place in the back of a gangster's limousine. Better the devil you know, especially one who owes you a very big favour.

Jenny's usual route into Blackstone Ley was blocked by roadworks, requiring her to follow detour signs through even smaller lanes, some with grass growing up their middle, that threaded through the fields to the east of the village. As the spire of the church appeared in the near distance, she turned the corner and passed the driveway to Blackstone House Farm, the home of the Grant family. A 'For Sale' sign had been erected on the verge outside, advertising an eight-bedroom family home with ninety acres of mixed farmland. Despite the fact that a DNA test had finally proven Simon Grant was not the father of Layla Hart's child, mud had stuck. Harry Grant, a man who had devoted his career to helping others remain in the shadows, and made himself enemies in the process, had found his family the unwelcome subject of prurient newspaper articles. Local teenagers had been persuaded to tell stories of Simon's sexual exploits with underage girls, and desperate to prove this wickedness was inherited, a tabloid had dredged up a former secretary who claimed Harry Grant had plagued her with lewd remarks and unwanted advances. As hatchet jobs went, it had been thorough and ruthless; Jenny had heard rumours that the Grants' already shaky marriage had been hurled onto the rocks.

It was a fresh and pleasantly freckled face framed by reddish hair that greeted her at the door of the Ashtons' cottage. The young woman was casually dressed in jeans and a practical shirt, but her sunny practicality immediately identified her as a nurse.

'Mrs Ashton said she was expecting you,' she said, after Jenny had introduced herself. 'I'll see how she is. I'm afraid she's very sleepy at the moment – she's on a lot of medication.'

Jenny waited in the hall while the nurse went upstairs to talk to Clare. The atmosphere had changed profoundly since her first visit. The house smelt vaguely of antiseptic and felt more like a clinic than somebody's home.

It was several minutes before the nurse reappeared and beckoned Jenny upstairs.

'Is it all right if I leave you alone? I've rather a lot to get through.'

'That's fine,' Jenny reassured her, and knocked lightly on Clare's bedroom door.

Clare was propped up on several pillows in the middle of the double bed. Her eyes were the only part of her that hadn't shrunk or withered, and they stared at Jenny from dark, hollow sockets; her skull was painfully visible beneath the powder-white skin of her face.

'Good morning, Mrs Ashton.' Jenny sat in the chair at the bedside. 'I don't know if you've heard all that's happened.'

'Philip's told me,' Clare said in a reedy, fragile voice. 'I had no idea. Though I suppose it explains a lot about her.'

Jenny waited for her to enlarge.

'I wanted to apologize, Mrs Cooper.' Her bony fingers scratched nervously at the edge of the duvet drawn up to her chest. 'You were only doing what you had to.'

'That's all right. I understand.'

'I thought I'd die that day, but – ' She let out a sigh. 'Well, I didn't. It wasn't going to be that easy.'

Her fingers continued to move for a moment longer, then stopped, as if something inside her had stilled. Her eyes seemed to grow even larger as she slowly turned her head and fixed Jenny with a look of total desolation.

'My daughter was a troubled child. She was born having a tantrum and never stopped. The doctors told me some are like that. They promised me she'd grow out of it, but when every day starts and ends with a screaming fit you struggle to believe it. In fact, you start to think that you've been cursed, or visited by some evil spirit. I loved her. Of course, I did. I loved her dearly . . . I just felt so helpless. So inadequate. If a mother can't even offer solace to a crying child, what use is she?' She paused and took in a breath, the effort of which seemed to drain what little strength she had left. 'She'd been having hysterics and acting up all morning. I was exhausted, my nerves were in pieces. I was trying to make lunch, peeling potatoes at the sink; there were boiling pans on the stove and Susie made a grab for one of them. She *knew* that frightened me more than anything else.' Clare briefly closed her eyes. 'It wasn't even conscious. Just a reflex. I slapped her cheek and she fell and hit her head. It raised a slight bump but that was all. She was perfectly fine afterwards. She even ate her lunch . . . But a short while later she turned pale and started to fit. Two minutes. That's all it took. She went limp and died in my arms. Even if I had called an ambulance I don't believe they would have saved her. It wasn't my fault, it could have happened to anyone, but somehow I couldn't see it that way. And I couldn't face explaining what I had done to Philip. Which is why I took the coward's way out, that wasn't a way out at all.'

Jenny said nothing. Despite the oppressive warmth of the room, a cold sensation crept over the surface of her skin.

Clare's voice took on a renewed clarity now that she had finally given voice to the truth. 'The only person I felt knew, really *knew*, was Kelly. How she did, I couldn't tell you. She recognized something in me, I suppose. She never said a word, but she played on it. She taunted me – a glance here, a gesture there. That's why I looked the other way when she and Philip – ' She paused to swallow. Jenny saw the movement of every muscle in her painfully scrawny neck. 'It was her way of telling me, I suppose. Telling me that she could do whatever she liked, because she knew.' Clare's face twisted into an expression of hatred that seemed both to consume and explain her. 'It was an accident, an *accident*. I loved my daughter just like any other mother, but that woman tormented me for years. She revelled in it.'

Jenny glanced at the tray of medicines sitting on the dressing table and reminded herself that Clare was under the influence of heavy opiates, and that nothing coming from her mouth could possibly be classified as reliable evidence. She would need some further proof.

'What did you do with Susie's body, Mrs Ashton?'

Clare dipped her head. 'I wrapped it very carefully and I put it in a bag. Then I hid it next door, in the church, before I called the police.'

'Where in the church?'

'There's an alcove with a wooden statue of a Madonna and child. The stone shelf it sits on slides away. One of the old churchwardens told me about it – Mrs Dawson, the one who gossiped to me all those years ago about Ed Morgan. It was where they hid the silver during the Civil War. It was a burial of sorts – the best I could do in the circumstances. I go in there often to offer a prayer. And to ask *why*?'

'And she's still there?'

Clare nodded. 'I've never disturbed her.'

Jenny heard the nurse emerge from the kitchen and start up the stairs.

'I've just one favour to ask of you,' Clare said. 'Can you keep this to yourself until – ' Her eyes flitted nervously to the door at which the nurse would at any moment appear.

'No, Mrs Ashton,' Jenny said, rising from her chair, 'you know I can't keep those kind of secrets. And I think that's why you chose to tell me now, isn't it?'

The nurse bustled through the doorway with a tray of tea and a breezy smile.

'Everything all right?' she enquired cheerfully.

Clare kept her gaze fixed on Jenny, then gave a hint of a nod before sinking back on her pillow.

'Yes,' Jenny said as she turned to go, more than grateful to be leaving Blackstone Ley for the very last time. 'Much better.'

# ACKNOWLEDGEMENTS

Writing is a selfish job. Each morning I sit at my desk and busy myself with this and that, while waiting – sometimes for several hours – for the real world to fade and the fictional one to take over. And so it continues, month after month. At the best of times this can stretch the patience of all but the most saintly partners and children. This year was a tough one, with illness in the family, and I have never felt that tension between the fictional and real worlds more keenly. There was a long stretch of time during which I fantasized about having a mechanical, untaxing profession, which would allow my thoughts to remain with those closest to me. Thankfully the fantasy passed and I accepted that life simply conspires to test us in the most unexpected ways, and shuts down the escape routes while it's at it. We are left with no choice but to keep on through the narrow tunnel until we reach the end, which, ultimately, is the best thing.

I want to say a heartfelt thank you to my editors, Maria Rejt and Sophie Orme, for cutting me all the slack I needed through a difficult time, and for being unfailingly kind, supportive and heroically elastic with the deadlines. My agent, Zoe Waldie, has also been a steady, understanding and reassuring presence throughout, for which I am hugely grateful. As always, the whole team at my publishers, Macmillan, has been a delight to work with. In particular, special thanks to Katie James, Geoff Duffield, Jodie Mullish and Will Atkins.

Lastly, thanks to my family for putting up with a husband and father who shuts himself in his study and mutters to himself all day, emerging only to tell bad jokes and eat all the biscuits. Couldn't do it without you.

October 2013